D0205072

KINTU

KINTU

Jennifer Nansubuga Makumbi

With an introduction by
Aaron Bady

**TRANSIT
BOOKS**

Published by Transit Books
2301 Telegraph Avenue, Oakland, California 94612
www.transitbooks.org

Copyright © 2017 Jennifer Nansubuga Makumbi
Introduction Copyright © 2017 Aaron Bady

First published in 2014 by Kwani Trust, Nairobi

ISBN: 978-1-945492-01-3
Library of Congress Control Number: 2016961684

Design & Typesetting
Justin Carder

Distributed By
Consortium Book Sales & Distribution | (800) 283-3572 | cbsd.com

Printed in the United States of America

10 9 8 7 6 5 4 3 2

All rights reserved. This book or any portion thereof may not be reproduced or
used in any manner whatsoever without the express written permission of the
publisher except for the use of brief quotations in a book review.

In memory of my grandfather, Elieza Mayombwe Makumbi, who told folktales and taught me how to tell them; my father, Tony Kizito Makumbi, who felt that all I needed were stories in books and who introduced me to Shakespeare when I was only eight years old. And to Aunt Catherine Makumbi-Kulubya, for holding my father's dream.

TABLE OF CONTENTS

Introduction

Aaron Bady

Ugandans have waited a long time for the book you are holding to exist. Since it was first published in 2014, after winning
the Kwani? Manuscript Project, the enthusiasm with which *Kintu*
has been received in Uganda has been difficult to describe but
remarkable to witness. Last year, I had the pleasure of trailing
behind Jennifer Nansubuga Makumbi at the Writivism literary
festival in Kampala, as readers and other writers caught at the
hem of her garment. In such circles, it is hard to overstate what a
rock star she is, and how precious this book has already become.
The book sold out immediately, and even those who hadn't read it
were talking about it and about where to get it. It's not hyperbole
to call *Kintu* the great Ugandan novel. It is, simply and obviously,
a plain fact.

Her reception in the UK, where she lives with her family, has
been very different. Even after winning the 2014 Commonwealth
Short Story Prize, Makumbi was told that *Kintu* was unpublish-
able, that it was much too African for British readers. Perhaps a
sprawling multicharacter saga like this one might work if the char-
acters were white, if the proper nouns were places like Oxford

or Southampton, and if their names were solid English names (and for goodness sake, only one name each!). In Great Britain, after all, who has even heard of Kintu, the mythical first man on earth and founder of the Buganda Kingdom? Who would know to pronounce his name with a soft *ch* sound, instead of a hard *k*? Perhaps British readers might be interested in the exoticism of the historical novel that *Kintu* starts off as being—the ninety pages or so that are set in the 18th century, before the rest of the novel reverts to 2004—but could the book-buying public be expected to care about the struggles of an extended family in present-day Kampala?

If you must write about Africa, then you write about dictators, ethnography, and war; these are the sorts of stories that confirm what people already "know" about Africa. And if you must write about Uganda, then you place a white character in the middle of the action. You write about Africans who have left Africa and migrated to the United States or Europe. You write about the legacies of colonialism. If you can't make Europe the hero of the story—and these days, you can't—then you can at least make Europe the villain. One editor rejected the manuscript because Makumbi didn't want to change it: to publish it, they would have to change it, and the novel is too good to change.

When Transit Books first read *Kintu*, they signed it immediately. They weren't concerned that American readers would be overwhelmed by the unfamiliar places and names, or that the novel was the wrong kind of "African." They put their faith in the story, trusting their readers to take that journey. It's a mistake to worry whether non-Ugandan readers will "get" this novel: as with any great work of fiction, this one teaches you how to read it. But it's a measure of the preciousness of the book you hold in your hands that I cannot help but burden you with a few words of advice, before you begin your journey.

The main thing to know, simply, is that this novel was written for Ugandans. This might seem obvious, but it isn't. What, after all, is a Ugandan? For one thing, a Ugandan might be someone for whom complex and indefinite extended families are more the norm than the exception, a world in which siblings might be cousins, parents aren't always parents, and everybody can have at least three different names, depending on who they're standing next to. A Ugandan might be someone for whom family is a much older and more permanent institution than the nation, and in which nothing is more political than sex and children. A Ugandan might also be someone who knows the name Kintu, whether or not they know what it means. At the highest level of abstraction, perhaps, a Ugandan is someone with firm ideas about what it means to be Ugandan, and who it is that isn't. But if Uganda is real, its borders are anything but clear and obvious: American readers might struggle to keep track of the names and relations that proliferate across the pages of this novel, but it's not like these things are easy for Ugandans. They are not. If family is the texture of everyday life, then everyday life is as confusing and indefinite (and borderline fictional) as family history itself.

More concretely, this book is for Ugandans because it's saturated with Ugandan words and places and names. From the hills and valleys that the urban jungle of Kampala now sprawls across—but that once looked out over the Buganda Kingdom—to the long roads and rivers that crisscross the country, *Kintu* is a novel about a singular and all-encompassing sense of place. And these references tell stories. You may speed past them on your way to your destination, but even a traveler who cannot understand the language—who can only look, see, and move on—will still feel the depth of the novel's engagement with Ugandan history. This is part of *Kintu*'s magic: you will feel more than you know. This also applies to Ugandans, especially those for whom "history" is the story of Europe in Africa.

As Makumbi has been quick to explain, *Kintu* flowed out of a desire to give Ugandans a taste of their own long and complicated history, to do for Ugandans something like what Chinua Achebe novels did for Nigerians in the 1960s: to make them look at a hill, for example, and know that the Ganda have been climbing it for centuries. To remind them that Uganda's history did not begin in 1962, when it gained independence from Great Britain, or even a few years earlier, when Europeans first "discovered" them. To place today's cultural politics—of citizenship, sexuality, and spirituality—into the deep and long endurance of centuries. Most of all, to tell a singular tale of Uganda as an expansive family saga, in which blood ties only mean as much as the stories we tell about them.

Makumbi began to write this story in 2003, in short bursts of frenetic, intense work that were followed by long fallow periods of distraction and contemplation. She was thinking about many things. One of them was a memory from her childhood, when she read Chinua Achebe's *Things Fall Apart*, in which a father kills his foster son. "It cut much too close!" she told me. "I was so young. I found myself looking at my father's hands and wondering, 'Would he kill me? Would he kill me?'" When her father lost his faculties, years later, she found herself dwelling on mental illness and the stereotype of Africa as a "mad place." And when she began a PhD in African literature, in England, she became frustrated at the insistence of her supervisors that "African Literature" be the story of Europe in Africa. As she began to write what she was then calling *The Kintu Saga*, she vowed to tell the story of Uganda with colonialism placed in perspective: not to say that the colonial encounter wasn't important, but that it wasn't the only thing that was.

A decade later, it's easy to find these biographical fragments in the final product. But as haunted as she might have been by Achebe's novels—about a father who kills his son and a father who goes mad—and as destructive as that legacy is, *Kintu* is a response to *Things Fall Apart* in which the story of a family curse is also a story of survivals. African literature is littered with patriarchal novels about how Africa's manhood was taken by Europe: it's one of Achebe's great themes. But while *Kintu* might be another story about men dying, it's also about families surviving (and often with women at the head). Makumbi insists that *Kintu* is a "masculinist" novel, and it is: focusing on the fragile edifice of paternity, she emphasizes the toll that patriarchy takes on the people who happen to be men. For that same reason, it's also one of the most feminist books one is likely to read. But when I asked her why she didn't call it "feminist," she laughed, and explained that I would have to wait and read what she was writing next. When I had, she said, I wouldn't have to ask; *that* would be feminist.

Makumbi is a scholar, and to write *Kintu*, she dug into the archives, asking questions about names and places and expressions and history. But Ugandan history is filled with stories that the archive won't tell, places where the historical record suddenly goes silent. To tell that history, she had to become a fiction writer attuned to silences. After all, Uganda is a family, and *Kintu* is the story of how all families are built out of silences and fictions: sometimes an uncle is really a father, or a cousin is really a brother; even mothers are never necessarily who you think they are. And sometimes the past separates us, and is better forgotten. *Kintu* is about creating family ties where none existed before, about making homes and families that can reach across the gaps of time and space; it's also about making up new truths when the old ones are lost or inadequate. It's about journeying far away to find out where you are from.

Take, for example, the long opening journey that begins the first book, as Kintu Kidda and his men cross the *o* Lwera desert on their way to the capital of the Buganda Kingdom. For him, the journey takes many days of hard travel across a barren and forbidding landscape. The governor of a distant province, and of suspiciously non-Ganda ancestry, Kintu is loyal to the Ganda *kabaka*, however far he is from the centers of courtly power. And so he must cross *o* Lwera to prove his allegiance; he must re-establish the links between the center and the periphery of the great Buganda Kingdom, must reassure the Ganda that he is part of it. As he travels—as he contemplates his situation, remembering his past and planning his future—we are immersed in his world, the courtly intrigues and domestic complications that consume him.

But we also follow him into the trials and tribulations of making family and nations out of strangers. Neither one is just *there*—both must be made.

Kintu Kidda is fictional, but the *o* Lwera desert is as real as the Ganda. Even today, the phrase "*Kulika o Lwera*" is a common greeting for travelers on their arrival in Kampala, a "well done!" for surviving the journey across its barren wasteland. It's not so formidable now. When she was young, Makumbi told me, she never understood why people said *Kulika o Lwera* to new arrivals; it was just something you said. The phrase survives as a relic of a time before planes and railroads and paved roads, when the barren stretch of land to the south of Kampala was still a fearsome barrier for travelers on foot. If you are traveling to Kampala on Masaka road today, you could be done with this journey in an afternoon. But it was not so long ago that it would make sense to congratulate someone for having managed not to die while crossing it. The world was much bigger a short century or three ago.

Today, the phrase has also taken on a new meaning: the overburdened Masaka road is an accident trap, a graveyard for automobiles and unlucky travelers. On foot or in a car, *o* Lwera is *o* Lwera. The historical resonance doesn't stop there: the road that a provincial governor might have taken to visit the capital in 1750 is the same road that Idi Amin's army took in the late 1970s when they set off to invade Tanzania and conquer a province that (he claimed) historically belonged to Uganda. It's the same road that Yoweri Museveni took, in the 1980s, when his army invaded Uganda from Tanzania, establishing himself as president until today (despite some who murmur that he is suspiciously Rwandan). It's the road that Rwandan refugees might take to Kampala, looking to find new lives in the capital, or the road they might take to return. And on arrival, they might all say the same thing, *Kulika o Lwera*.

Kintu rings with this sense of deep history, grounded in place while effortlessly leaping from past to present and to the past-in-the-present. It carries us from the courtly intrigue and sexual politics of the 18th century to the trials and tribulations of an extended family today, to the many and scattered descendants of the Kintu clan, united by a curse that may or may not be real and by the ghosts, stories, and memories that link them all together. Most of all, they are united by the place they all live in, the land that makes them all Ugandans, and the home to which they all strive to arrive.

Some of *Kintu*'s history is invented. Buddu province was not added to the Buganda Kingdom until later in the 1700s, for example, and Makumbi admits to moving a few landmarks to where the plot needed them to be. But then, *Kintu* is not history, and even "history" is not necessarily true. And this is also the point of *Kintu*, where families are made as much by hiding the truth as by disclosing it; why tell a son, after all, that he's *really* adopted? Why let it become true by saying the words? Indeed, this is the challenge of the historical novel: whether or not the stories are true might be the least important thing about them. History as it's written down in books is one thing, but history as it's *lived* is another.

Kintu belongs in the latter camp, and for good reason. When historians trained in Europe tell the story of Uganda, it's all about endings and beginnings, how Europe came and everything fell apart, or how independence came and colonialism fell apart; it's always the story of how the past recedes into the background as we race irrevocably forward. From that perspective, African history looks like a fast-moving train. "Tribalism" fades as modernity looms on the horizon. But on the ground, history looks nothing like this clash of nations and empires and states, however true and valid such stories may be on their terms; on the ground, history is the accumulated prejudices, hopes, and superstitions that we carry even if we don't understand how we acquired them, everything we don't know that makes us who we are. History is a fabric of memories and fear and forgetting, of longing and nostalgia, of invention and re-creation. History is bunk, and sometimes it's a good thing it is.

This is *Kintu*: the story of how the old pasts are forgotten so that new pasts, new families, and new nations can be remembered into existence.

What makes a Ugandan? A Ugandan might be someone who knows the story of Kintu, the mythological first man on earth, both the Adam of the Ganda creation story—with Nnambi, his Eve—and the legendary founder of the Buganda Kingdom. But as Makumbi explained to me, even this Kintu is already an ahistorical conflation, a Ganda-centric mythology placing that kingdom at the center of the world (and at the center of Uganda). At barely six or eight centuries old, the Buganda Kingdom is not *quite* as old as the human race; we may safely presume that the human race is a bit older than that. More to the point, Uganda is a nation-state that includes vast stretches of terrain and populations whose ancestors never spoke Luganda, who found themselves inside the Buganda Kingdom due to the usual machinations of state-building and imperial politics. But this historical land-grab is as good as any place to start to think about what it means to be Ugandan, now. And whether it's *true* is a lot less interesting (and illuminating) than why it's false in the way it is.

Kintu was written, then, for people for whom the name Kintu means something. Now you are one of those people.

Good travels. *Kulika o Lwera.*

KINTU

I profess accurately to describe naked Africa . . . If the picture be a dark one, we should, when contemplating these sons of Noah, try and carry our mind back to that time when our poor elder brother Ham was cursed by his father, and condemned to be the slave of both Shem and Japheth; for as they were then, so they appear to be now—a striking existing proof of the Holy Scriptures.

—John Hanning Speke, 1863

PROLOGUE

Bwaise, Kampala

Monday, January 5, 2004
There was a knock. Kamu's woman woke up and climbed over him to get the door. She picked a *kanga* off the floor and wrapped it around her naked body. Sucking her teeth at being disturbed so early in the morning, she walked to the door with the annoyance of a proper wife whose husband was at home.

The woman considered herself Kamu's wife because she had moved in with him two years earlier and he had not once thrown her out. Every night after work he came home to her, brought shopping, ate her cooking. He was always ravenous. When she visited her parents, Kamu gave her money so she did not go empty-handed. That was more than many certified wives got. Besides, she had not heard rumors of another woman. Maybe Kamu banged some girl once in a while but at least he did not flaunt it in her face. The only glitch in her quest to become Kamu's full wife was that he still wore a condom with her. With his seed locked away, she had not grown roots deep enough to secure her against future storms. A child was far more secure than waddling down the aisle with a wedding ring and piece of paper. Nonetheless, she would bide her time: condoms have been known to rip. Besides, sex with a condom is like sucking a sweet in its wrapper; Kamu would one day give it up.

The woman unbolted the door and pulled it back. She stepped outside on the veranda and stood stern, arms folded. Below her were four men, their breath steaming into the morning air. Their greetings were clipped and their eyes looked away from her as if they were fed-up lenders determined to get their money back. This thawed the woman's irritation and she moistened her lips. The men asked for Kamu and she turned to go back to the inner room.

The woman and Kamu lived in a two-roomed house on a terraced block in Bwaise, a swamp beneath Kampala's backside. Kampala perches, precariously, on numerous hills. Bwaise and other wet-lands are nature's floodplains below the hills. But because of urban migrants like Kamu and his woman, the swamps are slums. In colonial times, educated Ugandans had lived on the floodplains while Europeans lived up in the hills. When the Europeans left, educated Ugandans climbed out of the swamps, slaked off the mud, and took to the hills and raw Ugandans flooded the swamps. Up in the hills, educated Ugandans assumed the same contempt as Europeans had for them. In any case, suspicion from up in the hills fell down into the swamps—all swamp dwellers were thieves.

On her way to the inner room, the woman stumbled on rolled mats that had slid to the floor. She picked them up and saw, to her dismay, that the bright greens, reds, and purples had melted into messy patches, obliterating the intricate patterns her mother had weaved. In spite of the tons and tons of soil compacted to choke the swamp, Bwaise carried on as if its residents were still the fish, frogs, and yams of precolonial times. In the dry season, the floor in her house wept and the damp ate everything lying on it. In the rainy season, the woman carried everything of value on her head. Sometimes, however, it rained both from the sky and from the ground; then the house flooded. From the look of her mats, it had rained in the night.

As she laid the discolored mats on top of the skinny Johnson sofa, she felt a film of dust on her smart white chair-backs. The culprit was the gleaming 5-CD *Sonny* stereo (a fake Sony model, made in Taiwan), squeezed into a corner. She glanced at it and pride flooded her heart. Since its arrival just before Christmas, Kamu blared music at full volume to the torment of their neighbors. The booming shook the fragile walls and scattered dust. The wooden box on which a tiny *Pansonic* TV (also made in Taiwan) sat was damp too. If the moisture got into the TV, there would be sparks. She thought of shifting the TV, but there was no space for its detached screen.

The woman squeezed behind the sofa and went back into the inner room. Kamu was still asleep. She shook him gently. "Kamu, Kamu! Some men at the door want you."

Kamu got up. He was irritated but the woman didn't know how to apologize for the men. He pulled on a T-shirt, which hung loose and wide on him. When he turned, "Chicago Bulls" had curved on his back. He then retrieved a pair of gray trousers off a nail in the wall and put them on. The woman handed him a cup of water. He washed his face and rinsed his mouth. When Kamu stepped out of the house, each man bid him good morning but avoided looking at him.

"Come with us, Mr. Kintu. We need to ask you some questions," one of the men said as they turned to leave.

Kamu shrugged. He had recognized them as the Local Councillors for Bwaise Central. "LCs," he whispered to his woman and they exchanged a knowing look. LCs tended to ask pointless questions to show that they are working hard.

As he slipped on a pair of sandals, Kamu was seized by a bout of sneezing.

"Maybe you need a jacket," his woman suggested.

"No, it's morning hay fever. I'll be all right."

Still sneezing, Kamu followed the men. He suspected that a

debtor had perhaps taken matters too far and reported him to the local officials. They had ambushed him at dawn before the day swallowed him. It was envy for his new stereo and TV, no doubt.

They walked down a small path, across a rubbish-choked stream, past an elevated latrine at the top of a flight of stairs. The grass was so soaked that it squished under their steps. To protect his trousers, Kamu held them up until they came to the wider murram road with a steady flow of walkers, cyclists, and cars.

Here the councillors surrounded him and his hands were swiftly tied behind his back. Taken by surprise, Kamu asked, "Why are you tying me like a thief?"

With those words Kamu sentenced himself. A boy—it could have been a girl—shouted, "Eh, eh, a thief. They've caught a thief!"

Bwaise, which had been half-awake up to that point, sat up. Those whose jobs could wait a bit stopped to stare. Those who had no jobs at all crossed the road to take a better look. For those whose jobs came as rarely as a yam's flower this was a chance to feel useful.

The word *thief* started to bounce from here to there, first as a question then as a fact. It repeated itself over and over like an echo calling. The crowd grew: swelled by insomniacs, by men who had fled the hungry stares of their children, by homeless children who leapt out of the swamp like frogs, by women gesturing angrily, "Let him see it: thieves keep us awake all night," and by youths who yelped, "We have him!"

The councillors, now realizing what was happening, hurried to take Kamu out of harm's way but instead their haste attracted anger. "Where are you taking him?" the crowd, now following them, wanted to know. The councillors registered too late that they were headed toward Bwaise Market. A multitude of vendors, who hate councillors, had already seen them and were coming. Before they had even arrived, one of them pointed at the councillors and shouted, "They're going to let him go."

The idea of letting a thief go incensed the crowd so much that someone kicked Kamu's legs. Kamu staggered. Youths jumped up and down, clapping and laughing. Growing bold, another kicked him in the ankles. *"Amuwadde 'ngwara!"* the youths cheered. Then a loud fist landed on the back of his shoulder. Kamu turned to see who had hit him but then another fist landed on the other shoulder and he turned again and again until he could not keep up with the turning.

"Stop it, people! Stop it now," a councillor's voice rose up but a stone flew over his head and he ducked.

Now the crowd was in control. Everyone clamored to hit somewhere, anywhere but the head. A kid pushed through the throng, managed to land a kick on Kamu's butt and ran back shouting feverishly to his friends, "I've given him a round kick like *tyang!*"

Angry men just arriving asked, "Is *it* a thief?" because Kamu had ceased to be human.

The word *thief* summed up the common enemy. Why there was no supper the previous night; why their children were not on their way to school. *Thief* was the president who arrived two and a half decades ago waving "democracy" at them, who had recently laughed, "Did I actually say democracy? I was so naive then." *Thief* was tax collectors taking their money to redistribute it to the rich. *Thief* was God poised with a can of aerosol *Africancide*, his finger pressing hard on the button.

Voices in the crowd swore they were sick of the police arresting thieves only to see them walk free the following day. No one asked what this thief had stolen apart from *he looks like a proper thief, this one*, and *we're fed up*. Only the councillors knew that Kamu had been on his way to explain where he got the money to buy a gleaming 5-CD player and TV with a detached screen.

As blows fell on his back, Kamu decided that he was dreaming. He was Kamu Kintu, human. It was them, bantu. Humans. He would wake up any minute. Then he would visit his father Misirayimu Kintu. Nightmares like this come from neglecting his old man. He did not realize that he had shrivelled, that the menacing Chicago Bull had been ripped off his back, that the gray trousers were dirty and one foot had lost its sandal, that the skin on his torso was darker and shiny in swollen parts, that his lips were puffed, that he bled through one nostril and in his mouth, that his left eye had closed and only the right eye stared. Kamu carried on dreaming.

Just then, a man with fresh fury arrived with an axe. He had the impatient wrath of: *You're just caressing the rat.* He swung and struck Kamu's head with the back of the axe, kppau. Stunned, Kamu fell. He fell next to a pile of concrete blocks. The man heaved a block above his head, staggered under the weight and released the block. Kamu's head burst and spilled gray porridge. The mob screamed and scattered in horror. The four councillors vanished.

Kamu's right eye stared.

Kamu's woman only found out about his death when a neighbor's child, who had been on his way to school, ran back home and shouted, "*Muka* Kamu, *Muka* Kamu! Your man has been killed! They said that he is a thief!"

The woman ran to the road. In the distance, she saw a body lying on the ground with a block on top of its head. She recognized the gray trousers and the sandal. She ran back to the house and locked the door. Then she trembled. Then she sat on the armchair. Then she stood up and held her arms on top of her head. She removed them from her head and beat her thighs whispering, "*Maama, maama, maama,*" as if her body were on fire. She sipped a long sustained breath of air to control her sobs but her lungs could not hold so much air for so long—it burst out in a sob. She shook her body as if she were lulling a crying baby on her back but in the end she gave up and tears flowed quietly. She refused to come out to the women who knocked on her door to soothe and cry with her. But solitary tears are such that they soon dry.

The woman closed her eyes and looked at herself. She could stay in Bwaise and mourn him; running would imply guilt. But beyond that, what? Kamu was not coming back. She opened her eyes and saw the 5-CD player, the TV with the detached screen, the Johnson sofa set and the double bed. She asked herself, "Do you have his child? No. Has he introduced you to his family? No. And if you had died, would Kamu slip you between earth's sheets and walk away? Yes."

The following morning, the two rooms Kamu and his woman had occupied were empty.

Three months later, on Good Friday, the 9th of April 2004, Bwaise woke up to find the four councillors' and six other men's corpses—all involved in Kamu's death—strewn along the main street. Bwaise, a callous town, shrugged its shoulders and said, "Their time was up."

But three people, two men and a woman, whose market stalls were held up by the slow removal of the corpses linked the massacre to Kamu's death.

"They raided a deadly colony of bees," the first man said. "Some blood is sticky: you don't just spill it and walk away like that."

But the second man was not sure; he blamed fate. "It was in the name," he said. "Who would name his child first Kamu and then Kintu?"

"Someone seeking to double the curse," the first man sucked his teeth.

But the woman, chewing on sugar cane, shook her head, "Uh uh." She sucked long and noisily on the juice and then spat out the chaff. "Even then," she pointed in the direction of the corpses with her mouth, "that is what happens to a race that fails to raise its value on the market."

BOOK ONE
KINTU KIDDA

1.

BUDDU PROVINCE, BUGANDA:
The Moon of Gatonya, *1750*

Midnight

It was odd the relief Kintu felt as he stepped out of his house. A long and perilous journey lay ahead. At the end of the journey was a royal storm—the princes had been fighting for the throne again and weapons had not yet been put away. He could be carried back, his head severed from his shoulders—commoners tended to lose their heads when royals fought. Yet, Kintu Kidda, Ppookino of Buddu Province, was glad to step away from his home.

It was Babirye, his other wife.

Kintu had last seen her in the morning, taking the goats to feed on banana peels. Her eyes were angry and he had looked away. Kintu had never found respite in Babirye's eyes, not even on their wedding day. He thought of the fabled men who unwittingly married spirits but then dismissed the thought. Babirye was not a demon, just a dreadful woman. He shooed her out of his mind. It would be unwise to carry the extra weight of a glowering wife on this journey.

He paused at the threshold of Mayirika, his principal residence. The world was still. A spray of young stars streaked the sky on his right. On the left, a few lone ones, elderly, blinked tiredly. Around him, the midnight air was cold and calm. Darkness was thick. Fireflies tried to puncture it—on, off, on, off—in vain. Kintu was satisfied with the conditions. It was the reason why he and his men were setting off at midnight. They would make good distance before dawn broke and then there would be a short space when the sun was still lethargic. At midday when the sun started to bake the world, they would stop for the day and sleep until midnight when they would set off again.

From where he stood, Kintu could hear Nnondo, his headman, briefing the men below the courtyard, at the gate. He could not see them but he felt the feverish excitement of the younger men, probably impatient to start the journey. The older men were good at masking their excitement. Kintu touched his short spear, which he kept in a sheath near his stomach. He adjusted his barkcloth and then the leopard skin on top. He stepped away from his threshold.

As he walked across the vast courtyard, two figures scurried out of the older boys' house. His sons, Kalema and Baale, were late and had missed the briefing. Kalema was going to find work in the capital while Baale wanted to accompany his brother until daybreak when he would return home. Kintu shook his head as they ran past.

"You two should have been women."

As his men closed the outer reed gate, something made Kintu look back. The three main houses, now silhouettes, were silent. As instructed, everyone, including his twin wives Nnakato and Babirye, children, and servants, were in bed. Yet, he felt someone, something spying. He hesitated a moment then stepped into the journey.

Kintu was on his way to Lubya to pay homage to Kyabaggu, the new *kabaka*. Kyabaggu had grabbed the throne and announced Lubya Hill the new capital, claiming that Namugala had abdicated. No one believed him. The *ba kabaka* did not give away their thrones like that. Until Namugala was pronounced dead, the kingdom stood on its toes with apprehension.

Kintu was traveling with a modest entourage of twenty-five men chosen and led by his headman and trusted guard, Nnondo. All the men were warriors. Kintu did not know what to expect of Kyabaggu but taking a large group of *bambowa* was reckless. In any case, if Kyabaggu wanted to slay him, the men would not be able to protect him. As a new *kabaka* who had recently plucked the throne from his own brother, Kyabaggu would be jittery. Kintu was surprised that Kyabaggu had toppled his own mother's child. Normally, the mother was a binding force among sons, but then again, royals were hardly normal. These were terrible times to be of royal birth. Kings and princes lived the shortest lives. Any prince could stake claim to the throne at any time. The victor often massacred his siblings and cousins. Clever women did not declare their sons princes. Cleverer women watched the throne and alerted their sons when it was ripe for seizure.

In his service as Ppookino, Kintu had so far served five kings. He remembered Kagulu, the first *kabaka* he served. In his short reign, Kagulu had slaughtered more subjects than goats. In the quarterly *lukiiko*, the parliament sessions, governors watched their breath. Kagulu turned like the Nnalubaale Lake—now serene; now agitated; now deadly; now laughing. The gods deserted Kagulu after he put his half-brother, Musanje, to death for killing another brother, Luyenje, while wrestling. Fearing for their lives, Musanje's brothers, the ones he shared a mother with, fled led by their elder sister Nnassolo, taking Musanje's three little boys as well.

When Kintu next came for the *lukiiko*, Kagulu's palace at Bulizo was eerily silent. It was as if Kagulu was aware that his days were numbered. No one knew where Nnassolo and her siblings had fled. But everyone knew that she was a wrathful princess. Soon after Kintu returned to Buddu, news arrived that Bulizo was under siege. Nnassolo was back rumbling like Kiyira, the Nile.

Kagulu fled and Nnassolo pursued him. Kagulu was as swift as a kob on a savannah but Nnassolo was relentless: she wanted his jawbone. For a time, Kagulu hid in ditches and caves in Buto region. When he was captured, Kagulu who had put masses to the spear, would not face his own death like a man. Mercifully, Nnassolo had him drowned.

Nnassolo then installed the softly-softly older brother Kikulwe as *kabaka*. Kintu knew right away that Kikulwe would not last. History showed that kings who fought for the throne kept it longer than those who merely received it, and Kikulwe was naive. As if it would heal the kingdom, he brought music and merriment. He danced too far, too long from his throne and his brother Mawanda snatched it. Kintu laughed as he remembered Mawanda's excuse: apparently, the gentle Kikulwe had dug a staked pit to kill him.

Mawanda's reign, though longer and more prosperous, was dogged by rumors skeptical of his royal heritage. Eventually, Musanje's three sons, the ones he and Nnassolo had fled with, deposed Mawanda. Kintu sucked his teeth. Mawanda had brought up the boys himself! Then the three vipers went on to succeed each other in madness. The eldest, Mwanga, lasted only nine days as ruler despite sacrificing a maternal cousin to guarantee a long reign. The cousin's enraged father killed him before his buttocks warmed the throne. As Kintu set off to pay homage to Mwanga, Namugala, the second viper, was planning his own elaborate coronation at Naggalabi. During Namugala's eight-year reign, there was peace and quiet. But Kyabaggu, the youngest viper, was restless. Now, he had pounced. Kintu sighed. Abdication indeed: the way the monarch took subjects for fools!

Kintu put the instability of Buganda's throne down to the women. Unlike commoners, a *kabaka*'s children took after their mother's clan. Though this ensured the distribution of the *kabaka*ship to the different clans in Buganda, the custom bestowed immense power to a king's mother, the *namasole*. To protect their position, incumbent king mothers encouraged brothers to inherit the throne. The three vipers shared a mother, Nnabulya. Ruthlessly ambitious, Nnabulya had sowed yearning for the throne in all three young princes. Kintu saw her hand in the malicious slander questioning Mawanda's royal lineage. But what had she gained? Mwanga was dead, Namugala was exiled, probably dead too, and Kyabaggu was bound to die the same way. Kintu suspected that Nnabulya, who had held rivalling courts during Namugala's reign, had feared that half-brothers would easily depose her weak son and orchestrated the abdication story. In Kyabaggu, Nnabulya had a third chance to be king mother.

Kintu shook his head. Nnabulya reminded him of his wife Babirye. If only royals looked beyond beauty in their choice of women, perhaps the throne would be more secure. But then, royals were not renowned for their mental prowess. He saw no end to the bloodshed. In spite of all that, Kintu could not wait to get to Lubya and see the royal madness that would be Kyabaggu.

2.

The party formed a snaking retinue. They walked downhill from Kintu's courtyard, through cultivated plots on his land, past silent shadowy houses until they came to the bottom near the well where village residents collected water. The moon, as if shy, still hid behind a cloud. But midnight darkness was beginning to loosen. Kintu looked in the distance but the night yielded no horizon. Yet to him, the landscape was clear. He knew every rise and fall in the earth, every bush and thicket, and every old tree intimately.

By the time the party came to Nswera, a large stream that cut Kiyirika Village off from the rest of Buddu Province, the fireflies had gone to sleep. The moon now tailed them at a distance like a nosy little brother. It was good timing, the walkers needed light to cross the swamp. Nswera was in a huge basin: its edges were steep while the bottom was flat.

Ten men descended into the swamp before Kintu allowed his sons to follow. Inside the swamp, the snores of nature filled the air. Leaves rustled and insects whistled. Closer to the stream, frogs croaked as if hired to perform. The party crossed the stream without a problem and took on the incline to climb out. By the time everyone got out, the moon had drawn closer. Suddenly, Babirye, like an owl, swooped and perched into Kintu's mind. She loomed large and dark. Kintu contemplated her for a moment then dismissed her.

Four hours later, they were inside Nabweteme, a dense rain forest. The moon, now huge and low, sailed close to the canopy. Its light streaked through the trees. The forest was silent. When Kintu looked up again, the moon was racing ahead as if it had lingered too long in their company. He saw it sink behind the trees and thought, this is how we grow old: by letting the moon and the sun overtake us.

The first part of the forest came to an abrupt end and they broke out into a clearing. Daybreak lay in the distance. Kintu was peering at it when he felt cold air on his head, as if his hair had been swept off. He held his breath—there was no tension among his men. Were they being stalked? But the party was too large to be attacked by wild animals. His mind raced back home to his family but he felt no danger there either. Yet he was certain that something was wrong. He asked his sons, Kalema and Baale, who now trailed somewhere in the party behind him to walk close to him.

The horizon cracked into scarlet rays. The party had a few precious minutes to enjoy sunrise before entering the second phase of the forest.

Kintu's mind strayed to his wives, Babirye and Nnakato. He would rather have dealt with mutiny in his army than with Babirye, even though she was a replica of his beloved Nnakato. He never wanted to keep two women in the same house in the first place, not even identical twins.

Tradition claimed that identical twins were one soul who, failing to resolve the primal conflict in the self, split—and two people were born. The older twin, Babirye for girls, was supposedly the original soul. Nnakato, the younger twin, was the copy, the mutineer. But Kintu could not see how this could be true of his wives. For him, Nnakato was the original. Rather than being selfish, Nnakato was the pacifier who always allowed Babirye to have her own way. Surely it *had* to be Babirye who had fallen out with

Nnakato. She had pushed and shoved until Nnakato stepped out of the way. Babirye was born first and became the dominant twin thereafter.

They were inside the second part of the forest. The foliage was wet as if it had just rained. The canopy blocked the early sun. Still, Kintu could see well. Huge mahogany trees rose and soared, splitting into a canopy of dense branches. The shrubs below were lanky, making thin undergrowth. The forest floor was carpeted in a thick layer of decomposing leaves. Tiny hard black seeds littered the ground. Once in a while, they came upon an ancient tree with roots wide and webbed above the ground that towered over the men.

Kintu's mind lingered on the primal conflict that led to a soul splitting into twins. No matter how he looked at it, life was tragic. If the soul is at conflict even at this remotest level of existence, what chance do communities have? This made the Ganda custom of marrying female identical twins to the same man preposterous. It goes against their very nature, Kintu thought. Twins split because they cannot be one, why keep them as such in life? Besides, identical men did not marry the same woman.

But even as he raged against custom, Kintu knew that in the world of twins, things could be worse. There were people born as single souls only to bear twin personalities. More tragic were twins who changed their minds too late and arrived conjoined.

"Red ants," someone called and the men stood still.

"Lift your clothes up: these warriors seek out hairy regions first," Nnondo the headman called.

One by one, men jumped over the intricate ant processions.

"They are all over the place," someone called at the tail of the group.

The orderly convoy was abandoned. Luckily, they had come to the edge of the forest and soon broke out into the open. The men threw down their spears and loads, stomping and stripping.

Outside the forest, the vegetation changed dramatically. An expanse of elephant grass lay as far as the eye could see. A slight yellowing in the leaves indicated that the soil in this region was salty. The earth, previously a dark loam, inclined toward red. After the soft wet carpet of the forest bed, the ground was hard beneath their feet. The wind blew on top of the elephant grass and the leaves swayed like waves on a green lake. Kintu turned to his son Baale and told him it was time to return home.

From that point onwards, the party walked against the sun. They read its rhythm in the cast of their shadows and measured their energy against the cheerless posture of the vegetation.

Kintu married Nnakato first. He married Nnakato against counsel, against custom.

When he first whispered his desire to her, they were both young and Nnakato was shy. "You know you ought to court Babirye first," she had reprimanded wistfully.

Kintu shook his head, "It's you I want."

This implied difference between her and Babirye, the first in Nnakato's life, was so intoxicating that she failed to insist that Kintu court them both. Her parents, on hearing Kintu's proposal, initially rejected the idea of separating the twins. However, they then relented. If Kintu would not marry both girls, then he would wait until Babirye, the eldest twin, got married.

Kintu waited.

No man whispered to Babirye, not even in jest. Kintu's father died and Kintu became Ppookino. He then pressured the twins' parents to let him marry Nnakato. He claimed that as governor he was naked without a wife.

"True," the parents agreed. "However, as you know, our hands are tied. If you want our Nnakato, you must marry our Babirye first then come back for Nnakato later."

Kintu rejected the custom even though the twins were identical. The parents were perplexed, "They're one person. Surely if you want one, you want the other?"

Kintu claimed that the twins' eyes were different.

"I don't trust Babirye's eyes."

To support his views of Babirye he asked, "Why has no man married her?"

The parents, now cowering under Kintu's power, offered Babirye at half dowry, but Kintu still refused. Desperate, they offered her free on top of Nnakato, but Kintu would not have her. They resorted to threats.

"We don't wish you ill, Kintu. However, not only have you split our Babirye from her other half, you've humiliated her."

"If the girls didn't want to be separated in the first place, they should have not split into twins." Kintu was defiant.

The parents gave up, turned to the gods and prayed for mercy.

But after the wedding, Nnakato would not settle down to marriage. She kept going back and forth, back and forth, to her parents' house to check on Babirye. When, after many seasons she had not conceived, Kintu forbade her from visiting her sister. He declared that if the twins must see each other then Babirye, unmarried, should do the gallivanting.

Still Nnakato did not conceive.

The parents hung their heads in a *now-you-see* posture. But Kintu blamed Babirye for Nnakato's reluctant womb. Oh yes, twins might have an uncanny sense of each other, but to him, Nnakato's concern for Babirye was guilt and fear. It was this that locked Nnakato's womb. Kintu was certain that Babirye had punched Nnakato so hard while they were in the womb that Nnakato learned to make peace with her. He was surprised that Babirye did not devour Nnakato; such overbearing personalities often ate their twin and were born with a hunchback.

In the end, when Nnakato failed to conceive and Babirye failed to get married, Nnakato suggested that Babirye come and help her with conception. Even though Nnakato had abandoned her for a man, Babirye was keen to share her womb. At first, Kintu would not lie with her. However, as time passed, Nnakato's apparent barrenness began to compromise not only his virility, but his governorship. Expectant whispers: *Is the bride getting morning sickness yet?* turned from well-meaning to prying and finally petered out. Kintu gave in: better to have children with Nnakato's twin than with another woman.

Even though moments with Babirye were few and perfunctory, Kintu felt that she had jumped at the chance of becoming his wife. When Babirye conceived, she took over Nnakato's home with gusto, walking around the village showing off her swelling belly. Even when Nnakato explained to Kintu her agreement with Babirye—that on conception she would step back and assume the role of Babirye looking after her expectant sister, Kintu would not trust the older twin. To him, those first two years of Nnakato becoming a visitor in her own home, when Babirye became his wife, made Nnakato shrink. Babirye played her part well. Residents only noticed a slight change in Nnakato's' character. Apparently, her tone was sharper and she was impatient. Old women nodded knowingly: pregnant women were notoriously bad-tempered.

Babirye gave birth to twins. She nursed the babies until they started to run. Then she returned home to her parents. Over the years, she bailed Nnakato out four times. Each time, Babirye gave birth to identical twins. However, during the pregnancies, Kintu stayed away from home: either he traveled to the capital or toured his province.

Kintu was conflicted. He resented Babirye's claim to their marriage but prided himself in siring twins. His new title was Ssabalongo. The residents marveled, "As a sire, Kintu is chief indeed." Every time a set of twins arrived, they shook his hand, "A strong man may wake up late and still get to do as much as we who woke up with the birds."

Nnakato and Babirye were both called Nnabalongo, the children called both of them "Mother", but in her heart Babirye knew that when people called her Nnabalongo they were talking to her sister. She knew that the children called her Mother not because she had knelt down in pain to bring them into the world, but because she was their mother's sister. Babirye's eight children belonged to Nnakato.

It was midmorning: the sun was still amiable. Villages were now behind them. The further they traveled, the more stunted the vegetation became. Reeds had given way to *ssenke*, a sturdy grass accustomed to stingy weather. The ground was harder than before. Even to a novice taking the journey for the first time, the hardening of the ground, the yellowing sparseness, and thinning of vegetation indicated that they were moving further away from fertile land toward a more arid landscape.

3.

The party was now on its fourth day of travel. They had stopped
for the third break and changeover of tasks. The men refreshed
with water and fruit they had collected along the way, while Nnondo briefed them on the remaining part of the day's journey. They
were to watch out for anything bright-colored and slithering, especially monitor lizards and snakes.

Kintu took a swig from his gourd, the smoked flavor reminding him of home. He scanned the horizon for any dark cloud that
would shield them from the sun but the sky was a sterile blue.
He cut a slice of mango and ate: unripe but soft, it was tangy.
Normally, mango was fruit for children but Kintu and his men
were eating dried meat and roasted seeds. Meat was light in the
stomach and it kept hunger away, but it was obstructive to bowel
movement. Mango kept the stomach in motion.

After refreshing, the men stood up. Pacesetters at the head of
the convoy took over the migguggu of Kintu's sheets of barkcloth,
his regalia, skin robes, ceremonial wooden slippers, and other personal effects. Others carried food—especially meats hunted on the
way and dry-roasted, as they were soon coming to regions without
game or fruits. They now walked in the middle of the retinue,
while men who had been at the back took over pacesetting at the
top of the convoy. The ones that had been carrying loads now

took the rear. As they set off, Kintu ignored the nagging ache in his feet.

Soon the scenery gave way to huge cone-like hills covered in stone gravel. Rising off a flat plain, the hills were so close to each other that there were no valleys between them. The convoy walked around them through the narrow corridors. There was only a smattering of vegetation at this point. The hilltops were totally bare. The grass, only inches off the ground, was dewy, soft and wet, refreshing to the men's aching feet. For a while, the hills were a welcome distraction as they interrupted the horizon and kept Kintu's mind off the discouraging distance. But then a burning sensation—as if the air he breathed grated his nose—gripped him and tears came to his eyes. To ease the pain, Kintu held his nose and breathed through his mouth until they had left the hills behind.

Kintu married other women besides Nnakato. The women were brought to him as tributes: some from ambitious parents, others were daughters of fellow governors. His wives' homes were scattered all over the province for his convenience when he toured. The families, especially in far-flung regions of the province, were also a reminder to the local populace of his presence. Nnakato was in charge of the wives. When a bride arrived, she named and allocated her a role within the family—there were those good with children, creative ones who concentrated on crafts; those with a lucky hand in farming and who produced more food. When Kintu was away on *kabaka*'s duties, Nnakato visited the wives, checking on the children and the state of the land they lived on. When the children were older, she rounded the age groups up and brought them to Mayirika for instruction. She also garnered, informally, local moods and major incidents, reporting back to Kintu. Nnakato made sure that the wives met and visited each other regularly. The children visited each mother to meet their siblings. But to Kintu, the women were a duty.

At the thought of his wives Kintu gnashed his teeth. He felt bound. He was a prize bull thrown into a herd of heifers. He was Ppookino: Why did he have to mount every woman thrown at him? On the other hand, how could he not? He was a man, a seed dispenser. It was natural: he should enjoy it. For the *ba kabaka*, women brought to them were put away to entertain envoys, dignitaries, and other guests. Unlike a *kabaka*, Kintu was not above culture. Women given to him had to become his wives. In any case, Nnakato was an effective head-wife. She put in place a roster: every wife would have a child at least once in three years, ideally, once in every two years.

Kintu did his rounds; he spent a week with each wife. However, this sexual journey through his wives, *ebisanja*, was more arduous than the trek to the capital. Women waited moons to see him. Most were young with high expectations. They drained him. Despite Nnakato's potions, Kintu never felt fully replenished. In any case, Nnakato brought the wives who failed to conceive to Mayirika and asked him to double his efforts. Kintu winced at the thought of the potions. They were enslaving. Once you tried them, they confiscated what was naturally yours so that you depended on them. Probably, men envied him every time someone arrived with a shivering virgin, but he was not interested, not even in Babirye who writhed and made noises like Nnakato. He was no Ppookino, Kintu decided. He was a slave to procreation and to the kingdom.

Just as the eldest twins Kintu had with Babirye were about to get married, Nnakato conceived. Kintu could not travel to the capital because Nnakato's pregnancy was jittery: several times, it threatened to fall through. She became emaciated and haggard. Kintu cut down her duties and Babirye took over. Finally, Nnakato gave birth to a son, Baale.

That is when trouble started.

While to the family Kintu's love for Baale was mere indulgence of himself and his youngest son, Babirye saw it as Kintu wedging a distinction between her "own" children and Nnakato's son, that he never loved "her" children the way he loved Baale. Babirye, still living with her parents, threatened to tell the older children the truth. After all, Nnakato had her own child now. Nnakato was frightened, not of Babirye telling the children, but of the possibility of being partial to her son. She swallowed her hurt and asked Kintu to tell the children but Kintu would not hear of it.

One day, as Babirye prepared to return to her parents after a long visit, she took Nnakato aside and asked, "Nnakato, do you ever think about me?"

"Why, Babirye, how can you ask?"

Babirye was silent for a moment. Then she counted questions on her fingers. "Who carried those children for nine moons? Who labored on her knees to bring them into the world? Who nursed them for seasons? Who gives them up as soon as they are weaned? Have you ever wondered what happens to the mother in me as I pack to leave?"

When Nnakato did not answer Babirye said, "These breasts, they weep."

Nnakato choked. She had Mbuga—Nnakato called Kintu Mbuga affectionately—she had Mayirika and nine children. Babirye had nothing. Nnakato pleaded with Kintu to tell the children, but he threatened to keep Babirye away from his family. He felt that Nnakato fell too easily under Babirye's spell.

"Why didn't she bring her concern to me? Why ask you?"

"She is frightened, Mbuga. I am the one who asked for her kindness."

"But the children are mine: not yours, not hers. Mine."

"They are, Mbuga."

"When my children occupied her body, it was temporary. I'll pay for her services if that is what she wants. Tell all the other wives who might want to cordon their children off with a 'my' and 'mine' attitude that I will take them away from them."

"They know it, Mbuga. No one has cordoned her children off."

"That includes your sister. She's not special."

On learning Kintu's decision, Babirye screwed her face in tears and Nnakato cried with her. Before she left, Babirye whispered to Nnakato savagely, "Those children belong to Kintu because *I* said they do; if I change my mind they would not be his, would they?"

Nnakato held her mouth in shock. Babirye returned home enraged by the emptiness of her maternal embrace. Nnakato's guilt was exacerbated by the lethargy of her womb. After a while, she found a happy compromise and went to Kintu. "I've been thinking, Mbuga," she started. "Now that we're getting old, couldn't Babirye move in with us? She's given us the ultimate gift: why not share the rest with her? She will be mother to the children, Mayirika is vast, you're away most of the time and we'll keep each other company."

"You're asking me to marry her."

"You've already married her in every sense except in ceremony."

Kintu agreed to marry Babirye on condition that she kept quiet about the children. For Nnakato's sake, he married Babirye in a big wedding. The community applauded. "It was not right abandoning Babirye like that. After all, he's only a man. There's enough of him to go round. Whoever thought of separating twins in the first place?"

Kintu wanted to house Babirye away from his main home like the rest of his wives, but Nnakato insisted on sharing Mayirika with her.

There had been peace for a long while until recently. This time, Babirye accused Kintu of planning to make Baale next in line in spite of his older children. On this charge, Kintu was in a dilemma. All his sets of twin sons were identical. To make one twin governor was to ask for trouble: What would he do with the other? The Ganda never made identical twins heirs to an office; one could not be sure who was who exactly. Besides, with Babirye's disposition, who knows what she would do to Nnakato if he died and one of her sons became governor? Yet, there was no question of making another woman's child heir to the chieftaincy. That left him with one option: Baale.

Babirye had another complaint. Apparently, when her turn came to cook for Kintu, when he spent a week in her quarters, Kintu only came at night. He barely managed to stick a finger in her cooking, lick it and fall asleep. Babirye suspected that Kintu only visited her when Nnakato pushed him.

To Kintu, this complaint was immaterial. He never chose which wife to lie with and he did not visit his other wives more often than he visited Babirye. To him, while Nnakato continually worried about Babirye's welfare and begged him to spend more time with her even during Nnakato's own turn, Babirye complained incessantly.

Kintu made up his mind: One, he was going to build a house for Babirye away from Mayirika and move her. Two, Baale was his heir. It was time to start molding him. First, he would apprentice him and present him as his next in line to whoever would be *kabaka*. And when the time was right, he would get Baale married. Now Kintu adjusted the knot on his barkcloth decisively. The relief he felt was similar to that time when, after the long period of mourning his father as custom demanded, his hair had grown thick on his head. On the morning of his father's last funeral rites, his aunt shaved his head and Kintu had felt such relief.

Looking over the horizon, Kintu was grateful for the distance and space the journey had put between him and his home. Because of the recent royal turmoil, he had not traveled beyond his province for a long time. Such proximity to domestic politics clouded his judgement, he thought. Now that he had stepped away, everything stood in crisp clarity.

4.

The party was a week into the journey and their pace had slowed down considerably. In the absence of overhead vegetation or hills, they were exposed to the sun and to the heat. Although Kintu talked to his men, commenting on the weather and on the landscape, he kept counsel with his mind.

Now the men's laughter forced itself upon him. They no longer talked to those immediately around them as before, but as a group. It was a strategy to disregard the sun, to numb the ache in their heels and to maintain cheer. Kintu never took part in the morale-sustaining banter, partly because the men only ever discussed women and partly to maintain his distance.

Kintu turned his mind to the men's conversation. Gitta was the unfortunate subject. He had recently given Kiyirika Village the kind of gossip that sustained strenuous work because it did not die easily.

"At Gitta's age, a bride like Zaya would only hasten him to his grave," a voice said.

"But how was he to know that Zaya was a toddler? She was his height and had breasts on the wedding day."

"How was he to know? One, when he found out that his bride preferred children's company; two, when she continued to grow. Zaya's now head and shoulders above him."

"Zaya's not a child. She's one of those women who can't bear the touch of a man."

"In that case, Gitta is stuck with a man."

"What do you mean 'stuck with a man'? A woman's a woman."

"He should have made her pregnant first thing."

"How could he? The girl's a wrestler."

"Her family was negligent. Zaya wasn't sufficiently prepared for marriage."

The men threw opinions over Kintu's head like a bunch of women in a peeling barn. Kintu would have rather redirected the conversation but it had reinvigorated the pace. Gitta was a prominent elder. However, a very public error had felled him.

"I blame Gitta's eldest wife. When I bring home a girl like Zaya, I expect my eldest wife to take her on, groom her and let me know when she's ready," Nnondo the headman said.

"Depends on the first wife you married."

"Do you know what Zaya told my daughter?"

"What?"

"That Gitta is *rotten*, that she keeps a knife under her bed in case he gets rotten with her."

"I still can't make it out though. How did Gitta get his head stuck like that?"

"Apparently," a narrator started with relish, "this particular night, Gitta was to get his dowry's worth. When he got to her quarters, Zaya started her childish games of: *Leave me alone, I don't want.* Gitta gave her a few whacks to let her know that he was serious. Zaya stopped fighting. He made his move but Zaya went wild. She grabbed him—you know how huge she is now—swung him like a fibre doll and ran. Gitta, thinking he was still the bull he once was, gave chase. Zaya ran into the shrubbery behind her quarters, Gitta in pursuit. In the darkness, he ran into an acacia shrub. Somehow, the stems locked around his neck. When he pulled his head out, the stems tightened. Gitta panicked and roared."

"That wail, man. As if something was devouring him!"

"If you got to the scene after Gitta was dislodged, count yourself lucky. But there I was with a man old enough to be my father, his neck trapped between stems like a sheep because he was chasing young sex. I put laughter on hold and got working. But it was not easy. The women kept asking: *Why he was chasing her at this time of the night?* All Gitta said was, *Hurry, help me.* I looked long at Gitta, gray all over but still craving young cunt. I thought, surely there must be a point at which a man can say enough is enough and hang up his manly eggs?"

"My wife woke me up and said: *Your friend nearly died.* Which friend? I asked. *The aged bull that grazes among calves,* she said and I shut her up."

"What happens to Zaya now?"

An awkward silence hovered.

Zaya was now part of Kintu's household, but the facts were not clear. Unfortunately, the men could not speculate in his presence. The prolonged silence and the absence of Kintu's bland smile alerted the men that they had gone too far. The conversation died.

Actually, when Nnakato learned that Zaya was fugitive in her garden, she had invited her into the home and asked Kintu to let her stay while her marriage was sorted out. Kintu dissuaded Gitta from returning Zaya to her parents, reasoning that she might be a slow developer needing the firm but gentle handling of a mother. On her part, Zaya swore to kill herself if she was returned to Gitta. Kintu left Zaya with Nnakato and Babirye to groom and asked Gitta to give her time. Then he told his teenage sons to treat Zaya as a sister, but with the respect for a married woman. His sons had laughed. Who wanted Gitta's pugilistic bride, one who took strides like a hunter, whose feet grasped the earth like a man's, whose voice, when she spoke, carried the whole house on top of her head and who, as if her mother never breastfed her properly, said that she had dreamed of becoming a warrior?

As soon as she was let loose in Kintu's household, Zaya forgot that she was married and a woman. She joined Kintu's sons in laying traps to catch animals and shooting birds out of trees.

Boys kept reminding her that she was female and should not climb trees.

Kintu felt for Gitta. He knew the snare of being a man. Society heaped such expectations on manhood that in a bid to live up to them some men snapped.

5.

Just as the sun moved into the center of the sky to inflict its worst, *o* Lwera, a region of barren land came into view. For Kintu, *o* Lwera marked the beginning of uncertainty. The men greeted the sight of *o* Lwera with both excitement and dread. It was only the seventh day but they had covered a ten days' journey and could now rest for the night. However, *o* Lwera was *o* Lwera. Even at this distance, a dirge, the hum of its heat, was audible. Waves of radiation danced in the air warning: *You traverse these grounds at your own peril.*

Rather than stopping at this point for the night, Kintu decided that the party take on *o* Lwera for a short spell to give the men, especially those trekking for the first time, a sense of the moorland. There was a cave, not far away from where they were, where his father's entourage used to camp. They would spend the night there. Kintu feared that spending the night outside *o* Lwera's borders would enhance the men's apprehension. Still, the pace fell as each man battled with private doubts about traveling through *o* Lwera.

Kintu was a boy the first time he spent a night in *o* Lwera. He had traveled with his father. His father's head-wife's tyranny had led to the formation of cliques among the children in order to protect themselves. Kintu, an only child whose mother had died, had neither clique nor mother to protect him. Though his father later brought two other wives to the home to curb the woman's tyranny, Kintu never fit in. This led to a close bond between him and his father. That night, as everyone slept, Kintu had slipped off his sleeping skin and sat at the mouth of the cave. In his young mind, *o* Lwera was the son who, because of an intrinsic evil, isolated himself from his siblings and severed all intercourse with the family. Even at night, *o* Lwera seemed to turn its back to the moon and stars. It stood sullen, spying, and scheming. The following day, when he asked how *o* Lwera came to be, his father had explained, "*O* Lwera was the shallows of Lake Nnalubaale. But one day the sun, the lusty fool, attempted to kiss the lake and it shrank. *o* Lwera was formed."

Now, Kintu looked into its expanse and sterility stared back. The few scraggy shrubs scattering the landscape were nettled. Small parched weeds crawled the ground laying nasty thorns. *o* Lwera was level, its soil gray, thin, and loose as if a fire had caused the desolation. The ground burst intermittently into tiny gray bump-like anthills. Even the cool breeze from the Nnalubaale that soothed Buganda avoided *o* Lwera.

O Lwera played mind games. Its weapon was illusion. Distant objects seemed so tantalizingly close that gullible travelers set themselves impossible goals, often missing the right places to rest. Rookie travelers swore that when they lifted their feet *o* Lwera moved the ground so that they stepped back where they were before, that the sensation of walking but not advancing was frightening.

Kintu looked at his son. Kalema had kept to himself since Baale returned home.

"How are the feet, Kalema?"

"Still good, Father."

"Do you think you can wrestle *o* Lwera?"

"I am not frightened."

"Don't push yourself. If you're tired, we can take a rest."

"I am fine, Father."

Typical, Kintu thought. Kalema was at the threshold of manhood where the words 'I am not sure' did not exist. Shy hairs peered above his upper lip. His voice had dropped and his legs and arms had lost their childish flab. He was almost as tall as Kintu yet Ntwire, his biological father, was stocky. Kalema was born Kalemanzira but family tongues had reduced his name to the familiar and royal name of Kalema. At home, he was Kintu's son but older residents knew that Kalema was the only child of Ntwire.

One day, Ntwire had arrived in Kiyirika Village, distraught. In his arms was a shivering newborn, still covered in birth-blood. Between demonstrations and gestures, it became clear that Ntwire was a *munnarwanda* on his way to settle in the capital but his wife had died in childbirth. The residents took Ntwire to the governor. Nnakato, who had just given birth to Baale, offered to put Kalema on her breast. When Kalema grabbed it as if it were his own, Nnakato sat back in satisfaction: Baale had a twin. As a rule, a child in Kintu's house was a child of the house. Talk of different ancestry was taboo because it led to self-consciousness and isolation. In a house where all Nnakato's other children were twins, Kalema being Baale's twin never raised interest.

In appreciation, Ntwire pledged to lay down his life for Kintu. He would do any work for him. Ntwire took a piece of land that Kintu gave him, abandoned plans to carry on to the capital and started herding Kintu's cattle. However, while Kalema blended into Kintu's vast household, Ntwire hovered on the peripheries of the community. Unlike the Tutsis who found their way to the capital and who assumed Ganda names on arrival and married Ganda spouses, Ntwire stood aloof. Inside, he was torn between his needs as a lonely outsider who craved his son's love on the one hand and, on the other, he wanted to let the world take his son where happiness was. Otherwise, Ntwire was content to note that in spite of Ganda food, language and mannerisms, Kalema had taken after his mother: tall, regal, and with the most comely face that a womb ever sculpted.

When Ntwire found out that the governor was traveling to

the capital again, he came to talk. He had decided that Kalema should find a job in the courts of the *kabaka*. Kintu was surprised that after all these years Ntwire still thought that working in the palace was a good opportunity. It was true that settlers from other tribes found jobs and sometimes favor in palaces. To some *ba ka-baka*, surrounding themselves with people from different cultures was equivalent to traveling to these places. Mawanda used settlers as escorts to his envoys. Namugala employed them as spies. However, Kintu was uneasy. He knew the reality of the palaces, especially at such a time when a neophyte *kabaka* was still grappling for the security of his reign. In any case, there were many Tutsis in Kyadondo Province already. Despite this, Kintu understood Ntwire's dilemma. While Kalema the child had enjoyed the life of a governor's son, as a man, once Kintu's protective hand lifted, he would plummet to reality. Ntwire's refusal to take on a Ganda name and behave Ganda would always make Kalema a foreigner. Had Ntwire been a woman, mother and child would have been absorbed into the tribe as soon as a man made her his woman. Kalema would marry a Ganda girl: Kintu would give the children not only names, but his clan. However, Ntwire, the real father, was defiantly Tutsi and as long as he was alive, Kalema would be Tutsi in spite of his marriage and in spite of his name. Now Ntwire had chosen to send his son away. Kalema was on his way to the palace.

Kintu decided that if Kyabaggu did not need Kalema, he would put him in charge of the family estate on Lubaga Hill and let him carve out a future. Who knows? Kalema could become his eyes and ears in the palace. It would work out even better when Baale became governor. The two brothers would make a great team.

When Kintu told Baale about Kalema's departure, the boy was broken. Kalema seemed confused but he was a quiet lad who always did as he was told. Nnakato and Kintu had decided not to tell him the truth of his birth. If Ntwire wanted his son to know he would tell Kalema himself. But as far as they were concerned he was their son. All Kintu told Kalema was that he needed him to stay in Kyadondo to learn the ways of the *ba kabaka* court and that it would be useful to Kintu.

Baale and Kalema's parting was silent. Kintu had told Baale to return home several times. Each time, Baale had asked to go "just a little further." Finally, Kintu raised his voice and ordered him back. Everyone else stopped. Baale stared at the sky. Kalema looked down, drawing lines on the ground with his big toe. The pain on both their faces was heartbreaking but Kintu held his stern look. Baale turned abruptly—without a word to Kalema or to his father, without waiting for his escort—and ran toward home. Kalema too started to walk without looking back. He did not talk to anyone for a long time.

O Lwera's heat hummed. Kintu removed the leopard skin and passed it to the men carrying his clothing. Kalema walked in front of him carrying Kintu's drinking gourds. They were tied on a string, which Kalema had draped on his right shoulder. As he walked, they knocked each other noisily but he did not seem to be bothered.

"Snails are licking my heels. Pacesetters stretch your strides!" Nnondo called from the back. Kintu took the string of calabashes off Kalema's shoulders and carried it himself.

"There, you'll walk faster."

6.

The party finally arrived at the chosen campsite. At its threshold, *o* Lwera offered a few oases. Luckily, this one was close to a cave. The men rested their loads on the ground. Those carrying jugs took them down to the spring where water flowed, while others searched the cave for snake eggs or animal cubs. Kalema put down the gourds and stretched.

"I could've carried on," he laughed, shaking his hamstring.

Kintu clicked his tongue. "You're numb. One of these days, this journey will creep on you with such malice that even your tongue will ache."

As they sat down to eat, Kintu asked Kalema to get him brew. Kalema picked up one of his father's rounded gourds and ran down to the spring where the jugs had been rested to cool. He blew dust out of the gourd, tipped a jug with banana brew, filled the gourd, and took it to Kintu. After a sip, Kintu waved the gourd at Kalema, coughing. "Bring me water!" His voice was hoarse. "This is warm," he coughed.

Kalema ran back to the spring. He looked at the brew in the gourd, and for a moment was stuck. He could not pour it back into the jug yet all the other gourds were back in the cave. The other option, pouring the brew away, seemed like a waste to him. On the other hand, it was taboo to drink from Kintu's dedicated utensils. When his gourds cracked they were buried. Nonetheless, Kalema put his mouth on Kintu's gourd and started to drink.

Out of nowhere, Kintu's backhand crashed into Kalema's jaw. Kalema's hands let go of the gourd and it fell to the ground shattering into fragments. Kalema looked up at his father, surprised, but his eyes kept rising as if the slap had come from the sky. He started to blink rapidly and then sank to the ground. He made to stand up, but fell back onto a rock. He raised his right hand, trying to get up. His hand rose and rose, but then he fell forward, face down and thrashed. The force of his thrashing flipped him, turning him onto his back. The back of his head rolled in the mud. Small shards of the gourd stuck in his hair. His eyes stared wild. For a while Kalema writhed like a caterpillar whose hairs were set on fire. Finally, he slowed down until only his fingers twitched. A long rush of breath drained from deep inside him. Then he stopped.

"A*bange*," Kintu choked.

The men came running.

"Oh."

"What is this?"

"Ah."

"A snake?"

But none of them would question the governor by asking what happened. Nnondo looked in the distance, all around, as if he expected to catch whatever killed Kalema disappearing.

"He's gone," one of the men whispered as if not to wake Kalema. And the men stood and stared. To still his shaking hands, Kintu clasped them behind his back. Several times, he opened his mouth to say something but nothing came out.

"To say that just a minute ago this boy was—" a man started and stopped. Then he tried again. "Take a step back, just a minute back, this boy will be running."

"I chastised him—a slap," Kintu finally managed.

There was silence as if Kintu had not spoken.

Then a man said soothingly, "Journeying is like that. Some are allowed, some are not. We all slap our children. They don't drop dead."

The men sat down around the corpse. Kintu walked back to the cave; he had to hold himself together. He had been on his way to relieve himself when he saw Kalema drinking from his gourd. In panic, he had slapped the gourd off Kalema's mouth but instead caught his jaw.

In the cave, Kintu sat down. Not far from him, Kalema's food sat on a calabash as if he were coming back to eat it. The shattered fragments of the gourd flashed in Kintu's mind and he shivered. *Take a step back …* he had never struck a child, he had made all the right sacrifices for the journey, he had not offended any god. Take a step back indeed! He pulled a sheet of barkcloth from a pile and covered himself. *o* Lwera's heat had fled.

Outside, Nnondo rallied the men, "Come on! Let's get on with it." He made to lift Kalema. Custom dictated that trekkers who died on a journey be buried by the roadside. The other men hesitated.

"I'll ask *him* for instructions," one of the men said as he hurried toward the cave. When he got there he asked Kintu, "Can we still bury him today, Ppookino?"

"No," Kintu said. "Wash him and lay him on a mat. We'll bury him at sunrise." Kintu gave the man his thickest sheet and told him to wrap Kalema up well to keep him warm. On hearing these instructions, the men looked at each other. Any fool could see that Kalema was dead and there was plenty of time to bury him before sunset. But they could not question Ppookino. First, Nnondo passed his hand over Kalema's eyes and closed them. Then he straightened him and washed him. Finally, they laid him on a mat and covered him just as Kintu had instructed, with his face uncovered as if he were asleep.

Now Kintu remembered. He should have said something when he had that premonition. It was now useless to say, *My hair rose early into the journey. I felt something stalking us. Nnakato,* he wanted to call out and indulge in grief in the privacy of her chamber, but

Nnakato was far. Had Nnakato got the sensations, she would have sat down in the road; they would not have moved an inch further.

Memories came flooding back: the eyes he had felt watching as the men closed the reed gate at home, even that moon sinking when they were in the forest was now significant. Kintu would give his life to retrieve those moments because in them, Kalema was still alive. To think now that when he sensed danger he had brought Kalema close to himself, to think that Kalema, his gentlest son, should die at the hands of his own father. Nature had a cruel sense of irony.

Sleep is a thief: at dawn, despite staying awake all night, despite the death of his son, sleep stole Kintu away. While he slept, the men took Kalema for burial and left Kintu to rest. To them, *o Lwera* was mysterious. Once in a while, despite sacrifices, it swallowed a sojourner. They were as bound to nature's whims as the smallest ants. It was sad to bury someone so young, but a relief it was not one of them.

By not setting off at midnight, the party had lost half the time to travel to the next resting place. The men buried Kalema in a hurry. The grave was narrow and shallow. They used a stick to measure Kalema's length, but while the stick fit into the grave, Kalema did not. They crammed him in. They also stripped him of the sheet Kintu gave them to cover him. To them, it was too expensive to be wasted on the dead. In their hurry, the men did not even realize that they had buried Kalema beside a thorny shrub, *e Jirikiti*, the burial shrub for dogs. When they were ready to start, Nnondo woke Kintu up.

"Did I fall asleep?"

"You needed it, Ppookino."

"Did you lay him properly?"

Nnondo nodded.

7.

The men had not slept and they carried the extra weight of death. Kintu was worse: he had only licked on sleep. For a while, after being woken up, his body shook with the wrath of early sleep cut short. Even blinking was uncomfortable, as if there was sand under his eyelids. The sun gave them no respite. Nature's company were shadowy birds that croaked and menacing mirages that shimmered. The men had run out of laughter to mask their fears and *o* Lwera gave them nothing cheerful to talk about. The journey resisted them. Kintu tried to empty his mind of Kalema but failed. It wandered here and there, never anchoring on any subject.

A week later, they made it out of *o* Lwera, gaunt and sunburned. The vegetation started to thicken and to darken. The ground grew tolerant of their feet. It rained and the earth smelled fresh. At the sight of the green color of life, the men's spirits lifted. Soon the party was in Mawokota Province. At Kibuuka Town, Nnondo's relations awaited them. For a week, the party rested in Kibuuka until the blisters on their heels healed and the burned skin peeled off. When they set off again, cool wind soothed the sun-bite, it rained, and the air was filled with cheerful noises.

From that point on, Kyabaggu played mischief in Kintu's mind. Kintu had only met him twice before. As a prince, Kyabaggu was exceedingly haughty. Looking back now, to Kintu, the brothers had always seemed fond of each other, although it was clear that Kyabaggu was sharper than Namugala. Kyabaggu had once said to Namugala, in Kintu's hearing, "I'd take time to trust people from Buddu if I were you. Nyoro blood still runs thick in them."

"Did you hear that, Ppookino?" Namugala had laughed lazily. "Kyabaggu does not think you're Ganda enough yet."

Kintu had broken into a litany of allegiance, cursing any remnants of Nyoro blood in his veins. He also added, his eyes on the ground, "Those who betray the king, Ssabasajja, man above men, tend to be close to the throne. We commoners, whatever our blood, are nothing."

Now Kintu went over every word he had said on that occasion. It could mean life or death.

Fourteen days after Kibuuka Town, the party arrived below Buddo Bulungi Hill in Busiro Province where Namugala had been enthroned with new rituals and spectacle. From the traffic going up the hill, it was clear that Kyabaggu planned to be crowned in the same manner. The party pushed on until they came to the River Mayanja. There, as was traditional, the *kabaka*'s men, the *bakunta*, were waiting for Ppookino's party at the riverbanks. Kintu did not recognize any of the men. To him, that was the first sign that Namugala had not willingly handed over his throne to Kyabaggu as stated—otherwise there would still be familiar faces among the *bakunta*. Knowing that among Kyabaggu's men were spies and assassins, Kintu wore his most impotent look. No doubt, word had already reached the *lubiri* describing Ppookino's entourage. It was just as well that his men looked gaunt.

Kyabaggu's men led Kintu and his party through a new route. This way they cut Nateete, Wakaliga, and Lubaga off, and headed toward Mpiimelebela, across Kitunzi, through Bulange at the bottom of Namirembe Hill. This helped to avoid most of Kyadondo's steep hills and floodplains. To Kintu, Kyadondo was a foreign land. It did not matter whether it was the wet or the dry season: Kyadondo's valleys were always difficult to cross and the hills were painful to climb. Kintu had been up Namirembe Hill once when Namugala invited him to join him in a hunt for mpala antelope. Up there, the views over Buganda and Nnalubaale Lake were most magnificent. Only the *kabaka* was permitted to build on top of the hills. Each new *kabaka* vied to build a more magnificent court on a higher hill with a more spectacular view than his predecessor. Kyabaggu was expected to build a new palace on a hill not recently inhabited by a *kabaka* for hygienic reasons; however, Kintu was curious as to why Kyabaggu had chosen Lubya, a less imposing hill.

Even though Kyabaggu's escorts avoided the steepest hills and most wetlands, the party arrived at the foot of Lubya Hill out of breath.

8.

Up on top of Lubya Hill, Kintu could see a column of smoke rise steadily up the sky, indicating that the sovereign was at home. His heart turned slowly but he ignored the apprehension. *Just this one last climb and the journey will be over*, he thought. He asked for his leopard skin and draped it over his barkcloth. Nnondo passed him his ceremonial spear and shield. Kintu summoned all the energy he had left and holding his spear and shield in combat position—one never knows where the *kabaka* might be—he performed his allegiance and intention to protect the *kabaka*. Holding that position, Nnondo fell behind him and then the men. They marched up the hill.

The road to the *lubiri* was twice as wide as a commoner's courtyard. The periphery was lined with neat reed fencing. Kintu was sweating under his regalia but he held his warrior stance. As the retinue approached the summit, Kyabaggu's ambitions became clear. From what he could see, the palace under construction promised to be larger than anything Kintu had ever beheld.

At last they reached the summit. Kintu wanted to stop for a moment to catch his breath but the *bakunta* were hurrying ahead. Still he held his posture but looked around. The hilltop was vast and level. Perhaps this is why Kyabaggu chose it. Men were working everywhere—on gates, on the *kisaakaate*, the fencing, and on other structures. Kintu stood at the *wankaki*, the main entrance to the *lubiri*, and gritted his teeth. He stood right leg in front and his spear poised and performed fighting motions with the spear and shield reiterating that he was strong, he was fearless, he was loyal, he would serve and protect the *kabaka*. Then, without letting his guard down—even though his arms were quivering with pain—he led his men through the *wankaki*. The gatehouse for the royal drums was ready and the attendants stood in place. Behind him his men gasped at the size of the drums, the enormous gourds in the brewery, and the gigantic boats where banana juice was made. Before him, at the center of the *lubiri*, a sprawling reception area was ready. Two pillars ran along its face like a man's sideburns, curving back gently at the fringe. Men were smoothening the thatch, which ran from the top of the roof to the ground, covering the sides and the back of the building. Kintu's men walked, mouths open, turning around looking everywhere.

"Watch where you are going lest you turn your backs to the *kabaka*," Nnondo hissed at the men. "We're in the lion's den." The men fell back in line, quiet, wary. To Kintu, there was no doubt now that Kyabaggu had planned his ascension long before Namugala "abdicated." With the brevity of his brothers' reigns, one would expect Kyabaggu to commission something less elaborate, Kintu thought cynically.

The provincial governors' quarters, built on the western slope, had already been completed. A courtesan girl, Nnanteza, met Kintu at the arched entrance. Nnondo rushed to take the shield and spear from him and whispered, "You're still strong, Governor. You did not waver." Kintu smiled his relief. He wondered whether Kyabaggu had even seen his performance. The *bakunta* handed Kintu over to Nnanteza and Nnondo and Kintu's men were led away. Before Nnondo left, Kintu reminded him to procure the special Bwaise purple yam tubers that Nnakato loved and the medicinal *enkejje* fish powder for children.

When he walked into his lodgings, Kintu caught his breath. The walls were finished with the finest red earth only found on new anthills. The floor was underlaid with a soft layer of hay and then carpeted with white-and-black goatskins. The touch of goatskin under his feet was so smooth it was almost slippery. Kyabaggu was saying, "The real *kabaka* has arrived."

As he sat down, Kintu sighed. Starting all over again, getting to know Kyabaggu, negotiating his moods and whims, seemed like a mountain to scale. Then there were the "Worms" to watch out for —governors who would ingratiate themselves to the *kabaka* at the expense of others. No doubt, some had already brought virgin daughters for Kyabaggu to choose wives from.

There was also the tricky issue of explaining himself to Nnanteza: why he would not lie with her. Namugala had understood. He took no offence when he heard of Kintu's abstinence. Kintu had assured him that he was not averse to sex: just that *o* Lwera wrung the last liquid out of him. But then again, Namugala was always drunk.

Kintu looked at Nnanteza fussing over him and felt sorry. She had not made it to Kyabaggu's bedchamber as her parents had dreamed. Rejected, she would content herself with the casual use of royal guests. Nnanteza caught him staring and smiled. She was of the classical beauty: a long ringed neck, gapped front upper teeth, dimpled cheeks, large happy eyes, an aubergine skin, a wasp waist, and a firm earthen-pot bottom, all well assembled.

Now Nnanteza brought water in a calabash and knelt before him. Two *tutus*, short sturdy breasts, as if swollen, came close. Even when she leaned forward they refused to bow. Kintu stole a closer look: she had those rare breasts that are so wide at the base that there was almost no space between them—yet, they don't glut out. Five sons would knock them up and down and those breasts would bounce back, erect, Kintu thought.

"You know you're not only beautiful, Nnanteza, but you're blazing," Kintu said quietly.

Nnanteza looked up in disbelief.

"True—you belong in the arms of the *kabaka*."

Nnanteza's eyes fell to the floor. "Hmm," she said cynically.

"Kyabaggu will notice eventually," Kintu said softly.

"I didn't even get a royal viewing!"

"You did not?"

"I didn't make it past the king mother. Nnabulya decides who goes into his presence."

Kintu could only marvel at Nnabulya's shrewdness. She chose girls who would never threaten her position. "I'll not touch you, Nnanteza. In case Kyabaggu changes his mind."

Nnanteza smiled gratefully as she started washing Kintu's feet. Given the chance, he would mention her to Kyabaggu: a royal poking or two, a prince, become a *namasole*, who knows?

Among provincial governors, Kintu had the notoriety of failing to partake of the "fruits of the throne." He had had no esteem in Namugala's harem or the ones before. But Kintu was content with this reputation. To him, it was unwise to display sexual agility in the *lubiri*. His father had warned him that there was only room for one man in a palace, the *kabaka*. Besides, after his *ebisanja* through his wives at home, Kintu refused to perform in Kyadondo. After all, feeble performances were derided as well. As long as there was no concrete evidence, his "flaccid situation" could only be speculated upon, unlike those governors whose mediocrity was well established.

It was midmorning when Kintu stepped out of his quarters. The day was warming and he felt slow. He had been at the palace fifteen days but Kyabaggu had not summoned him yet. He spent the days catching up with other governors. Kintu yawned and considered visiting Kangawo of Bulemeezi. He had already seen Kaggo of Kyadondo and Ssebwana of Busiro. Because their provinces were closest to the palace, they arrived first and had already met Kyabaggu. Both men claimed Kyabaggu's graciousness, but offered no further information. Kintu had not expected it: governors guarded their thoughts on sovereigns.

Kintu decided to visit Ssekiboobo of Kyaggwe first, but as he set off, nature called and he took a detour to the back of his quarters. As he watered the back of an acacia, a cobra rose on his left.

In the corner of his eye, he saw it spread its neck, brandishing a thorny tongue. Kintu's leak died. The cobra rose higher, and shiny black scales glistened in the sun. A pattern, cube-like, on its throat wavered from left to right as it moved its head. Kintu waited until it stopped dancing. He then lifted his right foot and sat it softly on top of the left foot to keep still and look like a tree. The snake swayed belligerently again. Kintu closed his eyes and remained still.

Kintu did not know when the serpent lost interest. When he opened his eyes, it was gone. He went back to the house but Nnanteza was not in. He went to the royal guards and asked whether Kyabaggu kept pet snakes. They said he did not.

That night Kalema returned. He was much younger though. He stood shy, at a distance, his thumb in his mouth. His cloth had faded.

"You're dead," Kintu rebuked. "What have you come back for?"

Kalema crossed his hands across his chest and shivered.

"I am cold. It's chilly out there, especially at night."

"Nonsense, *o* Lwera is never cold."

"But I am, I am." Kalema was close to tears.

"But you're dead, you must stay dead."

"I am lying on my hand. It's numb. My leg is twisted. It hurts really bad. Won't people pile dead dogs on top of me? I am too close to *e Jirikiti*." Then he became excited: "Did you see me today, did you see me? Haaa, I was tall." As if realizing his father's lack of enthusiasm, Kalema added miserably, "People say I am not your son."

"You are my son but you are dead. Stay dead."

Kintu started to walk away but when he turned Kalema was standing at a distance, his arm was stretching out toward Kintu. It kept coming and coming regardless of how fast Kintu ran.

Kintu woke up, then froze. The snake was in the room: he could smell it. He lay still. He tried not to think about returning home, about breaking the news to Baale, to Nnakato, which language he would use to tell Ntwire. The thought made him hot and his skin grew wet with perspiration. The problem was not that Kalema had died—that is what people do—the problem was that he had killed him. It kept him awake through the night.

When day broke, he could not find the snake. Though the smell lingered, Nnanteza did not smell it. Kintu sent for Nnondo the headman.

"Did you bury the boy properly?"

"We tried our best, but it was as if in death he grew taller," Nnondo explained. "We misjudged him."

"What happened to the sheet I gave you?"

"We thought you'd need it."

"Did any of you see *e Jirikiti*?"

"*E Jirikiti*?" Nnondo was horrified that they had missed it.

Kintu sat cross-legged. His cloth covered most of his body apart from the right shoulder. He gnashed his teeth making his jaw dance frenziedly.

"Go away then," he whispered.

Nnondo walked a short way off, stopped and hesitated.

"The men and I can go back and bury Kalema properly, sir. We won't be long."

"Kalema is buried at the other end of *o* Lwera; you might as well go home."

Nnondo kept his eyes on the ground.

"I'll supervise it on our way back," Kintu whispered, realizing it was his fault for not overseeing Kalema's burial.

9.

The first time Kyabaggu summoned him, Kintu confirmed that Namugala was dead. It was there in Kyabaggu's eyes—the confidence that the challenge had been eliminated. Kyabaggu was so relaxed that there were only two guards on duty. For a moment, Kintu felt sympathy for Namugala: Did he die mercifully?

On this occasion, Kyabaggu was human. His smile reached the eyes. He talked about his ambitions for Buganda. As soon as Kintu was given liberty to speak, he broke into praises for the new palace, his quarters, and the sure prosperity that Buganda was going to enjoy because of Kyabaggu's expansive vision.

"Did the girl entertain you sufficiently?"

"That luxuriant beauty, Nnanteza? Ha! One look at her and I thought, is the *kabaka* testing me? I couldn't soil her. Me? Not with these commoner's hands!"

"Luxuriant beauty?"

"*Hwo*: you'd pour water on Nnanteza and I'd drink it."

"Nnanteza? Go fetch her." Kyabaggu snapped his fingers and a guard ran out. Meanwhile, Kintu expounded on the state of his province and illustrated his plans to extend Buddu beyond the banks of Kagera River to Kyamutwara. He assured Kyabaggu that, like his father and grandfather, he had no intentions of looking back at Bunyoro Kitara, the kingdom from whence his province was plucked six generations earlier.

Kyabaggu looked at Kintu condescendingly.

Kintu swore that the pitiful Nyoro blood—he spat—had been wrung out of his family, that no one was more Ganda than the people of Buddu. At that point the guard reappeared, Nnanteza in tow. Kyabaggu raised a hand and the guard nudged Nnanteza forward. She walked in a few steps, turned to face Kyabaggu, and slowly walked backwards.

"Turn."

Nnanteza turned but continued walking toward the end of the room, her back toward the king. She was visibly shaking and Kintu feared she would wet herself.

"Come back."

She turned and walked toward Kyabaggu. In the middle of the room, she stopped and dropped to her knees. All the while, she kept her eyes on the floor. Kintu heaved a sigh of relief—Nnanteza had been coached well.

"Look up."

She raised her face but her eyes were still focused on the floor.

"Look at me."

Nnanteza stole a glance at Kyabaggu and looked away.

"I see what you mean," he glanced at Kintu. Then he dismissed both Kintu and Nnanteza with feigned indifference.

Kintu was uneasy. The meeting had gone too well. Kyabaggu was too calm, too confident. Kintu was sure that his grovelling had worked. Kyabaggu was contemptuous. He hoped that he had laid a foundation for Nnanteza, as she never returned to Kintu's quarters. If she plays her *mpiki* well, Kintu thought, he would have an ally close to the throne.

On the second occasion, when Kyabaggu met all his governors as a *lukiiko*, he staged terror. First, the drums sounded to announce his entrance and the governors prostrated themselves. But instead of the king entering, Kintu heard a pair of footsteps, timid, come in and climb the podium. Up there, Kintu could not make out what was going on. Then the footsteps came down and scurried out.

The governors remained on the ground.

Then Kyabaggu and his *bambowa* entered. The men stopped at the entrance while Kyabaggu climbed the podium and walked to the namulondo. Kintu heard it squeak as Kyabaggu sat down. Then two men climbed up and stood on either side of the *kabaka*.

"Arise."

The governors raised their upper bodies and pressed down again in appreciation, like geckos, turning their heads to the left, to the right and to the middle.

When they sat up, shock ripped through the *lukiiko*. Some governors choked, others yelped.

In front of them, Ssentalo the *Ssabatabazi's* freshly severed head glared at them like a ghoulish trophy.

Twice, Kintu's nausea rose but he held it in his throat and swallowed. Ssentalo was the highest general in Buganda's army. He had served over eight *ba kabaka*, not counting Mwanga who had only lasted nine days.

Kintu was baffled. Ssentalo had been friends with Kyabaggu. Had he become too familiar? Ssentalo had been untouchable. His head was considered cemented onto its shoulders: Did some ambitious warrior take advantage to further his career? But Kyabaggu seemed too politically savvy to be manipulated. Was Ssentalo mistaken to harbor Namugala? Then, there was the issue of Ssentalo's reveling in his indiscriminate sexual tendencies. But as long as the kingdom's frontiers kept shifting outwards, his sexual avidity had not bothered earlier kings. Besides, he was always away looking for war. Ssentalo's beheading did not make sense.

Even in death Ssentalo's comeliness was still visible. He had been a *muvule* tree: tall and erect. He was charming, if a bit too good-looking and aware of it. The fact that he was a warrior who made both men and women groan beneath him had propped Ssentalo's manliness to unprecedented heights. Was Kyabaggu intimidated by Ssentalo?

Ssentalo and Kintu had been close. During Kintu's grooming, his father told him that Ssentalo was the only official he could trust in the *lukiiko*. The immense size of Buddu made Ppookino the most powerful governor, but Ssentalo was key to its expansion. He first introduced himself to Kintu when he succeeded his own father. He inquired about the "flaccid situation," and Kintu was alarmed that Ssentalo had misunderstood the path he walked. Seeing Kintu's panic, Ssentalo had said, "Don't worry. You're good-looking—but in a way that appeals to women. There's something gentle about you. When I want a woman, I go for a proper woman: soft, smooth, and round. When I want a man, I want hairy, sweat, musk, granite."

Kintu had smiled.

"Don't ever try men out of curiosity," Ssentalo had winked mischievously. "It's like a river: a one-way flow for many people, no return. Once you have heard the hoarse groan of a man, felt the moist hairy skin and drunk the scent of male sweat you will not want to hold a woman again. I have wives and I enjoy them. To the kingdom I've given a lot of children. Do you see what women do when they harvest cassava?"

"They replace it."

"Exactly: to avoid famine. As humans, we don't only replace ourselves, we multiply. Where there was one man, ten boys should grow. It's the ultimate law."

"I am not planning to try—"

"Do you enjoy women?"

"One of them—"

"Aha, Nnakato. I've heard that she was carved for you."

"Hmm."

"The others?"

"Sheer labor."

"What agony! This body," Ssentalo's hands had swept over his person, inviting Kintu to appraise it. "Was made to be enjoyed."

"Hmm," was all Kintu could say.

"If you want to make the arduous sexual labor through your wives bearable, here is the medicine. When you return home, rather than ravish Nnakato first, start with the wife that repels you most. Then work your way from the repellents to the favorites. Keep Nnakato for last. It's like eating sugar cane: the anticipated sweetness of the bottom pieces makes the top bits, which taste like tears, bearable."

Kintu had hoped to sound out Ssentalo of his decisions about Baale and Babirye and seek his counsel. Now, looking at his head dripping on a calabash, turning gray, while the *lukiiko* discussed raids on Busoga, brought pain to Kintu's joints. No doubt this was Kyabaggu intimidating the *lukiiko*. Kintu's shock melted and abhorrence took over. Ssekiboobo was discussing the best time to cross the River Kiyira, the size of fleet needed, and whether they could use the alternative route on Lake Nnalubaale. Listening to them was painful because all these campaigns were within the re-mits of Ssentalo's office. From then on, Kintu worked to mask his odium and maintain a frightened countenance. Meanwhile, Kyabaggu had made it clear that his eyes were set on the Ssoga people in the east. Annexing them to Buganda Kingdom would be his legacy. He wanted to know how many men each governor would supply for the invasion. Luckily for Kintu, Buddu was ex-empt because of the distance.

Kintu spent two moons at the palace. Soon after Kyabaggu's coro-nation, he returned to Buddu. Before setting off, he bought sheets of quality cloth from Lubaga. This time he oversaw Kalema's sec-ond burial. The party spent three days working on his grave. The men collected stones and piled them onto the grave until it stood out in the featureless *o* Lwera landscape. Then they planted the prolific *musambya* shrubs around the grave. When they finished, Kintu called Kalema and told him that he had done his duty by him as a father. He reiterated that in death as in life he was his son. However, Kalema had to stay dead. If he did not and chose to play mischief, Kintu would have his spirit bound.

10.

As soon as the trekkers reached their home territory and servants met them to take their loads, Kintu realized that Kalema had not made contact. For any traveler returning home with news of death, this was the first opportunity to disclose. But Kintu hesitated. He had hoped that the family would at least have an inkling that something had gone wrong on the journey so he would not break the news fresh to them. Anyhow, the furor over the safe return of the party so swept the urgency of a belated funeral away that even when Kintu set his first foot onto his courtyard, another moment to make the call of death, he did not. As moments right to disclose passed—he did not call Kalema's death as he stepped past the threshold of the main house either—Kintu realized that he would never muster the courage. When he sat down in his private lounge, he knew that he would never hold funeral rites for Kalema. He also knew that while Kalema's death was a tragedy, not holding funeral rites for the lad was reckless.

Before he even settled down Nnakato asked, "How was my boy when you left? I bet he—"

"Is he the most important thing in your life?"

"This tongue," Nnakato, though taken aback, cursed herself. "Such perils, *o* Lwera, Kyabaggu. *Ddu*nda has been merciful."

Kintu leaned against the wall and closed his eyes. He felt Nnakato hesitate, as if she were weighing her words.

"Are you still with us?" she whispered.

"Why not?" Kintu did not open his eyes. "After all, trekking from one arm of the kingdom to the end of another is blowing air through a basket."

Nnakato knelt before him. For a long time, she sat in silence. Her silence said she knew that something was wrong and she was waiting for him to tell her. Kintu did not open his eyes. Nnakato leaned forward, bringing her forehead closer until it touched his. Normally, this worked: either he smiled and whispered the problem or he pushed her away. Kintu did not open his eyes. He did not push her away either. Nnakato felt locked out. She sighed and stood up but then Kintu said, "I am not dying in case you're preparing to cry." Nnakato laughed because he expected her to. "But this journey will be my death," he added quietly. Still Kintu did not open his eyes.

"Kyabaggu might understand," Nnakato came back. "Instead of quarterly visits you could go twice a year."

"Governors twice my age still turn up all year round."

"But none crosses o Lwera. You trek across three provinces."

"Maybe I should get a wife that end," Kintu smiled.

Nnakato looked around to make sure that there was no one nearby. Then she whispered, "You could take Babirye and keep her there."

"Now you kill me," Kintu smiled and opened his eyes.

Nnakato fussed. The task of rehabilitating Kintu after trekking was hers. In order not to drown him in provincial and domestic issues immediately, she alone went into his presence. To help him recover, she had steamed small portions of bitter vegetables, which were good for repairing the body after a bad diet. Not to overwhelm his stomach, she had prepared juices, which he started with. Then she gave him ripe pawpaw, beaten to a pulp, to hasten his stomach and flush out the old food—later she would give him the medicines to drink for pain and muscle rubs for aches. Then she prepared his bath of crushed pawpaw leaves, tough on dirt, to scrub his body. After the bath, she massaged his muscles with crushed bbombo leaves. She dried him and laid him on the bed with his legs dangling. As he rested, she soaked his feet first then pressed them gently with fleshy banana fibers mashed into a spongy froth. When she had dried and oiled his feet, she laid them on the bed and propped hay pillows beneath them to ease the swelling. As Nnakato stood up to take the dirty water out, Kintu said, "Ssentalo didn't make it."

"Oh." Nnakato sat down. "I knew something was wrong; I knew it as soon as I saw you."

"Kyabaggu beheaded him."

"*Ddu*nda!" Nnakato swore. "How did Ssentalo offend him?"

"Who knows?"

"All that bravery, all that beauty thrown away just like that?"

"He brought Ssentalo's head along to the *lukiiko*."

Nnakato shivered. "What a shock for you, my one! You must have been paralyzed," Nnakato caressed his feet. When Kintu did not respond she added, "Maybe Kyabaggu asked Ssentalo to assassinate Namugala—"

"But he refused?" Kintu sat up. "You're quick, Nnakato. I see it now," Kintu said. "Ssentalo was stuck; either he killed Namugala, Kyabaggu becomes *kabaka* and kills him anyway—the obligation to kill his brother's murderer—or Ssentalo refuses to assassinate Namugala but Kyabaggu still gets his royal buttocks on the throne and Ssentalo has nowhere to hi—" Kintu was gripped by a fit of sneezes.

"Evening hay fever; I'll cover you," Nnakato fussed again.

Kintu poked a finger into his right ear and shook it violently. Then he rubbed his nose, clearing his throat.

"Funny though, hay fever never bothers me on a trek."

"Perhaps I should have used warm water to soak your feet."

"No, my feet were on fire when I arrived. It's the arrival of the night breeze. I'll soon adjust."

"Ssentalo was asking for it though," Nnakato carried on. "Displaying his magnificence like that? Only a sovereign should be that tall, that strong, that imposing. I hear Kyabaggu is short on royal looks."

"You read my thoughts exactly. Ssentalo reveled in the reputation of taking his four wives one by one in a single night, of being so manly women were not enough."

"You said he wore just a loincloth?"

"Or a skimpy skin, except to meet the king. Apparently, as a warrior the less he wore the better."

"Reckless."

"Now that you know what's been eating me tell me, any news?"

"Nothing but quiet since Kalema left. Kiyirika's not the same. Baale's drained of life."

"Baale's growing. Boys lose weight as they grow."

"You'd think they are proper twins. What am I saying? Of course they're proper twins."

"Hmm."

"I think Ntwire regrets sending Kalema away," Nnakato whispered.

"Has he said this to you?"

"A week after you left. He said he should have come along to see how Kalema settled in."

"Hmm."

"Funny though. I doubt Kalema knew of their true relationship."

Kintu pretended to be asleep. Nnakato sighed and stepped out.

Kintu did not sleep properly that night or the nights after. His failure to disclose haunted him. He should have announced the funeral as soon as he arrived; he should have gone up to Ntwire's house and told him, he could have sent one of the men ahead to break the news to the family. After all, there were all sorts of truths: snakebites, convulsions, truths that could have been more merciful than the truth, but it was now too late. How would he start—*Oh by the way I had forgotten: our son Kalema died?* Before the party arrived home, Kintu had told his men that word about Kalema's death should come from him first. Now it crossed his mind that perhaps he had said that because he had no intention of disclosing all along. Nnondo had said that they did not have to say anything at all. If the governor did not mention it, then none of his men would breathe a word.

11.

Ntwire, on his own on the plains grazing Kintu's cattle during
the day and alone in his hut during the night, dwelt more on the
difficulties of settling in Buganda than the advantages. Over the
years, the novelty of being in Buganda had eroded. In its place
was the contempt typical of alienated immigrants for their hosts.
The acceptance of his son as one of them, his life in their home,
of working for a generous but aloof governor, and the benevo-
lence of his twin wives were insufficient to ward off this contempt.
It was not his little knowledge of the language alone that kept him
apart: it was unease as well, born out of the Ganda's indifference
toward him. Then there was that obsessive cleanliness of theirs.
As a foreigner, the Ganda presumed that he was naturally filthy.
Even the most accepting among them would not allow him close
to their utensils.

After taking his child from him, no one looked back to ask
him how the boy should be brought up. At first, it was flatter-
ing to see Kalemanzira belong to the home as a son, but it soon
became clear that they had no intentions of letting the boy know
that he was his real father. It was wonderful to see his son happy
but painful when Kalema did not acknowledge him. He never told
Kalema the truth because he had heard that Kalema and Baale
once beat up a boy for calling Kalema a Tutsi. Ntwire could not

bear to see his son's disappointment when he found out that he was not Ganda.

In his isolation, little things like the Ganda's legendary ugliness gave Ntwire some satisfaction. Kalema stood out for his chiseled looks. Then there were things that the Ganda did that were just repugnant. For instance, for all their pride, art of language, and poise, the Ganda ate winged termites. It was not as though Buganda was without food. On the contrary, *matooke* rotted in the gardens unharvested. At any rate, the Ganda were fussy eaters who did not think that anything other than *matooke* deserved to be called food. Hence, to watch respectable men and women hankering after crawlies was abhorrent.

When it came to cows, the Ganda were impoverished. The only person with respectable herds of cattle in the region was Kintu. Milk was luxurious. The Ganda watered it down so badly that to Ntwire their hot milk *mujaja* drink looked like water. Every time Kintu held a feast, he slaughtered at least three cows to feed everyone in the nearby villages. Ntwire had never seen a people who loved meat as the Ganda did: they ate everything apart from the bones and skin. In fact, they sang songs cursing people who did not share meat with them. The men were such gluttons that they forbade women from eating chicken, eggs, mutton, and pork.

Because of his limited use of language, over the years Ntwire had developed a keen perception of body language. He could tell one who looked down on him even when they smiled. He could tell when they talked about him even when they whispered. He could tell a clear heart from a muddy one. He could tell when things had gone wrong. And now he was sure that something had happened to Kalema.

He had known immediately when the party returned. That initial eye contact when he smiled his gratitude at them for taking his boy to the capital and they had looked away. When he greeted them, they were abrupt, their bodies saying, "Don't ask." Often times, members of the party tensed when he walked past or they pretended not to see him. He saw it in their turned backs and in their veiled eyes. It was not one, not a few, but all of them. Ntwire was used to prejudice and contempt, but not to fear.

One moon after the governor returned, Ntwire deemed it polite to ask him about Kalema. But like a wary outsider negotiating a foreign language, he spoke without preamble. It came out brusque.

"I want my son back next time you travel."

"That will not be possible," Kintu looked at him levelly.

"Then I'll come along next time you travel."

"That will not be possible either."

"Because Kalema is dead?"

Ntwire's head tilted to the right until the ear touched the shoulder. It was a pleading posture.

Kintu was impassive. He did not refute Ntwire's assertion but he did not confirm it either. A flicker of hope floated across Ntwire's eyes. He thought that the governor was laughing. He waited for the laughter to break out so he could join in. When none came, Ntwire spoke up. It was as if he spoke his own language. His pain was harsh on the *b*s. *N*s became *ny*, *k*s became *g*s and *t*s were muffled yet what he said was clear. He pointed his shepherd stick at Kintu.

"You see these feet," then he pointed at his feet. "I am going to look for my child. If he's alive, I'll bring him home and apologize. But if I don't find him—to you, to your house, and to those that will be born out of it—to live will be to suffer. You will endure so much that you'll wish that you were never born." Ntwire's voice shook as he added, "And for you Kintu, even death will not bring relief."

But as he turned away, Ntwire still hoped that Kintu was only shocked at his audacity, that he would shout, *how dare you talk to me like that* and call him ungrateful because Kalema was fine and alive in the capital.

No word came after him.

Ntwire did not go back to his hut: he took nothing but the shepherd stick.

The rest of the family, not knowing why Ntwire had left suddenly, waited for him to return. Nnakato kept his house maintained and a tally of his cattle. She was sure that one day she would see Ntwire and Kalema on the horizon. Kintu kept silent. So did his men.

Kalema returned once in Kintu's dream.

"What did I say about you coming back?"

"It's so lonely out there," Kalema had gasped, out of breath.

"You died on a journey: you were buried according to custom."

"But I am frightened. I want to come home."

"First thing tomorrow, I am going to get you bound."

"Don't bind me, Father," Kalema had started to run away. At a distance he stopped and said, "Just bring Baale to see me one day."

But when he woke up the following morning, Kintu could not bring himself to bind Kalema's spirit. He considered taking Baale to o Lwera, to bid his brother goodbye, but he could not risk another son. Besides, to take Baale to bury Kalema was to bring the boy into the secret. It would not be fair on him. Instead, Kintu visited the strongest medicine man he knew and asked for protection. On top of sacrifices and ablutions, the medicine man directed that Kintu's children should never be slapped on the head as Ntwire was bound to revenge in a similar manner. Kintu made this a directive in his house; no child should ever be slapped on the head. If a child had to be punished then it would be on the buttocks where there was excessive muscle.

Kalema never came back again.

12.

It was ten years since his coronation, but Kyabaggu was still on the throne. In fact, there had been no royal uprising despite Kyabaggu's continual absence from the kingdom. Potential upstarts, nephews by former kings Mwanga and Namugala, were firmly in the control of their grandmother, Nnabulya. As Kintu had suspected, Namugala was pronounced dead soon after Kyabaggu's coronation festivities were over and the *lukiiko* had dispersed. Apparently, he had fallen to his death. But the nation knew that Namugala had been dead long before Kyabaggu's coronation. It was also known that Ssentalo was killed because he refused to assassinate Namugala on Kyabaggu's orders. Kyabaggu had taken over Ssentalo's warmongering and spent most of his time across the River Kiyira, terrorizing the Ssoga people.

Kintu was cynical about Kyabaggu's warring. On the outside, Kyabaggu seemed like a warrior *kabaka* seeking to subdue the obstinate Ssoga, yet he had not annexed any parts of Busoga to the kingdom. On the inside, Kintu knew that soon after his coronation Kyabaggu became an insomniac given to bouts of anxiety. Rumor had it that he had lured Namugala to Lubya Hill where he speared him. Namugala had fallen on the large rock outside the palace. Recently, Kyabaggu and his priests had consecrated the rock and made it holy. No doubt Namugala's blood was weeping. Haunted, Kyabaggu had fled the throne under the guise of war.

Kintu wondered what had possessed Kyabaggu to build a palace where he had assassinated his brother in the first place.

Meanwhile, Nnanteza had played her *mpiki* better than Kintu had hoped. She had found favour with Kyabaggu and so far she had borne him two sons, Jjunju and Ssemakokiro. Whenever Kintu went for the *lukiiko* in Lubya, Nnanteza insisted that Kintu's food be prepared by her own hand. Despite the circumstances of their first meeting, Kintu was always humble before Nnanteza. He had never discussed his role in her rise in status because words not only travel, but they acquire legs and arms along the way. And by the time they get to the person talked about, they are beyond recognition. Too many governors had lost their lives because of a rumor. Nonetheless, Nnanteza remained grateful. When she introduced Kintu to her family saying, "This is the man who rescued me," Kintu had asked, "Which rescue? I don't know what you are talking about." Nnanteza had resorted to sending the princes to visit Kintu every time he came to the capital.

Kintu smiled to himself—luck was so far on his side. His plans were moving well. All he had to do now was to get Baale married and then he would start to take him along to the capital.

At home, though the family still speculated about Kalema, Ntwire had faded from Kiyirika's memory. Kintu wondered whether Ntwire's curse had been just words from a grieving man or whether the protection from the medicine man had worked because nothing had happened to him or to his family. Not everything had gone according to plan though: Babirye still lived at Mayirika. Nnakato had refused to have her removed because she could not bear to see her sister "discarded' somewhere on her own. When Kintu insisted, Nnakato had started crying, saying, "Mbuga, you don't see Babirye's pain; it will kill us both." Kintu never raised the subject again.

Zaya had failed to transform into a wife. She was taller than most men and stood erect in spite of her breasts. Whatever made women feminine, Zaya had missed out on. She still begged the men to take her hunting, as joining Kintu's *bambowa* to go to war was out of the question. Gitta did not want her anymore but no man had come asking about her. Zaya did not even care about this "rejected" status of hers. She was happy to become part of Kintu's household. The family now treated her as a daughter who never got married.

Kintu was waiting at the fringes of the backyard. He stood near the *wawu* shrub whose coarse leaves the family used to scour pots. He was waiting for Baale. Father and son were going up the hill to harvest honey. The collection of honey was Kintu's chore. Normally, servants carried the torch on the way up and the honey afterwards on the way down, but this time only Baale was invited.

Baale joined Kintu with a lit torch and two large gourds. He was a man, taller than Kintu, though he still walked with a swagger. Baale had been reluctant to marry because he still wanted to *kulyabutaala* like an untethered goat. But then three moons ago he had surprised everyone by declaring that he was getting married soon and that no one was going to help him decide whom to marry. Baale had been a restless boy with a quick tongue and equally quick fists. Kalema had had a cooling effect on him. Every time the boys came home with Baale nursing a bleeding nose, Nnakato would ask Kalema, "What happened this time?" because Kalema's versions were more reliable. The fights had stopped about the same time as Kalema's departure. After the initial mournful stance, Baale had turned into a brooding young man who sucked his teeth at everything. Recently, his twin mothers were worried that he was getting too close to the gourd. Kintu was glad that Baale was finally getting married: a wife and a home would soon use up the excessive energy that made him swagger.

Kintu and Baale took the path leading up the hill. They walked quietly past the path that led to the gorge where the family collected water, past the twins' banana plantations, into the fallow land where goats and sheep grazed. At this point, the climb became steep and the path was covered in pebbles, some of them quite large. When they came to the huge mango tree that dominated the slope, Baale broke the silence.

"Is this mango tree male?"

"Why?"

"It only yields a mango or two in three years."

"If it was male, it would not yield any mangoes at all. I suppose it's one of those trees that wastes everything on appearance: handsome leaves, expansive branches but no fruit."

Just before the top of the hill, they came to a tree with a curious pink bark. It stood against a large rock. The tree had a straight trunk, but four meters off the ground it split into numerous branches. Kintu paused and touched it. He looked it up and down and shook his head. "There has always been such a tree in this place," he said distractedly. They walked around the rock. "It's always the same size though, I don't know whether it's the same tree or if one dies and another one grows." Baale, walking behind him, did not reply.

"So, Baale . . ." Kintu's voice rose, "You'll not wait for us to observe Ntongo. You're *on fire*. You must have her now."

"Who said I am on fire? I just can't see anything for anyone to observe for me."

"Exactly. You *can't* see! Let's say that where Ntongo is concerned, this thick emotion obstructs your view. But unlike you, we can see." Baale groaned. "Listen to me, Baale," Kintu said gently. "Let's imagine that Ntongo has a fiery temperament. We know how hot-tempered our Baale is. Would we be wrong to conclude that the two of you would set your house on fire? You shake your head? Good, because then we would either advise you to reconsider marrying her or we would prepare to put the fire out every time it broke out."

"There'll be no fire," Baale said tersely.

"What I am saying is that we're a very large family. Sometimes, what seems a private decision might have consequences beyond ourselves. For example, would Ntongo run an extensive home the way Nnakato does?"

Baale kept quiet. He realized that his father had asked him to come along not to help with honey but to discuss his impending marriage.

They arrived at the crown of the hill. Five trees similar in size and shape stood in a circle like quintuplets. The ground in the middle was clear. The trees had cavities like deep pockets into their stems. It was dark around the mouth of each hole which, at a distance, made the holes seem deep. Only one tree had bee activity, the others were quiet. A short ladder leaned against one of the trees. Kintu got the ladder and placed it against the tree with bees. He climbed two steps up and peered into the hole. "There is a lot," he whispered happily. He came down and took the torch. As he brought it close to the cavity, bees started flying out. Baale stood at a distance, watching.

Family lore had it that in the old, old days, a woman gave birth to a bee that settled close to home and built a colony. The colony was called Kayuki and it supplied the family with honey. But when, as a child, Baale asked Kintu about the story, he had replied, "My father did not pass on those details to me. However, he told me that the bees that live on top of Mayirika Hill are treated like a brother."

Baale had wanted the story to be true, to add magic to his ancestry. Even then, the way bees behaved around Mayirika was significant. Stray bees inside the house announced visitors. Dead bees were an omen. When a bee buzzed incessantly around a person, it indicated love felt somewhere.

"Baale," Kintu called. "Watch and learn; one day you might have to do this yourself. First, stand against the wind. That way, smoke comes toward you while the bees go the other way. Don't bring the torch too close to the mouth of the hive. You need to leave room for the bees to escape. Remember not to come in a foul mood."

When all the bees had gone, Kintu handed the torch back to Baale and climbed the ladder again.

"Sometimes Kayuki is in a mood. When the bees will not leave or when they're aggressive, go home; return when he's in a better mood." Kintu worked delicately. "The most important thing is to take only some, a half maybe. Just as you pick wild fruit and must throw back some to the wild, so must you leave honey for the bees." He withdrew a golden honeycomb and prepared to milk it.

"Do you know where you're going?" Kintu asked unexpectedly.

Baale remained silent. All that bee talk had been preamble. Here was the real thing. Kintu did not look up. He let the honey slide down into the calabash. Silence dragged on. Finally, Baale asked, "What do you mean where I am going?"

"Women."

Baale gave a short irritated laugh, "Of course I know where I am going."

"I am not talking about the breathless girls you steal with behind bushes. You know, the ones that challenge: *Show me your sun rising and I'll show you heaven.* Who, before you even get started, are quaking: *I hear someone coming.*"

"Father, I am known this village over, you can ask—"

"Who? The girls?"

"Of course not, but everyone knows I am—"

"No one knows anything, Baale, apart from you and the alleged girls. You forget I was once a boy." Kintu laughed. "We put about stories conjured in wet dreams. After all, girls always deny." Now Kintu looked at Baale, "I am your father. Is everything working?"

"Of course!"

"No need to raise your voice," Kintu looked around. "In the morning, do you wake up alert or . . . drowsy?"

"Alert. Father, I rise."

"So does my senile uncle," Kintu laughed. "Every morning, he gets out of bed. However, either we beg or cajole. Sometimes, he gets up, but moments later he's down again."

"I set off prompt. I am steady," Baale was beside himself.

"When all you have are a few stolen moments with a jittery

girl, anyone will set off fast and steady. I am talking about a real woman. When you have all night, when a woman makes you stand on your toes without relief. Do you know that a woman, while you are at it, can fall asleep? And when you are done and say, *Welcome back*, she snores at you."

Baale was silent.

"Come, hold this gourd for me. Put the fire out first. Take this gourd and place it near that banana leaf . . . Be careful, Baale. Now hold this one for me." Kintu noticed that Baale's hands were shaking. "Don't worry about women. I was like you but with time I worked them out. You see, we Ganda, we don't leave the propagation of the nation to chance. You must know what you're getting into before we place our bid on Ntongo's lap. Assure me that all's well and I'll assemble an impressive team made of my brothers, my older sons, and my friends. They shall descend on Ntongo's village and her family with style and pomp. But all that will be a show if you don't display something as impressive when she arrives."

"Obviously, I've never been married so I don't—"

"Now you talk like a man. Lift that jug. Are you sure you can carry it fine? We don't want to collect Kayuki's honey and pour it at his doorstep . . . Be careful, Baale. You know what, put it down, go home, and bring someone else to help us."

The way Baale fled down the hill made Kintu wonder whether he had been harsh. But he knew the pressures society put on men in marriage and he would never send a son into it unprepared.

13.

Two moons later, Baale, accompanied by his brothers and an uncle, paid an initial private visit to Ntongo's parents to inform them of his intentions toward their daughter. Not to seem desperate, Ntongo's parents told the party that they would "think about it." Now Kintu had received a message asking Baale to bring the dowry within three moons. Three moons would take the wedding into Musenene's rains, but Baale had refused to change the dates.

Kintu had a program for Baale's grooming. First, he had to take Baale away from his mothers and from Kiyirika Village so that he could taste life without them. Baale also needed to understand that not all women were kneeling yes-sir women. But most of all, something had to be done about that brooding energy.

Kintu summoned Baale and they went for a walk. They came to Nnondo's house and Kintu asked him to join them. As they walked, Kintu informed Baale that he was sending him away into the service of Princess Mazzi immediately. Nnondo, walking a step behind father and son, listened silently. Kintu told Baale that Mazzi, Namugala's youngest daughter, had recently traveled to Buddu. She needed dependable young men to run her temporary home.

"The princess will introduce you to public and royal etiquette—learn with diligence. Do not bring dishonor onto your mothers. Do whatever she asks with a good heart. Be open to new ways. Keep your ears and eyes open. Most of all, guard your tongue: if you must speak say good things only. I expect her to travel back to Kyadondo in a moon. She won't need your services after that, and you must return home."

"When do I leave?" Baale was excited at the prospect of travel. "Now."

"Eh?" Baale gasped at the haste. But Kintu did not offer any explanation.

"Go home and pack a few things."

As Baale left, Kintu held his hand and said, "Wait, you don't breathe a word to anyone—not even to your mothers. Do not bid anyone goodbye." Baale kept nodding. "When you are packed, come to Nnondo's house. You will set off from there."

When Baale had left, Kintu turned to Nnondo. He held in his hands a single cassava stem. It was short, half of what women used to plant cassava. It was thick but carefully cut at both ends. Now Kintu handed it over to Nnondo with both hands.

"This is a message to Princess Mazzi," he looked straight in Nnondo's eyes. "Don't give it to a servant; don't show it to anyone. If Mazzi can't see you immediately, keep it close to your chest. When she's ready to see you, present this stem with Baale. Tell her that this is the cassava that she craves, *the very stalk.* Tell her that Baale will be in her service for a moon and I would like her opinion of him. Do you understand?"

"I am a man, Ppookino."

"And, Nnondo, my son is in your hands."

Nnondo nodded.

Kintu added, "You know he will be Ppookino one day. Keep an eye on him, see how he carries himself over there, advise him, and bring him home safely."

"No word will rise off my tongue."

The two men turned and walked back to Nnondo's house. Now they talked about the Ssoga who had recently killed the governors Kyabaggu had appointed, again.

"Do you think that Kyabaggu is going to give up now?"

"And do what? He needs something to occupy him. He will go back to Busoga and the Ssoga will disappear into their bushes knowing that he would not stay long, otherwise he will lose his throne over here in Buganda. As soon as he returns to Buganda they will kill the governors and they shall go on like that until Kyabaggu gets tired or killed."

Nnondo sighed, "Then let's wait and see."

Soon Baale arrived at Nnondo's house carrying a small sack. When Nnondo and the men escorting Baale had left, Kintu returned to his home and informed Babirye and Nnakato that Baale had set off for apprenticeship.

Babirye kept silent. Nnakato was upset.

"He didn't even say goodbye to his mothers," she said.

"Baale's getting married soon. He will do things without informing us, unless he is taking you along to his marriage."

"That's not what I meant, Mbuga. Baale has never strayed beyond family."

"Now he has, as he should."

To indicate that the discussion was over, Kintu walked away. He smiled to himself. Nnakato would convulse if she knew that Baale had been sent to Princess Mazzi. Mazzi was notorious the world over. She had lasted only three days in marriage after the honeymoon because, as she lisped when she returned to her grandmother Nnabulya, "The husband wanted breakfast; I made it. He asked for lunch; I made it. Then he wanted supper and like a good person, I made it. For two days I suffered silently but then on the third day he was at it again—can you imagine the ash?"

From then on, Mazzi became a metaphor for spoiled brides in the kingdom. She refused to return to marriage even when she was given servants to take with her. Out of boredom, she now toured the nation.

One moon after Baale's departure, Nnondo returned without him. Nnondo asked to see Kintu in private. When Kintu saw Nnondo without Baale, his heart leaped into his mouth.

"Where's my child, Nnondo?" There was a slight tremor in his voice.

"The princess has had a change of plan. She won't leave until Musenene."

Kintu sighed with relief but was still confused.

"When the rain sets in? How will she cross the River Katonga?"

"I wondered too."

"Listen Nnondo, we've only got two moons to taking the dowry."

"I couldn't talk back to Mazzi. All she said was that I should come and let you know that Baale's fine. She also said that from the look of the stem, the cassava is a fine specimen. Baale is quick to learn in royal etiquette but some edges still need caressing into smoothness. Another moon, maybe a moon and a half would round him out."

"A moon and a half—did Mazzi actually say that?"

Nnondo spread his arms helplessly.

"How did Baale seem to you? Does he want to come home?"

"I hardly see him: the princess keeps him quite close. I think he's enjoying the attention."

"All right, Nnondo. Take a rest. In a week, go back to Mazzi and tell her that Baale is getting married soon and must return home. Don't let her take my boy."

14.

The Baale who returned from Princess Mazzi's service was unrec-
ognizable. Pensive and quiet, he was lean and had lost his former
bouncy gait. Nnondo reported that Mazzi would have taken Baale
along if Kintu had not been insistent.

Nnakato fussed. Baale ate less. For an apprentice, he looked
pampered. His skin had softened as if he spent most of the time
indoors, and he had the air about him of someone who had been
idle most of the time. What was more, Baale took time to readjust
to his old life. He did not return to his friends, however. Instead
he kept close to home, preparing his piece of land for the arrival
of his bride. Nnakato wondered loudly what had transformed her
boy into the reserved man, but Baale only smiled. Kintu was satisfied. If Baale had lost his heart to the princess then what better
way to break out of the cocoon of childhood into manhood than
through heartbreak? He hoped that by the wedding day, Baale
would have recovered.

A week after his return, Kintu called Baale to talk. This time,
he gave him a stool and a gourd of brew and said, "Now we shall
drink together."

Baale looked up at his father worriedly but did not ask why.

"Because," Kintu answered the question in Baale's eyes, "I
want to see whether you control your drink or it controls you."

Baale laughed shortly but he did not protest. He waited for his father to state why he had called him.

"How's your compound going?" Kintu asked.

"So far, on time. All the thatch for the roof has been brought in. It is drying now. I've been working on Ntongo's garden. I've planted *matooke* suckers further afield and her vegetables close to the house."

"And how was the princess?"

Baale looked at the floor. "She was leaving when we left," he said.

"I know she was leaving but how was she?"

"She was fine." Baale still looked at the floor.

"Do you want to return into her service?" Kintu stared at Baale intently.

"Me?" Baale looked up. "No. It's time to prepare for Ntongo."

"Do you still want Ntongo to come?

"Of course."

"I thought the princess had devoured your soul and Ntongo was no more."

"No, not at all. Princesses are like wind—they blow this way and blow that way. You don't want to blow with them."

"Thanks for the advice!" Kintu laughed. Then he became serious. "If that is the case, in fourteen days, I'll assemble men and women to accompany you to take Ntongo's dowry. Normally, the dowry day is the wedding day, but you want the wedding later?"

"I don't want the strain of doing everything on the same day."

"That's fine. However, on the eve of the dowry day all the married men we know will be here for you: your uncles, your brothers, my friends, and village elders will converge to talk to you all night. Don't drink or get yourself tired."

Baale smiled. The legendary groom sessions attended by married men only: he could not wait.

15.

Musenene's drizzles were relentless. The sun was in hibernation. The sky had dripped all morning, took a breath at midday, and started again. It had not stopped since.

It was beginning to get dark when men, including elders, governors, and friends of Kintu, started to assemble in the *kitawuluzi*, the large building set aside for meetings, consultations, and settling disputes. The *kitawuluzi* was circular. At the threshold, the thatch fell in such a fringe that there was hardly any headroom. But inside the hall, the ceiling of patched barkcloth was high. In one corner, embers smoldered. Kintu sat adjacent to the door, saluting guests as they arrived. Men who had arrived on time sat leaning against the walls. Governors sat close to Kintu. The women were in the guesthouse packing gifts for the bride's family. The rest of the villagers were in the tent making merry.

When Baale entered, the men clapped and cheered. He was adorned, on top of his cloth, with a black-and-white rhesus monkey fleece. On his upper arms, bands of bright, multicolored beads enhanced his biceps. His head was shaved except for the large crowning braid near his forehead, like all Ganda men. But Baale's braid, because he had been growing it for a long time, fell down the side of his face to below his cheek. The pampered glow he had acquired in Mazzi's service had not worn off yet. Kintu gave Baale a basket of smoked coffee beans to pass around among the men in welcome. As every man chewed on the coffee beans to reaffirm their brotherhood, Gitta leaned over to Kintu and asked, "Have we started pampering grooms for the wedding day? What's the world coming to?"

"It's not pampering—juices of anticipation have washed over him."

At that moment, women brought baskets of roast goat and jugs of *akaliga* brew. Nnakato stood at the threshold and called out the homecoming song, *Nyini muno mwali? Is the head of the house home?* And the men answered, *He knows not to discriminate relations, all these children, in this place, they are home.* As the song caught on, Nnakato withdrew.

When they stopped singing, Kintu thanked everyone for coming.

"Our son Baale wants to join the league of married men. Tomorrow, while his mothers and I will stay here anxious, you will accompany him to get him a wife. However, you will not bring the bride with you: she will be collected two weeks later. Apparently, only paupers combine the dowry day and the wedding these days."

"Wasteful," old men scoffed, while younger men nodded sympathetically.

"Before we send him into marriage, I've invited you tonight to help me enlighten him about manhood and marriage. We and Kiyirika have prepared him for the mundane aspects of life, but there are details to which we cannot get. Tonight, feel free to edify and share your experiences. As his father, I recently asked him if he has been with a woman and he answered: *Everyone knows, I have a reputation . . .*"

"Reputation? Did you ask him why only boys have a reputation?"

"They think that once they've pushed a girl upon the bark of a tree and heard her whimper then they know women."

Kintu realized that the introduction to the session had been plucked out of his hands. He sat back and let the talk flow spontaneously.

"Talk about cluelessness—recently we were talking about prowlers in our village when this young man said, *that's why my wife keeps waking me up. Three times this week she has woken me up. I checked outside, but there was nothing.* I asked him, *how long has your wife been waking you up? Two weeks maybe three,* the fool replied."

"For three weeks the buffoon has woken up but heard nothing outside his house and still went back to sleep?"

"I tell you by the time a woman starts 'hearing things' it's been a lot longer."

"Don't misunderstand me, young men, I am not saying don't check. There could be a prowler. Listen with her, you hear nothing, go close to the door and listen again. You hear nothing, come back to bed, ask: *Have prowlers disturbed your sleep, my good one? Yes,* she says. Then you give her something to put her to sleep."

"Baale, women don't ask for sex but it doesn't mean they don't want it. There will be times when you touch Ntongo and she yields. There will be times when she will pretend to be asleep, or kick you outright. Then there will be times when she will be restless. If you're the clueless type, she might burst into tears for no reason or become quarrelsome. I say to young men, watch the turning of the moon. Every woman has a pattern."

"Until you marry a second and a third and can't keep up with the patterns."

"Baale, if Ntongo makes you happy, why bring a second wife?"

"My father told me to watch my back if my two wives get on too well."

"When they turn against you—"

"Then don't cross them. My two wives live together in the same house. There is no boundary between the children. One has breastfed the other's children when she's unwell or has traveled. But of course when you fall out with them, you want to run out of your own house. But I am not about to marry a third because

I am frightened of them. My children are happy and that is what matters."

"Three women living in the same house turning against you: there's a frightening prospect."

"Don't put women in the same house."

"And separate my children? Allow my sons to grow up under a woman's influence?"

"You hear them, Baale? They can't even agree. As I said before, if one woman makes you happy—"

"A young couple I know suffered the 'restless' problem," someone interrupted. "However, it manifested differently. The woman hit the children."

"She did what?"

"One word to a child and the next was a blow. All of a sudden, the children had their father's ugly head and his vacant eyes. One time, she told a child to fetch something but before he stood up, she accompanied the request with a blow. I said: *Woman, stand up,* but before she stood up, I hit the ground so hard she jumped. I said, *I am not your husband, but hit a child again and I'll give you something else to hit.* She burst into tears."

"Ahaa!"

"I asked: *What is it?* She whispered: *Nothing.* I said: *Something is,* but she just wept. I took the husband aside and asked: *When was the last time you touched her?* He started: *You see, I've been clearing a virgin land. You see, the rains are coming. You see, I need to start planting . . .* I said, *Shut up. I see your home crumbling. Can virgin land cheat on you? Now go in there and fuck the steam out of her.* I took the children with me and handed them over to my wife. I told the husband to collect them the following day. When I saw the woman next, she whispered, *Thanks for your words—they were good.*"

"Imagine if he had three women and virgin land to clear!"

"I look at young men these days and shake my head. He's just married his first wife but before she's even pregnant, he's looking for a new one. You ask, how do they manage two young women?"

"Half their children belong to the village."

"I'll share a secret with you, Baale," whispered Kintunzi of Gomba. "Most marital disputes brought to us, the bottom line is sexual."

"True," agreed Kayima of Mawokota. "A sexually satisfied woman is a good wife, that's all I am saying."

"Baale, I've found it useful to listen to the noise she makes when we're in our moment—"

"The noisier, the phonier."

"Don't start me on noisy women!"

"It means you don't know what you're doing. Trust me, Baale: when you take a woman there, there is no way she's going to sing: *Oh, you're the pharaoh in my Misr*—I mean, she can hardly breathe."

"Often, the noise is a ploy to get you there quickly so she can go to sleep."

"Do aunts teach them how to sing?"

"I can't stand the noise, me. Sometimes I want to shout: S*hut up and let me get on with it.*"

"Silence? Aaah, it's like fucking a mattress."

"Same here, I need music to dance to."

"No one's talking dead silence. We're talking false noises."

"Noise or silence, Baale, the most important thing is for you to know how your woman behaves when she's actually into it. Learn to knock for as long as it takes for her to open up. However, if you can tell that she's not in it with you and still carry on just because she's screaming, that's entirely up to you. But I recommend that you hold her hand so that you both get there."

"Haa, there are some clever women; when she is not in the mood, she does not say no. Instead, she touches you here and there and before you have even started you have come. She turns around and faces the wall."

"Don't let her rush you—say, *don't touch that.*"

"As long as Baale knows that women are innate actresses."

"Until they get pregnant."

"Where do I start on pregnant women?"

"With the crazy cravings and bizarre—"

"My Nnabakka . . ." a man lowered his voice as if there were women nearby, "has the oddest craving when she's pregnant. I return from digging, sticky and stinking of sweat, but she wants me. I lie down and she buries her head into places and sniffs. If I take a bath and lie next to her, she throws up. At first, I thought, what sort of child is coming?"

"I thought sex stops when a woman's pregnant?" Baale asked. There was a chorus of groans.

"My Nnamale would claim: *I've not felt the child move all day, why don't you check and see?* At first I asked, *Check how?* She quipped, *How did you put him there?*"

"Mine cannot stand the sight of me. I walk past, she spits. She sees me coming in, she walks out."

"Baale, Ntongo will fall pregnant and you may not recognize her. Don't be alarmed. She'll return to normal as soon as the baby comes out."

"I went to a wedding fifteen years ago," Kintu started, and the room fell silent. "A friend's son was marrying. The lad had a 'reputation' like our Baale here. Dowry was paid, the bride was brought, the wedding went well until 'real marriage.' Just before midnight, the bride retired to the bedroom and soon afterwards, the groom joined her. The drummers signaled consummation and you know those drums won't stop until the groom comes out to signal that it's a deal."

"In fact, Baale—sorry to interrupt, Kintu—those drums are for you, to urge you on and give you rhythm. If the bride is erratic, as virgins normally are, ask her to respond to them, it helps with the nerves as well. Carry on, Kintu."

"When the fellow got to the bedroom, he fell asleep."

"He did what?"

"Fell snoring-asleep beside his bride."

An elder turned and knocked his head on the wall, "No, no, no."

"The girl, having been prepared for the wedding night, shook the groom's hand shyly, *Husband, husband; aren't we supposed to be doing something?*"

"I can't take this!"

"Don't hide your head, Baale. This is manhood under pressure."

"An hour later, in comes the girl's aunt to check on the couple."

"What about the drums?"

"Still going, presuming that the groom's stamina is phenomenal."

"*Wowe!*"

"First, the aunt listens at the door; no noises. She imagines it's done. She walks in to check the bed sheet. What does she see? The bride's sitting on the bed bemused, the groom's snoring."

"*Wololo*," a man cried.

"God knows the women people pick to be grooming-aunts: this one was evil. She woke the groom up and asked: *Do you imagine my girl came here to admire your backside? Whose girl do you think you're going to starve?* Before the groom could explain, she had reached for his manhood."

"Who reached for his manhood?" Baale hissed.

"The aunt. As you can imagine, the member had not stirred. *What is this*—she flapped him like a straw—*Have you ever got 'this' up?*"

"Women are ruthless."

"Before long, she was manipulating him, telling the girl to strip."

"Is it allowed for the aunt to touch him there?" Baale was alarmed.

"Is it allowed? Baale, it's decreed in Ganda law that when a groom fails to get it up, the aunt must get him going, that when a bride's having problems, the aunt must show her what to do. What do you think they have her there for?"

"Baale, most aunts will not let you make the mistake in the first place. Before they call you into the bedroom, she's stationed under the bed."

"Under what?" Baale stood up. "Do you mean *her aunt* will be under *our* bed?"

"Sit down, Baale. Nothing to be frightened of."

"My wife's aunt was under the bed on our first night. When I came into the bedroom, I gestured to my wife and she nodded. On the contrary, the idea turned me on. I thought, let me knock her girl so hard that by the time she gets from under our bed, she will be drenched. As I left the room, I said: *I am still running you know, can I have your aunt as well?*"

"The hag was under our bed too, but as I left afterwards, I called: *Aunt, how did you like that?* She was mute."

"That's the attitude. If her aunt is the nosey type, by all means give her something to remember."

"Mine could not fit under the bed. The bed-stands had been dug so deep into the floor that she could not slip underneath. I don't know whether I would have taken the pressure."

"I can 'ask' Ntongo's aunt not to be under your bed, Baale, as long as you won't fall asleep," Kintu laughed.

"I'll not fall asleep!"

"Either way, she will come in afterwards to check the bed sheets. You can't get out of that one."

Baale's hands were locked between his legs.

"I don't advise it, Kintu," one of Kintu's brothers said. "To bribe an aunt is to sow suspicion."

"Where did the reluctant groom end up?"

"I'll tell you three things I learned that day, Baale," Kintu started again. "One, our culture does not joke with sex. Two, being a man is no privilege because when things don't work you can't hide it—women are lucky: they can. Three, don't ever take your erection for granted. That aunt knew a few tricks. The groom finally rose to the task and she showed him what to do. But as he mounted the bride, he threw up."

"Threw up?"

"Emptied his stomach onto the bride."

"Kintu, must you tell this story?"

"Baale must know that sometimes manhood malfunctions."

"Was the groom drunk?"

"He does not touch alcohol."

"Oh."

"Draw the picture of that moment," Kintu stretched his legs. "The aunt steps out of the house and summons the father of the groom. Luckily, the bride's family has gone home and the rest of the revelers are drunk. The father calls me to help and the first thing I do is to tell the groom to step out and signal that it's a deal. Meanwhile, the bride is crying. The aunt, now packing the bride's bags, huffs: *We're going home child, there is no man here.* The father, as you can imagine, is speechless. I try to calm the aunt down: *Let's not be hasty. Let's talk like grown-ups*, but is she listening? I tell you fellow men: never negotiate with a woman. Their sense is not our sense. This woman looks me in the eye and says: *Before we talk, Ppookino, two bulls on the table for wasting our time.* I say: *Two bulls? For what?* She looks at me and laughs: *Then I'll return home with my child and that clean bed sheet.* She holds the bride in one hand, luggage in the other and walks to the door. I say: *Fine, fine, you have two bulls.* To cut the story short, we gave her two extra cows."

"Why?"

"She threatened to bring a cockerel to the groom's family in *broad daylight*, because he was a virgin."

"What humiliation!"

"Even then, after talking like grown-ups do, the aunt demanded that for the bride to stay, she would choose from among the groom's brothers whom she would have children with." Kintu shook his head helplessly. "Can you imagine a girl ticking off your sons one by one: *Not that one, no, I don't like that one, noo, yeah, that one!* Given a chance, women will kick you straight in the seeds. The shy bride chose the best-looking brother."

"Aha!"

"Give respect where it is due though, that aunt was thorough."

"The poor lad who was chosen—not yet married—was summoned and informed about the arrangement. Still, as if to make us feel her, the aunt insisted that the marriage be consummated *that* night. You can imagine, the young brother going in with a woman he had not anticipated for family honor. But as you know young men, he said: *Prepare her, I am ready.* So we hid the groom while his brother took over. The aunt got her bloodied sheet, and a goat, and left. She threatened that if the bride was not pregnant in two seasons, she would be back."

"I would rather die."

"The funny thing is that the couple is still together and had seven children the last time I checked. He's wealthy, the wife seems happy: no trace of contempt or anger."

"So what was wrong?"

"Who knows? Maybe the groom was asexual, maybe he was frightened of the dark depth or he walks the male path."

"That's what we brothers do for each other, Baale. After all, the most important thing, the children, are still blood," Kitunzi of Ggomba said quietly. "A brother will come and say there's a problem. He asks you to help with his wife. If his woman does not mind, then we do it. Men by nature don't have thin lips. We don't discuss each other with our wives. Even when you fall out with your brother, what must be kept from the tongue stays off the tongue. You don't say to a fellow man: *After all, I fuck your wife for you.* There, right there, you cease to be a man. We see you coming, we spit; we cross the road. The good thing about a woman: she will not disgrace her children by disgracing you."

"Baale, there are men born that way. They can get it up but they will not stick it into a woman. Others want a woman but it can't be bothered to get up. Sometimes, one that used to be enthusiastic loses interest. That is no reason to commit suicide. There are medicines."

"Baale looks crestfallen. Do you still want to marry?"

"Of course—it's just that no one ever told me any of this."

"Would you go back and tell your unmarried friends what you learned tonight?"

"Oh, that would be childish," Baale laughed.

"That's why no one ever told you."

"You'll be fine. If you treat Ntongo well and if you don't try to be perfect, things will work out in time."

"Besides, we shall be looking out for you. All of us here."

"And your mothers, they will be looking out for the girl. All you have to do is listen, watch, and learn. Soon, you'll work out what suits you."

"May I ask?"

"Sure, Baale. It's your night."

"I heard that . . . my friends say that a man must attempt at least three trips in a night—"

The session was thrown into uproar. Everyone spoke at once: some clicking their tongues in derision, some sucking their teeth.

"This is irresponsible—" but Kintu struggled to control his own mirth. "Our son wants to know whether three is the minimum journeys in a night. Who wants to take this one on?"

"Depends how long each journey is. If you're only going across the road like a rabbit—"

"If he's walking on his fingers—"

"Three trips? In your wet dreams, Baale."

"On the wedding night maybe."

"Get this, Baale—by the time you work out each other's rhythms you can't keep it up that long."

"But there are men like that: three hours later the bed is still creaking."

And the men went on into the night, remembering, laughing, sharing and disagreeing. They cited women's weird ways, feuding wives, keen mothers-in-law and all those issues that men considered their lot.

It was now a week since Ntongo's dowry day and another week until her arrival. Kiyirika was gripped with anticipation. Women and girls speculated on Baale's Ntongo—how beautiful she was. Men had put their own work on hold and were putting final touches to Baale's house. Unlike his older brothers who were scattered all over the province, Baale's house was close to Mayirika.

Apparently, Nnakato needed to keep an eye on Baale's home—Ntongo was coming from so far; she could get lonely; Ntongo was very young; she needed to be inducted into the family; the family was large: it could be daunting—all Nnakato's reasoning. Babirye, rather than ask why the same was never done for the older boys, rolled her eyes but kept her peace.

She knew the truth: Baale was being groomed to become Ppookino.

Baale came to the back of the house carrying a number of bales. One by one, he threw them up to the men reinforcing the roof. When he stopped, his hand flew to his face. His index finger skirted around a pimple. A sensation, pleasurable and tingly, threatened to turn into pain if he moved his finger closer. Gingerly, he placed the finger on the tip of the pimple and pain shot through the back of his head. He pulled the finger away.

Now Baale carried a pot of water inside the house. Men were plastering the walls with clay. With the roof on, the house was dark. It smelled of freshly dried hay. Soon, the warmth of his wife would wear the sharp edges of newness off the walls and round them into the familiarity of home. Baale looked at the floor. The hay carpeting was thin. He had opted for the scented *kisubi* hay. However, the rains would not let it dry. Now, he would probably leave the carpeting to Ntongo. Baale was happy. A whole moon of not working would be his to spend with Ntongo after the wedding: just the two of them on their own, in their home getting to know each other. They would wake up to be fed by his twin mothers and bask in the sweet morning sun. They would take lazy strolls at sunset. Then for another moon Ntongo would officially be allowed to move outside the bedchamber, but still she would not do chores. By then she would have morning sickness. Baale smiled. Nnakato and Babirye would fuss over Ntongo. He shook himself up and walked out of the house.

Before Baale realized, his finger flew back to the pimple, touching the tip. A sharp pain pierced his eyeballs and his head fell back. He had never had acne. For a huge pimple to grow right on the edge of his nostril, just before his wedding, was malicious. He turned to Kayima, his close friend, and said, "Look at this pimple for me."

Kayima tipped Baale's head. "Bend a bit, I can't see." Baale squatted. Kayima turned Baale's head toward the sun to get a better view. "Hmm hard: still raw," he said.

• • •

Three days later, work on the roof was finished. The bed-stands were dug into the ground and cemented in. Two men wove the flat of the bed using straps made from the bark of a *muvule* tree. Nnakato stuffed a sewn sheet with dried cow dung carefully fluffed out to get rid of the smell. Soon, the mattress would be done too. The men working on the bed were the only ones still in the house. The rest were out brewing. Drinking had already started. In the evening, after the chores, the villagers helped themselves to the brew before retiring.

Baale walked up to Kayima and asked him to look at his pimple again.

"It's ready," Kayima said. "Sit down, I'll squeeze it."

When he squeezed, a blinding pain gripped Baale. He pulled his head away and shook it. He blinked back the tears.

"The pain shot right through my eyes," Baale explained.

"I don't understand. It looks ripe but—"

"Try again," Baale said. Kayima hesitated.

"Maybe we should give it more time."

"No, it's two days to the wedding. There's no time. I'll bring a thorn."

Baale went behind the house to the lime tree and broke off a thorn. His friend started picking at the pimple's mouth but instead of yellow fat bursting forth, it trickled blood and water.

Kayima shook his head. "I don't understand: it looks all ripe on the outside, but it's raw inside. Let's leave it."

Baale passed his index finger on the tip. It was wet. He looked at the wet on his finger and rubbed again. He resigned himself to it, but a dull headache started throbbing in his left eye.

The following morning, when Baale woke up, his head was so heavy he struggled to get up. When he did, intense pain shot through his left eye into his jaw. He fell back on the bed. Finally, he sat up. Holding onto the wall, he walked outside. The sun cut right into his eyeballs. He shielded them with his hands.

Nnakato saw him first and screamed. "What has bitten my child?" She ran up to him. "Is this a spider's puff?"

"It's that pimple," Babirye caught up with her. "He wouldn't let it alone yesterday."

"What kind of pimple swells an eye?" Nnakato asked Babirye. "Look at the puffed face. I've seen acne before, this is not it."

Nnakato sat Baale down and gave him breakfast. When Kintu saw Baale's face, he made light of it.

"Do you reckon Ntongo will stay? One look at that face and she will be running home."

For the rest of the day, people poked fun at Baale's puffed face and he laughed with them. He did not manage to do anything at all. He blamed fatigue on the hectic weeks earlier.

The following morning, Baale did not get up. Nnakato went to check on him and found him in bed. His left eye had closed completely. He could not talk properly. The whole of his left side was dead. He could only move his right arm and leg. Nnakato was hysterical.

"This is more than a pimple."

That is when Kintu knew—Ntwire had struck. It took him by surprise yet it was no surprise.

Nonetheless, Kintu sent for his healer. All day long, the healer called upon the winds of the family to intercede but in the end he confessed, "Whatever it is, it's bigger than me. Only the dead can try now." He burned all sorts of herbs to wake up even the laziest family spirits.

As Kintu watched Baale's life ebb, the image of the shattered gourd that fell out of Kalema's hand flashed in his mind. Ntwire had lulled him into a false sense of security.

At the dawn of his wedding, Baale departed.

Nnakato, delirious, was locked up throughout the funeral. When the mourners returned from escorting Baale to the underworld, Nnakato had stopped crying. Kintu opened the door to check on her. When she asked whether her child had been properly wrapped, Kintu let her out.

Nnakato walked to where Babirye sat and pointed at her while she counted on her fingers.

"Babirye, you wanted a piece of my marriage, I gave it to you. You wanted my man; I shared him with you. You had eight children with him; I never begrudged you any of them. All I had was that one boy, a single sprout, but you begrudged him. You complained that he would be heir instead of your sons. You said that our husband loved him more than he loved yours. I never wedged a line between your children and mine. Yet you found fault with him. You found fault with our husband. You have complained and complained all our life but this is it. You can have it all: man, marriage, home, and family."

Kintu looked first at Nnakato and then at Babirye. The belligerent woman wore Nnakato's cloth but had Babirye's eyes. The woman sitting down, frightened, had Nnakato's eyes yet she had been Babirye all day. Kintu did not know whom to rescue from whom. Babirye was never frightened. Nnakato was always meek.

Nnakato walked away. Some mourners went after her. Clearly, her thoughts were in disarray. The things she said did not make sense. Babirye was childless; Nnakato had born nine children. However, Kintu called them back. He said that Nnakato needed to rage. Who else but her twin to take it out on? He did not want her locked up again. Instead, he asked Nnondo to keep an eye on her.

"Let her roam and scream everything out: then she will mourn. Locking her up will make her worse."

Kintu went to Babirye. It was as if he were talking to Nnakato,

"I know you didn't kill my son, Babirye. Baale had to go. Your sister will soon be back with us."

Babirye only stared, speechless.

That night, Nnakato returned home. She curled up in bed. Kintu sat on the bed opposite and sought out her eyes. It was Nnakato all right. Kintu sat silent, looking for words.

"Baale was a visitor," he said finally, "A fleeting moment. Remember we waited a long time for him?"

Nnakato did not seem to hear the words. Kintu moved to sit on her bed. He touched her feet, lightly at first. They were cold. He rubbed them, blowing on them until they were warm. Slowly, Nnakato uncurled and yawned. When she fell asleep, Kintu stood up. He lifted the sheets of barkcloth and covered her up to the neck. Nnakato shivered. He put his hand on her arm to steady her. Gradually, she stopped and relaxed in sleep. Kintu lifted his hand and went outside to the mourners.

At dawn, Kintu came back to Nnakato's chamber to check on her. She was not in bed. He checked Babirye's quarters; her bed was empty too. He sent for Babirye.

"Have you seen your sister?"

"No."

"She's not in her bed and I can't find her."

Babirye went out calling. At daybreak, everyone joined in the search, scouring the village, but there was no Nnakato.

Early on the third morning after Baale's burial, Zaya came down the hill howling. Kintu did not come out. He had become used to emotional theatricals in the aftermath of Baale's death. But then, Nnondo came to him and whispered that Nnakato had been found. Kintu came out of the house and followed him. Nnondo led him up Mayirika Hill past the path that led to the gorge, past the barren mango tree. On the tree with the curious pink bark, Nnakato dangled, her head bent forward. She was swollen. Her skin was patched black and gray. The rope had disappeared under her swollen neck. Her tongue hung out on the side of her mouth. Kintu looked at the large rock: Nnakato had used it to climb the tree. He felt betrayed by the rock and the tree. He looked at Nna-kato's feet and walked forward. His hand reached out to touch them but Nnondo stopped him. Suicide was untouchable. Kintu turned and went back home.

As with Kalema, there were neither mourning nor funeral rites for Nnakato. Those who could not help crying heaved in hiding. Nnondo hired men, strangers from a faraway village, to bury Nnakato as custom mandated. They arrived late in the evening and worked into the night. They dug a deep hole beneath Nnakato's dangling body. Then one of them climbed up the tree and cut the rope. Nnakato fell neatly into the hole and squatted. The rope, still around her neck, fell in after her. The men piled the soil on top of her as if she were a dog. When they finished, the men raced through the villages screaming to ward off the curse of suicide. Kintu wondered at Ntwire's sense of retribution—why kill Baale and Nnakato who had loved Kalema most?

A week after Nnakato's burial, Kintu came to Babirye's quarters. Babirye's eyes were distant but when he entered, she focused. Kintu squatted in front of her as if he were talking to his mother.

"Who are you?" he asked gently.

Babirye took some time to make out what Kintu had said. "What do you mean?"

"I mean, who, which one of you twins was buried?"

"Your wife."

"I know, but which one?"

Babirye hesitated. Here was the moment. Kintu, the family, Mayirika, and even Buddu Province hung on this moment: she could hold it or she could let everything crash. She had been Nnakato before. If Kintu—the only person to tell them apart—doubted then no one could be sure. All she had to do was bury childless Babirye and resurrect Nnakato and life would go back to normal. Finally, Kintu would worship her. But why should she die so that he could have his Nnakato back? He had not only separated them but had sowed suspicion in Nnakato against her. He had refused to love her even when she gave him eight children. Yet she was going to kill herself to reunite him with Nnakato?

"I am Babirye."

"It's Nnakato in that hole then?"

"Hmm."

"All right then," Kintu stood up.

He vanished that night.

Once, Kintu was seen in *o* Lwera in the cave near Kalema's grave, but his mind was in disorder. He said that Nnakato, Baale, and Kalema were in the cave with him, and that he could not abandon them. After that he was never seen again. Kintu would get neither a grave nor funeral rites.

Kyabaggu ruled Buganda for twenty more years after Kintu's disappearance. But the Ganda saying that *only character traits of the barren die with them* came true for him. Nnanteza's sons, Jjunju and Ssemakokiro, conspired and killed him. Jjunju, the eldest, became king. Nnanteza became king mother. Jjunju ruled for seventeen years. However, after becoming king, Jjunju fell out with Sse-makokiro. One day Ssemakokiro rebelled and, according to his version of events, he ordered the kidnapping of Jjunju. Unfortunately, the mission went wrong and Jjunju was killed in the scuffle. Ssemakokiro, unlike his father, was quick to appease his brother's blood. First, he banished all the men he had sent to kidnap Jj-unju, including their extended relations, from Buganda. Then he named his palace Jjunju. It worked for Ssemakokiro because he died of natural causes in 1814. Nnanteza lived as king mother for the rest of her life.

Three seasons after Baale's death, Mayirika, Kintu's main house, stood derelict because an heir to Kintu had not been chosen. The problem was that Kintu's body had not been found. All the young children had been returned to their mothers. It was Nnondo who kept grass from creeping to the threshold. A hundred yards away, Baale's house stood dark and silent. Bush had swallowed half of it. Babirye lived with Zaya in her wing. Like a witch, she spent her time gazing in space but Nnakato eluded her. She had not cut her hair for such a long time that the clumps had turned first into tufts and then they had formed ropes. Babirye had intentionally grown her hair before Baale's wedding. She, like other women in the family, had planned to shave it off on the wedding morning—the scalp would look clean and soft, not yet darkened by the sun. Shaving hair not only accentuated the skin, eyes, and lips but it made the shortest neck look graceful. Only ugly women grew their hair. However, since Nnakato's death Babirye had vowed to carry the burden of hair until Nnakato made contact. Nnondo had attempted to organize meetings with Kintu's children to choose the new Ppookino but the meetings tended to end in arguments and fights. Everyone voted for their mother's son. Babirye refused to take part. Wives had offered to take Babirye with them, but she declined. Zaya looked after her well, she claimed. When Babirye was asked about Nnakato's claims that she had eight children with Kintu, Babirye got very angry.

"How dare you say such a thing? Did you not see how Nnakato's head was confused when she lost her youngest son?"

In that, Babirye allowed Nnakato and Kintu to take the secret of her children with them.

One day when Babirye and Zaya had just had their evening meal and Babirye was settling into seeking Nnakato in the air, Zaya jumped. She held her stomach. Babirye looked at her enquiringly.

"Something moved in there," Zaya pointed at her belly.

"Moved—how?"

"I don't know. I've been bloated for a long time. But the last moon or so I am sure something moved in my stomach."

"Do you see the moon?"

"Not for a long time. I thought the moon comes and goes?"

"Let me see?" Babirye touched Zaya's stomach. "This is a child."

"A child? In there?"

"Yes; who?"

"But it does not show!"

"The first one never does. Whose is it?"

"Must be Baale then."

"Who?"

"Baale, the departed."

"How?"

"Way back, he offered to teach me how to be with a man, in case I had to go back to Gitta."

"Did he? How many times did he help you?"

"Once, ptsh," Zaya spat. "We went to Ntwire's hut. He told me to act like a proper woman: relaxed and patient but . . ." Zaya shook her head in regret.

"When?"

"Just before he was sent away for apprenticeship."

Babirye counted her fingers. When she got to the eighth finger she said, "Get up child, pack your things; we leave tonight."

Babirye looked at the sky and said, "I knew you would be back."

BOOK TWO
SUUBI NNAKINTU

1.
MMENGO, KAMPALA

Monday, January 5, 2004

At six o'clock in the evening, the door of Mulago Hospital mortuary opens and an attendant steps in. It is not a new arrival—it's a collection. Kamu has been in the mortuary for the last five hours. He was lucky to have been checked in, especially as he did not die in the hospital. Normally corpses like his, the ones that are brought by the police—car accident, collapsed on the road, murdered but no one has claimed them—are dumped outside at the door until there is space inside.

The attendant leads a group of three men and a woman into the *gwanika*. However they don't come in with him; they stay close to the door. The attendant slips a plastic apron over his neck and ties the strings at his waist as he walks toward the refrigerator. Then he pulls on a pair of gloves. He steps on a pedal in the wall, close to the floor, and a huge shutter rises like a curtain on a theatre stage, revealing large shelves inside the wall. The attendant tugs at one shelf and a tray with no fewer than ten corpses, like massive loaves out of a giant oven, slides out. The woman, seeing so many dead bodies with all kinds of expressions, holds her hands up to her mouth in shock.

The attendant walks around the corpses, checking the tags. He does not bother to read Kamu's. He knows who he is. Finally, he stops at the feet of one corpse and consults his clipboard. He checks the toe tag again and then the clipboard. Then he hooks the clipboard on the trolley, rolls the body onto it, and wheels the corpse toward the door.

There is something almost privileged about a corpse being sought like this—loved ones distraught, crying even, as they receive you on the trolley and their "thank-you-so-much" to the attendant, even though they have paid him a lot of money so that he does not lie to them that he cannot find you—it shows that you have lived a life worth the effort, that you'll be missed.

As the lucky corpse is wheeled toward its loved ones, the other corpses seem to stare forlornly as if waiting for someone, anyone at all who once loved them, to come and take them home. In three days, the haulers will come to clear out the old bodies and make room for new ones. First, they will inject the bodies with embalming fluid—the luxury of being unknown—identified corpses do not get this special treatment, unless their relatives pay for it, which is expensive, and they say that embalming keeps you intact for at least twenty years! Then they will be put into black plastic bags, which are tied at the legs, piled on a trolley, and taken out to be buried.

"Check and make sure he is your one," the attendant says as he stops the trolley in front of the men.

"He is our one: those are his pajamas," the woman says from the door where she stands.

"Other people have similar pajamas too," the attendant is impatient. "Check. I don't want to get out there and then be told: *Oh, he is not the one.*"

One of the men steps forward and looks. That one glance breaks him; he can only nod. The attendant goes back, pushes the trays back into the wall, steps on the pedal, and the shutter comes down.

Kamu's right eye stares.

• • •

Meanwhile at that moment in the city center, Suubi stood leaning against a pole outside the shops in the New Taxi Park. A glut in passengers had led to taxi frenzy. Brokers, who normally begged passengers to travel with them, now looked at commuters as if they were beans strewn on the ground. Vans drove in, brokers jumped out barely mentioning their destination and *pshooo*—the vans were full. Drivers then rushed to make as many trips out of the glut as possible while stranded passengers gnashed their teeth. Suubi watched the space where her taxis—*Bakuli, Mmengo, Lubaga*—normally parked. It was crowded with frustrated commuters. She would wait until the shoving and pushing abated.

Just then the cold breeze, the one that heralds the night, swept over her skin and she sneezed. When she stopped, her nose was blocked. That was it. Her hay fever would not wait for the fighting to stop. She wore the longer strap of her handbag across her chest and placed the bag on her belly where it was hardest to snatch. She then stepped out into the crowd. A van drove in and came toward the Lubaga crowd. Judging from its speed, Suubi anticipated where it would come to a halt and shoved toward that space.

"This *ka-woman!* She is small but the way she shoves!"

Suubi bit back her usual retort that thinness was not illness; she was focused on getting in that taxi. The van arrived and she maneuvered herself to the entrance.

"But this woman also!" The door opened.

"She has elbows as sharp as spears, I swear."

Suubi decided to show them what her "sharp as spears" elbows could do. She grabbed both sides of the entrance, blocking everyone else from entering, and climbed in.

"*Nyabo*; we're also going home!" She was the first inside.

"As if we came to spend the night here!" She sat next to a window.

"A*ha*, some women!" She checked her handbag.

"We're full: no more, no more." There was no tell-tale slash of pick-pocketing on her bag. The door slid and banged shut. "Wait for the next one." The driver swung the van toward the exit.

Suubi closed her mind to the *ehhu*, the *ahhaas*, and the *You can stand there until grass grows around your legs* that the passengers were lamenting to each other. She stared through the window thinking about how she was going to alight at Balintuma Road first, to pick up smoked fish, and then on to market for *matooke*. Opolot, her boyfriend, was spending the night and smoked Nile perch, cooked in thick groundnut sauce served with *matooke*, was their favorite.

The taxi stopped below Bakuli but Suubi was only half-aware. Her grandmother's story had intruded on her again. All day at work, the story, like an incessant song, had kept coming and going. Now that she was on her way home, Suubi gave in and her grandmother's voice flooded her mind.

In the beginning Buganda was serene. Our ba kabaka ruled the kingdom with wisdom. Buganda was huge; its borders touched Buule on one hand and Bweya on the other, reaching all the way into Tanzania! We had everything—rivers, lakes, mountains, animals, good climate, fertile land. Everything. There was food everywhere: matooke ripened in the gardens and was eaten by birds and monkeys. We did not eat cassava—we planted it on the borders of our gardens, in case of famine. There were no wars, people lived in such harmony that no one emigrated.

Of course, when a nation has plenty and peace reigns, foreigners start to flock in. And you know with foreigners: they bring their troubles with them. At that time, people from nations around Buganda had started to arrive, especially the Lundi, the Ziba, and the Tutsi.

Now, we Ganda were known the world over for our hospitality because we treated those who settled among us well. However, we asked for one little thing in return for our hospitality; one little thing—that everyone who settled among us became Ganda. You see, it was important that we were all one people—same language, same life, same everything—so that people don't stumble on each other's differences.

Then one day came a man who refused to integrate. He was Tutsi. His name was Ntwire. Ntwire stood away from everyone, from everything. He took part neither in the rites nor feasts, not even in funerals. He did not learn our way of life and he did not attempt to speak our language. Ntwire was a leopard, a loner with only one child. And what is a leopard with its cub like?

"Ohhhh, angry: always angry." Suubi was feverish.

Exactly, because its entire world hinges on that one cub.

Suubi gasped, anticipating tragedy.

Then one day, Ntwire's child misbehaved. When Kintu, our grandfather, saw him, he chastised him like any parent would do to his own children. In truth, Kintu did nothing much to the boy; he just nudged him like that. But the boy, ppu! He dropped dead—just like that.

"From a nudge?" Suubi was sure her grandmother had said it was a slap one time.

Who knows what ailment that boy suffered?

"And this was during the reign of Kyabaggu the Valiant? Tell me about Kyabaggu." Suubi was more interested in the *kabaka* than in Kintu.

Kyabaggu was a fighter namige who fought a lot of wars. In fact, it is said that when the Nyoro heard his name—the Nyoro were our greatest enemies at the time—they cried out in fear. He wanted to make Buganda even bigger, to swallow Bunyoro and all those tiny little kingdoms around Buganda. He subdued the Ssoga many times but because of the Nile he failed to annex Busoga to Buganda.

"How did the Nile stop him?" Suubi knew the answer but she still asked. This was her favorite part.

It was treacherous and took a long time to cross. When it flooded, the Nile would yira-yira, rumbling like Kiyiraaaaa, Kiyiraaaaa, Kiyiraaaaa.

Suubi would join in singing, *Bwowulira enyanja bweyira, yira, yira, nyabo!*

So many times, her grandmother carried on, *Kyabaggu subdued the Ssoga and appointed chiefs to rule them on his behalf, but as soon as he left to return to Buganda, the Ssoga would rebel and kill his chiefs. When he went back to Busoga, the cowards would disappear into the bush. As soon as he left they sneaked out and killed his chiefs again. That is why we say—as obstinate as the Ssoga.*

"What did Ntwire do when his son died?"

Child, what does a leopard do when its cub is taken?

"Ohhhh! It will not stop until it gets its cub back!"

Exactly! Ntwire, in his anguish, decided to flee Buganda. But as he left, he looked back at Kintu and said, "Kintu, I am leaving Buganda. One day, you and your descendants will search for me to undo your suffering but you'll never find me."

Kintu, knowing how hard it is to break a foreign curse, apologized and implored and pleaded and begged, "Ntwire, please, stay. I'll give you whatever you ask for."

But Waa! You know how vindictive foreigners are—Ntwire was inexorable.

So when he left, Kintu visited a medicine man, you know, to protect himself and his family. The medicine man told him to make sure that any child that comes out of him should never be slapped on the head: that Ntwire was poised to play the same trick. That is why in our clan we do not slap children on the face.

"That is why?"

Yes, because of Ntwire's curse.

"Then what happened to Kintu?"

Soon enough, his life unravelled. His children died. His wife committed suicide and he lost all his wealth. When Kintu died, he did not join the family spirits. He is still trapped here with us.

"But every story must end happily; Ntwire must be punished for being unforgiving and Kintu should be rescued and taken to the land of the spirits!"

Oh yes; you see, Ntwire thought that by trapping him on earth, Kintu would miss being a spirit—you know, not worshipped or offered sacrifices?

"Yes."

But because Kintu is still roaming the world, he is able to see Ntwire's wrath coming and often he protects his children.

"Ahhh! So Ntwire did not win?"

No, every time he tries to harm Kintu's children, Kintu is there to protect and to soothe. Up to this day Kintu is still protecting us, his children.

Suubi smiled at the story. How she had lapped it up—imagining Kintu blowing restlessly in the wind on the lookout for his children. How she had hated Ntwire, a devil on the prowl, looking for ways to harm Kintu's descendants!

Now she searched her mind for any other reminiscences from

her childhood but there was only blankness. Her grandmother was a morsel of memory hidden in a crevice somewhere in her mind. It felt as though someone had come with a broom, swept away all her childhood recollections, but missed her grandmother's voice. She could not even remember why she lived with her in the first place or when she left her. She could find no face, no house, no daytime activities, or even dreams from that life in her memory: just the voice telling that story and the tree they sat under when the sun glared.

Suubi jerked from the past and noticed that the taxi was not moving. Passengers were restless—some sucking their teeth, some scowling, everyone was peering outside to the back of the van. Suubi looked to see. A passenger had refused to pay the same fare as people traveling all the way to Lubaga because his was just half of the journey. The broker was blocking his way saying, "Me, you shall give me my money, sir."

Suubi shook her head. *There is always someone taking a stand and making everyone's journey more miserable,* she thought. Who does not know that taxis inflate the fare whenever there is a shortage? The driver turned off the engine, stepped out and banged his door as if to say: *We are taking no nonsense from anyone.* Seeing the driver coming around the van, the passenger handed over the money and everyone heaved a sigh of relief.

2.

At last, Mmengo Town, the last capital of Buganda Kingdom, came into sight. It was a compact town with only four streets. Whenever she got to this point, it struck Suubi that Namirembe Hospital kept Mmengo Town on life support. Despite the return of the *kabaka* from exile, Mmengo had not shaken off the mournful look of the decades when the kingdom was outlawed. A row of shops on the left slid along the road. The buildings that came into view were old—not in the proud ornamental way that the Kasubi tombs boasted of a heroic past, but with an embarrassed air, as if a grand plan had gone horribly wrong. Suubi wondered whether other people saw the town that way too.

The van stopped outside Namirembe Hospital and most of the passengers alighted. A few people going to Lubaga boarded the taxi and the hill started to slope. The Bulange, which housed the *kabaka*'s offices and the Buganda *Lukiiko*, came into view on the left. As the taxi approached Balintuma Road, Suubi called, "On Balintuma."

The taxi stopped and she stood up to alight. As her foot touched the pavement, her heart flipped and then shattered. Suubi knew immediately. It was Ssanyu.

This was the second attack. The first happened eight years ago on the morning after Suubi's graduation. She had lain half-awake in bed when a sensation of being "locked"—she could not open her eyes or move or scream—came over her. Yet she could see a young woman standing above her bed looking down at her. The woman looked exactly like Suubi only she was so emaciated that it was surprising she could stand at all. Her skin was dry, taut, and scratched. Her hair was in thick tufts. She even wore Suubi's floral blue dress with an elasticated waistband, yet Suubi had discarded that dress ten years earlier.

"Who are you?" Suubi had tried to ask.

"Who am I, who am I?" The woman was very angry. "I am Ssanyu, Ssanyu Babirye, you chameleon! Stop telling lies."

"What lies? I don't know you," Suubi tried to say but could not. Somehow the woman had heard.

"You're my Nnakato."

Suubi tried to shake her head to say that she was not a twin but could not. And how could Ssanyu hear her thoughts?

For a while she struggled to break free but not a muscle twitched, her eyes would not open but her heart pumped in her ears. It felt as if she had been buried alive. Ssanyu Babirye stood over her like a snarling guard dog.

Then she snapped out of it and sat up. There was no one in the room. She jumped out of bed and ran outside. For a long time she stood in the driveway, staring back into her room. Had she dreamed it? But she was awake when it happened. For weeks afterwards, every time Suubi remembered the face, she was gripped by panic. But as months went by and it wore off, she started to doubt what she had seen: it must have been a bad dream.

Now Suubi ran. Ssanyu Babirye was real and she was behind her. She hoped to get home before Ssanyu struck and locked her immobile again.

She crossed Balintuma Road and dashed past Esso, between the shops, past Mohamood High, heading toward the Christian Medical Centre. At the shortcut to Namirembe Cathedral, the road dipped and all she could see was the horizon. Then the high roof of the old colonial house near the school for the handicapped rose. Resolute not to look behind, Suubi chased the road ahead, but it seemed to run further. The colonial roof so dominated the horizon that her house, dwarfed, did not materialize immediately. Suubi's heart jolted, her legs wavered, she doubted she would make it and terror overwhelmed her. That was when she glanced behind. Ssanyu stood in the road. It was just a glance but in that moment, Ssanyu emptied her heart onto the road.

"The truth, Suubi," Ssanyu begged.

Though she stood at a distance, Suubi heard her words clearly. Ssanyu still wore Suubi's old blue dress. She still looked like she would drop dead anytime.

"Tell Opolot who you really are. Please."

Somehow this begging Ssanyu hurt more than the angry one. For a moment, Suubi was overcome by darkness, as if she had died. Then the darkness lifted and she reached for the electricity pole nearby for support. The pole felt warm and smelled of oil. But then she became too weak to stand and slid down to the grass. She leaned against the warm wood of the pole and closed her eyes. This had to be death.

After a long while, Suubi opened her eyes and looked back again. Ssanyu was not on the road. She stood up and looked around but Ssanyu was nowhere. Buoyed, Suubi turned and marched past a woman who had come to ask if she was OK. She distantly heard the woman say, "She's short-circuited that one," but Suubi ignored her. She walked back to where she had seen Ssanyu standing and shouted, "Tell Opolot what truth?"

After a short pause, when Ssanyu did not materialize, Suubi started to walk home. She looked around for the woman who had seen her madness: she was gone. The youth across the road looked straight ahead, the man on a bicycle was in a hurry, the schoolgirls might have seen something, they seemed nervous. Suubi waited for them to look back but they did not. Relief washed over her.

As she turned into her driveway, she was overcome by sneezing again. She sneezed so hard that her head felt it would split. As she lifted the wicket to walk in, she stuck a finger in her ear and shook it violently—the dreaded hay fever! She was still clearing her throat and sniffing when she opened the door.

3.

BULANGE VILLAGE, 1980

Whoever had dumped Suubi that April evening brought her early, for Kulata was not home to throw the child back. Kulata, who worked in Owino Market, arrived home at around six o'clock. At her doorstep sat five-year-old Suubi dozing like a chick dying of coccidiosis. On hearing Kulata's footsteps, Suubi looked up. Her eyes sat deep inside the sockets. She had no cheeks. The shape of her head was the shape of her skull. Kulata recognized her as her dead sister's child and sucked her teeth long and hard. She took Suubi's hand as if it were a diseased chick's wing, dragged her down the corridor to the back door, and dumped her below the steps. She then walked back and opened the door to her room. Thankfully, she needed the light coming through the doorway, otherwise she would have closed her door.

After drinking a glass of water, Kulata raised her voice. She demanded to know how the child came to her doorstep. When no answer came from the other tenants, she threatened to throw Suubi on the garbage bin. An irritated woman quipped, "Are you waiting for permission?"

Kulata burst into tears.

"Do you know why they picked on me?"

The tenants did not answer. "They" were her family.

"Because I don't have a child." She blew her nose. "Did they ask why I don't have children? No."

Now the tenants, some wearing concerned faces, some not bothering to pretend, came out of their rooms to hear the story.

"They presumed I didn't know how to make them," Kulata carried on. "Last time I went home to visit, they tried to force that child on me but I said no, I have problems of my own. Today they waited until I was away and dumped her here like garbage."

The tenants, now slightly sympathetic, swore they had not seen anyone abandon the child.

"If she is your blood," one of them said, "there is nothing you can do. Give her food while fate makes up its mind. Look at her: she looks half-dead already."

"What is she suffering from?" another asked.

"Who knows?" Kulata said. "She looked like that when she was born. Perhaps because she was the runt."

"She is a twin?"

"She is the Nnakato. Babirye was born full of life, but then suddenly *ppu*," Kulata snapped her fingers, "Just like that, she went. Then my sister also died. We waited for that one to die but *wa!* She is still here, blinking."

"What about the father?"

"The father?" Kulata made a contemptuous face, as if to ask: *How can anything like that have a father?*

"Hmm?" a woman prompted, anticipating a salacious story.

"I tell you my sister chose a family with the kind of madness that goes beyond having children with. And I am saying badly wired, short-circuiting, fuse-blowing mental kind of madness." Now she drew closer to the tenants and whispered, "The father, Wasswa, hacked his twin Kato to death."

The tenants gasped, "Oooh," as if it were a chorus.

"Asked: *Why did you kill your twin?*" Kulata carried on whispering, "*Because they were coming for him.* Who was coming for him? *They.* That kind of madness."

Everyone's face turned and stared at Suubi as if her father killing his twin was written on her body. Kulata continued to whisper, "The following day, thankfully, Wasswa committed suicide. And to me that was the best solution because what do you do with that?"

The tenants did not answer.

"The last I heard, this child was taken on by the grandmother, Wasswa's mother, but as the saying goes: *When it rains on a pauper, it does not stop to allow his clothes to dry.* The other day I heard that the grandmother had also died and I said to myself, what kind of misfortune does that family have? I did not expect this child to be still alive. I mean, look at her."

"Uhm uhm," a man shook his head and whispered. "She won't live. Don't worry about it."

"Is it true that dead twins collect the living one?" someone asked.

"If they do," Kulata answered as she made to enter her room, "then Babirye had better hurry up because I am not going to be saddled with this one."

Fate being fate, it started to rain. Suubi sat out in the rain without flinching. Kulata pretended not to see it until a tenant came to get Suubi in a manner suggesting that she was not a beast like some people. Before the woman got to Suubi, Kulata shouted, "Are you going to sit under the rain until you melt?"

Suubi stood up. For a gaunt child, her step was strong and steady. Despite being sunken, her eyes too were alert but no one noticed. She stepped into Kulata's world.

It was dark. Kulata lived in a single room in an unfinished house. The window was boarded up; sunlight from the corridor was thin. Soon, however, Suubi's eyes adjusted to the dark. In one corner of the room were pans, plates, and other kitchen essentials. In another were basins, soap, and bathroom objects. The other two corners accommodated Kulata's bed, screened by a net curtain. All the spaces along the walls housed bits and pieces of some sort. In the middle of the room were two basket stools, but Suubi sat on the floor. There was no ceiling above. Two electrical wires snaked along the beams to the wall and came down. One ended in a hanging socket, the other in a switch also unattached to the wall. Both were covered in dust and cobwebs. On another beam, a suspended wire ended in a lamp holder without a bulb. Kulata saw Suubi looking up.

"Don't you ever touch the electricity. Except when Babirye calls," she laughed. "Electricity hurts but it's a tidy way to go."

The following day, Kulata took Suubi to Mothers' Union Nursery School. She asked the teachers to keep her all day.

4.

As time passed and Suubi started to walk around the house, then the village, she discovered the world that was her new home.

The first thing she found out was that all the tenants disliked Kulata. However, they invited Suubi to their rooms. Sometimes, they asked her to run errands for them and gave her food. Suubi loved it when they chastised her. It made her feel like she was a proper child, like she belonged to them rather than to the corridor like a stray cat. Kulata locked her room in the day. She never left food for her. After school, Suubi came home to the corridor. Mostly she roamed the village, returning home just before Kulata arrived.

Bulange was a lethargic village, littered with modern but unfinished houses overgrown with shrubs or *matooke* gardens. In their unfinished state, the houses looked like ruins in a dying village. There were a few elderly houses, built between the 40s and 60s, which boasted of good days gone by. Tenants said that some of the old houses belonged to *Kabaka* Muteesa II's elite men and the families who first bought into British administration; others belonged to the landed gentry.

The landlady insisted that in the early 70s Bulange had verve and ambition. At the time, the village was fast becoming an affluent residential area. The old houses belonged to the landowners and the unfinished structures mostly to their sons and a few people they sold to. But then Idi Amin came and one by one, the men erecting modern houses disappeared. Her own husband had disappeared in 1977. Sometimes, she pointed at the incomplete houses naming their owners and the dates they had disappeared and she would cry.

The landlady was fat. Though her fatness was an illness—her limbs had shrunk beneath rolls of fat—the tenants were unsympathetic. They whispered that it was rather paradoxical for a widow to be fat. In return, the landlady called them cockroaches. She said that when they first came to her for a room they were courteous and humble.

"As soon as you settle in you forget yourselves, making me beg for my money."

This she said at the end of every month as she went around the rooms pointing fingers and threatening. The tenants, like cockroaches, would not stir. Once, overcome by fury over the nonpayment of rent, the widow stood in the corridor and let off a high-pitched lament.

"This world is a blender," she said. "Who would have thought that I, the wife of a high court judge, would beg for rent from cockroaches?"

If she saw a family eat fish or meat or even three proper meals a day, then they had better have her money ready at the end of the month.

"You've been feasting all month. I saw. You can't live like a cockroach and dine like royalty. I want my money."

The tenants called her unfinished house the Palace. Though an ordinary three-bedroomed bungalow, the Palace had over ten rooms. Each was rented by someone or by a family. The widow provided her tenants with a makeshift shelter, walls, a rough floor, and a door. There were also metallic frames in the windows but there were no panes. Some tenants filled the windows with bricks, some, like Kulata, boarded them up and the too-poor covered them with black polythene sheets.

A family of seven rented what should have been the sitting and dining rooms. They partitioned them with curtains and made a few more rooms. The kitchen and pantry were rented by a couple who behaved like strangers during the day, but the wife was always pregnant and nursing a baby.

Kulata rented one of the bedrooms.

The second bedroom was rented by a gaudy single mother, Balinda, who bleached her face. She had five kids who all looked about the same age. When she touched her face, Balinda's un-bleached hands seemed to belong to someone else. The tenants called Balinda Fanta-face, Cola-legs. Every morning, she painted her face, dressed up, and went to sell charcoal in the market.

The master bedroom, large and self-contained, was rented by a woman who brought home a different man every night and another during the day. She had a proper window with panes and curtains. She opened the window during the day and the curtain fluttered in the wind, like in a real house. The ceiling, en-suite bathroom, and toilet were painted white. Her room was painted a delicate cream. She had two beige sofas and her floor was covered with a brown carpet. She had wired her room with electricity and had a fridge, a TV, and a stereo. The landlady never quarrelled with her over rent. To Suubi, this was the queen's chamber in the anthill but other tenants called it "the office."

A youth, Toofa, rented what should have been the toilet, and a girl who slept during the day because she worked in a bar rented the would-be bathroom. There were pipes and gaping holes in the walls of the bathroom and the toilet. These holes were stuffed with newspaper; otherwise snakes looking for rats would crawl in.

A shy teenage girl lived in the garage, which faced away from the other rooms because it opened outside. She was kept by an old man who drove a sleek Mercedes. The girl had been in a boarding school when she stole herself away and came to Kampala with the old man who "parked" her in the garage. Apparently, her parents did not know where she was. When the old man came to see her, he hid his Mercedes behind the Palace. He never spent the night. Sometimes the girl was rich, sometimes she was broke, depending on how often the old man visited. In the evening, she sat on a stool at the door and stared at the road. When the Mercedes came, she jumped off the stool and ran into the garage. After parking the car out of view, the old man would go into the garage and lock the door. The women of the Palace would spit.

The evenings when the man did not come, the girl sat outside sighing. At around eleven at night, she would pick up her stool and lock herself in.

No one liked her, except Suubi—when she gave her food. The tenants whispered about the girl. Of course, they whispered about each other, but in the case of the shy girl, they whispered in unified anger. That a girl should escape from school, not let her parents know where she was and waste herself away on an old man was appalling. Even the slut allowed herself a piece of prejudice.

"Now that she has started with an old man, it will always be old men for her."

The landlady lived in a three-roomed annex set apart from the Palace.

5.

The first year in Kulata's home was tolerable, only head-bashing when she got in Kulata's way. To Suubi, life was daytime coming and going, night-time arriving and departing so that life carried her along. It had brought her to Bulange, to Kulata, to Mothers' Union Nursery School, and now Old Kampala Primary School. She did not resist it. She did not anticipate it. She did not hope. She did not regret. What she did resist were bad thoughts from the past because they hurt for nothing. Life soon taught her to forage for food in the market, especially during school holidays when there was no school lunch. Kulata only fed her at night when she returned home. In the market, women selling pancakes, samosas, bananas, fruit, and buns were most absentminded with their foodstuffs. But mostly her thinness was very useful. Market women would look at her and shake their heads.

"Does this one eat any food really?"

And Suubi would look down shyly. The next thing would be: "Here, take this," and they would pass on a cluster of *ndiizi* bananas or pancakes or other fruit. She knew not to wear out their kindness by frequenting too much. That was when she stole from the nonsense women who were not moved to kindness by her thinness. She did not steal from men because when they caught you, it did not matter how thin you were, men had no hearts.

Suubi knew she was going to die, everyone said it, but she had decided that she would not die during the day. She was vigilant not to fall asleep during daytime because then death would overcome her and she imagined that it would hurt. She was prepared to die at night just as her grandmother had. Her grandmother did not feel any pain as she died, Suubi thought, because Suubi did not hear her cry out yet they slept in the same bed. It never crossed Suubi's mind that dying was not easy.

Kulata was angry most of the time. It was not clear to Suubi why. She hated everyone. One tenant said: *That woman thrives on anger like maggots on shit.* But Suubi had heard women whisper. Apparently a man, a long time ago, gave Kulata the anger and then ran off with another woman, though the tenants could not agree whether it was the anger that he ran away from, or a lot of miscarriages. *You would think that after the man died and then the woman he ran off with joined him, Kulata would find a smile but no, she carries on being angry.*

And so everyone waited for Suubi to die, including herself. She had not put on any weight. The taller she grew the thinner she looked. Her kneecaps stuck out like tennis balls on two sticks. Her skin was still ashen. Kulata scrutinized Suubi's body for signs of the onset without shame. Sometimes she asked her if she had diarrhea. When Suubi shook her head, she would suck her teeth in frustration. One day she said, "You know, God's so evil He could let you live."

After a while, when Kulata did not see any deterioration in Suubi's health, she became direct, "Y*e*, when will she die?"

At first, thinking it was a rhetorical question, Suubi did not respond. Kulata tended to ask as they ate supper, after she had enumerated all Suubi's recent misdemeanors. Suubi kept her attention on food, feeling slightly guilty about still being alive. But one time Kulata kept such a steady gaze on her that Suubi felt obliged to respond.

"Soon," she promised—wiping her plate with her forefinger and licking it—as if she had felt death coming. "Probably next month at the latest. I'll ask Babirye."

"Did you say Babirye?"

"She sleeps in my bed sometimes."

Kulata slowly put her plate down. Suubi, now drinking water to fill the empty space in her stomach, did not realize that her aunt had stopped eating.

"If you ever tell lies again …"

Suubi looked up in surprise, "Which lies?"

Kulata threw her plate at her and missed. Suubi ran outside. She was confused. A woman had said that Babirye would collect her. Kulata herself had said that Babirye had better hurry. Why would she then doubt that Babirye slept in her bed?

The following day Suubi broke one of Kulata's only two china plates. Ranting, Kulata said, "God, when is she dying?"

"She's not: you are."

Kulata stopped. Suubi's eyes were so narrowed they were almost closed. She stood head defiant, chin pointed, eyes not blinking. Her chest rose and fell, breathing deeply as if she were out of breath.

"You will slim and slim slowly . . ." she caught her breath and then breathed out, "until you're bones only."

"Who told you?" Kulata reached to grab her. Suubi did not move. She pointed her index finger.

"Hit Suubi on the head again and I'll cripple your hands first."

"What is this?"

"Babirye. And you dare tell Nnakato that I came . . ."

Then Suubi sneezed a few times. When she stopped, she saw the shards on the floor and said, "I am sorry about the plate." She hurried to find a broom to sweep them up. But Kulata remained standing, staring at her.

After that incident, Kulata never hit Suubi again but she also stopped talking to her. Eventually she stopped feeding her altogether. Often times, Kulata did not let Suubi into her room for the night. Tenants gave Suubi food, especially the slut and the shy girl. In any case, Suubi stared hard at meal times. As soon as a family got ready for a meal, she crept close and pretended not to look at the people eating until a woman would say, "Suubi, why don't you wash your hands and join us?" and Suubi would start as if she had not been aware of them all along. Instead of saying, "I have just also finished mine," like polite people do, she would wash her hands and eat with the family. But when Kulata was around, the tenants did not feed her no matter how hard she stared. Instead they asked: "Suubi, your lips are cracked. Have you had anything to eat at all?"

"Of course," she would lie, all the while eyeing their plates in despair.

The nights were uncomfortable. Sometimes tenants let her into their rooms, but they had to let her out very early in the morning so that when Kulata woke up, Suubi was shivering sufficiently outside her door. Suubi was not frightened of being locked out of Kulata's room. There was no immediate danger to her life, as the outside door that led to the corridor was locked. It also gave her satisfaction that when tenants called Kulata thoroughly evil, it was true. Once in a while a rare moment came when Kulata was kind and fed her or she came looking for her and asked her into her room. These moments were as sudden and as unpredictable as madness. Then Suubi felt pangs of guilt for the things the other tenants said about Kulata. For those few days, Suubi tried to forget the bad past because remembering terrible things hurt in the teeth. Instead she focused on that day as the first day of her life. But then, like temporary insanity, the kind Kulata would vanish. The real Kulata would come home one night, open her door slightly and squeeze through. As Suubi ran to join her: *Welcome back, Aunty,* Kulata would bang the door and lock it as if she regretted her moments of lapse. Sometimes tenants saw her coming home and told Suubi to run to the door before she got there. Still, Kulata would open the door slightly, squeeze through and close it in Suubi's face. Suubi slept in the storeroom.

As years went by and Suubi outgrew the storeroom, Toofa, the youth who rented the toilet, took pity on her and sneaked her into his room. Toofa was kind. He bought her fried cassava chips and chicken or fried Nile perch with chapati. The door to his room could not open properly because his iron bed fit right into the doorway. Toofa hung his clothes on nails hammered into the wall. Magazine pictures of cars and motorcycles made his room seem crowded; the rest of his walls were covered in bloody guts of squashed mosquitoes.

While other tenants gave Suubi a mat to lie on and a piece of cloth to cover herself, Toofa let her sleep in his bed. When all the tenants had retired, he would insist that they take a bath first and then they ate together with his lantern burning lazily.

In bed, Toofa asked if he could rub himself on Suubi. At first, Suubi was not sure. But all he did was rub his hardness on her backside. Suubi did not mind as it made something not unpleasant flicker between her legs. Before long, Toofa would rattle like convulsions and make a stinking mess. That was the only problem: the slime and smell. Suubi was eleven.

Throughout her life at the Palace, Suubi went to school. From Mothers' Union Nursery School, her forms were forwarded to Old Kampala Primary School. Every morning, she washed her face, wore her uniform, which she hung on a nail in the storeroom, and went to school.

At school, Suubi was a different person. Her parents were in Britain. She lived with a wicked aunt who stole the money and the things her parents sent. Suubi took random items like video cassettes, shampoo, children's books, a vase, a makeup kit, all sorts, to school to prove her story: things she stole from shops and hid in the hedge.

This story of loving parents living in Britain and sending her things was not conjured out of air. It was built on a woman with no name. Once in a while this woman came to school and asked for Suubi. She only came in the morning before break time. Suubi would be writing when the teacher would say, "Suubi, you've got a visitor in the staffroom." And she would give the other pupils a knowing look, *a message from my parents again*, and sprint to the staffroom. The woman looked just like the women in the Palace, or in the market, or on the roadside, only that she was quite light-skinned. She was not rich-looking at all. But she had really kind eyes and the way they looked at Suubi, she knew that her mother would look at her just like that. The woman always had a bag. When she saw Suubi at the staffroom entrance she would say, "Eh, eh, she's here!" as if Suubi had worked very hard to be there.

She would scoop her up and hug her but Suubi had eyes only for the bag. The woman always whispered as if the two of them were thieves, which was intimate and made Suubi quite excited. In the bag she had *kabalagala* pancakes, *ebikyepele*, the huge pies stuffed with beans and the *mwana akaaba* buns all wrapped in newspapers. She always brought Suubi new knickers.

"I am sure you've run out of these," she would say and Suubi would smile at "running out of knickers" as if she ate them.

"Don't let Kulata see them," the woman would whisper as she stuffed the knickers, a jar of Vaseline, and money inside Suubi's school bag. It was all furtive, as if the teachers were against it. And then she would say: "Don't ever tell Kulata about me, my child." And Suubi shook her head vigorously. The woman would then look at her intently and ask, "Inside you, how do you feel yourself?"

Suubi would reach inside herself with all the feeling she could muster to feel herself. This would make her eyes roll, feeling, feeling. Finding nothing at all she would smile shyly because the woman's eyes were so intense. Then she would say, "Fine."

"Nothing at all?"

And Suubi wondered whether she should say that her heart was paining—people got frightened when someone's heart was unwell—perhaps the woman would give her more money and visit more frequently, but it would be too late because just then the woman would whisper, "OK," as if she did not entirely believe her but she was prepared to let it go. "Run back to class then."

It was all over in a few minutes. Suubi would run back to class, bag bulging, a discreet smile on her face. She would nudge the girl sitting next to her, partially pull out a pair of knickers, then some money, and show her on the sly. "My parents, in London," she would whisper with such contentment, as if for that tiny moment she would not wish to be anyone else other than herself.

Suubi did not ask who the woman was or why she was kind to her. Instead she took the woman's face and on it constructed first her mother, then her father, and then Britain. Every time the woman came, she had brought a message from her parents in England.

In any case, whenever names of school fees defaulters were read out to be evicted from class, Suubi's was never among them. She would smile smugly as the dismissed pupils packed their books, left their desks, and walked out of class. It was the only time that someone other than herself was the object of shame and it felt fantastic. And she would swing in her seat and look at the fees defaulters with the satisfaction of "*Yee*! You were laughing at me that I stink!" She would later explain to the pupils that her parents in Britain sent the tuition fees straight to school, "So that my aunt does not steal it."

Looking at Suubi's glowing school reports, the tenants would say, "Isn't it just like God to give her plenty of brains?"

Suubi loved this attention. Sometimes, to harness it, she got her books out and sat on the porch, where everyone would see her, to study. She knew that grown-ups loved the sight of a child working hard at homework. She would only put away her books when the sun went down. Suubi too started to believe that if life allowed her to live she would go far in her studies.

Only one thing bothered Suubi. Apparently, in class she stank so badly that no one wanted to sit next to her. In the playground, other children ran away from her holding their noses. Sometimes, when girls wanted to evict Suubi from their group one would ask, "Do you smell something?" And everyone would nod except Suubi. Then one girl would say, "I'll smell you all," to find the smells. And she smelled every girl's dress. When she came to Suubi she would smell from afar and say, "Oh oh," fanning her nose, and they would all run away from her.

But Suubi never smelled herself. No doubt, the girls were jealous because she came top of the class every term. She got back at them by working hard so that her name would be called on school parade at the end of term. And then Suubi was made to stand at the podium with the teachers, given free exercise books, textbooks, and pencils and the whole school would be made to clap for her.

• • •

One day, Toofa did not come home for three days. Suubi waited and waited, then she went and slept in his bed without him. The third morning, the police came and searched Toofa's room. Afterwards, they told the tenants that Toofa had been killed during an armed robbery. Suubi was envious that Toofa's day had come sooner than hers. That night, when everyone had gone to sleep, Suubi again crept into Toofa's bed. The following morning, she removed the sheets and blanket, rolled them together and put them in Toofa's bag. She hid the bag in the hedge first. As soon as it got dark, she took the mattress and the bag—she had picked up the lantern as well but then thought, *Hmm, can a child really own a lantern?* and put it down—to the shy girl in the garage and told her, "I've retrieved my bedding from my aunt's room. Can you keep them for me?"

Two weeks after Toofa's death, Suubi came back from school to find his room cleared out. A girl, a netballer playing for Coffee Marketing Board, had moved in.

One morning, Suubi was told that the shy girl in the garage had had a baby in the night. Suubi had not seen the girl's stomach swell. The attitude of the women toward the shy girl turned abruptly. They visited her in hospital, took her food, and washed her clothes. When she was discharged, they helped her with the baby. The landlady heaved herself up and went to the bush and collected the *kamunye* herbs to heal the girl's stitches, the slut woke up early every morning and helped her in the bathroom, the quiet woman collected herbs for the baby, boiled them in *ekyogero*, and bathed the baby every day until the stump of the umbilical cord fell off. Suubi heard her instruct the shy girl, "Not just the tit: put the whole areola into his mouth as well or he will suck the skin off."

The tenants now called the shy girl Maama Boy. Her baby was Boy.

Boy cried all night and slept all day. Maama Boy cried with Boy. The old man started to drip, drip in for a few minutes to visit and then he would leave quickly. Maama Boy started crying during the day when Boy was asleep. The landlady was unsympathetic.

"You chose to grow up too quickly. Get off that stool, find a job, and look after your child. Your man has had children since before you were born. Yours isn't special to him."

Kulata had started ailing—now she was up, working in the market and being evil, now she was down, shivering with malaria, making everyone feel sorry for her. At first, Suubi did not even realize that Kulata was dying because she spent most of the day at school. However, Kulata's malaria started to come and go too often. One time, it came back with such aggression that Kulata stayed down for a month. When she got up she had lost a lot of weight. The tenants started whispering, *What kind of malaria is that, hmm?* And then suspicion started to grow around the Palace. *That malaria is not alone; there is something else* and the suspicion spread into the village. People started to steal furtive glances at Kulata, looking for the symptoms of that something else.

It was at around that time that the quiet woman said to the other women that she had seen, as Kulata bathed in the communal bathroom, the *kisipi*, belt-like shingles people get on their skins around their waists when their immunity is weak. Everyone knew that the *kisipi* was the number one symptom for the new death. *The minute you see it, you say goodbye.* But as Kulata did not talk to the tenants, no one knew the real truth. Eight months after Kulata started ailing, her visits to the toilets accelerated and the tenants looked at each other with knowing looks. *She's started the sprints!* As if it were an athletic event. When her lips ripened like peeled tomatoes everyone said: *Eeeh eh there is no hope there anymore!*

But then Kulata would bounce back and carry on with life as if she had not been dying. It did not make sense to Suubi, the way Kulata went back to work in Owino with as much gusto as if she had a future. Every time she saw Kulata feeling better a question was on the tip of her tongue. She wanted to ask: *When are you dying?* Or to request: *If you get there before me could you keep my place warm?* But you can't say things like that to grown-ups, however evil.

6.

When death came to collect Suubi, it was ambivalent. It was eight years since she arrived at the Palace and heard that Babirye would collect her but nothing had happened so far. Her shoulder bones still showed through her school uniform. The skull still showed on her face. She still had no cheeks. Even puberty, which normally made girls round out, had not sprayed its sheen on her. Though no one had seen her fall sick, it was presumed that a proper bout of malaria could take her.

Suubi now spent her nights in the garage, tending Boy. The garage was infested with rats. Because Suubi wore neither shoes nor slippers her feet were so calloused that the crusts had cracked. When she fell asleep, rats fell upon the crusts on the soles of her heels and peeled them off. The rats were excellent surgeons. They breathed caressingly onto the spot they were peeling, deepening her sleep, while they sunk their teeth into the crust. They peeled layers and layers of skin, leaving her feet tender. It was not a problem when they peeled away just the dead skin but sometimes a zealous bite into the tender skin woke her up. Then she kicked at her bedding. The tenants advised her to get a rough stone to scrub all the dead skin off her feet but Suubi worried that if she did not have crusts the rats would bite into her feet.

Maama Boy insisted that she take a bath both in the morning

before going to school, and in the evening before going to bed, but it did not help. The rats kept coming back to her, never biting anyone else in the Palace.

Suubi had barely grown back the skin on the soles of her feet when it was nibbled again. It was a school day. Her heels were so tender they hurt. On the way to school, she lost heart. Children would laugh at her. Instead, she turned to the walkway that led to Namirembe Cathedral and mounted the steep hill. She thought of going to the grounds on the eastern gate near the cemetery where the view over the city was wider. The day before, in the history lesson, the teacher had made them read a passage by Harold Ingrams describing Kampala's landscape:

If you cast your mind back to the days you made mud pies and can imagine happily turning out, with no particular arrangement, a large number of pies from a round not very deep bowl on top of a flattish ground you will have a very fair idea of much of what this lakeside region of Uganda looks like. The social organization of these lakeside people seems to be based on this hill arrangement . . .

Suubi hoped that standing at the summit of Namirembe Hill would help her work out what mud pies looked like.

It was ten o'clock in the morning and Suubi was dodging grown-ups. A child in school uniform loitering outside school was everybody's business. A grown-up would take her hand, march her straight to the headmistress's office and say, "Here's your pupil. I found her truanting," and the headmistress, to justify the grown-up's initiative and to encourage him, or her, to do it again, would caress her buttocks with a cane before the do-gooder left.

As she made her way past the cemetery, Suubi's eyes caught sight of the *kabaka*'s lake. She stopped and sighed. The lake seemed so close. It was unbelievable that *Kabaka* Mwanga had it dug with traditional tools so long ago. Suubi must have lost herself in the view for she did not see the old man step out of the cemetery. He looked at her feet—Suubi never wore shoes to school. She stood on her toes to protect her heels.

"What happened to your heels, my child?"

Suubi jumped.

"The rats nibbled them," she recovered quickly hoping to deflect the man's attention away from her truanting.

"And no one cared to take you to hospital?"

For some reason, the words "no one cared" made Suubi burst into tears. It was the first time that someone had used the word "care" as if she, Suubi, could be an object of care.

"No."

"Where are your parents?"

"They are gone."

"Gone, where?"

"Kaganga."

"An orphan: who taught you to talk like that?" But he did not wait for her answer. "God knows what's happening to all the orphans we've made," he said to himself.

Suubi wept harder.

"Come child, come with me. I'll take you to Bata and get you a pair of shoes. Have you had anything to eat at all?"

Suubi shook her head and followed the old man. They walked down the hill, past Kayanja Primary School toward Namirembe Road. The old man bought her two fat vegetable samosas from a kiosk on Namirembe Road and they hopped onto a taxi going to the city center.

The car ride was soothing. Suubi had not been in a car for many years. She sat behind the man, eating her samosas. When she looked up, she noticed a thick fatty ring of scalp that fell above the man's neck like a collar. He is rich, Suubi thought. Only rich men get their scalp rolled into fatty collars. Maama Boy's old man had one and he had a Mercedes. Suubi was reassured. They alighted at Blue Room and went into a Bata store. It smelled of new leather and privilege. A wonderful feeling spread over Suubi at the prospect of getting new shoes and showing them off at school. The man looked around but said he did not like the shoes in that branch.

"There is a branch on Entebbe Road where I bought my granddaughter's shoes, let's try there."

It was a mild day, soothingly gray as if lazy rain was coming. Suubi and the old man walked past Nakivubo Stadium, across the canal into the former UTC bus park and then into the taxi park. They caught a taxi bound for Kajansi.

As familiar landscape disappeared behind her, a nagging doubt crept up Suubi's back—hmm maybe—but the car ride was so beguiling, the concern of another human so intoxicating and the man's age so reassuring that she did not allow her doubt to form. They alighted before Kajansi Clay Works, just after the colonial gymnasium with the muscly statue outside.

It was drizzling in Kajansi.

As soon as they alighted, the old man started to run. He crossed the road, went down a shrouded path, and disappeared into the eucalyptus woods below. Suubi followed him down the slope presuming that he was running because of the drizzle. When she got to the bottom and heard the cars on Entebbe Road whizz above her head, she stopped.

"You've abducted me. You're going to rape me."

The old man opened his eyes in shock and disbelief.

"You? My child, look at me. I am an old man. Why would I rape a child?" He stopped and thought. Then he added, "If you're worried that I'll rape you, go back to the road. I'll go to my house and get more money. I've only realized I don't have enough, my house is just after the woods."

Suubi turned and walked back toward the road.

"Wait," the old man called. "I should give you money for your fare."

Suubi noted that the man shouted as if she were deaf. He frantically checked his breast pockets, then patted the hip and the back pockets.

"Wait here, child," he screamed. "I'll run home and bring the money."

Suubi started to walk again, heading back. Then she heard another call. When she turned, two men were upon her. She yelped.

"Girl, stop. Don't you want your shoes?"

It was no use screaming. The young men held her.

"She's old," one of them said breathlessly.

The other threw up his hands in frustration, panting like a sprinter beaten to the line. The old man caught up with them.

"How do you mean 'old?'"

"Those legs, she can't be less than eleven." He turned Suubi's head and saw the hidden straws in her earlobes. "Her ears are pierced as well. Even if she was the right age, she's blemished."

"I didn't see them. I doubt they'll see the holes in the ears."

"Girl, how old are you?"

"Thirteen."

"I told you. Let's get out of here."

"Have you been with a man?" The old man was not giving up yet.

Suubi started to shake her head but the young man thundered, "Don't lie, we'll find out."

"It was Toofa who did it to me all the t—"

The young man did not wait for her to finish.

"I knew it as soon as I laid eyes on her."

"Besides, she looks half-dead," the other young man said.

"We can still try—"

"You heard the man: he doesn't do orphans or street kids, he wants a proper child."

"Who cares, it's not like there is a stall selling proper children."

Suubi looked at the ground. The smell of grass was overpowering. The ground was wet. It still drizzled. She realized that her last view of the world would be this damp morning, the narrow path in the woods with a pungent smell of grass. Fancy waiting for death and ending up under a sacrificial knife. All the insects she had killed crawled into her mind, mocking.

Two other men, standing at either end of the path, now joined the young men. They kept their faces averted. The old man stared at Suubi like a starving child forced to throw away a bowl of porridge because a fly had hopped into it.

"Do we leave her here?"

"Do you want to take her home?"

Suubi must have blinked, for when she opened her eyes the young men had vanished. The old man stood petrified. Then Suubi saw cows coming. The old man put his hands on Suubi's shoulders. The hands shook. His voice rattled.

"Run, child. Do you see the cows? They belong to a spirit. These are her woods, she hates trespassers. If she catches you, you're dead."

He turned and the bushes swallowed him.

Suubi recovered and ran as if the soles of her feet had not been nibbled. She did not stop until she broke out of the woods into short thick bushes. She realized that she had run away from Entebbe Road but she could not see the end of the bushes. Luckily, she could still hear the cars. She could only go back where she came from. She looked back into the woods: no witch, no cows came her way. She waited for a while, then ran back.

As she finally came to Entebbe Road, a woman carrying a basket on her head and a baby on her back came down the slope. She had not seen Suubi yet. Suubi hid. She knew that spirits preferred wearing bland disguises like that of a woman carrying a child on her back. The woman walked past. Suubi expected her to melt into nothingness but she walked on in human form. It did not make sense. Surely if the spirit wanted to see her, it would have?

After a while, Suubi emerged and ran toward the road. The noise of the cars grew louder. She climbed the incline and the muscle-bound statue outside the colonial gym came into view. As she came to Entebbe Road, she heard from down below, "There's a girl. Girl, stop."

Entebbe Road was too close for Suubi not to try. She ran.

"Wizards! Abductors!" she cried out. "They want to sacrifice me."

People from across the road—some working in their gardens, some doing household chores and others tending roadside stalls—came to her aid. But when they held her, Suubi fought, convinced that they were all part of the spirit world. One of the men calling from below caught up.

"We only want to talk to her. We've caught some suspicious men. Why were you in the woods, girl?"

Suubi, sure that the spirit had come in multiple guises, screamed and shouted until a woman said, "Give her to me. She's frightened."

Another group of people from the woods came up. They held the old man and two of the young men. Suubi stopped struggling and pointed at the old man.

"He brought me here. I was on my way to school," and she told the crowd about the rats, showing them her feet, the old man, the shoes, Bata, and the young men. She told them her age, about the straws in her ears and the woods' spirit. She left Toofa out. Young men laughed at the idea of the woods belonging to a spirit, someone asked how stupid she was to be led into the woods to buy shoes but the woman holding Suubi rebuked,

"Would you laugh if she was your child? Just imagine the number of children they've abducted so far."

"Look how far they brought her," another woman added, "All the way from Mmengo!"

"You're at home thinking that your child is in school studying," a woman broke the *lusolobyo* she had been using to cut banana leaves into two and gave the other half to another woman, "While she's been abducted by these—" and brought it down on the head of one of the men.

"Wait, people. We need to get off the road."

The crowd turned, heading back to the woods, some breaking branches off trees, others picking up wood, some calling others, "They abducted a child. We've found her. We've got them!"

The crowd swelled. They came carrying *mbukuli* clubs, hoes, and sticks. Women were hysterical. They held firewood and stones and hoes. They started stoning the abductors but one of the men cautioned, "Hold on, the police will see us."

"If you don't know what to do with them, hand them over," a woman cried. "That child was on her way to school," she added, as if going to school was the most moving aspect of Suubi's story.

As the crowd turned off the road onto the path that led down into the woods, the old man begged, "Take me to the police."

"Police, my womb," a woman screamed. "We're taking you back where you brought her."

The last part of her sentence must have stirred her for she threw a stone at the old man, the men holding him ducked and the women fell onto the old man, hitting him wherever they could. The men pulled him away, insisting that they would not have women kill a human. One woman, incensed by this statement, squared her shoulders and challenged the men.

"Do you know the pain of a child, hmm?"

"We need to interrogate them. They'll lead us to the priest," one of the men pleaded.

"Pregnancy is a promise," the woman's voice shook. "The child in your hands is the real thing. The longer we hold onto them the more chances of the police coming along. We'll catch neither the other two nor the shrine man. And that will be a miscarriage."

"Instead, we'll be arrested for abduction, grievous bodily harm, and intent to murder."

"And in two days, these men will be back prowling the streets for other children. Do you know how much they make out of a child?"

The women must have swayed the crowd because when they pounced on the men again, few people restrained them.

"Women can be savage. I can't watch," a man said.

In the process, Suubi's hand was let go and she joined the people running back to the road. She heard a guttural cry, "*Maama nyabo*," and she stopped to look back. A woman hitting one of the young men screamed, "Call your mother again. Let me hear you call her."

"You abducted the wrong child this morning."

"Yeah . . ." agreed another and, for emphasis, she raised her club and brought it down on one man adding, "She's protected by a strong taboo this one."

"She is your last."

A man retched. Suubi slunk away. When she got back to the road, where the people down below could not see her, she ran. She was certain that someone would come to her and say: *You led those men to their slaughter.* The men's spirits could haunt her at night. She was supposed to die. Suubi had never known that her life was so precious that total strangers would kill for her. She decided that the women down below were only scaring the men. They would not kill them. It was useless to think about it. She should forget. She must not remember. It did not happen.

It took her all day to walk back home. She did not even realize that her heels did not hurt anymore. Along the way, she skipped and sang joyously. *Think good thoughts only, good thoughts only.* Every time the memory of what had happened tried to come back to her, she blocked it and sang louder and thought about her parents in Britain, how they would soon send the woman and how she would hug her. If she allowed bad memories to return, her molars would hurt. *I wonder why I am hungry when I had lunch at school? Suubi, you are becoming a glutton!* She hastened her pace so that night-time did not catch her away from home. *I am a nalubili, my thinness is natural, and it runs in the family. Thinness is not sickness, sickness is not thinness, thinness is not sickness and sickness, is not . . .* She was happy, walking in places she had never been. She had had a good time at school and she was on her way home. When she saw blood on the back of her uniform she thought, *perhaps my periods have started, most of the girls in my class have had theirs*, but Suubi had not seen hers. She was happy that her periods had finally arrived. *I am normal. I'll have children when I grow up.* By the time she arrived at the Palace the incident had been pushed out of her mind.

The following day when Suubi went to the toilet, she noticed that flesh on her inner thigh had been torn away. At that instant, the wound started to hurt and she limped out of the toilet. She could not remember how she got injured. When she got back in the garage, she tore a piece of cloth from a rag and bound the wound.

A month later, during the second-term break, the landlady called Suubi to the annex and told her, in a congratulatory way, that she had found her a temporary job. Suubi looked at her in consternation—she had not asked anyone to find her a job, she was young, she was still studying. The woman explained, "Look, such a chance does not come every day. You don't have a home, you don't have anyone. Your aunt Kulata is on her final lap. Where will you go when she dies? In any case, she has never cared for you. You could be knocked down by a car and that woman would walk past your corpse. As a house-servant you'll at least live in a proper home, you'll be fed, and there will be grown-ups to watch over you. You can save your money toward a stall in the market."

Suubi broke down and cried. She could not help feeling sorry for herself.

"It is OK, if you don't want to go," the landlady pretended to give Suubi a choice. "But I don't want to see you around my house except if you are living with your aunt. She dies, we pack you with her corpse on a truck and you will be taken to wherever she will be buried. You don't come back to my house."

Suubi cried like a spoiled child, as if what the landlady had said did not make sense, as if she did not know that getting a job in a proper home—to eat proper food, to sleep in a bed, to have grown-ups in her life—would be the best thing to happen to her in a long time. Nonetheless, she cried because she had only finished her mock exams and had hoped to go to secondary school.

The following morning a long gleaming Volvo arrived. Suubi wore her beautiful blue floral dress, with a thick elasticated waistband, which the slut had given her—the tailor had made it too small for the slut. Suubi got into the car but she was uneasy. She did not like cars.

7.

MAKINDYE HILL, KAMPALA

December 1988

Inspect the house: make sure everything is perfect before they return. Dishes washed and put away in the pantry, the sink is empty and dry, lunch is ready, and the floor is spotless. Close the kitchen door behind you. The dining table is laid for lunch—tablemats, glasses, cutlery, plates—everything is in place. Ah, peace and quiet when they're not here: this becomes your home then. When there is no one to remind you who you are, then you belong. It's a great feeling. This could be your home, they your mother and father, they your siblings. You're younger than Katama and Kula. Their father calls you Kaama: nice of him. Close the dining-room door behind you.

Perhaps because they are my parents returned from London?

No, no Suubi, don't start that!

Ssanyu Babirye had started whispering to Suubi when she arrived at the beautiful house in the long Volvo six months ago. It was a vast house surrounded by a tall hedge of fir. Suubi had only seen such beautiful homes in white people's magazines. When she stepped out of the Volvo and into their house, three delicate children had stared at her as if she were a rat crawling out of a pipe. Their eyes languid, their skin pampered, they had never seen ugliness, never known foraging. Their father had glanced at her and quickly looked away. Their mother smiled a lot. The house was quiet as if there were no children. Suubi had never known air in a house to be so weightless. Everything was clean. The family spoke in delicate tones, whispers almost. That day, Suubi's tongue could not move. At night, she was dazzled by the beautiful curtains flowing to the floor in the sitting room, by the bright lights that left no shadows in the rooms, by the food that smelled like restaurants she had walked past, by the clinking of cutlery that sounded so civilized, by how everyone ate with a fork and knife so efficiently while her fork chased her food around the plate. The family ate such tiny portions yet the food was so tasty. And the way the children were indifferent to it all! Suubi felt the urge to roll on the soft carpet in the opulence surrounding her because, to her, to be rich was to be spoiled and to be spoiled was to roll on the soft carpet with no care at all.

Ssanyu whispered the following morning when Suubi started working. She told her what to say and what to do.

You're getting absentminded again, Suubi!

Suubi carried on inspecting the house. *That curtain is askew, use the tieback. Run, the player is chewing the cassette. Press STOP, now EJECT. Take the cassette out slowly.*

Suubi had been listening to UB40.

Use a pen to roll the tape back into the cassette: it is that rewinding of "Red Red Wine" over and over that made the player chew the tape. Turn off the player. Close the dining door behind you. The hallway is silent and clean. The toilet mat is straight, straighten the hand-towel. The bathroom is perfect . . . Who strangled the toothpaste? Squeeze it upward, there. Close the bathroom door behind you. Five months you've been living in this place but I still have to remind you to close the doors! The girls' bedroom is clean. No, you're not going to try on Kula's dresses: she smelled your sweat on them last time. Katama's bedroom is neat and tidy. The master bedroom is locked: nothing you can do about that . . . the horn! They are back. Run to the gate.

Suubi opened the gate and a picture of a Westernized family in a maroon Volvo Estate—Dad driving, Mum in the passenger seat, three children in the back looking fed up and a boot weighed down by shopping—drove through. Suubi locked the gate. The car parked outside the garage, which meant that the family or the parents would be going out again. Mr. Kiyaga stepped out, then his wife, Muwunde. The children, Katama, the eldest, a boy of fifteen, Kula, a girl of fourteen, and Katiiti, a girl of ten, scrambled out of the back seat. Kula and Katiiti were squabbling over who should sit next to the car doors.

"You're the youngest and must sit in the middle," Kula shouted at Katiiti.

"But I booked first. Mummy said I can if I book fir—"

Stop staring, Suubi. They would not take you along because you're a servant. There are only three seats in the back of the car. That's why they have three children only. Now open the boot and take out the shopping.

"Welcome back," Suubi started but the children ran past her.

They're excited. Try again when you get to the house.

When she had brought all the shopping into the kitchen Suubi asked the children, "Where have you been this morning?" She had put lightness into her voice but the children glanced at each other and scampered off to their parents' bedroom giggling.

They don't play with servants.

"Lunch's not yet on the table, Suubi?" their mother asked.

"I'll get it."

Put matooke on the big plate, rice in a dish, greens in a small dish, and meat in the large dish. Put the dirty pots away. Now go and call them.

"Food's on the table."

The family came out and headed toward the table. As they sat down, Katiiti observed, "There's no juice?"

"Oh sorry, I forgot! I'll get it."

"Can't you get the juice from the fridge, Katiiti?" their mother's voice came. "Suubi's made it, surely you can get it."

As she sat down again, Katiiti started, excited, "Uhh, I can't wait to go—" she gasped the rest of the words. Eating stopped. Spiky eyes tore into Katiiti. They each stole a glance at Suubi, then darts at Katiiti again.

All right, something is going on and they can't talk about it because you act like you're their abused stepsister. You're making them nervous.

"Are you all right, Suubi?" Kula was observant.

"Yes, why?"

"You're staring at your plate like you'd break it."

Laugh, roll your eyes.

"That's funny."

"She scares me." That was Katiiti. Katama, the boy, never talked to Suubi at all.

Your jealousy is showing!

After lunch, the children went back to their parents' bedroom but their father stayed in the sitting room, reading the newspaper. Suubi knew as she cleared the table that something was going on—a party somewhere, a trip to Nairobi, a sleepover somewhere—otherwise the children would have been sent off to bed to have their mandatory afternoon siesta. Rather than start to wash the dishes, Suubi went outside and sat in the frog, the old Citroën. Ssanyu pleaded, *Suubi, you're not Cinderella. Go back and wash the dishes.*

Something in Suubi refused to do the dishes. She did not know why she chose to sit in the old abandoned car, but it felt right. It smelled of oil, there were nuts and bolts in the foot wells, the leather on the seats was cracked, and the speedometer, clock face, and glove compartment had all been pulled out from under the dashboard: it was a shell. The grime and the dirt and smell calmed her down. When she lay down on the cold leather on the back seat, she felt at home.

Next she heard, "Mummy, she's here. She's sleeping in the frog."

Suubi sat up.

The sun is setting.

"Why are you sleeping in the car, Suubi? Don't you have a bed?" Mrs. Kiyaga asked.

"It was so quiet and cool in here. I sat down for a while. I must have fallen asleep."

"We've been looking for you for hours."

"I am sorry. I fell asleep."

"Come with me," said Mrs. Kiyaga.

Now you're in trouble.

"The rest of you stay here. I want to talk to Suubi alone."

Close the door behind you. Sit down on the carpet.

"Suubi, you seem unhappy with us," Mrs. Kiyaga started. "Often, you forget that you came to work. It's as if you're here on holiday. You're how old?"

"Thirteen."

"Children younger than you run homes larger than this, but you're struggling. Because you're young, we share everything with you, which we never do with other servants. Maybe that is the problem."

"No!" Suubi was alarmed.

"If someone came and found you sleeping in the abandoned car, they'd think you're being abused. Suubi, I can't take you everywhere we go. I don't mind living with you until we find proper servants, but your behavior worries me. Let me know if you want to leave."

Don't even cry. Do you want to go back to the Palace? You're not their child. Is not being part of them the worst thing that has happened to you? Like you had a car, like you had a bed, like you've ever belonged. Close the door!

"Mummy, why does she live with us?" Katiiti asked.

"Shhhh, she's helping us."

"Then she must sleep in the annex. All servants sleep in the annex. We're crowded. There're only four bedrooms."

"She's young."

"What if she dies in our house?" Kula whispered.

"Yeah, Mummy: she looks like she's about to die." Katama's voice seemed to embarrass him. When he spoke, it started deeply but ended in a squeak.

"I don't want to hear that talk again."

Focus on the beautiful things like their bathtub, rich food, and they do Christmas like in films. But you can't be their child.

8.
MAKINDYE HILL

June 1989

"Didn't I say that I wanted that girl removed before I left for work this morning?"

Suubi had walked into the pantry to get a glass from the shelves and get water from the fridge. She had been constantly thirsty all day. When she heard Mr. Kiyaga's voice, she stopped. *Someone has annoyed Daddy,* she thought.

No answer came from his wife. Mr. Kiyaga carried on, "I don't want her mixing with my children anymore. We now have three servants and that's enough. Besides, you know that things have been disappearing since she arrived."

"What do you want me to do," now the wife's voice came from further in the house, "throw her out on the streets? I took her back where I found her but her aunt had died. She doesn't know her relations."

"She's lying. Where did she come from? How can she not remember where she came from?"

"Suubi was very young when she was abandoned and no one had seen any relations visiting. I can't just send her away; she's too young."

"Then take her to the police."

"And where will I say I found her?"

"You should've known she was underage when you employed her."

"Like you came up with any options! I've put announcements on the radio. Someone will claim her."

Someone is coming, run! Get out of the house before they see you!

"Here she is, Mummy. You're not allowed in here. Go back where you came from. You are making Mummy and Daddy argue."

"Yeah, they never quarrelled before you came."

"Let's go, Katiiti. We're not supposed to talk to her."

What are you smiling about, Suubi?

I am happy.

Shhh, they'll see you talking to yourself.

I have my own bedroom in the boys' quarters, I mean the annex. Daddy says that "Boys' quarters" is a colonial word. I like "Annex," it is an educated word. The annex is not really bad. Mukasa the *shamba* boy who doubles as our askari at night sleeps in one room. Daddy says that Mukasa is not a "*shamba* boy," another colonial word, but the gardener. Mutono, our *ayah* and Naiti, who is our cook, all sleep in the annex. I'll lie down for the rest of the day . . . some children in Africa go without food. I've seen them on TV.

Now you're properly unhinged. Stop calling him "Daddy." He's not your father. What were you thinking sneaking back into their house? You've been told to stay in the boys' quarters until your relatives come to claim you.

It is the annex and I was thirsty. I think a headache is coming on.

You could have waited for Naiti to bring your food and asked for water but no, you must be in their house. Now you've set him off.

It's the servants: they won't even let me touch a book, they're terrible. Before they came everything was fine. Naiti hates bringing food to me. Oh, I told her that her name is spelt N-i-g-h-t: she didn't know. How ignorant! I think she's been telling lies about me and turned the family against me. That's why everyone has changed suddenly. Before the servants came, everyone loved me.

They asked you to leave the house because you stole things from the children, you wore their clothes, and you kept calling them Mummy and Daddy.

You make things up. I slept in that big beautiful house and watched films and listened to music. I read a lot of beautiful books and I was very, very happy.

Remember when Mrs. Kiyaga took you back to the Palace? You cried all the way. The landlady wouldn't have you back because Kulata is dead.

I'll go back to school! I'll catch up. I brought my books and uniform with me. Now I understand why Mummy gave me all this money. It's to buy things I need for school. I need a pair of shoes, socks, knickers, another uniform, a school bag, books, and pens. It's a long way to school but if I set off at five-thirty in the morning, by eight I will be in Old Kampala. It's seven or eight miles away but from Makindye to Ndeeba is rolling down hill, from Ndeeba to Namirembe Road is a flat straight walk, the only climb, Namirembe Road, past the mosque and I am at school. When I bring home a good school report, they will forgive me, they will love me again, wait and see. There is a funny taste in my mouth. I am so tired I want to sleep.

That money was your pay. Save it. Find another job and save some more. In the end, find a market stall and sell second-hand clothes while you wait to find a man and marry.

What is that itching up my leg?

The scar, you got it when you were abducted: the only mark you've failed to erase.

You lie: I have never been abducted. Suubi was almost screaming now. Stop coming to me.

And so Babirye did.

When Suubi sat down on her bed, tiredness spread all over her body like a wave. She felt like lying down but instead picked up a magazine she had already read and flipped through the pages. In the end, she lay on top of her bed and felt pains in her neck. She remembered that she had felt similar pains earlier in the day. Perhaps her head had slipped off the pillow awkwardly the night before. She put down the magazine and closed her eyes.

A wave of shivers hit her. They gripped her skin first and then exploded like fireworks of chilled tiny darts leaving a spread of goose pimples. She held her arms across her chest as if to trap the fleeing heat. She looked outside to see whether rain was coming. There were no clouds. She rocked her body to regenerate heat.

She was leaving the toilet for the third time that evening—the problem with drinking a lot of water—when the shivers launched another attack. This time, they crept right through the skin, through the flesh, into the bones and froze the marrow. By the time she got to her room, her legs were numb and her teeth chattered. Curiously, the three steps to her room seemed higher. Her chest was hot. As she reached for the doorframe to steady herself, hot tears started to stream down her face, yet she was not crying.

She got into bed and coiled tighter than a poked millipede. Still her body shuddered. Her breath was fiery so she breathed into her hands, which were icy. Then she grew hot and threw the blanket off. The T-shirt she wore was drenched in sweat. Her heart raced so fast she heard it pumping in her head. She tried to get up and take off her T-shirt but a new onslaught of chills overwhelmed her and she sank back into bed. It started all over again; the burning in her eyes, in her mouth, on her breath, and in her feet. Yet her skin was covered in goose pimples and her bed was icy. She stretched, pushing her legs as far away as they could go, arching her chest, and pulling her head up and away from her shoulders. As soon as she snapped back, she shivered again. Cold hands touched her and she jumped.

"She is burning."

Naiti's eyes were estranged from her face. At first they floated in the air. Then suddenly they darted here, there, like insects. Then they multiplied and grew bigger. They started to menace. They were coming for her, forming more eyes, growing larger. They dashed like millions of bats, screaming. Now the eyes surrounded her and then lost shape. They were a thing but were still eyes and millions of them but the thing was leaping.

She sat up, gulping for air.

All the servants were in her room. They stared. Their stares were worried. Naiti was talking.

"What is it? Why did you scream?"

"Your eyes; they are fine now but they tried to kill me."

She collapsed back in bed. She intended to keep her eyes open and look out for the eyes but then she was sitting up in bed. Naiti knelt beside her.

"You screamed again."

"I did not. I was awake," but she was breathless as if she had been running.

She must have fallen asleep again, for next she felt a wet towel on her forehead and she winced.

"Shhhh, you're burning." Naiti kept wetting the towel to keep it cold.

Soon the pounding in her head ceased but then she shivered and turned on her side. Then she curled up and covered her head. At that point she felt layers and layers of blankets piling on top of her.

"Aren't you people supposed to be in the house?" she asked the servants. They looked at her.

"It's only me, Naiti."

"I thought I saw all of you." There was silence and she added, "Thanks for staying with me, Naiti."

She was woken up. Mrs. Kiyaga was shaking her. The room was crowded with a lot of people but there were no screaming eyes. The sun had come down into her room: she shielded her eyes from it. Mrs. Kiyaga whispered something to Naiti. Then she bent down and smiled.

"How are you, Suubi?"

Suubi looked at the woman: it was the stupidest question.

"You are Suubi, aren't you?"

Suubi nodded her head.

"Who am I?" the woman asked.

What's wrong with her? But she said politely, "Mrs. Kiyaga."

"Right, let's get you out of here."

She and Naiti held Suubi's underarms and hoisted her up. When she stood up she tottered. Mrs. Kiyaga held her with both hands as Naiti put a thick jacket around her. Mrs. Kiyaga laughed, "You're surprisingly heavy."

Suubi smiled at being called heavy. She held both Mrs. Kiyaga and Naiti around their shoulders and they held her around the waist.

"When did you start feeling like this?" Mrs. Kiyaga asked as they walked out of the annex toward the large house. It was night. Suubi wondered where the sun in her room had gone. She looked back; her room was dark. "Suubi," Mrs. Kiyaga spoke again. "When did the fever start?"

"An hour ago. Where has the sun gone?"

"It's two in the morning."

"Oh. Around four or five or six."

"Have you eaten anything since?"

Shook her head.

"Would you like to eat something?"

Shook her head.

"Something to drink maybe?"

God, keep quiet! The voice sliced through her head.

Shook her head.

"Can we rest awhile please?" Suubi asked. They were halfway to the house.

"Come on. You're a strong girl; I'll let you rest when we get to the house."

They climbed the steps to the house into the kitchen. It was a long way to the bedrooms. When she finally got to bed, Mrs. Kiyaga told her not to lie down yet. She gave her two Panadols and water. Naiti brought a jar of juice, a glass, and a side table. Suubi shook her head.

"You will drink a glass!" Mrs. Kiyaga was stern. "You are not going to lie down until you've drunk."

Tears came into Suubi's eyes as she poured passionfruit juice mixed with pineapple down her throat. She was not sure why she was crying but she could not stop herself. Everyone around her was whispering.

"Don't fuss; I am supposed to be dying."

She fell back into bed and slept.

She was woken up again. One of Kula's dresses was laid out on the bed. Naiti was shaking her. Suubi had never seen Naiti being consistently nice to her.

"Get dressed."

"That is Kulabako's dress."

"She said you can wear it. Here, let me help you get dressed. They are taking you to hospital."

"What will they do when I die?" she whispered to Naiti.

"Shhh, don't say things like that!"

"Everyone says," her teeth were chattering again. "They say that I cannot live because I am too skinny."

"Stop talking: the fever has gone to your head."

When she was done, Suubi fell back into bed. Then Mr. and Mrs. Kiyaga were holding her—was she sure it was them, really? They were walking her to the Volvo. She fell asleep on the back seat. Next they were helping her out of the car. Next there were the blasted stairs again to climb. She sat on a bench but decided to lie down. Before she had caught her breath, a nurse came and helped her up. *If only they would realize how tired I am!*

"Come with me," the nurse says, and she holds her around the waist.

They come to a large room divided into small cubicles using plasterboard. The first one has a microscope and a table lamp but they walk past it before she sees anything else. In the next one, the curtain is closed. They walk into the third one. It is cold in this one. The nurse turns on the light and it is too bright. There is a long narrow plastic bed propped high, right in the middle of the room. A sharp smell of aspirin mixed with other medicines pervades the air. The nurse shakes a thermometer violently, now peering at it intently, now shaking again. Finally, she sticks it under

Suubi's arm. A man comes in. He takes a needle out of a wrap and says, "I am going to take a drop of blood; just a prick."

But there is no time to negotiate with him, for he grabs Suubi's middle finger on the right hand. He presses the ball so hard that it has gone red and then he pricks, the monster! He has picked up a glass slide and is rubbing drops of blood on it. When he is done he presses a cotton swab on the finger and takes the slide to another room.

"You can lie back on the bed now." It is the nurse's turn to do things.

Suubi's eyes are closed tight as the nurse pulls up her dress. The cold metal of the stethoscope darts then stops and she listens. Then it moves lower, listening and searching the chest and the stomach. Then the nurse taps her belly and listens as if searching for ripening jackfruit. Afterwards, she pulls the thermometer out from her underarm.

"Forty degrees!" she says to Mrs. Kiyaga and walks out.

Suubi falls asleep. Mrs. Kiyaga watches her.

"It is the falciparum strain, Mrs. Kiyaga." The nurse is back. "That is why it went to her head. Other than that there is nothing wrong with her. Of course we can do more tests if you want."

Suubi does not open her eyes, but she can hear the punishment for being 40-degrees hot and having the falciparum strain of malaria prepared. First, there is the crinkling of polythene paper and then tearing. *She is getting the needle.* More tearing. *She is getting the syringe.* Something thin, metallic touches a metal bowl. Then the sucking sound: *The needle is sucking medicine from the little bottle,* then tapping on the syringe, *to get rid of the bubbles.* Suubi cannot bear the silent torture any longer and she opens her eyes. A long, thick needle, pointed in the air. The nurse pushes the medicine up the syringe to get rid of the bubbles; she squirts the excess in the air.

"Can't I have tablets instead?"

"No, I am afraid not."

"Don't get me wrong; it's not that I fear injections. I hate them." Tears are coming again.

"I am glad to hear that because I am going to give you two."

"Oh, why?" Mrs. Kiyaga asks.

"Her temperature is too high to leave it to tablets to bring it down in the case of cerebral malaria. The first injection will bring the temperature down and when it is low I will give her quinine. Chloroquine won't work on this strain and it causes terrible itching."

The injection lies in a bean-shaped metallic bowl like a giant engorged mosquito. Suubi rolls over. She is weeping shamelessly. Mrs. Kiyaga holds her hand.

"I'm allergic to quinine." Suubi tries one last attempt. She had heard people say that at the Palace.

"Everyone is allergic to quinine, child. Now, if you'll turn around; we don't have all day."

Suubi swears not to embarrass herself any further. But as the cold swab cleans that part of her buttock, she clenches the muscle. The nurse stops.

"Relax the muscle. If you clench it will take longer and it will make it more painful."

A short, piercing pain is followed by an intense burning. Suubi squirms. The needle is out. The nurse massages the spot. She gives her two Panadols as well to swallow.

Suubi was not sure what was worse: quinine or malaria. The shivers had ceased, so had the retching, but her head was spinning. Her tongue felt swollen and numb. She did not taste the juice she drank. Food was still out of the question. In any case, the fever had burned her lips so badly that they had burst into sores like blisters. The ringing in her ears was incessant and she was partially deaf in her right ear. Her stomach was an empty room and wind whirled from one end to another. She was still weak and stayed in bed for most of the time. In the evening, the children came in and said hallo and stared and smiled. And Mr. Kiyaga, in his gruff way, said she had to eat because she did not have any weight to lose. *And put that cream on those lips!* He put it on the table. And Kula gave her a lot of her clothes she did not wear anymore and Naiti helped her to the bathroom.

When Suubi recovered and went back to eating at the table with the family, and everyone made sure she ate properly, and she was not sent back to the annex with the servants and she wore what used to be Kula's dresses, she decided that her parents had returned from London. One morning, she woke up early and walked back to Old Kampala Primary. She told the headmistress that she had been unwell and joined the primary seven class. At the end of the term when she brought home a fantastic school report, her parents could not believe that a child could walk so many miles to school and still manage to study so well. "Katama, Kula, Katiiti, look at this report!" Mummy said to Suubi's spoiled siblings.

There is nothing that parents love more than a child who brings home a fantastic school report.

9.

MMENGO, KAMPALA

Saturday, February 14, 2004

Suubi finished bathing and reached for the towel. Instead of drying her body, she wiped away the steam on the mirror and looked at herself. Her collarbones were so prominent that water would collect in the dents. Her stomach curved in and the bones of her pelvis stuck out. She was twenty-nine years old but retained a childlike kind of thinness. It did not matter what she ate, her body was as indifferent as a pipe to water. She turned and looked at her backside. From this view, when she was naked, it looked shapely and respectable but one time a colleague she had fallen out with described her as that "I-sit-on-my-back-like-a-dog" woman. Of course Suubi waited and later as the colleague walked past her, she said, "You've dropped something, Katana."

The woman stopped, looked back, saw nothing and looked at Suubi questioningly.

"Oops, sorry," Suubi said, "I really thought I saw something fall; must have been your arse."

Sometimes Suubi felt that she was above the whole notion of "she does not fill the space she occupies" as people described skinny people but other times it hurt.

It was Saturday midday. The previous night, as usual on Friday evening, she and Opolot had gone out with his friends in search of a kafunda, watering holes in Kansanga that hosted live bands, but had ended up in Bbunga. At around three in the morning all the friends had squeezed into Opolot's Prado and Suubi, who did not drink, dropped each friend back home. It was coming to five when they got home. Opolot was still sleeping when Suubi came to the bathroom.

She dried her face first, then her arms. She flipped the towel onto her shoulders and, tugging at it, dried her back. She was wiping her right leg when a nail clipped the scar on the thigh. The pain was so dramatic that she clenched her teeth. As the pain ebbed into itching, she passed a finger around the scar. The finger caressed round and round. At the edge of the pain was a fragile pleasure. Suubi bent over to look. The scar was a dent in her thigh as if flesh had been scooped out with a tablespoon. The skin on top was as thin as on cooling milk—soft, smooth, and wrinkled. She blew on the scar for as long as she could sustain her breath. She blew repeatedly until the pain faded. Then she fastened the towel above her breasts and stepped out of the bathroom.

Opolot lay reclined on the bed when Suubi walked in and she smiled at him. He was already dressed and was reading the previous day's paper. Normally, Suubi would make something to eat, either breakfast or lunch, then at around four they would go to his house where he would change clothes, and at around seven they would go out again. Now she asked, "Should I cook?" but before Opolot answered she added, "Do you have a program for today?" Suubi walked around the bed to the dressing table.

Opolot put the paper away and yawned.

"No, no proggie," and he stretched. "Perhaps Half-London. Kijjo and the others will be there." Kijjo and others were friends with him when he had attended St Mary's.

"I'll make *chai*—got some fresh milk yesterday and there is half a loaf of yellow bread."

"That'll do for me."

Opolot liked his milk straight from the cow—pasteurizing kills both the taste and the flavor, he claimed—and hardly diluted. Since meeting him, Suubi had acquired a taste for fresh milk, *conc*, especially when spiced with *tangawuuzi*, ginger. *Omujaaja* weed would be best but it was rare to find anymore and so she settled for cinnamon.

Suubi did not sit down at the dressing table. She picked up a bottle of lotion, opened the lid, and squirted some in her palm. She rubbed it between her hands, applied some on her face and then on her arms. She squirted some more and lifted her right foot and placed it onto the lower shelf of her dressing table. She had started to rub lotion into it when the towel fell off her back. A strangled cry escaped her. Opolot, who had been watching her rub lotion on her legs, whistled and crossed his own, "Now the proper show begins."

But Suubi sank onto the floor and buried her face into her lap to hide the scar. She remained on the floor, her head curled into her lap.

"Eh?" She heard Opolot sit up, perhaps beginning to realize that she was not fooling around. "Now what?"

She did not reply. The air in the room bristled. Opolot sucked his teeth.

She heard him get off the bed and his feet walked around, coming to where she knelt. He stopped behind her, picked up the towel, and she felt it spread over her back. But then he hesitated. Then he squatted and she felt her butt exposed—the towel had been lifted.

"Hmm, is this what you are hiding?" his voice was cheeky.

The next thing she felt was her butt being raised off the floor.

What are you doing?" Her arms reached for the floor to steady herself.

"Just checking what you're hiding. Is it down here?"

He lifted her buttocks so high that her head touched the floor like a Muslim praying.

"Opo— Wha— Sto—"

He rubbed his crotch into her butt, one cheek first, "Is it

here?" then on the other, "Here?" then in the middle, "Maybe here?" then all around, "Or everywhere?" the way she liked him rubbing himself on her. Suubi clenched her teeth but between her legs she was swelling with sensations. She felt him starting to coil in his pants and she clawed at the floor looking for something firm to hold on to and lift her head off the floor. Luckily, with his every thrust, her head got closer and closer to the dressing table. Then she saw its legs, pawed at them but only managed to place her hands onto them.

"Tell me to stop, Suubi," Opolot taunted. "Beg your man to stop right now. Eh? This woman wants me to kill her *dala-dala*."

"But you . . . bastard."

"Eh? Did she call us bastard, soldier? Let's kill her right now." He thrust harder.

"Say, *Opolot, my sir. Say, Chief, please you're killing me.*"

Suubi managed to ease her upper body up.

"Ooh no, she is stubborn this one; she likes it when I rub my soldier on her butt and my soldier stands at atteeention!"

Suubi bit back a moan as she manoeuvred herself upright. Finally, her feet were placed firmly on the floor. Opolot was forced to hold around her waist, his legs apart. By now, Suubi's butt felt like a million fireflies all lit up. Each needed to be rubbed critically. She held onto the sides of the dressing table and eased herself into a position where she would anticipate Opolot's thrusts and twist her butt to give every inch of it a feel of his groin. But then he pulled away.

"What?" Suubi spun around. There was such a riot of sensation between her legs that she could feel the slipperiness between her thighs.

"It's a new belt and I—" Opolot fidgeted.

Rather than help, Suubi spread her legs around Opolot's and, using her pelvis and arms, forced him to walk backwards until he stumbled and fell back on the bed.

"Suubi, bannange, wait. Let me get out of these trousers," the chief was gone. "We'll mess them up." But Suubi had undone his fly, pulled him out, and she was helping herself to his soldier.

"You started it," she giggled evilly as she rubbed him on her every desperate inch.

Opolot was pulling off his shirt, to feel her skin on his, when Suubi thrust herself onto him. She ripped his shirt open and lowered her breasts onto his chest. She nuzzled her head in the side of his neck and the chief was reduced to deathlike gurgling. She had intended to ask him to beg her to stop but she only remembered when she was done.

"Don't ever hump my butt when you are not ready," she tapped his chest.

Opolot opened his eyes weakly. She sat on him smiling with triumph. As she eased herself off him, she looked at the damage to his trousers. "Y*roou*, Opolot, you're disgusting!"

He raised his head, looked at the slime, sucked his teeth and fell back.

As she stepped onto the floor Opolot saw the scar and reached to touch it. Suubi pulled away.

"That must have been a nasty wound," he said with concern. "What happened?"

Suubi looked down at the scar and for a moment panic came to her eyes. "I don't remember," she turned away. "I was very young."

She picked up the towel and wrapped it around herself. She pulled out a drawer and took out one of the soft thin muslin cloths she had bought for this purpose. She took it to the bed and started to wipe Opolot. She smiled at his closed eyes, "If I twist like this, round and round and then again, the soldier could wake up again. Oh oh he heard me! He has heard right now! Tsk, tsk, tsk," she shook her head in mock disapproval.

Opolot lifted his head again, looked at his half-hearted hard-on with pride, but gave it up, fell back, and smiled through half-closed eyes. He loved being wiped like this. Sometimes, when Suubi was prepared, she boiled the kettle. When they were finished, she wetted the cloth with warm water and when she touched him with it he would lie back, stretch his arms and *ahhh*.

Now Suubi tucked him back into his damp Y-fronts and zipped his wet trousers. She buttoned his shirt and pulled it down to hide the patch.

"There, no one will see it as you get out of the car."

She went to the bathroom and threw the cloth in a basin. She examined the scar as she washed herself. It was good now that Opolot had seen it. She did not have anything to hide anymore. Maybe Ssanyu Babirye would leave her alone now.

When she went back to the bedroom, Opolot was snoring. She carried on moisturizing her skin.

10.

Suubi felt beleaguered now that the toothaches had started. The aches were mild, only the crowns hurt—as if heavy metal objects were scratching each other—but the discomfort was mounting. Every time she connected Ssanyu Babirye's return to dating Opolot the pain came, creeping to her front teeth. She had considered giving up Opolot for peace of mind but she knew that there would be no such thing. Theirs was a calm relationship—without the complication of the intense emotions she had seen other couples display. It was only when she considered terminating it that its intensity became aggressive. Suubi was now convinced that she was possessed by a jealous spirit that did not want to see her happy with a man.

Dating Opolot had not only conjured Ssanyu Babirye out of hell, it had also pressured Suubi into telling the story of her life. She had to have events and anecdotes at her fingertips to dispense in conversation with him and his friends. This is what brought on the pain in the teeth. It had always been like that with friends. They always wanted bits of her past: answers to tiny questions, musings, or wonderings. Suubi did not mind people talking about their lives or childhoods as long as they did not expect her to join in.

"You don't talk much about yourself, Suubi."

"I have lived an ordinary life," she would say. Inside, she wanted to scream, "I am here. Let's start here, now."

Most people, she presumed, grew up dispensing bits of their lives over and over. Eventually their stories flowed easily. However, she had never made friends as a child and so she had not had the chance to rehearse her stories.

Suubi had known Opolot for more than two years but previously, when he probed, she distanced herself. However, nine months ago it became ridiculous to say: *This won't work*, when he countered with: *How can it work when you've not given it a chance?* Perhaps this was why their relationship was quiet. They had been in a repressed love for two years, both knowing that the other felt it as keenly as they did. Neither had tried to date other people. When Suubi finally plunged herself into it, because she could not hold out much longer, it felt like they had been together all that time.

Suubi wished she could say to Opolot that her memory was a scratched disc, that it jumped and skipped. Sometimes it didn't play at all. Nevertheless, when questions about her past presented themselves she answered them as faithfully as she could. Little by little, a story of her life had taken form.

"My full name is actually Suubi N. Kiyaga.

"N is for Nnakintu but I don't use it really. Nnakintu is the feminine version of Kintu. The name 'Kintu' is clanless, any clan can use it. Things like clans don't matter to me really. Luckily, you're Atesot: we can't be related. Yes, clans are about identity, but essentially they're a measure against inbreeding. Yes, Suubi means 'hope' but my parents never told me what they were hoping for. I have no attachment to names really.

"Katama is the eldest. When we were young and got in trouble together, he always got blamed, 'And you too, Katama, a big boy?' He hates his name; it suggests that he is tiny. Yes, he's quiet but I would not say haughty. It was easy for me being a middle child. Maybe I was a little neglected sometimes, like all middle children, but nothing to be traumatized about.

"Kula is the second-born; her name is actually Kulabako which means 'beautiful to look at.' Kula is the hot-headed one of all of us. She makes up her mind fastest and loudest. She says it exactly as she sees it and can be offensive. But she'll give you her last shilling and won't remind you if you go back for more. She is generous in that way—just don't start a fight with her.

"Then there is me, the second last-born. At home they call me Kaama. I guess it's all about the 'K' names: rather embarrassing really. Kaama is from a proverb. It says that a destitute child is like *Kaama*, a wild yam. Unlike other yams that are tended and nurtured in a garden because their stems are delicate, Kaama—just as delicate—must fight its way in the cruel jungle. But then I could be Kaama—a whisper. The difference is in intonation.

"Katiiti is the last-born. She's the pretty one: her name means 'love-bead.' I desperately wanted that name when we were young! Katiiti is oblivious: nothing bothers her; nothing matters; she floats through life. She can be mean though. Daddy said we used to fight, me and her, when we were young. I guess because she comes after me.

"I look different from my siblings? I guess it is because they look like Mum . . ."

"Apparently, Dad was not my biological father after all. I only found out last year, after his death. You know the Ganda have a saying: *Your father is never truly yours until your mother is dead.* It came painfully true for me. When Dad died, we took pride in the fact that he didn't saddle us with half-siblings. And then I find out that he's not my real dad? It's still hard for me.

"I suspect Mum and Dad broke up at one point and in the gap Mum got pregnant with me but they made up regardless. I don't know. Maybe Mum didn't know that Daddy knew.

"No, Dad was good to me. I don't have a bad word to say about him. People say I was his favorite. I mean, that could be the reason why Katiiti and I don't get on. I brought home the best school reports. Katiiti struggled in school. I was the one who was never sent to boarding school because I could pass in any school.

They envied me for staying close to our parents. At sixteen I was given my own room in the annex because I was so responsible while they slept close to Mum and Dad.

"No, I never suspected anything at all. On school forms, I filled in his name as my father. You've seen my graduation pictures: he stood beside me with Mum. He threw a great graduation party for me. Actually, people say I looked more like him than anyone else in the family. I still use their family name though.

"Of course anyone would want to know their biological father but it is no big deal for me . . .

"When Mum was diagnosed with cancer, my sisters would not leave her side. But I was always with Dad because he also needed someone. He was the one who was going to stay behind on his own. Someone had to be there for him too. When she died, I checked on him every day. Even when I discovered, two months after Mum's death, that he was seeing someone else, it didn't matter. The others were incensed that he had been seeing the woman behind Mummy's back while she was ill. It could have been true, but you know, the relationship between Mum and Dad had nothing to do with me. That, I think, led to a rift between us.

"Dad had a stroke two years after Mummy's death. When he died, we mourned together as a family. At his burial, the number of his children was not mentioned, I thought, hmm, that's strange: we are only four.

"Now that you mention it, the number of children was not mentioned at Mum's burial either. Then the clan meetings for Daddy's last funeral rites started.

"Anyway, one day, Kula rang to ask me to drop her home for the clan meetings to arrange for Dad's last funeral rites. I thought, drop her: why not go with her? Why wasn't I told about the meetings? When we arrived, the uncles and aunts, Dad's siblings, were not only surprised to see me, but frowned at Kula for bringing me along. They would not look at me throughout the meeting. You could see they resented my presence.

"We set a tentative budget for the rites. Some clan elders wanted us children to contribute equal amounts of money but I suggested that we should contribute according to our means. However, while everyone else's contribution was met with approval, mine was met with a stony silence, yet it was quite substantial compared to everyone else's. You see, Kula, a teacher, is a single mother, and Katiiti didn't have a man at the time, which meant she was broke. Katama doesn't part with money easily, even though he is the eldest, the heir, and the only son.

"I found out during the rites. The family was invited to the reading of the will. But the elders insisted that only the children from Kiyaga's 'leg,' as they put it, should attend. I didn't realize what was going on until Kula whispered: *That coward's talking about you, Suubi. As if you don't know that you're not Daddy's child.*

"Can you imagine? I turned to stone. Why didn't Mum tell me? How come everyone else knew? From then on, a gap opened between my siblings and me. They've avoided me since.

"Yes, they can be haughty as you say, but they're fine when you get used to them.

"Finding my father? It's kind of you to offer to look for him but you don't have to.

"I would like to know him but I won't have sleepless nights over it. Why hasn't he tried to find me?"

11.
BULANGE VILLAGE

Saturday, March 13, 2004

Bulange was built up. The houses along Nabulagala Road, designed in the 90s style of crannied tile roofs called the French Cut, made it look like a new village. But the main road through the village was covered with murram. Suubi looked at the house that Opolot had brought her to see. Its 70s extended porch made it stand out from the rest. From across the road, the building looked similar to her home in Makindye. The fencing around it was a red-brick wall at the bottom with metallic bars on top of the wall. She walked close to the gate and looked through the bars. The house was beautiful and neat with a whitewashed porch and pebble-dashed walls. Suubi looked to the left. A narrow drive led further along to the neighboring houses. On the other side of the feeder road was a hedge. Suubi took the road, walking along the fencing, toward the back of the house. Opolot followed from behind.

Suubi's mind was focused on the house when a woman wearing a *busuuti* with a headscarf on her head came toward them. She was either in her forties or fifties. She looked at Suubi intently. There was a hint of hesitation on her face, then she smiled broadly. Suubi smiled back politely but there was no recognition in her eyes. The woman's smile turned to apologetic embarrassment, as if she had mistakenly smiled at a stranger, and she walked past them.

"Do you know her?" Opolot whispered.

Suubi shook her head, her face screwed up in a scowl.

"She seemed to know you."

Suubi shrugged her shoulders.

She had been reluctant to come to see the house but Opolot had insisted. He held the traditional view that everyone must know where they come from, no matter where it was, that to know where one comes from was to know one's full self and where that self was going.

Suubi was skeptical. To her, it was a worn-out view passed down through generations by people who could not be bothered to question things readily embraced. What difference would a good or bad past make? Everyone wants a bright future regardless of their past. But she would not say to Opolot that he was better off coming up with his own views than slotting into the lazy and tired views of the past. What she told him of was the foreboding she felt about going back to look for her past. If her family had wanted her they would have found her.

"To go looking for them is to go looking for heartbreak."

"They don't have to love you, Suubi, and you don't have to love them. All we need is to know. It will give you peace in your heart. Get rid of this, 'I am *Nnakintu, ati,* I am *Kayiga, ati,* I don't know who I am.' It's not good for your well-being."

"You are so traditional for someone whose first language is English."

"I speak English on principle. Otherwise, Luganda would be my first language. There are those that imagine that Uganda is synonymous with Luganda and that, to us non-Gandas, is infuriating."

"Except in the markets and shops."

"English is costly in markets."

They came to a side entrance to the house. It led straight to the garage. While there was a lawn in the front yard, the rest of the compound was covered in concrete slabs. The annex was at the back. Suubi stopped and turned to Opolot.

"You are sure this was once my home?"

"Apparently."

Suubi stared at the house again. There was nothing familiar about it.

"Keep looking," Opolot encouraged. "You might recognize something."

Suubi shook her head apologetically.

"I don't remember living here at all."

Opolot was disappointed that nothing had jolted Suubi's memory. It was such a beautiful house to forget. He had seen nothing in her body language to suggest that she was hiding anything. Now Suubi stopped and said,

"Maybe we should go inside. I might recognize something."

"We can't," Opolot explained as they made their way back to the car. "The widow who owned the house died and her sons sold it to an army general."

"I must've been very young, no more than four or five perhaps," she said casting a final look at the house.

"According to the couple I talked to, it was a long time ago. The village has changed since."

Just then, someone tapped Opolot's shoulder. He looked back. The old woman who had smiled at them beckoned him quietly and slipped back into the hedge. Suubi did not see her and carried on walking. Opolot said to her, "Just a moment, Suubi," and ran back.

Suubi stopped to wait. She stared at the hedge where Opolot had disappeared.

"Sorry to disturb you, son," the woman said as soon as Opolot arrived. "Is that Suubi you are with?"

"Yes, do you know her?"

"Oh, *Katonda watu!*" she clapped her hands.

"Wait here," Opolot said. "I'll go and call her."

"No, wait, maybe we should talk first."

"Then I'll go and open the car for her, she's waiting by the roadside. I'll be back."

Opolot ran back to Suubi.

"I've just seen the couple I talked to over there," he pointed beyond the hedge. Why don't you wait in the car while I go back and ask them some more questions?"

Thankfully Suubi did not suggest coming along with him.

"I won't be long," he said as he clicked open the central lock.

The woman stepped out from behind the hedge as soon as she saw Opolot coming and led him down the road to a small unpretentious house tucked behind its more affluent neighbors. The house was new. The burned mud bricks used to build it were bare. It had small glass windows and a corrugated iron roof. The woman was tall and might have been very light-skinned had she led a comfortable life but right now she was sunburned. When they turned into her walkway, she stopped and looked at Opolot.

"Sorry to bother you like this," she apologized again. "I couldn't talk in front of your companion."

"Yes?"

"That is Suubi, really?"

"Suubi Nnakintu."

"Suubi *Nnakato*," the woman corrected. "Not Nnakintu, though it is also our name."

"A twin?"

"Identical."

Opolot sighed and then walked around but came back to the same spot.

"*Yii yii*, who would have thought?" The woman clapped her hands and then held her chin. "I knew my eyes were not lying." Now she threw up her hands in disbelief, "Suubi lived!" She shook her head. She talked to Opolot as if she had sighted *Bikra Maria* herself. "I saw the image and I said to myself: *Hmm, isn't this my real child?* So I smiled and when she smiled all the other images, all of them came—her mother, her father—they were all there! And she's a real person now. Who would have thought? And so accomplished-looking!" Now she lamented, "But, *maama*, she did not recognize me. I don't blame her though." Now tears came to her eyes. "It is such a long time," she sniffed. "When I last saw her she was this tall," she indicated the height of a ten or eleven-year-old. *"Yii yii,* this Suubi child! Her mother named her well. Whoever saw the dying little mouse?"

"You knew Suubi's parents?"

"Knew them? He asks! Suubi is my very own child: one who came out of me, *bbe nghi!"* She made a pushing motion as if giving birth. "My brother Wasswa was Suubi's father. I came after the twins: that is why I am Kizza. Nnyonyi, her mother, was my best friend."

"Then why don't you come and meet her?"

"My child, there are all sorts of reasons in this world. Where do you start to explain and where do you stop? But tell me, is she all right properly?"

"We were trying to find her family. Someone said she once lived here so we came to look."

"Yii yii?" Kizza clapped her hands again. "If yours was a cry for help, you screamed right at the police station. I am her family."

"So should I go get her and introduce you?"

"Not yet. As I said before, these are things you don't rush. If she forgot maybe it is not wise to shock her too much like that. There are reasons for her forgetting, traditional reasons. You're sure she is all right: it is just this forgetting?"

Opolot spread his hands to show that he was not aware of anything else wrong with Suubi.

"Then that is fine." Now Kizza became pensive. "But if you notice something not right, if she appears disturbed or restless, bring her to me. For me, this is where I sit." She pointed to her house and smiled. "You want to see me; you just walk in and call *Ssenga Kizza.* That is me."

"OK, I shall bring—"

"Oh, I had forgotten, child. Isn't this good luck or is it providence?" Now she was talking to herself. "Because where would I have found Suubi to tell her?" Now she looked at Opolot. "Child, next month is *Apuli* isn't it?"

"It is."

"We're in *Maachi* now?"

"Yes."

"This is serious because I don't know how we are going to do it. I think we just have to tell Suubi the truth because during the Easter weekend, that is Good Friday, Saturday, Easter Sunday, and Easter Monday, our whole clan is going back for a reunion and Suubi must come. We hope to sort out the clan. Suubi's forgetting could be helped there. And it is important that she comes to meet the rest of the family. But you and I, we need to do this gently so we don't frighten her. When you find a good moment, tell her about me. Tell her I want to meet her, then bring her. I will tell her about everything myself. What do you think?"

"It is a good plan." Opolot smiled. "I am happy you are going to take her home."

"We're all happy to go home. Here is my phone number," and she proceeded to spell out the digits while Opolot keyed them into his phone. When he finished she said, "Now call me."

Opolot rang the number. The phone rang somewhere in her breasts and she giggled.

"That is where I hide it! No one can steal it from in there."

Opolot looked away as she reached into her bra and scooped out the phone. She looked at the screen and smiled.

"Eh, even yours. I have it now."

Opolot nodded.

"Now go before Suubi comes back looking for you."

As Opolot walked away the woman called, "Wait, son, how," now she made her voice sound mellow. "How are we related to you?"

It was a direct question. Opolot knew what the old woman was looking for. He tried to find a way of putting it delicately.

"Me? I am with Suubi," and he looked at her directly.

"Oh," the woman laughed shyly. "That is very good!" and she gave him both hands to shake and bent her knees in a gentle curtsey. "Very nice. Good to see you, son. I can see already that you are a good person." Now she talked to him like he was already an in-law.

Opolot smiled. Kizza was a typical Ganda aunt. She finds out you are dating her niece and she treats you like you're an in-law already so you marry her girl.

"Son, one last little thing."

Opolot looked at her.

"Where do you come from?"

Opolot smiled.

"Soroti, I am Atesot. My name is Opolot."

"Haaa, Atesot! That is why you are exceedingly handsome! Your Luganda is good," she said as if it were a compliment. "But there was slight skidding here and there," she added with a knowing smile. After a pause, as if she were remembering she blurted, *"Ejakait."*

Opolot smiled politely but did not return the greeting. Tell the Ganda that you are Atesot and they will fling *Ejakait* at you as if it summed up the whole of being Atesot. Some of them cannot even be bothered to learn your name. They will just call you *Ejakait*.

BOOK THREE
KANANI KINTU

1.
BUKESA, KAMPALA

Monday, January 5, 2004

It is already ten o'clock but the police have not arrived in Bwaise to collect Kamu's body. Idlers, like sightseers, come, stare, and then leave. They form a semicircle a few meters away from the corpse. Sprinkles of dust—thrown by passers-by, mostly strangers mumbling, *I've not walked past you stranger; I've buried you*—are strewn on Kamu's feet and on his trousers.

The idlers are subdued. Some have their hands folded at the chest, some at the back, some bite their nails but mostly they shake their heads, sigh, and suck their teeth in disbelief. A teenager standing by, out of sheer idleness rather than necessity, spits on the side and everyone turns on him, "You do not spit for the dead! Not even when they smell." And there is indignation at such a lack of decorum.

The air in Bwaise has turned. Once Kamu died and the LCs disappeared, horror and disbelief arrived. *Is a human slayable just like that?* And the whole notion of taking a human life became so heavy that Bwaise stared incredulous as if some other place had done it. *How do you go to bed at night and sleep when you've killed a whole human, hmm? The world died a long time ago . . . Everyone hates himself. People are not human anymore and all the buntu is gone.*

The women in the market, even some who had waved their

hands saying that they were fed up with thieves, now click their tongues at how quickly it had all happened. *At one moment the LCs were leading him down the road right, right here, the next he was wuu, dead.* They have already sprinkled dust on Kamu saying: *Kamu, you know I've buried you,* to absolve themselves from guilt. The same women now whisper the names of the killers and their whispers drift everywhere like smoke on wind. By midday, everyone interested will know who hit Kamu where, with what, and whose blow made him swallow his last breath.

At that ten o'clock, Kanani Kintu and his wife Faisi stepped out of their house to go sowing. Kanani stood below the veranda while Faisi tugged at the front door—the rains had made the wood swell and it was hard to open or close. Kanani faced a dilemma. He could offer to help Faisi at the risk of being brushed off impatiently, or he could look on, holding the padlock and the keys, while his wife struggled.

Just then, Faisi stepped back and wrenched with both hands. The door slammed with such force that the roof rattled. She wedged the bolt into the staple and motioned with her hand at Kanani. He passed on the padlock. She slipped it through the latch and pressed it. Kanani passed on the keys, this time unbidden. Faisi selected a key, stuck it into the lock and snapped it twice. Then she unzipped her handbag and tossed the keys in. She drew up the zip to close it but it got stuck along the way: the edge of the Bible stuck out. Kanani was about to offer to carry the Bible when Faisi pushed the book deeper into her handbag and the zip sailed past. She slipped her right hand through the straps, pulled them up her right shoulder, and cradled the bag between her arm and ribs. Faisi looked up and stepped off the verandah. Kanani followed.

Faisi was already in mode and Kanani knew not to disturb. He would not say that the Holy Spirit was upon her—only the brazen new churches from America made such claims—but once in mode Faisi was under Holy Guidance. Faisi was six foot two, slender and straight. She was not the kind of wife who, contrite about her lofty stature, shrunk to enhance her husband. Faisi walked tall even though Kanani was only five foot six and skinny. Now walking behind her, he wondered how, at the age of sixty-five, Faisi's backside could still be so pert. Suddenly, she stopped and he bumped into her. She removed the Bible from her handbag and Kanani gestured for her to pass it on. The straps on Faisi's handbag were frail. The patent leather, once tight, smooth, and shiny, had crumbled and flaked off. Kanani smiled: a lesser woman would have discarded the handbag a long time ago, but not Faisi.

When the two came to Makerere Road, Kanani asked, "Should we wait here for a taxi or should we walk?" But Faisi was already walking toward Naakulabye Town center. "Disciples worked in more hostile conditions," Kanani muttered to himself as he hurried to catch up.

It was a steep walk to Naakulabye. While Faisi looked straight ahead, Kanani noticed that the smell of garbage welcomed them into the town. The overflowing skip in the open yard of the market was as much a landmark of Naakulabye as the ancient *muvule* tree at the market's edge. When they came to Total Petro Station at the top of the road, women selling *matooke* across the road called, "Come, customer: take a look. Today's food is—"

"Leave those two alone," a woman interrupted. "They're the Awakened couple from that old house near Kiyindi."

"Do the Awakened still exist?"

That is true testimony, Kanani thought to himself; the world knew that he and his wife walked in the Lord.

By the time Kanani and Faisi came to the center of Naakulabye, the sun was severe. Kanani saw the unsightly tenants of the paved town circle and shook his head. Two fat cows, urban in bearing, occupied the space where flowers once grew. One cow lay on the ground chewing the cud, the other stood swishing its tail languidly, oblivious to the traffic circling around it.

"Africans . . ." Kanani hissed.

He remembered the neat paved walkways, manicured hedges, blooming plants, and the dustless streets of colonial Naakulabye and despaired. As a child in the 30s, Kanani had seen Kampala City take shape in the magical hands of the British. When it came to carving out landscape, the white man was a wizard. First, the mpala antelopes, which the *ba kabaka* had hunted for generations, were banished from the hills. Then the hills were measured and marked, then dug and demarcated into Streets, Roads, Lanes, Places, Squares, and Mews. The roads were tarred and paved smoother than mats. Trees and plants of agreeable species were planted at the roadside at precise intervals, then flowers of all colors. Suddenly, there were palm trees in Kampala. Streetlights sprang up between the trees and lit up in the night. Kampala's hilltops were enhanced with beautiful structures. Namirembe and Lubaga were crested with magnificent cathedrals, Kikaya was crowned with a beautiful Baha'i Temple, Nakasero with the tall Apollo Hotel, Kololo with a huge TV mast, Makerere with majestic university structures, and *Lubiri* with a modern royal palace. There was hope then. There were systems. There was order. Uganda was on its way to civilization.

Then independence came.

Kanani was pessimistic right from the start. Ugandans related to the land and to the hills, but not to the art drawn on them by the British. The land was theirs but the city belonged to the British. Kanani had watched, wary, as one by one, Europeans packed and left their city behind. Excited Ugandans, dizzy with euphoria, took their places. He remembered Rev Mackenzie, the senior accountant at Namirembe Cathedral at the time. Kanani was his assistant. He was in Mackenzie's office helping him pack his books in boxes when Mackenzie exploded, "You're a good person, Canaan." British people pronounced Kanani's name properly. "No doubt you'll do a good job. But mark my words: these buffoons are going to destroy your country."

Not even Mackenzie's pessimism prepared Kanani for the ineptitude and later, the sheer greed that consumed the city after independence. Through the decades, Mackenzie's words had come to pass like a prophecy. Luckily, churches were unaffected—right from the start churches had belonged not to Europeans but to God. For Kanani, that dry and dusty town circle in the middle of Naakulabye occupied by fat urbanite cows was emblematic of independent Uganda.

A taxi van bound for the city center came along and Kanani and Faisi boarded. As soon as he sat down, Kanani closed his eyes in prayer. But instead of prayers, images of his twins, Job and Ruth, floated past. Then Paulo Kalema, his grandson, came into view. The image of Paulo's face was close and large. It stayed immovable, blocking Kanani's prayer. He opened his eyes, blinked a few times and closed them again. He started to pray again but the images returned. Kanani was troubled. When prayer did not sit properly in his mind, it did not reach heaven. He ignored the images and mumbled on but Paulo's picture widened and darkened. No matter how fast Kanani prayed, Paulo's image remained a thick dark shadow he could not see past. Kanani gave up praying.

Lately, the fact that Paulo insisted on using Kalema as his surname had begun to bother Kanani. The coincidence of the name was too close to the curse. Yet Kanani's father and even his grandfather had been confident that if the family remained steadfast in the Church and kept their faith they would be safe. Sometimes though, especially at moments like this when his prayer had been blocked by the wandering of his mind, Kanani wondered whether they were. He found solace in the fact that both his father and grandfather had told him that the curse was specific: mental illness, sudden death, and suicide. He had not seen signs of mental illness in his family, and the twins, whatever their faults, were not suicidal. He pushed the thought out of his mind. The curse was nothing but the work of the Devil and Jesus had trounced all evil at Golgotha.

2.

Kanani and Faisi were going to "sow the seed." Normally, Faisi sowed alone but Kanani was on forced leave. At seventy-four years of age, there was grumbling within Namirembe Cathedral administration that Kanani should retire. He was awaiting the trustees' decision.

Faisi and Kanani Kintu were Awakened, an old sect within the Anglican Church. The Awakened were based at Namirembe Cathedral, though they had other churches all over central Uganda. For decades, the Awakened claimed to be the only people on the right course to heaven. They had declared other Anglicans Asleep, and Catholics were pronounced heathen for worshipping idols and a woman. Moslems were a primitive tribe.

Kanani and Faisi were a model Awakened couple. They lived a basic life. In fact, they wore poverty like an ornament. Faisi's ankle-length skirt was thick and woolen. Bought second-hand, she had worn it for the last ten years. There was neither adornment nor paint on her body. Her hair was cut so close that she brushed it with a shoeshine brush. After paying the tithe, Kanani and Faisi still spent most of their earnings on God's work.

Since the arrival of the deafening and predatory Pentecostal churches from America in the 80s, the Awakened had become an endangered species. The Pentecostals had drowned them with their discothèque music, frenzied dancing, and ecstatic prayer.

Kanani and Faisi had disagreed with the Awakened's decision to "withdraw from towns and cities to go into the hills." The brethren had pointed to the "signs of the times" and declared: "When you see false prophets you know the end is nigh. Get out of Babylon."

"But no one knows the day or the hour except He," Faisi had argued. "The world needs our true witness now in the age of false witness more than ever."

But the brethren did not listen. Now that prophecy had come to pass with cruel irony. The end had crept upon the Awakened sect but there was no Christ in sight. Kanani sucked his teeth in anger.

They alighted in the new taxi park and Kanani looked around. Because his life had rotated around Namirembe Cathedral, which was close to his house, this was the first time in a long while that he had looked at the new taxi park properly. The new shops, small and box-like, looked like shipping containers. No doubt the city engineer had a cave-like architectural vision. Kanani chastised his mind for wandering into worldly issues. He looked at Faisi and envied her unwavering focus. Faisi now had a spring in her step and a cheerful smile played on her face. It was as if an invisible hand guided her. A taxi broker saw them coming and asked with respect, "Kyengera, Nabbingo, Nsangi, old ones?"

Faisi smiled in agreement.

"If you sit at the back of the van you won't be disturbed," the broker advised helpfully.

From his vantage view at the back of the van, Kanani watched as one by one passengers climbed in. He contemplated the reasons why these passengers had been chosen in particular. This could be a pertinent point to put to them. Why you, why today? But then a thought intruded on him: is this how those suicide bombers felt as their victims boarded the American planes? Did they sit there wondering, *why him, why her, why today?* Kanani shook the thought out of his mind. He was vexed that his thoughts kept straying that morning. In any case, he and Faisi were agents of life, not death.

The last passenger hopped onto the van and as they drove out,

Kanani felt Faisi gearing up. He slipped the Bible into her hands. After ten minutes of driving when the passengers sat back to enjoy the cooling air wafting through the windows, Faisi launched.

"Praise God, brothers and sisters."

The air was stunned. Passengers' shoulders sagged.

"I thank God for He saved me."

Faisi clutched the Bible as if it were a battery powering her.

"God has sent me with a message for you."

The passengers whimpered simultaneously. It was the whine of a people who had given up on anything good happening to them.

"I was a sinner but He set me free."

While other passengers decided to ride out the onslaught silently, a lad sitting a few seats away from Faisi turned and laughed. "Why do you still look trapped?"

Rather than Faisi, the passengers vented their frustration on the lad. Faisi raised her voice above their annoyance.

"I was an evil woman." Faisi had a strong alto.

The passengers glared at the lad, their eyes saying: *See what you have done now,* but no one else seemed moved. Confession to evil was not potent anymore. People had hardened. Nonetheless, Faisi had cleared the field. Kanani waited to see how she would plough.

"I was a slut."

A woman sighed contentedly.

"I preferred married men. I aborted three of my unborn babies."

A man cracked his knuckles but the women were not moved. Shock had not worked either. Kanani became anxious.

"Eventually, I settled down with one married man. But God punished me. I couldn't have children. In a rage of envy, I killed his wife's children." Faisi paused for effect, "All three of them."

The passengers were still.

It was a moment of balance: the passengers could believe her and get angry or they might not and laugh. Kanani sat on the edge of his seat praying that they would get angry. Wind whirled through the windows.

"No one knew about me. The children dropped off one by one and within five years, they were finished."

Kanani worried that Faisi had overdone it.

The lad, now nervous, glanced at Faisi. A man sitting to her left shifted, but there was no room to move. The van's engine purred. She had them, Kanani wanted to clap.

"I did," Faisi choked. "And for what?"

Looking at her, Faisi was an old woman seeking respite from an old sin. Words came from far beyond pain. "Because of a man … a mere man," her lips trembled. "Those children, I remember them, especially the little girl. They died because of …" the words trailed away.

After a measured pause of sniffing, Faisi infused her voice with optimism.

"But then I saw the light and I confessed to my husband. He did not believe me and I left him. However, God had plans for me. He sent me another husband. I confessed to him as well, but he married me and we have two children. Now I serve the Lord."

A sign for Buddo Hill, Buganda's traditional coronation grounds, whizzed past. Kanani sensed the passengers slipping out of Faisi's hands. If a passenger stopped the taxi to alight, it would be impossible to recover the ambience.

"Whatever you've done . . ." Faisi's voice soothed, "God will forgive. No sin is bigger than His mercy. However, you can't hold on much longer. You don't know what the next hour might bring."

She paused to allow the passengers to contemplate whether they would make it to the end of the day alive. As the van drove through Nabbingo Town, Faisi concluded, "That is the message God's sent you today." She took a short breath and called, "Getting off right there."

The driver stopped the van.

As Faisi and Kanani paid their fare, the passengers hurled,

"They should swing from the gallows!"

JENNIFER NANSUBUGA MAKUMBI

"They commit crimes and claim God's mercy!"

"That's why I keep away from churches . . . they're full to the rafters with criminals I swear . . . including the pastors . . ."

Faisi smiled patiently. Kanani closed his ears but not before he heard someone ask, "Is that the fool who married her?"

When the taxi drove off, Kanani and Faisi crossed to the other side of the road. They waited for a taxi bound for the city.

"Oh," Faisi held her forehead in anguish. "I forgot to quote the Bible."

"Never mind," Kanani soothed. "You did well; your timing was impeccable."

"It was God's mercy." Faisi never took credit for anything.

"I like the way you rounded up the message with a sound of hope."

"But a quote would have washed the Word down beautifully."

At that moment, a van came along. Kanani made to flag it down but Faisi stopped him.

"Not that one, it's half-empty. Wait for an almost-full one."

It was Kanani's turn.

3.

As they walked home after sowing, doubt beset Kanani. Doubt was a cancer—you pray, it could go away; you pray, it could stay. Kanani and Faisi had prayed but doubt had stayed. For all their piety and evangelism, they doubted that they had a place in heaven. But Faisi and Kanani could not share their doubt with the brethren at church because there was no space for doubt among the Awakened. Doubt was worse than sin for it destroyed the soul.

Faisi had never killed anyone. Kanani was the only man she had "known" her entire life. Her evangelical confessions were a ploy to elevate her audience to a higher moral ground while she came across as the lowest of humanity. The deeper her transgressions seemed, the greater God's mercy manifested.

Faisi and Kanani doubted their place in heaven because they indulged as man and woman. Even after menopause; sometimes on Sundays as well. Sex was the one act during which the human in humanity was erased and man became beast. It was selfish gratification. It crushed them. In fact, there was a school of thought within the Awakened that believed that to acquire a certain level of sanctity one had to abstain altogether. Sex was permissible for procreation, but to be avoided otherwise.

In the fight against lust Faisi and Kanani failed dismally. At the beginning of their marriage they attempted to sanctify it with prayer. But prayer before sex dropped off trembling lips. The prayer after sex, breathless, was bad breath to the Lord.

For some time, Kanani and Faisi hid their toxic desires behind procreation even though they were not keen on children. Then it became clear that God meant them to have only two children—both at once—but Faisi and Kanani continued to indulge night after night.

The hardest part for Kanani was Faisi's self-hate. She was Delilah, he Samson. It was true Kanani never asked for "union." When Faisi said that they should abstain, he did. But then came nights when Faisi would get restless. Resolute, she would turn to the wall and pray. Sensing her distress, Kanani would get so worked up it physically hurt. After a while, having failed to sleep, Faisi would whisper wistfully, "Maybe … I don't know. Maybe we can, as long as you don't go very deep."

That is where Kanani failed. His teeth chattering, he would justify their desire with the quote, "Hebrews 13 verse 4 says that *the marriage bed is undefiled,*" and they would pounce on each other. In the ensuing madness, the Holy Spirit fled. In the absence of the Holy Spirit, Faisi was wanton. She arched and arched, seeking Kanani out until she swallowed him. When Kanani was swallowed, common sense flowed toward their groins. Then they ground each other until they were so inflated they burst.

As humanity returned, a deep ugliness settled on them. When Kanani came to—he took longer to recover—Faisi would be sobbing.

"Why are you crying?"

"Because I am a temptress."

It was to no avail that Kanani explained that he was equally to blame. Without her, Faisi cried, Kanani would not fall. Kanani, a man, was at the mercy of his body. As a woman, the onus fell onto her to fight the good fight.

"It's a demon, Kanani," she would say. "It brings seven other demons every time."

Kanani, not knowing what else to say, would suggest they

kneel down to pray. God would look into their hearts and forgive them. Surely, He would see how pained they were. And yet, Kanani doubted that God would forgive a sin they had perpetuated through the decades.

Unfortunately, Faisi and Kanani's concern was so focused on God's judgment of their lust that they neglected the well-being of the twins in the next room. Their house had no ceiling because in the 50s, when Kanani had it built, Jesus was coming soon. At the time, the Awakened believed that the world would end in less than a decade. It was therefore wanton to spend so much money on a house they would not live in for a long time while there were people in the world that needed saving from destruction. Kanani and Faisi did not realize that their lust spilled over the walls.

Now, as they came down the steps leading to their house, images of the twins Ruth and Job reeled across Kanani's mind again. Although they were now forty-seven years old, the image of the twins that haunted him was of them as teenagers. Yet, his grandson Paulo, thirty-three years old, came to his mind as an adult. It was unnatural, Kanani thought, for Paulo's picture to look older than that of the twins.

4.

When Faisi brought supper, Kanani's other regret in life raised its head. Forty-nine years of marriage but he had not got used to Faisi's cooking. The rice on his plate was boiled, soggy, and white as she never spiced it. Whatever Faisi cooked she drowned: vegetables, Irish potatoes, even *matooke*. She never steamed food traditionally in banana leaves. When they first married Kanani would joke, "The pieces of meat are swimming," or "I need a fishing rod to catch these beans," but it fell on deaf ears.

As time passed, Kanani felt coerced because he would not dare cook for himself. The Awakened had shaken off most of Ugandan culture yet aspects of traditional manhood persisted. Cooking was unmanly. In the 50s, when he first joined the church administration, he envied European men who wandered in and out of their kitchens without restriction. When missionaries invited him and Faisi to barbecues and dinners, Kanani saw white men help their wives cook. Some openly confessed that their wives were hopeless cooks and that when they wanted a decent meal they made it themselves. Yet, for him to let slip that Faisi was unimaginative in the kitchen was to undermine her as a woman. Instead he would say, "In our culture the kitchen, especially the cooking stones, are taboo to the man of the house."

"Really?"

"As boys if you wander too often into the kitchen doubt is cast over you."

"What would you do then if Faith—Europeans said Faisi's name in English—was as hopeless as my Jennie?"

"It would be my cross to bear."

"Rather harsh, wouldn't you say?"

Kanani missed his mother's cooking. He was brought up on European soups and gravies. His mother was a housekeeper for a missionary, Mr. Lane, who lived on the western slopes of Namirembe Hill. Mr. Lane was the Headmaster of the School for the Handicapped. The school, run on British charity, had long closed down. Kanani sighed as his childhood returned and his appetite fled.

At the time, he could only describe Mr. Lane's house as a whole village. "Rooms and rooms, all huge, each with its own toilet and bathroom, cupboards and wardrobes and carpets, I swear." The floor in Mr. Lane's vast sitting room was not carpeted as the rest of the house; it was made of tiny wooden panels, parquet. Kanani always helped his mother to varnish it because it was hard work. He especially remembered the square dining table, which was partitioned into four equal triangles. Each triangle had its own chair. If the family wanted to dine together then it became one table: the pieces locked together perfectly. But if you wanted to dine on your own, then you took a triangle and a chair wherever you wanted to sit.

When Mr. Lane's sachets of sauces expired, they had to be thrown away but Kanani's mother brought them home and they tasted fine. She explored new ways of cooking Ugandan food with British sauces. Hence, before marrying Faisi, Kanani had been used to eating thick gravies and soups, crunchy vegetables and traditionally steamed foods.

Every time Mr. Lane returned from his holiday in England he brought toys and sweets for Eileen's children—Mr. Lane called Kanani's mother Eileen. Kanani especially loved the self-assembling red plastic buses. Once every term, Mr. Lane opened the vast stores where he kept bales and bales of children's clothes that arrived every month from England. He would ask Kanani's mother to pick as much clothing as her family needed. Even when Kanani and Faisi had the twins, his mother still brought clothes from the school.

Unlike other missionaries, Mr. Lane stayed long after independence. When Amin expelled all non-Africans from Uganda, Mr. Lane stayed even though he was quite old. Children with disabilities were brought from all over Uganda to this luxurious boarding school, given wheelchairs and crutches if they needed them. Their parents only came to visit and to take them home during holidays. As far as Kanani could see, the school was a paradise for disabled children. Mr. Lane left when his cancer worsened. That day, he asked Kanani's family to come and take whatever they wished from his house before he locked up. Kanani had picked the partitioned table first, then a fridge and a cooker. Afterwards, Mr. Lane had taken the keys to the new headmaster.

But no one took Hio, Mr. Lane's donkey, or Sheba, his tail-less dog, with an unkempt striped tiger coat. Mr. Lane cried the day he left and so did Kanani's mother. Luckily, she was kept on by the school as a cleaner. She looked after Sheba, who had been evicted from Mr. Lane's house by the Ugandan headmaster. Sheba died a year later of sadness and of the kawawa flies, which had perforated his ears. Hio, on the other hand, did not notice Mr. Lane's departure. He continued to roam the vast grounds and fields of the school.

A discreet knock on the door came and Kanani looked up. Paulo stood at the door. Shrouded by the night, Kanani could only make out a silhouette of Paulo's face. But then he leaned forward and placed two heavy carrier bags on the floor, coming momentarily into view before withdrawing back into the shadow. As usual, Paulo was not coming in, but had come to check on his grandparents before he went to his quarters.

"How did the day treat you, Paulo?" Kanani had refused to call his grandson Kalema.

"Nothing new, Grandfather. Maybe yours was interesting." Paulo, now holding the door, looked away from Kanani, out into the night.

"Ours was exciting. We went sowing."

"I hope it went well," Paulo smiled.

Kanani pushed his food away and stood up. He came toward the carrier bags Paulo had placed on the floor.

"Oh, the success of sowing is not ours but His," Kanani answered wearily. "We are only His humble vessels. Is this food?" Kanani checked the groceries. Then he sighed as he saw rice and beef. "Why do you keep buying food you won't share with us?" He picked up the plastic bags and answered his own question, "You've been out with friends and have already eaten." He sighed like an old man who did not understand. "Now get out of the dark and get to bed."

"Sleep well," Paulo said as he closed the door. "Greet Grandmother for me."

Kalema closed the door and walked to his quarters in the new wing of the house, which had been added for him by the twins.

5.

The twins' names should have been Wasswa for Job and Nnakato for Ruth but Faisi and Kanani named them after biblical figures. They would not even allow themselves to be called Ssalongo and Nnalongo for that would be courting the Devil. The twins were hermaphrodite: one side was boy, the other girl. As babies, people thought they were identical—sometimes boys, but mostly girls because when they smiled, which was rare, Ruth and Job had such disarming dimples. Their hair was cut close to their scalps. Faisi and Kanani were unconcerned about gender.

"Children are children; they're neither male nor female," Faisi would say as she made Job wear Ruth's knickers. The only thing that Kanani insisted upon was that Faisi would never slap the twins on the head. When the twins started school, Kanani informed the teachers that due to a medical condition, his children should never be slapped on the head.

Often times, because they looked so alike, Ruth and Job were "borrowed" by brethren, first as flower girls then as bridesmaids at weddings until they were ten years old and Job's angry jaw could no longer be concealed under bridesmaids' rouge.

As children, the twins were timid and shy. But they were not quiet with each other. Even before they started to talk, the twins were in sync. When one gurgled, the other gurgled back. When one cried, the other joined in for sheer volume. Once the twin in need was identified and tended to, both fell silent.

As soon as Job took his first step, Ruth followed closely behind. As they grew older and misbehaved, it was useless to ask who was in the wrong because they would look at each other as if puzzled. Faisi found a solution: she punished both. It was just as well because when one twin was punished the other bawled even harder.

So Job and Ruth crawled together, sat together, and sucked their thumbs together. Ruth pinched her nipple as she sucked her thumb, Job pinched his foreskin. After a heavy bout of bawling, Job would stick his right thumb into his mouth and heave. His left hand would reach into his pants. Ruth would follow suit, her left hand seeking her left nipple. When they started to talk, each said that the other's thumb tasted better because the other seemed to enjoy their thumb more than they did their own. It was Ruth who asked first, "Can I taste your thumb?"

She licked it tentatively at first and then sucked hard. Job's thumb was sweeter than hers but when Job tasted hers he said, "You're joking, yours is better than mine."

Sometimes, when Ruth cried and Faisi refused to attend to her, Job stuck his thumb into her mouth, which would pacify her. Faisi slapped the little thumbs out of the mouths, the hands out of the pants and from behind dresses, but as the twins grew older, they found safe places to indulge. In any case, they only had to wait for Faisi to go sowing and they would do whatever they wished. Ultimately, it was at night, in their shared bed, that the twins pinched and sucked to their hearts' content.

In primary five, when they were twelve, a teacher attempted to break what she regarded as an unhealthy relationship, even by twins' standards. To foster independence, she put the children in different classes. After five minutes of separation, Ruth stopped crying but she did not stick her finger into her mouth. A stream of water snaked to the front of the class from under her desk. Then she fell off her chair and thrashed on the floor. Before the teacher could do anything, Job, whose class was on the other side of the block, was at hand.

"Don't touch her!" he screamed.

Yet he stroked Ruth's hand saying, "I'm here, I'm here."

When the school nurse arrived, Job insisted that the worst was over, that all he had to do was to give Ruth a wash and put her to bed. The teacher and the nurse stared as the brother washed his sister and then made her lie on the bed in the dispensary. The twins could not be taken home immediately because Faisi would be out sowing.

"She'll be all right," Job assured the nurse. "Even if Mother was home, I look after Ruth better. Mother will tell you herself."

Ruth was kept in the school dispensary for the rest of the day for observation. Job did not go back to class either. The school nurse was suspicious. She had found no trigger for the convulsions. And how did the brother know that his sister was ill? She knew that traditionally twins were complicated—easily offended and hard to pacify. When the school van took the twins home that evening, she explained what had happened at school, but neither Kanani nor Faisi showed concern. This deepened her suspicion. She went back and advised the teacher who had separated the twins to protect herself as soon as possible.

"God is God and I am a Christian too, but there are other forces as well," she whispered. "The way I saw it, there is something about those twins. I would check on our ancestors if I were you. It will not make you less a Christian."

The teacher, being Asleep, lost faith and consulted a traditional healer who asked, "Were the twins given second birth rites?"

"They're Christians, they were baptized."

"Ah, bound to the skies."

"Yes."

"Then why come to me? The Church owns the skies."

The teacher slumped in helplessness. The healer took pity on her.

"An angry lightning hangs over these twins," he warned. "They'll burn their parents first."

He gave the teacher leaves to crush in her bath and others to burn at the threshold of her house to ward off the twins' wrath.

The following morning, the twins sat together in Job's class. Ruth slipped her hand into Job's who held it close to his ribs in defiance. They did not relax their stance until the day after when it became clear that the teachers had given up separating them.

Ruth and Job sat together at break time. They whispered even when they were alone in a classroom. They did not play with other children. They did not join in drama performances, not even the nativity play. They did not join the school choir. They took part only in what they could not escape doing. The other children called them "the Kintu twins with soft heads."

At home, they avoided their parents, referring to Kanani as "He" and to their mother as "She." Job would say to Ruth, his lip curling in resentment, "She wants you to sweep the yard and me to wash the dishes." And they would both start sweeping the yard. At which Faisi would ask, "Didn't I say Ruth to sweep the yard and you to wash the dishes?"

Ruth would stop sweeping and look at Job worriedly, but he would pause long enough to say, "We're doing both together, it's quicker," and they would sweep furiously to prove that they worked best together not apart.

This led to Kanani Kintu's house being split into two worlds: the twins' and the parents'. Most of the time, the house was silent except when the twins and parents came together in prayer. At thirteen, the twins still shared the same single iron bed. Faisi and Kanani had either forgotten to buy another bed or they did not want to waste God's money. Whatever the reason, the twins did not complain. They continued to suck each other's thumbs at night, as they had done in the womb.

6.

Kanani and Faisi continually thanked God that the twins were never problem children. They had so far not received bad reports from school. In Sunday School too, the twins behaved well. In church, they sat between Kanani and Faisi who made sure that they did not run up and down the aisle like other children. The twins did not go to the toilet during the service, making grown-ups stand up, because Faisi sent them to the toilet before entering church. In fact, other parents said to their children, "Why can't you be like the Kintu twins? They don't disturb."

At thirteen and fourteen Job was a bit confrontational but it was nothing that prayer wouldn't eliminate. Hence, Kanani and Faisi did not see the Devil coming. He arrived early in 1968 and camped in the twins' world. The twins were eleven years old at the time.

On Wednesdays, school closed at midday. Normally, the twins went back home and played outside the house until Faisi returned from sowing to open up. One Wednesday, however, the twins walked from school as they normally did but rather than turn to Naakulabye to go home, they crossed Bukesa Road and rolled down the hill until they came into the narrow valley called *ewa* Namalwa.

The valley was flooded. Frogs croaked among the yams. There were no houses. The twins walked past a well and stood on a dry patch near the muddy road. They looked up Makerere Hill. All they could see was bush. The track was undefined: rainwater from the university came down the track more often than people. On the left, ten minutes of walking would take them to Old Kampala, which was now considered the Indian capital. Apart from Fort Lugard, a forlorn and lonely monument for Kapere Lugard (named after Captain Fredrick Lugard—fabled for being the most stupid person the Ganda have ever met and who was responsible for children being called *kapere* if they were silly), there was nothing exciting in Old Kampala.

The twins turned to the right and walked toward Makerere Road. At the top of the road they stood at the junction wondering whether or not to cross it. On the other side, beyond the shrubbery, was Kiwuunya, the only place on earth that replicated hell. Every day between 8:00 a.m. and 1:00 p.m., the twins heard shrill squeals and grunts as pigs were butchered. Children at school said that pigs made a lot of noise because they did not have necks. In the evenings, the smell of death, thick and rotten, fell like a blanket over Naakulabye.

As the twins were about to go home, they saw, on their right, children from their school scurrying around a church, peering and giggling. Ruth explored first; Job was wary of churches. Ruth followed the other children to the church doors and stood still. Before her were grown men and women singing, clapping, and dancing, their piano raucous. Job joined her and he too gaped. The pianist now knocked, now tickled, now caressed the keys like a heathen playing drums. The piano grunted and squealed and whooped as if it were not European. The songs being sung were Christian, yet heathen. The twins knew all of them but in their holy versions. When a kindly woman came and led the twins inside the church, neither Ruth nor Job resisted. They sat on the pews and watched. There was no sermon. In their church, the sermon was the main course of a service. This congregation indulged mainly in singing, a side dish, sprinkled with short readings from the Scriptures. The twins expected God to empty a wrathful bowl of brimstone and fire on the church but they did not leave. It felt wrong and right at once, like stealing with your mother.

By the time the twins emerged from the church, it was the end of the school day. Faisi was already home when they arrived but she did not notice that it was Wednesday and that the twins should have been home earlier. The twins went back to Ggug-gudde's *Mungu ni Mwema's* Church the following Wednesday and many Wednesdays thereafter. Ruth was the first to let go. Until then, she had never realized that she owned dancing energies. Her eyes shone as she nodded, swung, and clapped. The familiarity of the songs in dance versions must have unlocked her inhibition. Job, on the other hand, was stiff. He clapped and swayed but only to egg Ruth on.

Then one Wednesday, the twins arrived at Gguggudde's to find the congregation howling. The worshippers threw their hands in the air, pulled their hair, beating down on their thighs, wailing. Without hesitation, the twins launched themselves into crying. Even Job threw his arms in the air and had a hearty howl. Every bad deed, evil thought, and ill feeling was exorcised. It was so personal, this wailing, that the twins did not even share with each other the agonies they howled.

Finally, the piano whispered softly and the congregation calmed down. Then singing started, melodious and soothing at first, then it rose and rose until they were singing to fill the church up to the roof for the Lord. They clapped and danced with as much abandon as they had howled. Leaving Gguggudde's that afternoon, the twins were lightheaded. For the following three years, until they went to secondary school, they sneaked into Ggug-gudde's and joined in the abandonment of worshipful howling.

The Devil revealed his true intentions just after the twins sat their primary leaving exams. There was a man, Kalemanzira, a water-man who fetched water for the family. Initially, Kalemanzira annoyed the twins by claiming that the family had Tutsi roots.

"You're too good-looking to be Ganda. Look at that slender nose," he pointed at Ruth.

The family ignored him but Kalemanzira carried on asking, "Are you sure there is no Tutsi blood in your family? Look at Nnakato: look at that shape, those legs. Ganda women have such twisted legs that they make a ram's horns jealous."

"Her name is Ruth," Faisi admonished.

"Don't talk about her," Job was so angry he choked.

Then one day, Kalemanzira was so tempted by Ruth's voluptuous body he sneaked a finger to poke her bottom. Job was so incensed he picked up a stone and hurled it at Kalemanzira's head. Kalemanzira passed out.

Kanani was paralyzed with fright.

It was Faisi who called an ambulance. After recovery, Kanani gave Kalemanzira so much money that the water-man went back to Rwanda.

Shortly after Kalemanzira's departure, Ruth was taken to Namirembe Hospital with a fever. The rest of the family came along—Kanani to make sure that a doctor, who was a friend, saw Ruth quickly so he could go to work, Faisi to guarantee that whatever the problem she would still go sowing, and Job to be together with Ruth. Hence, all four were stunned silent when Ruth was pronounced pregnant.

7.

Kanani parted with the family in the hospital foyer. "There's nothing else for me to do here, is there?" he asked no one in particular. He took the back gate of the hospital, which opened into Namirembe Cathedral's grounds. Faisi and the twins carried on walking through the wide corridors of Albert Cook Ward until they came to the main road that ran through the hospital. But Faisi walked away from the twins as if she did not know them. When they came to the main gate she said, "Gone to do God's work," without looking back.

By the time they got home, the twins had become indifferent to Ruth's condition. It had only been a question of time before either followed into their parents' sinful footsteps. Even then, getting pregnant was nowhere near as horrible as the twins had anticipated. As Ruth pushed the front door, which was stuck again, she said, "I've committed my worst sin but I didn't kill any child."

"Lucky you," Job clicked his tongue. "Maybe I'll kill them." Ruth laughed as Job mimicked Faisi: *I was so depraved I killed my parents, and for what?*

"You need to be contrite about it otherwise it doesn't count."

"Then your pregnancy does not count: you're not contrite."

"It would count if I abort and then confess."

"Like her?"

"Never."

The twins fell silent as they contemplated the sins they would commit and confess on buses, in church and markets when they started to sow the seed. That night as they lay in their bed, they heard Kanani and Faisi whisper,

"It's the Devil, Kanani. He hoodwinked us."

"But my children?"

"That is how the Devil works, Kanani." There was a hint of impatience in Faisi's voice. "Remember Job in the Bible? When the Devil failed to make him denounce the Lord, he used his family against him."

A week later, Faisi called the family to get together in prayer. Instead of Kanani, she led the prayer and beseeched God to give them wisdom so they would make the right decisions. When they got off up their knees, Faisi smiled as if she had had an epiphany. First she wiped the dining table with her hand even though it was clean, then she announced that Ruth was going away to live in Nakaseke-Bulemeezi for the time being. Kanani's heathen cousin, Magda, had married there. Magda was heathen because she had defied her father. She had refused to be confirmed in church with the name Magdalene.

"Why was I named after a woman who leaked?"

Everyone in the family had expected Magda's father to get *omwenyango*, a shrub with fiery leaves, and scrub her lips. But Magda's father was a weak man. Instead he offered to name her Victoria, a beautiful name, which was not yet common in Uganda. But Magda would not have it either.

"The whole world is full of Victorias: the lake, the falls, and streets. Isn't that enough?"

Then Magda had named herself Mukisa and asked the family to call her Blessing if they wanted an English version. But the family agreed that she was far from a blessing. In retaliation, Magda took Mukisa in its heathen form, Bweeza. The end result was not surprising; Magda fell away from the church and was living a heathen life.

Only Kanani accompanied Ruth to Nakaseke because Magda

was his heathen cousin. Faisi could not bring herself to go the Devil's lair. Besides, she had sowing to do.

When they arrived in Nakaseke, Kanani looked more lost than Ruth. Nakaseke was rural and traditional in ways Ruth had never known. They alighted at Nakaseke Hospital and took a narrow path up a steep hill. The path was stony but covered in dense vegetation. The world here was quiet save for twittering birds, the odd guinea fowl scratching frenziedly, or slithering lizards. As they came down the slope, they would stumble on a house here and there. The houses, sometimes as much as a kilometer apart, built with mud and roofed with corrugated iron, looked squat to Ruth. On either side of the doors to each house stood two large metallic barrels, sometimes dug into the ground with two long steel funnels on either side to trap and channel rainwater. Sometimes, skeletons of the houses showed through thin mud. Reeds looked like ribs and poles like bare bones where mud had fallen away. Doorframes were at wrong angles and made the houses look like a child's careless drawing. The windows were small: Ruth was worried that it was dark inside the houses. Goats were tethered under trees near the dwellings. Children, especially boys in shorts whose fabric had worn away at the buttocks, played in the yards. Once in a while they came across a man wheeling a bicycle, women speaking in low tones, or a child rushing along the path. Villagers smiled and stepped aside for Kanani and Ruth to pass saying, "Seen you there," or "Greetings." Nakaseke looked and felt like a heathen world.

Finally, they joined a wider track. Ruth's curiosity was piqued. Someone along this track owned a car: the track was made up of two permanent tire trails with an island of long grass in the middle. Shortly after, they came to an open field of green bulbs like poppies.

"What are these?" Ruth gasped the words before she could stop herself.

"Cotton," Kanani said. "Look ahead, the other field has exploded."

Ruth stopped walking. The miracle of cotton growing on shrubs had so lifted the dense air between her and Kanani that she skipped when she started moving again. The bulbs in the field that Kanani had pointed at had burst into fluffy balls of cotton. At the bottom of the field, women were picking the balls and throwing them over their shoulders into the baskets strapped to their backs.

They came upon Magda's house suddenly. It was vast. Ruth had expected a small dark hut shrouded in an evil-looking bush. Magda's home was a landmark in the village. Beside the main house, there were two other structures. One was built wholly from roofing aluminum. In front of it was a lorry. Men ferried sacks of coffee out of the structure onto the back of the lorry. Boys hung around excitedly. Just as Ruth and Kanani turned into the courtyard, the loading stopped. The wooden flap was lifted and the back of the lorry fastened. The engine started and some men climbed in the back and sat up on the sacks. When the driver pulled out, boys ran after the lorry yelling. They leaped and hung onto the wooden back for a while then yelped before leaping off triumphantly. Ruth shook her head at their audacity. She had turned to look at the men bringing in the cotton sacks when she heard excited girls calling, "Visitors! Someone open the reception room … go call Mother … Can't you see they've come from the city? Take their bags!"

Magda's home was bursting with so much noise and movement it was dizzying. Before she realized, Ruth's bag was taken.

"I am not going to sit," Kanani tried to stem the excitement. "Is the mother of the house in?"

The children stopped running. Clearly, they didn't know what to do with a city visitor who would not sit down. An older girl said, "Bring a mat and folding chair outside," but Kanani was firm.

"We're not taking seats, I am leaving soon."

The children stopped again. Ruth, who could see their concern, marveled at Kanani's thick skin.

"Mother's coming. She's gone to a garden further away," a girl explained.

The children started to greet them. They were numerous. It was awkward standing while the children knelt down.

"Bring a mat for her," Kanani pointed at Ruth. "I'll be fine."

To Kanani, taking a seat even outside Magda's house was like shaking a leper's hand. You still catch the leprosy even though she is a relative.

When Ruth sat down she looked around. The whitewashed main house was elevated. Five steps led to a wide verandah, which together with its balcony, skirted the house. On the right was a massive concrete water tank with two taps. The funnels channeling rainwater were held up below the roof all around the house and then down into the tank. The windows, open, were large and wooden with closed screens of mosquito meshing. The roof was ridiculously high, like a church's. The outdoor kitchen was as big as Kanani's entire house. On the other side of the main building were the toilets and bathrooms. In front of the aluminum building, where the lorry had been, Ruth saw a wide concrete slab of at least twenty-five square meters. Spread on it were coffee beans, some still red-ripe, some grayish-dry. Children were sweeping and collecting the beans into heaps; older boys were packing them into sisal sacks and carrying the sacks into the aluminum building. The smell of drying coffee was everywhere.

"Stop staring, children. Have you no manners?"

Magda stepped from behind the house. She threw her arms in the air and hastened in joy, "Oh, whom do I see? My brother and, oh: is this our child Nnakato?" She was clearly overwhelmed. "My rude children have not offered you a seat?" She stopped in shock, looking at Kanani. "I'll kill them today . . ."

"No, no, no, I told them I would not sit," Kanani said quickly.

"What have I done to deserve this visit?" Before Kanani answered Magda pulled Ruth to her bosom. "I am sorry but I am a mess with happiness."

Ruth stared. Magda was Kanani in a feminine form. Kanani began to say that he was not staying long but Magda, joining Ruth on the mat, turned to face her.

"Nnakato, how you've grown, my child!" Then she looked at Kanani. "Where is our wife Faisi and our son Wasswa?"

"They couldn't come."

"They don't know me. My own children," she looked at Ruth sadly. "You would walk past me on the street, wouldn't you?"

"You look like Father exactly," Ruth hoped to reassure her aunt.

"Aha, well said, child. He calls me cousin, the English way, to distance unwanted relatives. But blood speaks."

"I need to whisper, Magda," Kanani said impatiently.

Magda chided the still-staring children for lingering. The children laughed and scampered away.

Magda was only too happy to help but she enjoyed the tortured look that had replaced Kanani's enduring righteous face. Finally, he and his crocodile of a wife had realized they needed blood relations after all. The fact that Kanani and Faisi could not handle a simple situation like teenage pregnancy made Magda feel validated: they had come to her. And then there was the snub—Kanani would neither sit down nor have refreshments in her home. He had talked to her standing like a tree. Hence, Magda could not help adding a touch of pepper to Kanani's sores.

"Do you want it plucked?"

"No, no, no, all we ask is for you to look after Ruth until . . . she is . . . untied."

"I am sorry I asked," Magda said, clearly not sorry. "But you know, we're family. No one needs to know." Now Magda whispered, "I know someone who can pluck it out just like that." She snapped her fingers as if flicking a speck of dirt and Kanani stepped back.

Even as he asked for her help, Magda noticed Kanani's eyes darting around her home. She knew he was looking for signs of heathenry like traditional earthenware, barkcloth, herbs, or a prayer basket with smoked coffee beans and coins. Magda wished she had a traditional smoking pipe with three heads to puff and mutter beneath the smoke to confound him.

Yet, as Kanani bid his daughter goodbye, Magda could see his pain. "Ruth," he said. "God is with us even in our darkest hour."

Ruth nodded but she did not seem to see the darkness. However, Magda was not letting Kanani off easily.

"What do you want me to do with the baby when Ruth is … untied? I can keep the baby if you want."

"I want to bring up my child," Ruth protested quickly.

"Send me a word and I'll collect Ruth and the child. I'll send money every month with the Zikusooka bus driver. Give him any letters you want to send."

"I was only checking. You never know with you civilized people. We don't want our blood wandering rootless in an orphanage."

Kanani turned away. Magda knew that her words had knocked him hard. For a moment, she wished she could call them back, but Kanani was walking away from her house, his stance discouraging any inclination to walk with him. As she watched him go, Magda wondered how thought rolled in that head of his. Christianity messed with the mind: how else would she explain Kanani who had frozen all his humanity to turn into a walking Bible? She turned to Ruth. "My name is Bweeza but you can call me Magda."

"I will call you Aunt Bweeza," Ruth smiled.

"Then, I'll call you Luusi, your English name."

Magda promptly put Ruth on a traditional antenatal regime of crushed herbs in her morning bath and an herbal mixture to drink. Ruth acquiesced without complaint, without enthusiasm. Magda grabbed every opportunity to pass on scraps of family history.

"Did you know we're descendants of a great Ppookino in Buddu?" When Ruth shook her head she asked, "So you know nothing about Kintu our ancestor?"

"No."

Magda decided not to divulge the information about the curse. If Kanani had chosen not to warn his children, then it was up to him.

"But you know that we don't slap children on the head?"

"Yes, we have a medical problem in the head."

"Is that what you were told?" Magda laughed.

Ruth nodded.

Now Magda's face clouded. Three months of looking after her but Ruth would not discuss the man who owned her condition. She had asked a few times, but Ruth was not forthcoming. Magda was tempted to ask again but she let it pass. Probably it was another child who was as confused as Ruth. Instead she said, "I know your parents each have one foot in heaven already but what right do they have to take away your twin names?"

"I don't know."

"The day I meet a white man called Kintu is the day I'll call myself Magdalene."

"It's all Christianity," Ruth now knew the right words to say to Magda.

"It is, child. Our family dived too quickly, too deeply into Christianity."

Magda told Ruth about their ancestor, Nekemeya, the first Christian in the family who became a teacher. "But ask yourself," Magda said, "How was he a teacher around the 1890s? Christianity arrived in 1877: thirteen years later Nekemeya was a teacher? Sometimes I fear that we descend from the very first Ganda to sell the nation to the white man."

"It's hard to tell who was what back then," Ruth said.

She felt no guilt for selling out Ganda tradition for Christianity. She felt nothing for naming, for culture, or for the grand patriarch Kintu. What she felt was a profound regret that she was born at all and had to bear her parents. Now, in the absence of Job, the only thing Ruth hinged her life on was the tadpole in her stomach. Lately, she had felt it swim noisily across her womb.

When Magda's efforts to familiarize Ruth with family history failed, she focused on Ruth's pregnancy. She showed her herbs to slacken her pelvic bones and ease birth, herbs to galvanize a newborn's skin, and the clay, *emumbwa*, for strong bones and teeth. She woke Ruth up early every morning and sent her on a four-mile walk.

"Don't let him sleep all day. You don't want to work with a lazy child during labor."

On her return, Bweeza would strip Ruth for a cold bath during which she rubbed herbs at the base of her belly with downward strokes. "The baby is properly aligned," she would remark with satisfaction. In the evening, she would ask if Ruth had felt the baby move. When Ruth said that she had not, Bweeza would say, "Go down to the well and fetch water in a pan three times."

Even the day that Amin took power from Obote, Ruth went to walk. That morning Ruth found all the repressed Ganda anger over Obote's exiling *Kabaka* Muteesa II spilling in the roads everywhere in villages and trading centers in songs, dancing, and poetry. All this was new to Ruth. She had been unaware of the anger—her parents never discussed politics, as all worldly concerns were nothing but wind.

When she got back home, Bwanika, Magda's husband who had spent the week with the family, was preparing to return to the main farm in Kapeeka where his first wife lived. Magda's husband had three homes. Each home had a wife and a farm. Magda had coffee and cotton *shamba*s, the first wife reared cattle while the third lived on the poultry farm. Bwanika spent two weeks with his first wife and a week each with Magda and the third wife in Ssemuto. During Bweeza's week when he was around, Bwanika inspected coffee and cotton *shamba*s, paying the workers. Then he went around the village talking to the residents.

Magda was a different woman in that week. Her words were

few and mild. She wore her non-work clothes. She did not work in the garden and did most of the cooking herself. Bwanika was treated with reverence by the family whenever he came. When Ruth saw Magda kneel before him an image of Faisi kneeling before Kanani crossed her mind and she burst out laughing. Although Bwanika was friendly and tried to talk religion with her, Ruth preferred him away. She sensed a slight strain in the air, as if the children, not used to having him around, did not know what to do with him. As soon as he left, the air relaxed and the noise picked up. The pensive look on Magda's face did not last. Soon she was vivacious again, her attention focused on Ruth.

8.

On May 21, 1971, Ruth woke up in the middle of the night. She was sure she had felt pain in the back, around her waist, but it was gone. As she fell asleep again, the pain struck again and she sat up. It came and went as fast as a flash—no lingering pain, just a mild need to open her bowels. She remained sitting up in the dark wondering whether it would return.

The toilets were outside, shrouded in the coffee *shamba* at the back of the house. Then the pain came back. It was as if a tiny metallic fist had punched her in a nerve. This time she was sure she needed the toilet. She decided to wake up one of the older girls to escort her.

They lit a hurricane lamp. Two children, who needed to relieve themselves, joined them. But when Ruth squatted on the latrine, nothing came out. As they walked back to the house, she did not tell the others that she had woken them up for nothing. She blew out the lamp and she prayed that the pain would not come back.

She had fallen asleep when it hit again. This time it was so intense that she ran outside without a lamp on her own. She squatted on the latrine again. Nothing came. She decided to stay on the toilet until the new pain came. In the meantime, her eyes grew accustomed to the dark. When the pain came, she stood up and grabbed the door instead of opening her bowels. As it subsided she squatted and pushed. Nothing.

She walked back to the house, found the matches, lit the lantern and took it to her room. It was as she sat on the bed that the thought crossed her mind. Perhaps the baby was coming! But wasn't it three weeks too early? Perhaps she should wake Bweeza up. The problem was that the pain felt like diarrhea. It would be stupid to wake her up for that.

She did not go back to sleep. Whenever the pain came she was sure she should wake Bweeza up but when it went away she did not want to fuss. For a while Ruth hovered in the corridor between her door and Bweeza's until a no-nonsense pain gripped and wrung her nerve. She gripped the door and ground her teeth. As it let go, it spread all over her stomach. Then her innards, as if made out of butter, were melting on a fire. She ran to Bweeza's room and shook her, "*Ssenga* Bweeza, *Ssenga* Bweeza, *Ssenga* Bweeza!"

"What is it?" She sat up.

"It is my stomach. I think it is the *bisa* pains coming. It might be diarrhea but when I go to the toilet nothing comes out."

Bweeza yawned. "How does it feel?"

"Urgent."

"Urgent where? Is it in the back, in the front, or all over?"

"In the back first and then all over."

"Is it a pushing pain, as if you must poo all your intestines?"

"No."

"Well then, there is nothing to worry about. Could be something you ate. Don't worry. You will eventually open your bowels, probably not tonight though. Get one of the metallic basins and put it in your room. When the pain comes, squat on the basin. Don't go out to the latrine again."

Ruth felt stupid as she walked out.

"Tell me if anything else happens." Bweeza was already settling back to sleep.

Bweeza did not go back to sleep as she had made out. She had not been asleep when Ruth woke her up. She had heard her waking the girls up to go to the toilet. And when she ran out again, Bweeza had got up and kept an eye on the toilet. But she was not about to let Ruth know that the baby was coming because day-break was still far away and, according to the intervals, she was still far off. Let her think it is just a stomachache, Bweeza told her-self. I am not going to entertain hysterics for the rest of the night. According to the doctors at the hospital, Ruth was three weeks early. Bweeza sucked her teeth in contempt.

At about five o'clock Bweeza got up, had a bath, packed a bag with a few *kangas*, a razorblade, and other things she would need if they did not make it to the hospital. Then she made breakfast.

Ruth would not eat.

At around six o'clock Bweeza said, "OK, Luusi, time has ar-rived."

But instead of hysteria, Ruth said, "I knew it. I am getting fed up with this pain."

"Come and show me how far gone we are."

Ruth ran to her bed and spread her legs. She was glad that her aunt was taking a look.

"Hmm . . ." Bweeza said as she turned her head to have a better look. "Good dilation . . . things are moving properly . . . yeah, you're doing fine." She patted Ruth's legs. "Now get dressed. Someone in there is getting ready to come out." She spoke as if the whole thing was a mild headache.

Bweeza asked a lad to come along with a bicycle in case they needed it. She had arranged for Bwanika to come around by the due date but the dates were wrong! Now she insisted that instead of riding on the bicycle, Ruth walked. Walking would hasten the birth. She put their bags on the bicycle's carrier and they set off for hospital.

"In the past, I would've made you comfortable at home, called a few friendly women, and we would have sat and waited with you. Now we have to go to the specialists." She threw her arms in the air.

Ruth did not respond.

And it was like that throughout the journey; Bweeza conducted a one-sided conversation because Ruth was in her own world while the lad wheeling the bicycle watched Ruth nervously.

"You are a tough girl, Luusi," Bweeza said. "Me, I'd be howling by now."

Either Ruth did not hear or she was saving her energy.

"When you feel it coming on, stop and grab me or grab a tree until it lets up."

But when pain gripped, Ruth would go down on her knees and Bweeza would pull her off the ground saying, "Hang on me, the ground is dirty."

The lad would stop wheeling the bicycle, grip the horns, and look into the bush. When it let go, Ruth would run past him as if she had not been dying a few moments before.

"See you at the hospital," she would say.

"Isn't this a party?" Bweeza panted as she tried to keep up with her. "Here is a story to tell, young man."

"Had I known it goes like this I wouldn't have come."

"Oh, it goes like this, young man. Remember that next time you make a woman lie on her back."

When they arrived at the hospital, Ruth was examined by a nurse who determined that the baby had engaged. She was taken to a large ward where women in all forms of pain and states of undress were kept. Still, between the throes of pain, the women managed to ask Ruth how old she was. As soon as Ruth's pains started again, she began to push as well; she screamed, "Something is coming, it is pushing!" but the nurses did not rush as she had expected. One of them brought a wheeling bed and took her to the delivery room.

"Primigravida, fourteen years old?" A no-nonsense nurse asked as she pushed a trolley with all sorts of instruments laid out on it toward them.

The nurse wheeling Ruth nodded.

"Strap her in! I am not going to have her holding my hands and throwing herself about."

Ruth did not care what the nurses did to her. She just wanted the thing out of her because, at that point, she had decided that whatever was inside her could not be human.

She was helped into a chair with straps on the armrests and footrests on its legs with straps too. Her hands were strapped on the armrests, her legs spread wide and tied at the ankles on the footrests.

"When the pushing pain comes, push. No playing around in this place!"

Perhaps it was the nurses' attitude—*If she is still a child, why was she sleeping with men*—toward her that made Ruth strong. The pushing pain came once and the second time a baby boy was out.

By evening, the nurse suggested that Ruth and the baby could go home if they wished. Magda went to the roadside and hired a car. On the way home, she made sure that there were no roadside stoppings by curious women. As soon as they arrived, she fed Ruth and put her to bed. Then she performed all the birth rituals she wished for the child. By the time word got round the village that Ruth had unknotted and women started streaming in, Magda had protected the baby against any conditions, deliberate or accidental. The following day she asked Ruth, "Do you know his name yet?"

"Yobu."

"Ah, after your twin?" Magda was surprised. Most girls would give their child a fanciful name or name them after the boyfriend. "I like the Ganda version better," Magda smiled.

In the first two weeks, Magda would wake Ruth up to nurse the baby, have a bath, eat her porridge, and then go back to sleep. There were so many eager hands in the home yearning to carry Yobu and to do the laundry but Ruth wanted to keep the baby close. She insisted on putting him in her bed, she checked on him if he slept too long, and she looked anxious as he was moved from one set of hands to another. However, Bweeza was insistent: Ruth's task was to recover.

Bwanika and his other wives arrived when little Yobu was

three weeks old. They brought baby clothes and money. They also brought chicken and meat to celebrate.

"I heard that my European wife was brave and I wondered: do my wives howl just to make me feel horrible?"

Bwanika called Ruth his *muzungu* wife because she grew up in the city and did not understand traditional things.

Bwanika's wives went straight for the baby. The Ssemuto wife, the one who kept livestock, whom the children called Maama Ssemuto said, "We heard about the newborn and we thought what a perfect excuse to visit!" as she reached into the Moses basket to pick up Yobu. When she saw the baby's face the woman added, "What a neat nose: there's Tutsi blood in your family, Bweeza, don't deny it."

"How can I?" Magda laughed happily. "This child is proof."

Bwanika and his wives stayed the weekend, cooking, eating, talking about the children, and gossiping. There was a sense of festivity especially when hordes of village women started to arrive and more cooking was done and the women stayed longer than they had intended. Each put money into Yobu's tiny hands. When he gripped it, they laughed in admiration. "He recognizes money, doesn't he?" as if Yobu was the cleverest newborn they had ever seen.

"May you have strong hands to earn your living," they prayed.

"May you have luck the way millipedes have legs." Ruth smiled happily as women wished her child good luck and cracked jokes.

Magda was in her element telling the women how, because of her vigilance, the baby simply slipped out, "No complications and none of that stitches nonsense." The women decried the hospital midwives. "They don't give you a chance; they snap and slit and stitch at will." And the women agreed that the lazy midwives who did not allow a child to arrive in its own time were perfect for the lazy city women who lie on their backs as soon as they fall pregnant.

"I am going to replenish Luusi's blood and help her body repair itself before I send her back to her parents. I doubt that that mother of hers knows what to do," Magda told the women.

Ruth's face darkened at the mention of her mother. Magda, misunderstanding her, quickly added, "But the human in me cannot blame Faisi. My brother's wife has never known blood relations. She grew up in an orphanage."

There was a moment of silence as Ruth looked up in surprise. The women squirmed in discomfort but Magda carried on regardless. "It must be hard not knowing who you are. But it's no excuse to drive away your husband's relations."

"Sometimes when we lack something, those who have it seem to flaunt it at us," a woman explained.

Ruth smiled to reassure Magda that she was not offended. Still, she was surprised to hear that Faisi came from nowhere but an orphanage. She had presumed that her mother, like her father, had discarded her relations. In any case, even if Faisi had relatives, she would have thrown them out of her life if they were not Awakened enough. In the past, before Magda was mentioned, their extended family were the Awakened. But the Awakened were controlled. They did not visit each other unnecessarily and they did not fuss over each other's children. The church was like a bus and brethren were passengers on their way to heaven rather than a family. Ruth remembered the last time Faisi talked to Kanani's uncle who had brought news that the most senior clan elder had died.

"We don't have relations that don't walk in Christ. Don't come back here telling us there's this funeral rite or that death. Our Lord said, "Let the dead bury their dead!"

Ruth, who was six years old at the time, had watched the old man climb the steps from the compound into the road. She had felt sad for a man who was already dead going to bury the dead.

"I would like to wait before we tell my parents," Ruth told Magda. "Until I am fully recovered."

"You do?" Magda could not contain her gladness. Ruth might have as well have said she preferred Magda to her parents.

That weekend, Ruth noticed that some of Magda's children

resembled the other wives but she could not be so rude as to ask. Life in Nakaseke was not as simple as it had seemed. Counting how many children there were in the house was to invite death because only death counts people. You don't ask visitors whether they will eat or have tea because you are telling them to say no. It was taboo to ask who was cousin, niece, or nephew. Only Ruth was niece in the house and only she called Bweeza aunt.

On Monday as the two wives and Bwanika drove away in his Opel, Magda could not contain herself. She whispered to Ruth, "Did you see how possessively elder wife sat in the passenger seat?"

Magda made stiff motions with her neck as if the elder wife were a turkey. Ruth looked at her with surprise because she thought they liked each other. Magda relented and said, "They are generous, my fellow wives, but Maama Kapeeka always wants to show that she is the first wife."

Ruth and little Yobu soon fell into Nakaseke's rhythms. In the morning, when the children were at school, she looked after him. But as soon as they returned, Yobu disappeared. They attempted to plait his slippery hair. Village girls lingered saying, "We've come to carry the baby for you." Sometimes Ruth sent them away, "Come back later, he is sleeping." Magda, seeing Ruth worry would say, "Let them enjoy him while he is still here. It is good for him to be loved by so many."

9.

Yobu was lifting his butt off the floor, leaning forward to start crawling, when Kanani arrived to collect them. When Magda saw Kanani's lack of interest in the baby she remarked, "When I saw the baby's features I said, *hohoho that Tutsi lad of old has popped up in the family again. Fancy him falling right into my hands!*"

Magda was only knocking Kanani with family history in jest, like throwing a stone into a thicket to see what might fly out. His response astonished her. "The child's father is Rwandese."

Ruth, who was dressing Yobu, looked at Kanani sharply. It was as if she too could not believe that Kanani had said it. Then she felt Magda staring at her questioningly and she smiled in agreement.

"Is he one of your church people?" Magda asked.

"He's not," Kanani snapped just as Ruth was about to nod.

"But why choose Luusi?" Magda smiled at Kanani's discomfort. "You would think that if the lad wanted himself reincarnated he would go for a male's child."

"You know how empty those beliefs are, Magda."

But mischief was still on Magda's face as she answered her own question. "Well, what do we know about the world of the dead? Maybe over there they don't erect boundaries between daughters and sons."

"But the Bible—"

"The one written by the white man?" Magda snapped.

"It could've been written by anyone. Remember there'll be no color or creed in the new world."

"Is that what God says these days? Oh well, God has seen the light," Magda threw her arms in the air. "The last time I was in church Africans were an accursed crew."

"That was a wrong interpretation."

"And this one is right?"

"That's it," Kanani was fed up. "Ruth, pick up your bags, we're going."

"Luusi," Magda turned to Ruth, "Let no one make you feel sorry. Yobu being Tutsi was no mistake and you're lucky to be chosen to have him."

Ruth kept a straight face.

"Give me the bag." Kanani reached for Ruth's bag. "Get the baby. Let's go."

But Magda was not finished. "Watch out, Kanani." She pointed a finger at Kanani. "The ancients are on to you for some reason. First you had the twins, now the Tutsi? I am jealous!"

"My daughter having a Tutsi child has nothing to do with it. There are Tutsis in this world. That's the end of it."

"Nnakato!" Magda suddenly realized the implication of Ruth being a Nnakato. "That's why he went for a daughter," she gasped. The Tutsi lad is seeking his mother Nnakato of old." Magda looked at her arms and said, "There are goose bumps all over my arms. I can't believe this is happening, and to you of all people!" Now Magda closed her eyes and hissed, "For once in your life, Kanani, open your eyes and see what lies at your feet."

Kanani turned and walked out of Magda's compound. Magda ran after him. Kanani hastened his pace as if the Devil was close to his heels.

"I warn you, Kanani," Magda whispered so that Ruth would not hear. "You might think that because you are a Christian the curse will not touch you but I am telling you this child is not a coincidence. Ignore him and you'll pay dearly."

Kanani stopped walking and turned to Magda. "The curse is with us, Magda. You are the curse. You are the madness looking for things where they are not."

Kanani started to walk again. Magda threw her arms in the air again and called. "Oh wizard that bewitched my brother Kanani, let him go I beseech you!" but Kanani ignored her. Ruth followed her father. She wanted to laugh at Bweeza's insistence about Yobu being Tutsi, at her turning a mere anthill into a mountain. Eventually Magda gave up and walked quietly with Ruth until they came to Nakaseke Hospital where they would catch the bus. Kanani walked ahead, alone.

After a brief wait at the hospital, a Ganda-owned bus Sulemani Serwanga, arrived. Magda kissed Yobu over and over, reminding him that she was his grandmother and that she had brought him into the world. Then she hugged Ruth but stopped herself from saying, "Don't forget Nakaseke, Luusi."

As he prepared to get on the bus, Kanani handed Magda an envelope. When she opened it, Magda smiled through her humiliation and said, "I would've paid you, Kanani, for the chance to look after Nnakato and our grandchild." She removed the money and waved it. "This will help to fix the rituals for little Yobu's Rwandese situation."

To contain himself Kanani jumped on the bus.

"Buy the children some sweets or cakes with the money," Ruth suggested.

As the bus pulled away, Ruth stuck her head through the window and waved until Magda was out of sight. When she sat back, Kanani said, "I can see she treated you well," rather sheepishly.

Ruth only nodded. She felt herself slip out of the carefree Nakaseke mode. The city mask fell back.

"Her father was my father's real brother," Kanani was saying, "But he was Asleep." He sighed deeply. "Now see what happened: Magda married a heathen with two other wives. I doubt they go to church at all."

"The children did at Christmas and on Easter."

"That is exactly the nature of the Asleep. For them, God switches on for Christmas and Easter but he is off for the rest of the year."

When Ruth did not respond, Kanani continued less passionately. "I remember Magda's father coming to visit us when I was young but my father never returned his visits. Magda and I went to the same school. She was quick in class, quicker than me in fact, although I was older than her, but she was not interested in studies. She could have become a nurse or a teacher."

After spending a year in Nakaseke where strangers asked about her child like their own, where Yobu had been called the newcomer as if he had moved into a house in the village, where everyone's business was everyone's business, Ruth was shocked by Faisi's distance and lack of interest in the baby. As she and Kanani came down the steps, Ruth saw Faisi sweeping the side yard. Something about Faisi told her that she had seen but was not ready to acknowledge them. Finally, Faisi looked up from her sweeping as if seeing them for the first time but there was no hint of welcome in her eyes. Faisi smiled at Kanani and glanced at Ruth. She took the bags off Kanani and carried on as if there were no baby. Ruth was overwhelmed by tears. The mantra, *there is no sin too big for God,* which Kanani and Faisi dished out to strangers, had not been offered to her.

After Bweeza's vast and noisy home, her parents' house seemed small and hushed. Ruth headed straight for the bedroom she used to share with Job. Their bedroom had been cleared out as if she and Job had been evicted. The metallic bed they had shared all their lives was now folded. It stood upright leaning against the wall. There was a second bed, a new Banco. Its stands were still wrapped in plastic covers. It also stood leaning against the wall. Everything else in the bedroom was neat.

Kanani came into the bedroom carrying a Moses basket and put it down on the floor. Then he looked at Ruth. There was an awkward moment as if he wanted to say something but then he decided against it, turned, and walked out of the bedroom. A few moments later, he returned with a bundle of baby clothes.

"These were yours and Job's. Thank God your mother never throws anything away," he said miserably.

Then he helped Ruth bring down one of the beds off the wall and set up the bedroom. He said nothing to Ruth all the while. Faisi did not come to the bedroom to help.

The night before Job was due back from school for Christmas holidays, Kanani informed Ruth that the following year, she would be going to Gayaza High. They were in the sitting room. Instead of jumping up and down with joy (Gayaza High, a boarding school, was the best Anglican girls' school in the country) Ruth asked, "What about Yobu?" She had no intentions of leaving him with Faisi.

"I'll look after the child," Kanani said. "I've piled up leave worth a whole year. I am sure the church will allow me to take at least six months at once. You must get a good education."

The air in the room went still. Kanani's offer had come out of nowhere. It was clear that he had not discussed it with Faisi, for she asked, "What about God's work?"

"You'll carry on with your work," Ruth snapped.

"I mean money for God's work."

"It'll be paid leave," Kanani explained.

Faisi picked at the table even though it was clean. She stood up and went to the kitchen as if to discard the invisible dirt she had removed from the table. Ruth knew that Faisi was stifling something she wanted to say. She feared that Faisi was not yet done. Suspecting that she would suggest that the child be taken to Ssanyu Babies' Home, Ruth began to heave. Kanani looked at her and asked, "Why are you crying now? I said I'll look after the child."

"Thank you for not taking Yobu to the orphanage." And she stood up and went to her bedroom.

• • •

Job arrived late the following afternoon. The red-and-white school bus with a red lion emblazoned along its side dropped him outside the house. Tears rolled down his face as he threw down his wooden suitcase and attempted to lift Yobu in one hand and Ruth in the other. Faisi looked away.

Kanani was clear. The twins were not to start another family in their bedroom. As far as he was concerned Ruth and Job were still children: he would not have them behave like parents towards the baby. Job was told to sleep in the sitting room, leaving the bedroom to Yobu and Ruth. And two weeks before the twins started school, the baby would move in with him and Faisi to get him used to being with them. As if she had been waiting for an opening, Faisi added, "Now that everyone's here, it's time we thought of an appropriate name for the child."

"He's got a Christian name already." Ruth looked at Kanani for support but Kanani kept quiet. Faisi shook her head.

"Yobu, even in its Ganda version, is wrong for this child. I suggest we call him Nsobya."

"*Nsobya?* As in *error?*" Ruth glared at Faisi.

"Sin is a sin and we must call it by its proper name," Faisi glared back.

"I don't care about Nsobya as a surname," Job said. "But there is nothing wrong with Yobu as his Christian name."

"We shall baptize him Saul. It will give him a chance to turn into Paul."

Kanani, who had kept an uncomfortable silence, now spoke up.

"I name my grandson Paulo. His Ganda name will be Nsobya. That's the end of the matter." He sat back in the chair and crossed his legs.

There was silence. Its echoes hovered about the room.

Faisi, cut off by Kanani like that, sat back in her chair and propped her chin with her hand. The twins looked at each other, stood up and went to their bedroom where they jumped up and down soundlessly. It was a relief to see Kanani assert himself. The miserable look on Faisi's face was priceless. Ruth whispered to Job, "I don't know why, but he's been clipping her lately. First, he did not send Yobu away; then he offered to look after him. Now he has crumpled her 'sin' view."

"But when we leave, she'll override him."

"I told them I'll kill myself if I find my child gone. You should have seen how frightened he was!"

Sunday, February 2, 2004

Paulo parked outside the Redeemed Gospel Church on Sir Apollo Kaggwa Road and turned off the engine. He waited for Ruth in the car. Outside, the sun was stretching toward one o'clock. He reminded himself to tell Ruth that Kanani had been cut off from work. He was worried about his grandfather. The change he had seen in him in just a month was dramatic. Perhaps he was imagining it; perhaps he had never noticed his grandfather looking so lost because he had never seen him idle. It was not the loss of his job that was killing Kanani, Paulo knew: it was the loss of the Cathedral. Kanani had been the Awakened's last hold onto Namirembe Cathedral. There were no young Awakened in the church anymore. Most of the children of the Awakened, like the twins, had deserted the sect for the new Christianity. Others had abandoned the faith totally. According to his grandparents, the Church was now in the hands of the Asleep.

When he looked up, worshippers had started streaming out of the church. Ruth emerged. It seemed as though she was heading straight to the car, but then she stopped to talk to two women. Then they were joined by still more women and Ruth settled into chatting. Uncle Job too emerged from the church and went to where Ruth stood. Ruth turned to him and said something. Aunt Kisa, Uncle Job's wife, also came out and joined the group. Paulo sucked his teeth. He had hoped that Ruth would come straight to the car so he did not have to go and greet the twins' friends. Now he stepped out of the car and walked along the road. As he approached the church gate, someone recognized him and called, "Ruth, your brother's here."

Both Ruth and Job turned. Job said, "Paulo's not our brother, he's our son; how many times shall we tell you?"

Ruth smiled and came to meet him. She held Paulo's hand and whispered, "Sorry, they never listen."

"Ruth stole that boy," someone said. "He's only slightly younger than her."

"Where does Paulo go to church?" another asked suspiciously.

Paulo's jaw squared. This nosiness was exactly why he hated greeting the twins' friends.

"Paulo's not into church yet," Uncle Job came to his rescue. "We're still praying for him."

"Come, Paulo, say hello to my friends." Ruth nudged. Then she whispered in his ear, "Give your uncle a hug."

Paulo obliged. After embracing him, Job, smiling with one side of his mouth, his most affectionate smile, looked Paulo up and down as if making sure that he looked fine. Then he said, "I don't see you often, Paulo." It was an accusation, as if Paulo were purposely avoiding him. "What are you up to these days?"

While Paulo's relationship with Ruth was close and laid back, Uncle Job was a proper father figure. The problem was that Uncle Job left home as soon as he went to University, while Ruth stayed even after University until she built her house in Bbunga. Uncle Job had paid Paulo's school fees, come to school to check on his progress and behavior, and was always officious with the teachers. Ruth, on the other hand, was more interested in how Paulo felt, how he dressed, what he wanted and, whenever Uncle Job was gruff or being no-nonsense, Ruth was there to say, "But the boy is . . ." softly. That was why hugging and chatting with Uncle Job did not come naturally.

"I am fine, nothing much," Paulo scratched his head.

"Then we should see you more often," Job said.

Paulo glanced at Ruth as if asking her to rescue him from his uncle.

"Go say hello to Aunt Kisa." Ruth steered Paulo toward Job's wife. "I'll meet you in the car in a moment."

Paulo's surname was no longer Nsobya. It was Kalemanzira. He was sixteen when he changed it. He was in boarding school, just before he registered for his O-level exams. The name had been bothering him since that day, when he asked his grandfather who his father was.

"Your father was a man called Kalemanzira," Kanani had explained as he cut the hedge.

"Kalemanzira? Was he a *munnarwanda*?"

"Hmm." Kanani carried on clipping twigs and leaves without looking at Paulo.

"Where does he live?"

"I don't know. He went back to Rwanda I suppose." Now Kanani started clearing away the cut twigs from the ground. "What I know is that this Kalemanzira worked hard all over this village pushing a cart, helping people to fetch water from the well."

He picked up as much as he could carry and walked away from Paulo toward the rubbish heap in the *matooke* garden. Paulo picked up the rest and followed him.

"He fetched water?" Paulo could not hide his consternation at finding out that his father was a cart-man.

"Yes. Unfortunately, he was attracted to Ruth because he thought we were *bannarwanda* like him. One day, Job got so angry with him that Kalemanzira almost died. When he recovered, Kalemanzira never returned to the neighborhood. Kanani dropped the twigs on top of the heap and rubbed his hands to clear them. He rubbed them for a long time saying, "We searched to tell him that he had a son *nga wa!*" Kanani blew in his hand and let it fly away. Then he turned to walk back to the hedge.

Paulo chewed this information like a piece of plastic then followed his grandfather. He was not letting the story go yet because it had not made sense to him. And it seemed to him as if he were chasing after the story; he would have preferred that his grandfather stopped walking and talked to him properly. After a polite pause he asked, "Why was Uncle Job angry with the water-man?"

"Because he was getting too friendly with Ruth." Kanani barely turned.

"Oh," Paulo laughed. He could almost see Uncle Job's grumpy face. "And why is my name—?"

"I named you after Paul, the rock on which Christ built his church," Kanani snapped.

But Paulo was not asking about his Christian name. He wanted to know why he had a Ganda name when his father was Rwandese. However, it was clear that Kanani was fed up with the questions. Paulo dropped the subject.

At sixteen he decided that he could not carry Ruth's error on his head anymore. But mostly, it was a fraud to be Rwandese and pass himself off as Ganda. That was what bothered him most. In the end, he went to the headmaster of his school and explained the situation. Then he asked if he could change his name. The headmaster explained that he could not until he was given permission by his mother.

That was first time that Paulo called Ruth mother. He wrote, "Dear Mother," and explained that he would like to be called by his father's name and that the headmaster had agreed. But he needed his mother's permission. He signed with, "Your Loving Son, Paulo."

Ruth and Job came together to the school and changed Paulo's name from Paulo Nsobya to Paulo Kalemanzira. But at the end of the term, when he handed his school report to his grandfather and Kanani saw "Paulo Kalemanzira" as his name he shouted, "What is this name?" Kanani's hand shook. "Where did you find this name?" he glared at Paulo as if he had stolen it.

"Ruth, I mean my mother, and Uncle Job gave me permission

to use my father's name. They came to school and changed it. You can ask them."

"You're playing with fire, you hear me?" Kanani's right cheek twitched. "You, your mother, and whatever you think you are, are playing with embers."

Kanani threw the report on the table and went to his bedroom. Faisi walked into the dining room from the kitchen. She picked up the report, looked at it, and threw it back on the table. She did not look at Paulo as she wiped the spotless dining table with her hand. Then she wiped her hands and went to their bedroom. It crossed Paulo's mind that his father was a bad man: the way he had disappeared like wind; the way he left no traces of himself like a ghost; he must have done something terrible for Kanani to hate him like that. Nonetheless, he insisted on being called Kalema if Kalemanzira was too much for his family.

Presently, Ruth came to the car.

"It's funny with church," she sighed apologetically as she sat down. "You can't wait for the service to end, but once you step outside you can't pull yourself away. Can you imagine we used to sneak into this church as children?"

"You've told me."

"But everything has changed now. The whole of this," Ruth waved her hand over the place, "Was just bush. Down there was all swamp and yams. Over there was a well; now it's all dry—look at the houses. People should not build on the flood areas. But tell me, how are He and She?"

"Grandfather was stopped from working."

"Oh," Ruth said unconcerned. "To be fair, he stayed on too long."

"He's lost. I don't think he knows how to live without his job."

"He can join her in sowing."

"You don't care about them."

Ruth laughed.

"I care in my own way, especially for him. But mostly, I am proud of you for loving them."

"They're not that bad."

"Hmm!" Ruth was cynical.

"I know Grandmother seems like a wall sometimes but she's not forced me to take on their way of life."

"Do you know why?"

"I don't care why," Paulo laughed.

"She thinks you're already damned."

"I know, because I don't go church."

"You're generous," Ruth looked out of the window, leaving silence to settle in the car. As they came to Bat Valley, she sighed as if regretting the silence. "You know, the whole of those *kalitunsi* trees were once covered with millions and millions of fruit bats. Even the traffic couldn't drown their chatter. These slopes were open fields."

"What happened to them?"

"War. Bats don't like gunshots."

"It must have been tough for Grandmother. That childhood, moved from one family to another."

"Who told you that?"

"Grandfather. First, she was adopted by a Dutch family but when they were returning to Europe they passed her on to a German family and then a British one. She ended up with an Awakened family."

Ruth yawned. "I thought she grew up in an orphanage. In any case, she is only too happy not to have relations. Ask yourself: how many times does she ask you about me or your uncle?"

"She is indifferent but not in an evil way. It is bizarre though. You would think that she would be used to my presence by now. Sometimes she stares at me peculiarly."

"How does she look at you?" Ruth's laid-back air was gone.

"I don't know—never straight. I catch her staring and she looks away or she leaves the room."

"Wait till I tell Job."

"It's not malicious," Paulo tried to reassure her. "I suspect she still sees in me evidence of how her daughter was forced to have a child before she was ready."

"Ha, Faisi worrying about anything else apart from her place in heaven!"

"I don't know about that." Kalema was unconvinced about Faisi's selfishness. "I mean, she cleans and tidies my quarters every day."

"Does she?"

"Washes and irons my clothes too."

"Maybe she's getting senile; maybe she is bored. She was never like that with us."

Ruth did not say another word until they came to Bbunga. They turned into the murram road off Gaba Road leading to her house. When they came to a shopping center, she asked Paulo to drop her at a bar where she normally went to drink in the evening. "I don't fancy going home on my own now. Don't worry," she quickly added when she saw guilt spread across Paulo's face, "My friends will drop me home."

As Ruth stepped out of the car, Paulo dropped his hand in frustration. He had upset her by his defense of his grandparents but he did not know how to soothe her.

"Mother," he called.

Ruth stopped.

"What did they do to you?" Paulo was close to begging but there was a tinge of exasperation in his voice.

Ruth smiled at him like he was a child. For a moment it seemed as if she was not going to answer. Then she changed her mind. She returned to the car, bent low at the window, and asked, "Have you ever sat on a bus and listened to your mother confess to strangers, to being a slut, to abortions, and to killing innocent children? Have you ever sat in a school chapel with the whole school present listening to how your father started his sinning career by stealing eggs, then chickens, progressed to bestiality, and graduated to raping women?"

There was a long pause.

"When you have gone through all that, come back and tell me how to love my parents. Now go."

Paulo did not drive away. He did not go after his mother either. Ruth was on the verge of tears; it would be stupid to follow her for she would explode. He stayed in the car. Having grown up in boarding school he understood that his grandparents came from an old, austere school of Anglicanism whose approach was old-fashioned. Despite that, they had been good to him. Just the other month, because he had no father to give him ancestral land, Kanani had told him that when they passed on, their land and house would go to him. That never happens among the Ganda. Daughters' children never inherit land from their grandparents. But when he told Ruth about it she had only shrugged her shoulders. Another mother would have said, "Oh, how generous of them," or she would have gone over to her parents to thank them, but Ruth had just sighed, "We don't have any sentimental attachment to that place. You can sell it if you want." It was that kind of insensitivity on the part of the twins that had made Paulo protective of his grandparents. It was the reason he was willing to stay with them through their old age.

Now he was conflicted.

He got out of the car and joined Ruth outside the bar where she sat drinking. She looked away from him. They drank in silence. Paulo was too contrite to break the silence. All he asked was, "Another one?"

And Ruth would nod and look away from him.

When it came to alcohol, the twins were the proverbial pastors' children who drank on behalf of their parents. But the thing that puzzled Paulo most was why they kept going back to church when it was clear that they were not really Christians. To him, the twins' Christianity only went as far as turning up for service on Sunday. Unlike other Christians, they never talked about their love for God, or witnessed about the wonders Christ had done for them; they had never asked him to get saved and he had never seen them pray outside the church. Mostly, they had utter contempt for the zeal of new converts: "They've only just met God—they're wont to overdo their love," the twins would sneer, turning their noses up at the enthusiasm of new church members.

When Paulo asked her why they didn't just give it up Ruth was surprised.

"It is our tradition."

Paulo had nothing to say to that.

Now, as he returned from getting Ruth her Nile Special she said, "I know you're itching to ask more questions, so go on, ask."

Paulo smiled. "No, I thought I should just stay with you tonight."

"I mean it, ask. I am not angry with you."

Paulo considered his mother's state. Perhaps she was getting tipsy. Perhaps this was the right moment. He tendered, "Hmm, was my father Tutsi or Hutu?"

There was a long pause as Ruth stared at him. She sighed and lifted her bottle. She took a sip and put it down. She sighed again.

"Where did that come from, Paulo?"

Paulo spread his hands and he adjusted himself in his seat. "I am not just a *munnarwanda*, I am something specific."

"I guess he was Tutsi from the look of him." Ruth picked up her bottle and sipped looking up at the sky. When she put it down she asked, "Why ask now?"

"If I am to start a family I'll need details."

"You're half-Ganda: give the children our names."

"I am not one of those Tutsis who hide their ethnicity."

"You don't even speak the language."

"How old was Kalemanzira?"

"I guess twenty, twenty-five, I am not sure."

"He was young!"

Ruth turned in surprise.

"Yes, well, you could say 'young' now, but for me at fourteen, twenty-five was quite old."

"All along I had this picture of a rough, burly man stinking of sweat. Did he live alone?"

"I don't know, I was not his friend," Ruth said. "I only saw him in the morning when he came to collect the empty *ndebbe* and returned them filled with water."

"That's what I find most exasperating: no one knows anything about this Kalemanzira. Not even Grandfather who employed him."

"He was a freelance water-man."

"Then more people should know him."

"But you know how foreigners keep to themselves. If anybody knew anything it would be fellow Rwandese."

"So where are they?"

"Remember I was only a schoolgirl at the time," Ruth said.

"I am sorry he forced you."

Ruth stopped. Paulo was mortified. "Forgive me, I shouldn't have brought that up." Ruth remained silent.

"I am sorry," Paulo said again.

Ruth burst out laughing. It was clear the drink was taking effect. "He apologizes for his father!" It was such a deep laugh that her stomach shook. "I am not!" she said. "Look what I got." And she waved her hands over him.

Paulo rubbed his nose.

"It's Nyange, isn't it?" Ruth said. "She's pushing you to marry her."

"No, it's not her . . . Yes, it is about her I suppose. I've told her I am Rwandese," he smiled. "She thought Kalema was the royal name. And you know how bigoted people are. My own family can't bear to call me Kalemanzira. We must Gandarize it to Kalema."

"I don't care what you call yourself. You insisted on that name."

"But if I ask Nyange's family to marry her, I must name at least four generations of my paternal grandfathers."

"Paulo, you're Ganda. I am your mother." Ruth held her heart as if Paulo did not believe her. "Job has been your father in every sense of the word. What more can we do?"

"I appreciate Uncle Job, but he's your brother."

"But where your father is not, Job is. If you're my son, Paulo, then you're Job's son. We're one person."

Paulo shook his head, but Ruth continued.

"You're the one who insists on this Rwandese thing. You can start your own Kalemanzira clan. You can buy a plot of land in Kigali if you want and spend some time there. But don't dig this up. Many Tutsis are without roots but they have sprouted their own and made a life. Immigration is like that. It breaks things up—tribes, families, even races." Ruth took a breath and then asked cheerily, "So are you planning to marry Nyange?"

Paulo shrugged his shoulders. "I am thinking about it."

11.

Sunday, February 22, 2004

Paulo had heard a lot about Magda, a cantankerous heathen according to his grandparents and a radical traditionalist according to his mother. Since nothing had been heard of her since 1971, it was presumed that she had died during the bush war of the 1980s. Thus, he was surprised to open the door to a woman so like his grandfather. She looked startled to see him as well, as if she had not expected anyone to be at home.

"Are the elders in?" the woman asked.

"It's Sunday, they're at church. Please come in and wait for them."

"Wait for them? No, blood relatives don't wait in this house. I've only brought a letter for my brother." She gave Paulo a brown envelope and insisted, "Make sure you give it to the husband, not to the wife."

"I'll give it to Grandfather."

That was when the woman stopped and said, "Don't you dare be little Yobu, Nnakato's son."

It took Paulo a moment to remember that Ruth was Nnakato. He shook his head.

"My name's Paulo Kalema, I mean Kalemanzira, and yes

236

Ruth is my mother. But my name was Nsobya before I changed it to Kalemanzira."

For a long time, Magda stared at Paulo as if he were an apparition. Then she said, "I need to sit down, bring me a mat."

Kalema went inside the house and brought a mat. He laid it on the verandah. Magda bent painfully, both hands reaching for the floor. After she sat down she repeated counting on her fingers, "You're Nnakato's son, who was named Nsobya but is now called Kalemanzira?"

"Yes. Well, Kalema." Magda stopped. She looked away from Paulo and made clicking noises in her throat.

"Bring me a gourd of water, Kalema. My throat is parched."

"We only have glasses," Paulo said.

Again Magda stared at him. Then she asked, "Do those words mean anything to you, Kalema—I mean, bring me a gourd?"

"It's the old way of asking for a drink." Paulo was now getting uncomfortable.

"Get me a glass of water then."

When he brought the water, Magda muttered something under her breath and drank. Her old throat trembled as she swallowed noisily. As she put the glass down, Paulo noticed that her hands were quivering. She took a breath and said, "Glasses rob water of taste."

"Grandmother does not smoke the pot anyway," Paulo smiled.

"No, Faisi would not do such a thing. Now tell me, Kalema, has anyone ever told you about Magda?"

"Magda who is also Bweeza of Nakaseke," Paulo laughed in awe. "That's where I was born."

Bweeza clapped her hands happily. "Do they call me by both names? How you've grown, Yobu!"

"Yobu?"

"Yes, Yobu. That's what Luusi named you, after her brother. Is she fine, your mother?"

"She's fine."

"Married?"

"Not yet."

"Come here. First, I am going to carry you on my back, then sit you on my lap." But she hugged him. "They kept you away from me. Me, in whose hands you dropped?"

Paulo grinned.

"It is good that my children know both my names but that Magdalene is what your Christian family wanted. My real name is Bweeza."

"Then I'll call you Jjajja Bweeza. I am not Christian."

"Ah aha," Magda exclaimed. "Come here again." She held out her hands. Then she whispered, "I prepared your first bath: I included lweeza for good luck." She said this as if it were the reason Paulo was of no religious inclination. She kept stealing glances at him as if she did not believe he was real. Finally she said, "You know, Kalema? You belong to your mother's family in ways you might never know. This is why I am angry that they're not allowing daughters' children at the family reunion."

"Family reunion?"

"The letter I gave you is an invitation for Kanani. We are organizing a meeting for the wider family to come together." Magda's eyes lit up. "We're going home, back to the base." Now she sighed. "But Kanani's too mad to attend. I wish you could come though. I am convinced that you're significant."

"I am a daughter's son."

"That is where I get impatient with tradition. If a man cannot be sure of his sons except by the word of a woman, then a daughter's children are more reliable. Do you see how tradition shoots itself?"

In a way, Bweeza was as fanatical as his grandparents.

Magda was keen to leave before Kanani and Faisi returned. Paulo drove her back to her home and she told him the story of his birth along the way. When they reached Nakaseke Town, she asked him to stop the car while she went to the market.

The main road in Nakaseke was still murram because it only led to peasant towns that had no commercial traffic. A handful of brick blocks had sprung up on either side of the road. But between the new blocks, old mud structures still clung onto life. Yet the new buildings seemed out of place the way rich people are when they visit poor relatives. Paradoxically, the mud structures were alive with activity—people were going in and out of the shops making a lot of noise. They sold everything from boiled maize, boiled eggs, matchboxes, and pancakes to cooking oil and kerosene measured by a funnel, bar soap cut into pieces, gourds, and calabashes. Ropes and traditionally smoked coffee beans in fiber sachets hung down the doors. *Maama Paatu's Hare Saloon*, where women had their hair straightened or braided, threatened to collapse with activity. All sorts of synthetic hair weaves and second-hand clothes hung on nails or metallic hangers by the door. Women, some waiting for their turn, some scrutinizing second-hand clothes, clogged the doorway. Next to *Maama Paatu's* salon, loud music boomed from an impossibly tiny strip of a shop selling audio- and video-cassettes.

The new shops had an ostentatious air about them as if saying to Nakaseke, *modernity has arrived can't you see?* Here, hardware merchandise including cement, nails, paint, and bolts were sold beside skin lotion, toilet soap, combs, make-up, bleaching creams, and other skincare products. One shop sold plasticware in all sorts of bright colors but on the shelves, lanterns and wax candles sat next to exercise books, biscuits, scones, and *kitenge* garments. Even *Michelle's Beauty Salon*—which had proper sinks, wall mirrors, padded chairs, and modern driers—was empty. Paulo smiled at the war between the new and the old. He wondered how long Nakaseke's loyalty would hold out against the lure of modernity.

At the end of the block on the right was the market, but Paulo could not see Bweeza anywhere. The market stalls were made out of sticks and planks topped with straw shelters. The stalls heaved under huge jackfruit, pawpaw, *uju*, and other varieties of vegetables and fruit. One stall had just Bwaise yams. The last stall sold protein: sacks and sacks of dried *nswa*—flying termites—by the mugful. It also had powdered groundnuts and a few molding dry fish. Paulo looked around for a butcher: there was none, not even pork. In the absence of meat, he thought, Nakaseke needs its *nswa*.

Bweeza reappeared. But instead of shopping, she came back with friends. She introduced Paulo to them. Those going in the same direction as she was, she offered a lift. "Squeeze in. We don't leave each other by the roadside, do we?" Then she told them about Paulo. "You remember my girl Luusi who had a baby here in the 70s? This is the boy. Yes, so grown and driving me in his own car. Fruits of a long life, what can I say?"

Paulo asked Bweeza to help him choose good Bwaise yams to take home but she scoffed, "Why would you want these anemic ones in the market when I have proper yams in my swamp?"

"City people," a woman in the car smiled. "They can't tell the difference."

When they arrived at her house, Magda quickly got out of the car, grabbed a hoe, and asked two girls to get the large baskets and follow her. They disappeared behind the house. Paulo, now on his own, looked around the compound. He could not believe that his life started here. Magda's huge house was old. It might have been affluent in the 50s and 60s but with age and disrepair, it looked decrepit. She lived with three grandchildren, which made the house look like a vast nest when the birds have flown. An old Bedford lorry with a skinny steering wheel in a black rounded cabin sat on its hinges next to a tank. Its bonnet was a thick nose ridge. Its flared nostrils were covered with fins like a radiator and the wood on the back had rotted and fallen off.

Magda and the girls came back carrying baskets full of yams on their heads. They rested them outside the kitchen and Magda peeled the clay soil off the yams with the back of a knife. Then she washed the rest of the soil off and cut off the tendrils. She divided the yams into three heaps and packed them in bags. She instructed Paulo that one bag should go to each of the twins' houses and one to her brother Kanani. "But don't tell your grandparents that

I sent the yams," she said, "Or they might not eat them." Magda filled the rest of the boot with all sorts of fruit for Paulo.

Paulo felt ashamed. Magda had cared for Ruth through a tough time but his mother had never bothered to return or taken him to visit her. He wondered at Magda: she loved people regardless of whether they loved her back. To compensate for Ruth's oversight, he promised to come back soon. Before he left, Magda made Paulo promise that he would make sure that Kanani read the letter.

When he opened the letter, Kanani was instantly suspicious. Firstly, it was written in Luganda. Secondly, it named four generations of his grandfathers. He put it down and looked at Paulo.

"Who brought it?"

"Someone slipped it under the door."

"Why don't you read it first and see what it's saying?" Faisi suggested.

The letter named Kanani as the head of a branch of their clan. Then it invited him to an elders' council to arrange a family reunion of Kintu Kidda's descendants. The council would determine the nature of the reunion. Dates and venues of the council's meetings were provided.

Kanani threw the letter on the table. He could not believe the tenacity of the clan. Decades after cutting himself off, they still clung onto him. It was preposterous that he was expected to take part in organizing a heathen function. Faisi picked up the letter and read it. First, she asked Kanani to join her in prayer. Then she said, "You know, Kanani, God works in mysterious ways. This letter is a calling in disguise."

"How?"

"I see a multitude of relations hungering for salvation. I see you well placed as a clan elder, as God's chosen, to feed this multitude."

"But you know that in his hometown, among his relations, a prophet is without honor," Kanani argued.

"Now you're being a Jonah," Faisi stood up impatiently. "Remember God will send a whale and you'll still go."

In spite of Faisi's compelling argument, she was not a blood Kintu. Kanani knew the family curse. Maybe he should have warned the twins about the evil inheritance but then to tell the twins was to suggest that he did not trust God to take care of the family. In God, the curse is obsolete, Kanani told himself. Nonetheless, doubt plagued him. Had God withdrawn his protection? Was Paulo a coincidence? Kanani was ashamed of himself. How could he think that his grandson was anything but just his grandson?

He sighed.

Sometimes he had a distinct feeling that he and his family were naked, without God's protection. That was why he was not keen on a head-on collision with the family curse.

As he sat down on their bed, Kanani mourned the fire that once burned in him. As a young man, he would have thrown himself into this quest without question. He would have gone to the reunion and he would have torn down the Devil's bastions. Now, at seventy-four years of age, all he wanted was to work on his place in heaven. It did not matter whether his crown was without the stars of people he had led to heaven anymore: as long as he was inside when the pearly gates closed.

Kanani deferred the decision. The family reunion was still seven weeks away.

BOOK FOUR
ISAAC NEWTON KINTU

1.
BANDA, KAMPALA

Monday, January 5, 2004

It is ten o'clock at night. In Mulago Hospital, the door of the mortuary opens again. It has to be a new corpse—either rich or unknown. The attendant has to have been paid a lot of money to come to the *gwanika* at this time of the night for a mere collection. In any case, poor people, when their loved one dies in the hospital, ask for the body not to be brought to the mortuary. Checking into Mulago Hospital's mortuary is like checking into the Hilton Hotel. The bill would kill the loved ones. Poor people take their loved one home, buy a needle and syringe, and inject their dead with paraffin so that they don't stink of anything worse than kerosene before burial.

It is a collection! The attendant is talkative; they've given him good money. He is with a woman, her teenage son, and older daughter. These three are confused. They don't know when their loved one—father and husband—died, how he died or even whether he is dead at all. He disappeared a week ago. They are checking to see whether he died somewhere and has been brought here. The attendant goes to the extreme end of the room on the right where the oldest dead are stored. The shutter goes up, the trays slide out, and it starts all over again.

"Come and see," the attendant calls.

"Stay right there," the woman says to her children. They are strong, her children, no flinching.

She walks to where the attendant is. He stands at the head of a corpse while the woman stands on his right. He lifts the head of the first corpse several inches off the tray. The body rises like a log.

"This one?"

The woman shakes her head.

The man lets go and the body falls, *ddu* like the stump of a banana tree.

"This one? No?" *Ddu.* "This one?" Ba *ddu*. He works fast; the refrigerator is huge and there are many bodies to go through.

"Look carefully," he says to the woman. "The dead change looks."

"Ours has a beard and he is not so old," the woman says unhelpfully.

There is a knowing look on the face of the attendant, a cynical smile almost, as if he knows that this loved one disappeared with a new loved one, but he is not going to throw away good money by telling these people. They can enjoy their denial if they want but it will cost them.

He comes to today's corpses. He looks at Kamu's tag and laughs at the day-shift attendant's sense of humor.

"Kamu Kamugye?"

The family smiles. They don't even bother to shake their heads.

"He was killed at Bwaise this morning. Mob-justice. Take a look, he might have been mislabeled," the attendant insists.

"Ours has a beard!" The woman is indignant and her children have lost their sense of humor at the insinuation that their loved one could be the thief.

"He is not here," the attendant says as he pushes back the last tray. The family is visibly relieved. The attendant pulls off his gloves and apron, throws them in a bin, and locks the door. Kamu waits.

• • •

It had been forty-four hours since Isaac last slept but sleep was beyond him. He sat on Nnayiga's dressing-table stool, his back against the mirror. As he turned, he caught sight of her wig hanging on the top right edge of the mirror frame. Spasms gripped him. He picked up a coat-hanger and prodded the wig until it came unhooked. It fell with a light thud, like a dead pigeon. Nausea rose in his throat. He hoped the hair was synthetic. He spasmed again as he used the hook of the hanger to lift the wig off the floor. He dropped it into a plastic carrier-bag, tied the bag, and rolled it tight. He then slipped it under the dressing table where Nnayiga's sisters would not find it. He would bury the wig later. Unable to contain himself any longer, he ran to the en-suite bathroom and retched.

The state of his bedroom mirrored the turmoil in Isaac's mind. The mahogany double bed, disconnected from its side drawers, stood upright on its headrest. Turned like that, the back of the bed looked coarse, like the underbelly of a dead dog. Nothing on the bed had been removed. It had been turned over—mattress, sheets, and blanket. He had found out that morning that tradition demanded that the marital bed be flipped on the death of a spouse, until after burial. Isaac shook his head. What did they think: that he would climb on the bed and masturbate while his wife lay stretched out in the sitting room? He stepped out of the bedroom and locked the door.

The corridor was dark. He must remember to buy a bulb tomorrow. He opened the door to the first spare bedroom on the right: it was crammed with people he did not recognize. He apologized and closed the door. He went to the other spare bedroom but it was occupied by Nnayiga's sisters. Isaac smiled but before they smiled back he had closed the door. He checked Kizza's bedroom door; it was locked. Everything that could be stolen had been moved in there. Most mourners mean well but some have light fingers.

Isaac came through the door that opened onto the sitting room and caught sight of the coffin. A strong, sappy odor hung in the air, which meant that the timber used to make the coffin was immature. Too much business for coffin-makers meant there was no time to wait for the timber to dry, Isaac thought bitterly. He was perturbed by the coffin's shape. The two ends were too narrow, as if Nnayiga's legs had been tied together at one end and at the other her head had no room to turn.

"The womb rattles with memory."

Isaac wrinkled his nose at his mother-in-law's theatrics. Where do women learn the art of mourning?

"You've got to eat something, Mother," someone called to the woman. "Here's a mug of porridge: pour it down your throat then cry all you want."

When Isaac walked into the room, all the noise died. The coffin lay on the floor in the middle of the room. It was surrounded by women dressed in *busuuti* and a few in *kitenge* prints. They had covered their lower bodies and sat on the floor out of respect for the dead. Furniture had been removed to make room. Nnayiga's mother, flanked by her sisters and friends, was the chief mourner. All soothing energies—shaking of heads, melting eyes, and stories of other bereaved mothers—were directed at her. Isaac had heard her tell about the omens—her eyelid had twitched all week and an owl had hooted outside her house two nights in a row.

"A child's passing is like no other," an elderly woman had soothed.

Isaac knelt before the coffin and peered through the glass above Nnayiga's face. He ran his hand across it.

"Death titivated her, didn't he?" Nnayiga's mother asked, as if reading Isaac's mind.

"Hmm," he acknowledged her, stood up and walked out. He walked to the end of the corridor into the garage. Nnayiga's wheelchair, pushed into a corner, looked like wasted effort. Women, mostly elderly, slept along the walls of the garage. Isaac walked through the double doors, out into the compound.

• • •

Outside, the number of mourners that had come for the vigil took Isaac by surprise. The compound heaved. In the middle of the yard was a makeshift tent, with hissing bright pressure lamps at its four corners. Close to the garage, Isaac's mother sat with a group of women from the market where she worked. At the far end, clan elders and his father's relatives camped. Away from the tent was the funeral hearth surrounded by teenagers, mostly Isaac's cousins—for them, the funeral was a sleepover. Small groups of young men in thick jackets and women wrapped in colorful *kangas* were everywhere. Elderly men in mackintoshes sat together in more comfortable chairs under the tent talking in low tones or dozing. The hymn sung by the choir from Nnayiga's church wobbled like a cassette on fading batteries. Closer to the gate was the MTN camp—Isaac's colleagues were drinking.

Isaac saw the ramp unoccupied and made for it. As he walked across the compound, he saw mourners glance at him. It was as if he could hear their thoughts: *He's killed her, poor Nnayiga; she sat at home faithfully while he sniffed under every bitch's tail . . .*

As he sat down, Isaac's eyes started to run. He cried not because he too was about to die, not because Kizza was motherless but because he had lost her. He had been weeping for a while when he saw his colleagues Habib, Lule, Kaaya, and Mugisha coming toward him. They squatted around him. For a moment, they were silent as Isaac blew his nose. Lule spoke first.

"*Kitalo*, Isaac."

"God's will," he sighed. "Nnayiga's turned her back on me."

"Word's going around that your wiring is coming loose," Habib joked.

"And you've come to tighten it," Isaac smiled through his tears.

"No, tighten funeral arrangements, so you can run raving mad."

Isaac turned to Lule. "Have you seen her, Lule? Nnayiga's never looked more beautiful."

"He's seen her, Isaac." Habib gave Lule a warning glance.

"Death likes his brides beautiful."

"I also hear you've not eaten, Isaac." Lule changed the subject.

"I've got no energy to eat."

"You don't need energy to eat." Habib stood up. "I am going to get you food."

"I had spared her. I swear, I thought I'd spared her."

Habib shook his head as he walked away. He had heard the story countless times.

"When I found out, I said to myself, Isaac, stay away from Nnayiga."

"How did you find out?" Kaaya asked.

Isaac stopped heaving and looked at Kaaya. "How do people find out? You just know. With this thing you just know."

"So you did not take any blood tests?"

Isaac shook his head. "Blood tests bring nothing but certainty. We could not handle certainty. When all you have is a tiny doubt, you hang onto it."

"When did you first find out?"

"About myself? A few months before Kizza was born." Isaac counted his fingers silently, "Kizza's four now—almost five years ago."

"Why did you suspect?"

"A woman from the past died. I had gone 'live' with her."

"Four years ago you still went 'live?'"

"It's too late to be shocked, Kaaya," Mugisha interrupted quietly.

"That's when I decided to stop going with Nnayiga."

"Have you shown any symptoms yet?"

"No, nothing."

"So … when did you find out about Nnayiga?"

"She was sickly around Christmas 2002 but we did not take it seriously. Then in January last year she started to freeze and shiver, *I am cold, I am freezing*, especially at night. Slipping into bed with her, I swear, was like getting in bed with a corpse. From then on, the disease accelerated—night sweats, fevers, fatigue, a funny rash on the left arm, sometimes her mind went, and her feet hurt. She suffered from this, that, everything. Then her weight dropped. Before we knew it she had lost her hair. Then her feet hurt so much, I put her in a wheelchair. From the wheelchair Nnayiga hopped into the coffin—kidney failure."

"Maybe, you should've told her about your suspicion," Kaaya said.

"I wouldn't do that to her. *I said to myself, Isaac, unknown troubles don't keep anyone awake: leave Nnayiga in peace.*"

"Why not use condoms?"

"Condoms?" Isaac stopped for a moment. "You know what women are like: she would ask why, when we've only got one child?" Isaac paused to sigh. "By the time I stopped, I had given it to her."

"We understand your guilt, Isaac, but at the moment, you have to put it away for Kizza."

"Besides, someone gave it to you; you did not find out until it was too late. Someone gave it to that person and she didn't mean to give it to you. What do we do, form a queue of the guilty and hang ourselves?"

"We're all dead, Isaac. All of us. It's a question of who goes first," Lule said.

At this point, Habib returned with a plate of food and passed it to Isaac. "Shove the food down," he said to Isaac.

Isaac balanced the plate on his lap. Lule asked Habib to keep Isaac company while he and the others made inquiries about the following day's arrangements.

"Thank you, people . . ." Isaac said as they walked away. Kaaya turned and said, "Today's yours, tomorrow's ours. We're only helping ourselves."

Isaac pushed the food into his mouth and in no time, it was gone. He put the plate down and whispered, "You have no idea what the sight of your woman lying in a box does to you."

Habib shook his head and said, "I look at my Zulaika, the way she is with the children, the way she handles the home and things, and I pray to Allah that *Alhamdulillah* if it is to come, it is to come. But for the sake of my children, let it take me first."

Isaac watched as his three friends moved from group to group talking to elders. As they approached his mother, Habib remarked, "Your mother is young—"

"And beautiful," Isaac interrupted. "And you're wondering what happened to me. Go on, I am used to it."

Habib was saved from denying this by the return of the others. Lule and Mugisha sat on the ramp while Kaaya squatted in front of Isaac and said, "Everything has been arranged."

"Food, transport, church service, and the construction of the grave," Lule added.

"Your mother insists that she'll move in with you for the time being—"

"To give Kizza some stability," Kaaya added quickly.

"My mother?" Isaac asked in disbelief.

"Yes," Mugisha said. "She said to us, 'Don't worry about Isaac, I'll take care of him and Kizza.'"

Isaac stifled a cynical laugh. At forty-three, he was finally going to be mothered. He had long made up his mind that nature was a woman. She stands at the gate of the world and as souls step in to start life, she hands them a bag of tools—loving parents, a stable home, health, brains, good looks, luck, and opportunities. But when he came along, the woman was in a foul mood. She tossed him a bag almost empty, and still he had made life out of the nothing she gave him. But just as he was beginning to make something of it, the woman had snatched his life back.

2.
KATANGA, KAMPALA, 1967

Isaac sat naked on the floor. His buttocks were numb from sitting too long on a cold concrete surface every day. His chin dug deep into his chest as he leaned forward to see past his distended belly. He pulled back the foreskin on his little penis and a pink worm jutted forth. He let it go. It slunk back into its sheath and the wrinkled foreskin pouted. He thrust it forth again. Fascinating: the worm had a mouth. He let go and the foreskin swallowed it again. But he had to see his worm pop out just this once. He pulled back the foreskin, it popped out, gleaming. Isaac was engrossed in this now-it's-here, now-it's-not game when a rush of air swept across his face and a slap disengaged his hands. He started as if chilled water had been thrown at him. It was not the pain of the slap, not even the fact that he had been caught at it that made him jump, it was because he had not heard her coming. Isaac lifted his eyes slowly but could only see as high as her knees. He could not risk looking further, the movement could provoke her. His head turned owl-like and went down. A ray of sunshine streaking through the window illuminated his thin wavy brown hair.

"Stop playing with that maggot."

Isaac's eyes darted back to his penis but it had shrunk beneath his belly. He sighed. This was the end of the peace he had enjoyed that morning. He waited for the next assault. He did not know in what form it would come.

"If I catch you toying with it again, I'll cut it off."

Isaac's little fingers did a slow dance with each other like the legs of a dying cockroach. Then he remembered and closed his eyes. His mind chanted, "Leave the room, leave, leave . . ." His concentration was so intense that he rocked back and forth.

It worked. The air relaxed and he heard the inner door close. Isaac opened his eyes and smiled. He looked down for something to occupy him. Two thin legs came into view. They wandered from beneath his belly and stretched before him. At the end of the legs were two feet, unused, baby-like. Isaac looked at the legs as if seeing them for the first time. He leaned forward and touched his knees. The scabs, thick from crawling, deadened his touch. He felt his knees distantly. He gave up touching himself.

The lounge was devoid of furniture. In one corner, pans, yellow enamel plates, cups, and a matching teapot sat on a wooden tray placed on top of a metallic pail. In the corner adjacent to him, mats in dazzling colors leaned against the wall. On his right, two meters away, was the door to the other room, the bedroom. In the bedroom was a single bed, his grandmother's. At night, the bed brought forth all sorts of bedding and the floor, both in the lounge and in the bedroom, was besieged by sleeping bodies. In the morning, the bodies woke up early, gathered their bedding, tied it into bundles and the bed swallowed them again.

Each morning, someone pulled Isaac off his heap of rags before he woke up. He was tossed in this place where he watched, through the window, hordes of fruit bats swarming as if someone had thrown them out of bed, too. The rags, always wet, were tossed out to dry making them thicker, crustier, and warmer at night. Isaac had grown so used to the smell that when he was thrown back onto the heap, a sharp wave of old urine hit him and mellowed into a delicious intimate smell making him yawn.

He would grope and slither, half asleep, into heavier and warmer rags. A tattered shirt, a dress, whatever, Isaac snaked his arms or legs through. By the time he was through with thrusting and tossing, he was asleep, the smell too cozy, the rags too familiar, the luxury too overpowering to keep his eyes open.

"Look, he's peed again!"

Isaac started. Where did she come from? He looked down in panic. A rivulet snaked from beneath his belly between his stretched-out legs toward his feet. He turned and looked behind him; there was only the wall. It was his water. He sighed as if to say: Guilty, do as you please, and clenched his head in anticipation. The smack did not come. Instead, his grandmother's voice called from outside, "Take him out and squat him on the latrine. He might shit as well."

The girl panicked and wrenched Isaac up.

"Oh no, he has!"

She let Isaac's body fall back into its shit. The pain cut through his numb buttocks. A sharp breath escaped his mouth but he sunk his chin into his chest and strangled the cry. He had not felt his body defecate.

"You're going to sit in that shit for the rest of the day."

"Tendo, Tendo, TENDO!"

"Yes, Mother?"

"Clean him right away."

"Can't we throw him into the latrine with his dung?"

Isaac flinched: falling through the latrine-hole was his nightmare. He had no doubt that Tendo would do it when his grandmother was not watching. He imagined himself spending the rest of his life in the ponging darkness with people dropping dung and susu on top of his head and shivered.

"I am not laughing, Tendo."

Tendo's legs, their hairs bristling, went out of view. Isaac heard her rummaging in the inner room. Then she was coming back. Isaac looked through the corners of his eye and saw her feet, in thong sandals, come into view. They stopped in front of him.

Above his head, paper ripped. Then an exercise book fell on the floor. It opened at the middle and Isaac saw squared pages with figures and scribbling. Then he heard her crumple and wring paper to soften it. He was jerked off the floor, stood on his feet, and leaned against her legs. He bit his lower lip as the crack between his buttocks was savaged. Despite Tendo's attempts to soften the paper it was a scourer: his crack was on fire. She thumped him back on the floor in a different place and scooped up the shit.

"Phmnnn, this boy's rotting."

Tendo ran out of the house as if she were carrying a spreading fire. Isaac heard her spit heavily on her way to the latrine. Then she came back with a rag, soap, and water. She scrubbed his behind with the wet rag and then mopped the floor. She let him down with a final thud and walked out, spitting some more. When she returned, Tendo stood away from him.

"You dare shit again," she hissed, "And I'll stitch your anus."

Isaac sucked in his anus.

"Did you squat him on the latrine this morning?" his grandmother's voice came.

"I did and he had a go. He eats a lot."

"Was it loose?"

"Mother, he's always running loose."

"Remind me to buy Mebendazole. It could be worms."

"I'd stick a pin into that balloon belly of yours," Tendo whispered to Isaac, "But shit and worms would explode everywhere—*phrooooooo!*"

Isaac saw fragments of his stomach, like a balloon's, scattered all over the floor.

Tendo walked back outside.

"I don't understand it," his grandmother's voice was now faint. "Six years old but he stays mute and unable to walk?"

"He's not unable, Mother. He doesn't want to. The doctor said there's nothing wrong with him," Tendo said.

"Then we shall be patient."

Isaac crawled back to where he had fouled earlier, sat in the exact place, and settled down to exploring his body again. He sunk his index finger into his navel and felt crusts of tight dirt lodged in secret creases. The finger nudged and teased until a sliver of dirt came loose into his nail. He pulled the finger out. He prized the dirt from under his nail and rolled it between the balls of his thumb and forefinger. He lifted the finger to his nose and sniffed. The smell was deep, ugly, and intimate. Isaac rolled his eyes in shocked pleasure. He exhaled the smell and snapped the dirt into the air. He sunk his finger once more into the dent, seeking more folds, more old tight dirt.

Thus Isaac passed his time exploring rotten parts of his body, carrying their decay on his finger to his nose. There was so much ugliness on his body. From behind his ears to between his toes he explored every crack, crevice, and fold until the smells stopped shocking him. Other times, he amused himself with insects that trespassed on his floor. Insects, especially ants, made him feel powerful. He crawled after them, sometimes getting on his feet without realizing it, to catch them. Usually, he plucked the hind limbs and let them go. He marveled that when dismembered, ants never opened their mouths to cry out. Instead, they dragged their bodies, now moving in circles. Sometimes, he squashed the abdomen and watched as the insects did a chest dance. Other times, he flooded them with his urine and watched them wading, gasping until they drowned. If he didn't have urine, he put the ant in his mouth, closed it and flooded it with saliva. Then he listened as it wriggled on his tongue tickling it in its death throes. Sometimes, an ant squirted something disgusting on his tongue in revenge. As soon as it stopped kicking, he spat it out. Then he waited for dusk when multitudes of fruit bats filled the sky, happy to be free in the air, going to a feast.

3.

Isaac had no excuse to come into the world, except if you count his mother Nnamata's backside, as illustrious as a 1957 Plymouth's and as round as an earthen pot, a reason.

In the early 60s, Nnamata was her father's favorite child because out of a litter of six, she was the only one with a "bright future." Nnamata's parents, Ssemata and Ziraba, were as ambitious as any Ganda commoners who had grown up under the British Protectorate. You found yourself on earth without design on your part and there was no option but to grow up. Along the way, you found out that there were three human species in the world and that you belonged to the worst. You were told that if you got baptized, then confirmed in church, you might have a chance. You got baptized in case the Europeans knew what they were talking about. Some children, mostly boys, had a stint in school. Royals, governors, and the children of proper Christians stayed on, while for commoners, for whom school was a waste of time, the only thing left to do was to get married. A woman then dropped as many children as she was fated. Every child was born with its peculiar luck. Parents showed their children the right way and watched as each child's destiny manifested depending on how the child interpreted the world.

Ziraba and Ssemata abandoned rural life in the 40s for the opportunity of a better life in the city. But because Kampala was looking for skilled people, they fell into Katanga—a fissure between Makerere, Nakasero, and Mulago Hills—and formed a family. Whenever it rained and the water from the hills overwhelmed Katanga, Ziraba would say, "God is sweating. We're armpit hair." Katanga was so named by Makerere University students. To them, the valley was as rich in female flesh and cheap alcohol as Katanga Valley in the Congo was in minerals. Katanga serviced and watered the largely male students at the university.

For a long time, Ziraba gave birth to boys until Nnamata came along. Then, a friend led her to a traditional healer who "tied" her womb. All the healer, a woman, asked for was a pad soiled with menstrual blood. Ziraba never saw exactly what the woman did with the pad but she was eventually shown where it was buried in case she changed her mind.

After independence, Uganda—a European artifact—was still forming as a country rather than as a kingdom in the minds of ordinary Gandas. They were lulled by the fact that *Kabaka* Muteesa II was made president of the new Uganda. Nonetheless, most of them felt that "Uganda" should remain a kingdom for the Ganda under their *kabaka* so that things would go back to the way they were before Europeans came. Uganda was a patchwork of fifty or so tribes. The Ganda did not want it. The union of tribes brought no apparent advantage to them apart from a deluge of immigrants from wherever, coming to Kampala to take their land. Meanwhile, the other fifty or so tribes looked on flabbergasted as the British drew borders and told them that they were now Ugandans. Their histories, cultures, and identities were overwritten by the mispronounced name of an insufferably haughty tribe propped above them. But to the Ganda, the reality of Uganda as opposed to Buganda only sank in when, after independence, Obote overran the *kabaka*'s *lubiri* with tanks, exiling Muteesa and banning all kingdoms. The desecration of their kingdom by foreigners paralyzed the Ganda for decades.

As Buganda faded and Uganda started to take root, it became clear that education was paramount in the new nation. Attitudes toward the schooling of children among commoners started to change to the point where educating children was the same as putting money away into a pension fund. By the late 50s, fathers close to European civilization realized that an educated daughter made for a better pension fund than an educated son. Apparently, sons, after sucking their parents dry, fled the family nest without a backward glance. Ssemata and Ziraba tried to educate their children. However, term after term, their sons brought home uninspiring grades. One day, after looking at his brood's school reports Ssemata said, "Only my girl takes after my sharpness, the boys opted for their maternal dimness."

Ssemata's sons, having been vexed by study, asked if every successful man in the world was educated. When the answer came back negative, they dropped out of school. Besides, education took too long to yield results. They could start trading slowly-slowly. Ssemata laughed, "I've put food on your plates but you couldn't pick it up to eat: what makes you think that you will hunt, cook, and feed yourselves?"

"Nonetheless, it still rains in the desert." Ziraba, accused of being the source of the boys' dimness, now defended them.

And so the boys prowled Kampala streets looking for opportunity and luck while Nnamata sailed through the classes. At fifteen—they started primary school at nine in those days—she was in her final year of primary school. Ssemata planned to sell some of his land in the village so he could send her to a Catholic boarding secondary school for girls. There, she would be safe from the potential landmines of puberty. He was not a demanding father: Nnamata was only a girl. If she could become a nurse, a teacher, or even a secretary and catch a rich husband he would be content. Educated men now wanted their wives neither "raw," without education, nor "well done," with too much schooling.

But before Nnamata got to the nuns' boarding school, puberty set in and upset Ssemata's plans. She rounded out into a body made for pleasure. Her skin smoothened and shone. Her rear was generous and provocative. When she walked, it rose in such sharp challenge and then dropped in scornful regret. Men, convinced that she shook it on purpose, twitched their legs as she walked past and swore under their breaths, "If I ever get my hands on her . . ."

Katanga was not the place for a young girl to possess that kind of body if she wanted to put nature on hold. Some men still thought that to keep a girl in school past the age of fifteen was an act against nature.

Ssemata watched this dialogue between Nnamata's body and the men with a sharp eye. First, he put her in long shapeless skirts, then under curfew. He made it known all over Katanga that he kept a sharp machete at the ready by filing it publicly every evening. Once, he chased a lad wearing just his briefs. The lad, thinking that Nnamata was bathing in the communal bathroom, had put his case to her in poetry. Ssemata had listened in silence. When he could no longer take it he had whispered, "Wait there, I am coming." He barely managed to get into his briefs and pick up the machete. He chased the lad down Katanga's muddy corridors swearing, "I'll kill someone if you don't leave my girl alone."

As clever as she was Nnamata was not strong in mathematics. Mr. Puti Kintu, the math teacher at Bat Valley Primary School, offered to give her free private tuition.

"Nnamata is our star student this year," he had told Ssemata on parents' day. "But math is a problem. I am ready to sacrifice an hour every day after school if she can stay behind."

Ssemata bowed and bowed in gratitude, forgetting that teachers were not shepherds, that even if they were, once in a while shepherds had been known to eat the lambs in their care. To Nnamata, Mr. Kintu was a teacher, a grown-up, and he was helping her. So when he pushed her against the wall breathing, *hmm, you girls always say no. Yet you shake your buttocks like that?* Respect, gratitude, and fear paralyzed her. Afterwards, the math lessons continued and Nnamata kept quiet. Normally, silence washed things like that away, but this time it watered it and the deed grew. It was not long before Katanga was laughing, and, like everyone else in Katanga, her father did not buy Nnamata's story of rape. *If he raped you, why didn't you tell us?*

At first, in private negotiations, Ssemata said to Mr. Kintu, the math teacher, "I am a fellow man: I come to you with understanding." But Mr. Kintu thought it was ridiculous that he should be asked to pay a father and marry a girl who had not completed her primary education. He would look after his child, no doubt about that, but there was no way he was marrying a slum girl. Mr. Kintu did not realize that the issue had nothing to do with defiling a minor. Rather, it was about theft from a pension fund. Had Mr. Kintu paid the money to the wronged father and married his daughter, Ssemata would have congratulated Nnamata for pulling a teacher so easily. When he did not, Ssemata, at last, believed that Nnamata was forced. By 1961, when Isaac was born, Mr. Kintu was serving time in Luzira Maximum Prison. Contemplating his children after the tragedy unfolded, Ssemata spat, "Such wasted sex. I should have slept instead!"

The English saying that a man shouldn't place all his eggs in the same basket suddenly made sense. A few months later, Ssemata left Ziraba to find another basket in which to place his eggs.

Ziraba had another daughter, Tendo. The pregnancy took her by surprise. When she asked the friend who had taken her to the healer what happened, it was put to her that sometimes a determined child can hoodwink even the strongest medicine.

Nnamata, whose last lesson in school was on the law of gravity, named her child Isaac Newton. Because her math teacher was Mr. Kintu, she baptized him Isaac Newton Kintu. In the name Isaac Newton lay all Nnamata's vanished dreams. But Isaac Newton was an ugly baby. Even Nnamata agreed with her brothers, "Yes, mine's the ugliest child the sun has ever shone on." For a while, assured by her mother that all newborns are hideous, she waited for Isaac to transform. Six months after his birth, when Isaac Newton failed to turn into a cute baby, when Nnamata could not find anything on the little body to anchor her love, she ran away into the night.

4.

Isaac was eight when Ziraba first saw him talking to someone invisible. He stood under the avocado tree next to their house. He waved a long stick angrily. Ziraba looked about but there was no one. She let it pass. Isaac was too young to have run mad. In any case, for once, he seemed passionate about something. There was nothing threatening about a child who talked to the wind. Even then, every time she saw him talking to himself, Ziraba looked about.

Then, one day, she heard Isaac arguing to the point of crying. No one had ever aroused such emotion in him. Ziraba came out to see. Isaac was pointing a finger at someone close by. Whoever it was, was taller than him because Isaac was looking up.

"You can go back wherever you came from, if you don't want to play by the rules . . . I don't care! Go away. I didn't call you . . . Hmm hmm, not my fault . . . Not my problem, leave me alone!"

Ziraba ran out of the house, whisked Isaac off the ground, and ran back inside. After a while, she peered out of the window and listened. Nothing happened—nobody came, no sound but the wind. She turned to Isaac.

"Who was that?"

"Where?"

"Who were you talking to?"

"Where?"

"Just now, there, outside."

"I haven't been talking to anyone."

Now his grandmother's fear frightened him.

"You were arguing."

"Oh, that one," Isaac wiggled out of her grip. "He's my friend."

"Who is he?"

"I don't know," Isaac shrugged.

"Where does he come from?"

"I don't know. From around I think."

"Do you know his name?"

Isaac shrugged again.

"When did he start coming?"

"He's always been there."

"Since when?"

"Always."

"Where's he now?"

"Where is he now?" Isaac looked at his grandmother with exasperation. "I don't know. He's gone, I shouted at him."

From that day on, Ziraba watched Isaac closely. She must have whispered to her friends for they watched him as well. He heard the women saying, "Why don't you find his roots? Take him to meet his people. Some clans have all sorts."

"Especially undeclared children: blood cries out for its own."

"It's the burying of the dead close to the house that encourages them to return and haunt you," Ziraba answered cryptically. "I've no money to find his clan."

It was his friend's coaxing that made Isaac leave his cozy corner in the house to go outside and play. The first time Ziraba saw him outside, she gasped, "Oh, my kapere is done now," as if Isaac had been indulging in a particularly long sulk.

"Yes," Isaac had said, holding onto a wall unsteadily.

"Then I suggest you spare the neighborhood your nudity."

Isaac started walking and talking on the same day. But Ziraba had no time for indulgent notions of trauma. She only remarked to her friends, "Nnamata's child is finally ready to face the world." And that was that.

Ziraba had begun to doubt her fears about Isaac's "friend" when one day she heard him giggling and whooping with laughter. There was no one else in the house to laugh with. Tendo was married—that is, she had fallen pregnant and moved into the guilty man's room. The boys had long scattered. Besides, no human could elicit such merry laughter from Isaac. Ziraba went to see. The hair moved off her head.

There, on the floor of the lounge, was Isaac playing with an enormous snake. It wound itself around his waist as he crouched on the floor laughing merrily. Then he raised his torso off the floor and balanced on his toes and hands. The snake caressed him with its coils, around his stomach and down his chest until it was in his face. Isaac stuck his tongue out at it and once again collapsed into laughter as it copied him.

That was when Ziraba remembered to scream.

"What is it?" Katanga called.

"A snake is killing my child."

Katanga was so close-knit that neighbors could hear each other farting. Everyone cared. As one of the men tried to get into the house, the snake balanced on its coils and widened its neck. It charged toward the steps and the men scattered. Isaac, now catching their terror, screamed too. Ziraba shouted in the window, "Don't move, Isaac! Stay still," but Isaac shrieked and shrunk into a corner.

When the men scattered, the snake pulled back its neck, sank to the ground, and turned to Isaac. The men regrouped and came back with more courage. This time, the snake coiled itself once and launched into the air. The men fled. The snake glided back to the house but turned, slithered along the wall, past the latrine and disappeared into the swamp.

The neighbors advised Ziraba to sprinkle her rooms with kerosene and to kill the rats because that was what brought snakes. But she was suspicious.

"Was that your friend, Isaac?" she asked.

"I thought he was but—"

"But what?"

"It was a snake, wasn't it?"

"Was that the first time it visited you?"

"No. Sometimes he sleeps in my bed."

"Don't worry, Ziraba," a neighbor said. "In nature, snakes don't harm children, especially ones that live in a house."

"It'll try to come back. Make sure you get a mason to cover all the holes and cracks in the wall, floor, and roof," another advised.

"Don't worry, snakes are like that. You can live with them for years and years without knowing. Once they get your sleeping pattern, they slither in and out unnoticed."

"Oh, I don't know. Could be family things, you know. Has the boy been taken home yet?"

"That's why we don't kill house snakes—you never know."

"That boy has a strong taboo on his head. I'd be careful if I were you, Ziraba. He sat silent for seven years, then suddenly he walked and talked in one day?"

"No wonder it fought gallantly."

As each resident shared their snake stories, Ziraba relaxed. That night, she sprinkled the house with kerosene and the following day a man filled in the holes in the wall. She planned to go to Luzira Maximum Prison to talk to Mr. Kintu the math teacher but she never got around to it.

That day, Isaac was not given the chance to tell them that they had got it wrong. His friend did not come as a snake only: sometimes he was a lizard, a bird—all forms. When he came, Isaac knew it was him. Once he was crying when a leaf floated through the window and fell on his hand. It was not an avocado leaf yet there were no other trees around. Isaac had stopped crying at once. Even though he had navigated childhood without the intimate touch of love—no one ever tickled him or rubbed their cheeks against his or blew into his tummy to make him laugh, he never fell asleep with his head cradled between a loving neck and shoulder—he instantly knew the love of his friend.

The following year, at ten years old, Isaac started primary school.

5.

Isaac reversed out of the packing yard of MTN headquarters. Because he was the on-call engineer for mast repairs in western Uganda that week, he drove a double-cabin Hilux truck. He did not know why or when he had changed his mind, but he and his son Kizza were on their way to the Joint Research Centre to take the blood tests.

Isaac was back at work. To him, the phrase "life goes on" after the death of a loved one meant that time drags you along. Kizza was in the back seat. Though he had wiped his mother's forehead ritually to say goodbye, and had watched her coffin lowered into the grave, he seemed unscathed by her passing. He had only asked once when they would pick her up from the grave, and when Isaac explained that they would not, Kizza had kept quiet. Isaac hoped that as Nnayiga had been ill for over a year and had been unable to look after him, Kizza had detached himself.

They came to the top of John Hanning Speke Road near the top of Nakasero Hill. It was an affluent area with plush hotels, expensive cars, few pedestrians, and hideous Marabou storks. When Isaac turned into Speke Road, he realized something was wrong with the birds. Some had perched on the walls of Standard Chartered Bank, their gular sacs hanging down their necks like long scrotums. Others strutted Speke Road pavements like they paid tax. As he came down toward the General Post Office, he saw why. Urchins, looking like black vultures themselves, were up the trees pulling down the birds' nests. Others were on the ground hurling stones, cans, and obscenities at the storks. Pedestrians kept close to buildings, watching nervously. A fight between street kids and the storks was a family affair: it was volatile and you didn't interfere. Probably, Isaac surmised, an urchin had died in the gutters and the storks had found him first.

It was two weeks after Nnayiga's burial that Kaaya, a friend who checked on Isaac every evening, broached the question of blood tests. Apart from the sappy smell of the coffin timber that still lingered in the sitting room, the house was back to its old self. Kaaya chose the moment when Isaac's mother was present, to enlist her support.

"This time, Isaac, we're doing things right. We need you to take a blood test so we can start treatment."

There was a moment of silence as irritation crossed Isaac's face. His mother looked down at the floor.

"What's the use of a blood test?" he finally asked. "What didn't you see?"

"There was no post-mortem—"

"Have you just arrived from New York? Post-mortem indeed!"

"And there was no comprehensive diagnosis apart from the unexplained kidney failure." Kaaya carried on despite Isaac's sarcasm.

"Yes," Isaac's mother now picked up the thread, "the vast majority of us decide we have 'it' because a partner died." Kaaya shook his head sadly. "That is Africa. People who've never seen the inside of a lab make diagnoses: *She has it because we saw her with so-and-so who is dead.* And what is incredible is that these diagnoses are never wrong because if a person does not exhibit any symptoms they're either on a fattening diet or are labeled a 'carrier' of the virus who gives it to partners but never suffers from it."

"But most people pointed at end up dying nonetheless," Isaac said.

"Dying of what? Probably some die of the anxiety that comes with being 'diagnosed.'"

"It's as if before this thing came there was no death," Isaac's mother said evenly.

"All I am asking, Isaac, is for you to take a blood test. No one doubts that it is what you think, but it helps to have ink on paper."

"Tell him, Kaaya," Isaac's mother said. "Maybe he'll listen to you. I ask myself, if an educated person like Isaac can hold backward views like that, what chance do we illiterates have?"

"It's now possible to live another fifteen to twenty years just by changing your lifestyle and starting treatment early. In the past, we used to see this disease walking up and down the streets, now you can't tell any more. Give your child and yourself a chance."

"Can't I start treatment without a checkup?"

"Start what treatment for what condition?"

"I tell you, my Isaac can be rawer than a peasant."

"To get treatment you need to present the results of a blood test. Even then, not everyone receives the same treatment. It depends on the strain of the virus and how far gone your condition is."

"Don't talk to me like I've no common sense, Kaaya. It's not that I don't understand diagnosis and medication. I've told you before: I don't want to know. I don't expect you to understand but I don't want this certainty that you want. In my mind, I am certain that I have it, but in my mind I am also certain that I don't. Don't take my doubt away."

For a moment, it seemed that Isaac was about to cry.

"Isaac," Kaaya started softly. "We understand that certainty will kill all hope for you. But it'll kill false hope. Even if you have hope today, who knows what you'll suffer tomorrow? Doubt might give you a week of hope in a month, a month out of six, but think about it. Is that a way to live?"

"Tell me why I would get out of bed to go to work if I knew that my boy was dying?"

"You'll be given sufficient counselling before and after the test. Some of the people offering counselling have got it themselves. They'll show you how to live with it."

There was silence for a moment. Then Isaac said softly, "I could come for the tests to get you off my back, but I cannot bring Kizza."

"That's a start and brave of you but the test will be of limited use. Hear me out, Isaac. It's possible that you have it but not him and equally possible that Kizza has it but not you."

"Have you ever wished your own child dead, Kaaya?" When his friend stared blankly, Isaac continued. "Well, every day I pray that Kizza dies before I do because there's no one in this world I can leave him with. The idea of leaving him in this horrible, horrible world is cruel."

There was silence. Kaaya pretended not to see the tears running down Isaac's mother's face. She plucked straws off the mat she sat on.

"All right, Isaac. As long as there's a plan, I'll leave you alone."

At that point, Isaac's mother stood up and left the room. Kaaya turned to Isaac. "Just because you think you're dying does not give you the right to treat your mother cruelly."

"It's the truth. I don't want to leave my boy with anyone."

"But don't say it in her face. Not when she's in your house trying her best."

"I'll come for the blood test, Kaaya. But I'll not bring Kizza. That's the best I can do."

Later that evening, Kaaya was joined by the rest of Isaac's friends from MTN who, since Nnayiga's death, brought their beer and roast goat to Isaac's place instead of going out.

• • •

Isaac turned off the engine, stepped out of the truck and helped his son down. The *kabaka*'s palace stood above the Joint Research Centre. Looking up, Isaac could only see part of the palace complex. The gleaming copper dome that crested the palace tower seemed to be floundering against the empty skyline. The sprawling grounds that rolled down the hill were overgrown in parts. He wondered whether the *kabaka* ever lived there at all or whether he lived in his smaller residencies. He held Kizza's hand and led him toward the entrance of the research center.

6.

At school, Isaac discovered two things. One—that studies were so easy, especially mathematics, that he did not understand why anyone struggled. Two—that he was ugly. The latter explained why no one loved him. The six-year-old girls in his class recoiled from him to such an extent that he wondered whether they had a different humanity. The first girl he sat next to in class broke down in tears. When asked why, the creature replied, "They're laughing at me. That I am his wife," she pointed at Isaac.

"But you're not Isaac's wife."

"He's old and has such small red eyes and—"

At which the rest of the class burst out laughing and the crying girl reluctantly joined them. It was the practice in lower primary to make a girl and a boy share a desk as, at that age, they could not stand each other: it kept the class quiet. The following term, when Isaac was moved to another place, the girl he was made to sit with this time sat at the edge of the bench and sulked for the rest of the term. But as boys did not flinch from him, Isaac grew wary of girls. He had heard men in Katanga say things like, "I must have met a woman first thing this morning: my effort was barren all day," or "Women are a curse." Now he understood why.

In 1978, at the age of seventeen, Isaac sat his PLE, primary school leaving exams. He was the mathematics genius in the school. But when the results came out, his math grade was missing. He got 85 percent in English and 87 percent in the General Paper but without a Math grade, he could not proceed to secondary school. His teachers tried to track down his marks, but Nakivubo Primary, a slum school, was too insignificant to warrant effort from UNEB officials. Isaac resolved to sit the exams again the following year but by then, the Tanzanians were fed up with Amin's antics and were on their way.

The wonderful thing about being Katangese, as Katanga residents were called, was that Amin's brutality flew above their heads and toward the hills, especially Nakasero and Kololo where the elite resided. Sure, the army were deadly when they got drunk and many times they did not pay for their drink, but Katangese knew not to insist.

Amin had turned the tables against the intellectuals. Makerere University had become the haunt of failures. Intellectuals stood out. A mournful and persecuted demeanor, a battered leather bag full of paper and worn-away soles of shoes were the classic signs of an intellectual. They tended to be alcoholic. The term "professor" was synonymous with a lack of common sense. Isaac heard Katangese poke fun at lecturers as they asked for crude Waragi on credit. The plush hotels in Nakasero were now haunted by army generals and the Mafta mingi businessmen. Graduates worked in markets and denied their stint at the "Hill of Knowledge" to avoid ridicule. People in Katanga said, "Amin has no problems with us. It's them the 'I-Knows' who are trouble." Yet, despite these discouraging echoes, Isaac put his faith in education. Ziraba insisted, "Certificates don't rot: they only collect dust. Amin will go."

For some time, war anxiety did not bother Isaac: his grandmother did the worrying. Yes, there were fresh bodies in the streets every morning, but all Isaac had to do was cross the road. Yes, there were nights when he heard angry noises and pleading cries but in the morning they would discover that it was none of the slum-dwellers. The bodies, dumped in the yam fields or gutters of Katanga, tended to come from Kololo or Nakasero. To Isaac, Ugandans were like ants. You swept away the ones that were killed the day before and still others came out the following day. As he was yet to find the corpse of a child on the roadside, Isaac had no fear. He wore his school uniform everywhere.

When the war arrived, the Katangese stopped laughing. Isaac had seen young men from Katanga and poorer backgrounds rush to join Amin's army because of the power and quick wealth it brought. But as death became imminent, the army grew angry. Soldiers asked why they should die for the rest of them and made everyone feel their pain. When Isaac saw trucks carrying stony-eyed soldiers to the frontline, he understood their brutality.

It rained continuously during the war. Vegetation all over Kampala thrived on a combination of abundant rain, decomposing bodies, and the absence of humans. Marabou storks migrated to Nakasero Hill while the bats in Bat Valley went into exile. Only funereal songs played on the radio. Continual announcements said that the enemy had been repulsed, but people whispered that the BBC said otherwise. Tanzanian anger cracked the skies at night relentlessly. Rockets, just before they exploded, squealed like a giant cat whose tail had been trodden on. Now Isaac was frightened. Rockets exploded in the back of his house, but in the morning people said it was up in Kololo Summit View. Now, guns and army uniforms that the army fleeing had discarded lay strewn on roadsides.

One night, the rockets exploded without pause into the following day. At around four in the afternoon, as Isaac opened the door to sneak to the toilet, a huge German Shepherd crashed into him and went straight into the inner room. Isaac shut the door. The dog curled in the furthest corner under Ziraba's bed. *"Gettaut, get-taut,"* Ziraba shouted in English but the dog would not budge. It whined silently and quivered. Its eyes were all black, its coat thick and glossy. Isaac could not help laughing, "What were you think-ing you rich bastards—that your day would not come?"

Ziraba was beside herself with anger. "How can anyone keep

a dog that eats more than two humans do a day?" The following day, worried that it would foul the room, Ziraba moved her bed and hit the wall so hard that the dog bolted.

"Fahkin you," she spat in English. "Go die your own death, rich dog. We'll die our own." As Ziraba shut the door she remembered that being nasty to dogs brings bad luck and said, "I'm sorry! Poor creature, either the owners have been killed or they didn't buy an air ticket for it."

Isaac's phobia of hair cut off the head started on the first day he stepped out of the house after Kampala fell. A neighbor called at their door, "Ziraba *wuuwu:* are you still alive?" When Ziraba called back that she was, the woman rebuked, "The world is out here getting rich and you're locked in the house?"

When Isaac opened the door, Ntulo, their neighbor, whizzed past carrying a sack of shoes, all similar. She did not take a breath when she dropped it in her house but ran out immediately.

"Are you waiting for church bells?" she asked as she ran past the dazed Isaac and Ziraba. "Come on, come with me, I'll show you. These people up in Nakasero lived like kings, wait and see! Yesterday was theirs: today is ours."

At the turn into Kyadondo Road, the path on the roadside was so overgrown that people kept on the tarred road. But Isaac had walked this path often. As he turned the corner, he saw a skeleton. Its clothes lay flat on the ground as if the body had melted. There was no smell. Yet the hair, black and thick, was intact. It had moved a few inches away from the skull as if shaved. Isaac was so shaken by the non-putrefaction of the hair that he failed to pull away his eyes. He was used to corpses: fresh ones, swollen ones, even those that had burst open, but this hair washed off the skull was hard to take.

That day, as he carried the looted items home, the image of the hair haunted him. Two days later, outside the Fairway Hotel, Isaac came across another skeleton. (Isaac was lucky at Fairway

Hotel. He was right there when the liberators broke into it. He got blankets, sheets, and towels.) He could tell from the clothes that it was the skeleton of a female. The cranium was bleached white. A few inches away was thick hair plaited together in mounds. It remained there unchanged, as though its owner had not died. Isaac crossed the road and retched until he felt as if his innards were coming up as well. From then on, he kept away from bushes. Whenever he saw a barber's shop ahead, he crossed the road lest he look in and see hair on the floor. Isaac kept his own head bald.

In search of Amin's remnant army, the liberators seemed to hate the rich as much as the looters did. They broke into shops and houses and let the hungry loot. The soldiers would have their pick first, normally of small things—watches and jewelry. When looters came to a rich home that was unoccupied, the absence of the owner signified guilt. The people would shout, "Amin's man!"

"*Wattu wa Amin?*"

"Yaa," and the doors would fall away. Looters, like termites, would strip the house of anything movable. In no time, Ziraba's room was filled with an assortment of things—a sack of shoes from Bata, which Isaac later discovered were all for the right foot and could not be sold, a kettle, an iron, a hotplate, car and bicycle tires. There were a few other gadgets he didn't know—when the doors of depravity fell away, there was no time to ask: *What's this? What does it do?* Instead, he took home whatever he got his hands on and later someone who had worked as a domestic in rich homes would explain, "That is a toaster: it roasts bread . . . yes the same usual bread . . . No, they don't cook it again. It makes it crispy . . . yeah, too much money."

Two days later, as Ziraba wandered the Industrial Area looking for opportunities, she came across a crowd hanging about the Tanzanian liberators expectantly. They were about to break into a warehouse. When the doors opened, there was sugar—the real white sweet stuff. Ziraba, who had not seen sugar in three years, grabbed a 20 kg sack, dragged it to the side and sat on it. When the warehouse had been stripped empty she asked a man to help her put it on her head. The man shook his head and said, "My old one, you won't manage. If you agree to share half-half, I'll carry it for you."

"Do I look stupid? What if you walk away?"

The man lifted the sack and put it on Ziraba's sixty-year-old head. Ziraba made it across the rail lines, Jinja Road, De Winton Road up the roundabout below Shimon Road. She even made it to the island in the middle of Shimon Road, hoping to get to Kitante Road, when she felt tired. But as she made to throw the sack down, she collapsed under it. Someone relieved her body of the sugar, saw that she was dead and said, "Every dog has its day: today is hers, mine is coming," and made off with the sugar.

At home, Isaac waited. Then he searched the city. He worried that his grandmother had been killed by a stray bullet. Many people who had made it through the war became careless and lost their lives during the looting. The fleeing army had strewn the city with bombs disguised as tiny radios, torches, balls, clocks, and toys. Often, looters, mainly children, picked them up and they exploded. Nonetheless, when Isaac cooked, he made food for two. For a month, he searched hospitals in vain. Neighbors came by to check on him but without a corpse they sucked their teeth, shook their heads, and walked away. That was all the mourning Ziraba got for her stint in the world.

Finally, Isaac accepted that his grandmother was not coming home and climbed onto her bed. He had a cooker, a fridge, a TV, an electric iron, a dryer, and electric kettle. Even though there was no chance of electricity straying into his house, the sight of the gadgets made him feel rich.

Even after all that bloodletting, neither peace nor prosperity came to Uganda because as people believed, the expelled Asians had cursed the country. The liberators fell out with each other and there were coups and counter-coups. Tendo slunk back home with two young children in tow. Isaac reverted to his mute days. He could not even look at them. Tendo and her little ones ate right through everything he had looted, and soon the house was back to its pre-liberation emptiness.

Isaac got a job. He worked in Port Bell as a laborer on a fishing boat. He worked in the night and slept between four o'clock after school and eight o'clock. Tendo and her children lived off Isaac's fish. He did not begrudge them the food: it was given to him every morning along with his pay. Tendo justified her presence by keeping the house clean and cooking the meals. But Isaac could not open his mouth to speak to her. She seemed to understand, for there was a perpetual look of mortification on her face.

It was not until 1980 that Isaac was able to re-sit his exams. UNEB, the Uganda National Examination Board, demanded that he re-sit all three subjects. The earlier results, however good, were now void. At nineteen, Isaac had to wear a short-sleeved shirt and a pair of khaki shorts even though his arms and legs were over-grown with wild hairs. The other pupils stared and whispered, "Grandpa." This time, the results in all three subjects returned but the excitement had gone. Isaac was invited to the top two schools in the country but as he could not afford a top school's fees, he sold copies of his results to rich kids and started at Kololo High.

Life was bearable until his employer bought a larger boat and turned from fishing to transporting people. As if that was not bad enough, Isaac's mother Nnamata returned. She had a litter of five children and they stank of poverty. Isaac looked at her once and looked away. "You've turned out well, Isaac," he heard her whisper but he did not look back. Luckily, Tendo and Nnamata didn't get on. His mother found a stall in the market and moved out as soon as she was able.

7.

Isaac got his first break during his O-level vacation. Sasa, a deejay who owned a mobile disco, took him on for lifting and handling. But Sasa had a restless tongue, especially after he had been drinking, which was most of the time. Isaac soon found out that deejaying was a trade that attracted transient, laid-back, but arrogant people. Sasa's assistant deejays came and went so fast that he became suspicious of Isaac's loyalty. After rowing with an assistant, Sasa would ask Isaac, "How come you're not leaving with them? You must be robbing me somewhere I don't see."

But Isaac would just shake his head and carry on with his work. In time, Sasa came to rely on him. He started to apologize after a shouting bout. "Don't listen to me, Isaac, it's the drink talking." Gradually, as deejay after deejay abandoned him, usually just before a performance, Sasa asked Isaac to help. He became familiar with turntables and vinyl. He learned beatmatching, phrasing, and slip-cueing.

When it was announced on the radio that the O-level results were out, Sasa insisted on going to Kololo High with Isaac to pick up his results. When he looked at the slip and saw eight distinctions, Sasa cried. Isaac, being cried over for the first time, melted too. That day, Sasa took Isaac to the Speke Hotel for a meal. Then he invited Isaac to come and live with him. A month later, Sasa came home with a second-hand three-piece, pin-striped suit, a bowler hat, and a walking stick. When he tried the suit and the hat on, he looked like a broke black gangster from an American film. The following day, Sasa walked in front of Isaac like a no-nonsense father all the way to Makerere College School.

When their turn came to see the headmaster, Sasa walked in and slapped the results slip on the headmaster's desk. "There," he said as he pushed the slip in front of the headmaster. "My name is *Mr.* Sasa Kintu, my son Isaac Newton has achieved the best results you'll see in a long time. We selected your school as our third choice. Kings College, his first choice, wants him. Namilyango, his second, wants him. But we have chosen to come to you. Ask me why."

Isaac expected the headmaster to tell them to leave his office but instead he clasped his hands and asked, "Why, Mr. Kintu?"

"Because I am a single father. My wife died when Isaac was born. I have this one only child," Sasa waved his forefinger. "A single matchstick—you light it wrong, ooopi! You're plunged into eternal darkness. Do you get me, Mr. Headmaster?"

"I understand."

"I've brought him up on my own and in spite of this old suit, I am poor and don't want him to go away because he runs the family business. I understand you have a non-boarding section in your school."

"Yes, Mr. Kintu. We, unlike other so-called First World schools, are not entirely boarding."

"So, what can you do for my son?"

"Isaac has a place with us as a non-boarder."

"Is that all?" Sasa threw his arms in the air in disbelief.

The headmaster looked at Sasa, bewildered. Isaac squirmed. He had not discussed anything of this with Sasa prior to coming. Isaac had imagined that Sasa was only escorting him. Sasa clarified their position.

"You mean you have no schemes or bursaries for such poor high-fliers like my son?"

"Oh, I get you, I get you, Mr. Kintu. Leave it with me. I'll get in touch within a week or two. Meanwhile, don't look elsewhere."

Sasa turned to Isaac and growled, "You see this kind gentleman? You see the chance he has given us?"

Isaac nodded.

"I suggest you come to his school. Join the rich boys and make trouble, I swear upon your mother's grave I'll take you to the school assembly and caress your backside with this stick like I've never—" Sasa turned to the headmaster and said, "He won't be trouble," and shook his hand. Leaning heavily on his walking stick, Sasa snapped at Isaac. "Let's go, lad." They walked in character all the way home until they got into the house and collapsed into laughter.

Their relationship did not, however, improve entirely. Oftentimes, Sasa threatened to throw Isaac out. But Isaac never talked back. If it hurt, he never showed it. Later, Sasa would say, "That's why I love my man Isaac: he knows me. When I rage he keeps quiet, saying to himself, *Sasa doesn't mean a word he says.*"

Isaac's eyes were so set on Makerere University that Sasa's rants were nothing. Besides, his own family had been worse. So what if Sasa, a stranger, screamed? He knew that Sasa asked him to move in with him so he would not leave him, but it suited Isaac. He had not only walked out on Tendo and her children, but he paid no rent and did not buy food. In any case, Isaac suspected that he loved Sasa no matter how flawed their relationship. Apart from his grandmother, no one had ever shown him this level of care.

Isaac received his admission letter to Makerere College School and started his A-levels. At school, he was shy, unable to look a girl in the eyes. He worked hard at his studies especially on those nights when they did not have a gig. Thankfully, sex was one of the fringe benefits of deejaying. After years of being shunned and called ugly, followed by shame and disgust at his soggy, sticky dreams, Isaac had stopped trying to figure out girls. They frightened him, yet the way his body wanted them alarmed him. For a long time, he relied on his imagination. However, disco music, a darkened room with dancing lights, large headphones across his head, him hiccupping in the mic, and his phenomenal dancing, kept a steady supply of sex. But it was sex in shadows against walls with dark figures who were, more often than not, drunk.

One weekend, Sasa had such a bad headache that he could not bear to be anywhere near music. Isaac hired an assistant and a pickup truck to transport the equipment. For the two nights, Friday and Saturday, while the helper played his selection, Isaac manned the door and took the collection. On Sunday, when he showed Sasa the take, Sasa was not interested. On Monday, when Isaac came home from school, Sasa was so weak he could not walk to the road. Isaac hired a taxi and took him to Mulago Hospital where he was admitted. On Wednesday, the doctor explained that Sasa had a rare strain of meningitis and asked if Sasa had ever taken an HIV test. Isaac had no clue. Was Sasa sexually active? Isaac had never seen him with a woman but he could not be sure. How old was he? Isaac did not know. Should we carry out a blood test? Isaac said if necessary. That week, Isaac tried not to think about the fact that he did not really know Sasa at all. He went straight to hospital after school to nurse him. When he asked Sasa about his family, he replied by crying for his mother. Sometimes, when he was delirious, Sasa cried in a language Isaac did not understand. Hearing a grown man crying for his mother was heartrending. Isaac would go home and cry too because this man with a skin darker than night, with tribal scars on his cheeks and a gap between his front teeth, wanted his mother.

The following weekend, Sasa was unresponsive. Even though he was sedated, Isaac explained to him that he had to go to work to pay the hospital bills. On his way to perform on Saturday evening, he visited to bring juice, but by then Sasa had lapsed into a coma. The HIV results were not back yet. When he returned at midday on Sunday, Sasa's bed was occupied by another patient.

Relatives of other patients said, "You're late, lad! Your father left early this morning."

Isaac was too frightened to cry. He had not anticipated Sasa dying. What was Sasa's real name? Sasa is a Swahili word for "now." What was his tribe? He suspected, because of the way he twisted words and the scarification, that Sasa was either Kakwa, Amin's tribe, or Nubian. It now occurred to Isaac that Sasa could have been one of Amin's people who fell from grace after the war. It explained the name, the fact that no one had ever visited Sasa in the two years Isaac had known him and why he never talked about his past.

Isaac slunk from the hospital like a thief because he did not intend to pay the bill. There was something fraudulent about paying a huge medical bill only to take home a corpse. In any case, where would he take Sasa's body? Isaac went home and packed his bags, ready to run in case Sasa's kin turned up.

He mourned quietly. For a week, he sat outside their two-roomed apartment and stared at people and cars and clouds going past. The silence in the house was oppressive. Sasa's nicotine smell was thinning but his clothes, hanging on the wall, were difficult to ignore. For the first time, Isaac looked at the trees around the house. There were long nandi flames on the roadside but close to the house was a eucalyptus shrub. They were indifferent to his plight. Their leaves shook at the slightest breath of wind as if Sasa, who had lived so close to them, had not died. Isaac wondered where his grandmother was buried. He cried alone in bed because he had told no one about it. Then he went back to school. If Sasa was watching somewhere, he knew that Isaac had mourned him like a son. But Sasa would also know that he owed him. It was only fair that he made as much money as possible before the scavenging relatives turned up.

A month later, not a single inquiry had been made about Sasa. By the end of two months, Isaac had made so much money he did not know what to do with it. He opened a grocery shop in the market where his mother worked and asked her to operate it. The money was to help with her children's school fees but he would be keeping an eye on it. Then he opened an account in a bank and deposited the rest of the money.

During his A-level exams, Isaac put away the music and concentrated on his studies. He had no doubt that Sasa's relatives would come one day. If they did, there was money in the bank and he still had the whole set of equipment to give them. When he thought about the things other people would have done with Sasa's money, Isaac was not sure whether to marvel at his own goodness or to cringe at his stupidity.

After the exams, Isaac took the ageing decks and speakers, sold them off one by one and replaced them with new ones. He changed the name of the disco from Sasasounds to Isaac New Sounds. He moved out of the house in Kavule to Banda. He turned up regularly at the grocery shop to balance the books, stock-take, and help with wholesale purchases. But he did all this silently. Afterwards, he would tell his mother how much money she could put to her children's school fees without hurting the shop. Then he would leave, despite his mother asking him to stay and eat with them, despite his siblings' gratitude for his kindness—Isaac remained uncommunicative.

8.

Isaac met Nnayiga the same year he finished his course at university. It was February 1990. In September 1986, he arrived at Makerere University to read Electrical Engineering. His disco business had expanded so well that he bought a pickup truck. He now had two sets of equipment. The largest and newest he hired to a nightclub, the older set he hired out to prepaid gigs. He still turned up at the gigs and made record selections but he did not deejay anymore.

When he arrived at Makerere, despite the sense of achievement, Isaac felt detached from the euphoric freshers. At twenty-five, he had nothing in common with the nineteen-year-olds. The kind of girls who cried when he sat next to them in primary school, who watched TV while he wrestled with fishing nets, who made their demands to doting parents with tantrums and sulks while he fed an aunt and nephews, now seemed blind to his ugly self because he was well off. Yet Isaac knew he had not changed physically: his eyes were still small and red, the skin on his face was gravel and he had knock-knees.

At first, he tried to enjoy this new acceptance but he soon discovered that the delicate girls were not to his taste at all. They were too keen sexually. It was like being with a fellow man. Their desire made him feel like he was the woman. In the end, he ran back to the darkened discothèques and grabbed some insecure girl whom he never looked in the eye, whose body he never saw, whom he gave money to appease his inner demons.

Isaac met Nnayiga in a discothèque. Sitting alone, sipping a Fanta orange, Nnayiga looked shy and vulnerable. She carried a school bag and had that lost and raw look of a girl just arrived from a backyard village.

Isaac asked her to dance. Three records later, he went to the bar and bought her a beer. Nnayiga refused it.

"I am not sure I should drink that."

Isaac's eyes lit up. "You don't drink?" Nnayiga shook her head. "Try."

She took a sip and wrinkled her nose. "It's horrible," and pushed the beer toward him.

"Never mind, I'll get you wine."

He brought her some red wine and assured her it was sweet. When she tasted it, Nnayiga frowned.

"Don't you like it?"

"It leaves a burning sensation down the throat." She cleared her throat. "But it's sweet. I'll try it."

After two glasses and more dancing, when she started to laugh less self-consciously, Isaac said, "I am going now. Would you like me to drop you home?"

"Oh, can you?"

"You live in Kamwokya?"

But rather than taking Luggogo bypass to go to Kamwokya, Isaac carried on toward Nakawa. Nnayiga's childish voice vanished.

"Where're you taking me?"

Isaac kept quiet: he hated girls who pretended not to understand what was going on.

"Where are you taking me?" she repeated. "I am going to pick something up from my house," Isaac played along.

Nnayiga smiled, "For a moment, I was afraid you wanted to kidnap me."

Isaac stole a glance at her. Was she really that green?

"Why would I do that?" he asked.

"I don't know. Sex or sacrifice."

Isaac was silent for a while. Then, he stopped the car and swung it around.

"What are you doing?"

"Taking you home."

"I thought you were picking something up."

"Not with you thinking those ugly things."

"Oh, ignore me. I was afraid that I would have to stab you." Nnayiga pulled a blade from her schoolbag. Isaac stepped on the brakes. Nnayiga moved closer to the door and faced him. Isaac rested his face on the steering wheel for a while. Then he laughed.

"That's almost a machete."

"First you give me beer, I refuse it, then you give me wine. When you think I am drunk you offer to take me home. Along the way, you remember to pick up something from your house. It's eleven o'clock in the night and I am alone in your car."

She is really green, Isaac thought. "Did I say I was picking things from my house?"

Now Nnayiga looked confused, "I thought you said home."

Isaac laughed. "You misunderstood me. I was going to pick things up from a friend, not my home: I don't live at Nakawa. Now, I see why I alarmed you."

Nnayiga smiled with relief but did not put the knife away.

"So," Isaac tried to make light conversation, "Do you live with your parents?"

"No, my parents are in the village. I live with my older sister."

"How long have you been in the city?"

"Three months now. My parents told me to carry a knife."

"Where do you study?"

"I finished my A-levels in the village this year but I didn't pass well enough for free tuition at Makerere University. So I came to Kampala to see what my sister can do."

"So your sister will put you back in school?"

"I hope. If she doesn't, I'll re-sit next year after saving up."

Nnayiga told Isaac that she worked at a takeaway on Johnson Street.

When Isaac stopped outside her sister's house, Nnayiga smiled contritely and thanked him. "I am sorry I doubted you."

"It's all right." Then he hesitated. "Nnayiga, if a man offers to drop you home, don't accept. Getting into his car might mean something else to him."

"Really?" She looked frightened.

Sure, Nnayiga lived with her older sister but they shared rent. Yes, she did not drink beer but that was because she did not like it. She had done her A-levels in the village, but that was three years ago. Nnayiga and her sister would not describe themselves as twilight girls but their neighbors did. They had an understanding with their men: no demands, no questions. It was just that the men were generous in the morning. At any one time, they each held two or three such relationships. Now she listened at her sister's door; on hearing a male voice, she made her way to her bedroom. It had been an unfruitful night but at least she had cast bait.

Meanwhile, Isaac went back to the discothèque every night but Nnayiga was not there until a month later. He immediately sat with her and asked if she came regularly.

"Once in a while. If my sister finds out, I'd be in trouble."

"How's your sister?"

"She's fine."

"But you're here and it's getting late."

Nnayiga smiled wickedly. "She thinks I am working late."

This time Isaac did not ask what she wanted, he bought her wine. When it was time to go he asked casually, "Would you like me to drop you? Though, I should warn you, I am going home first."

"I trust you now. Besides, I still have my knife."

Isaac took Nnayiga to Lumumba Hall.

"You're a student!" Nnayiga's surprise was genuine.

"In my final year."

"What are you reading?"

"Electrical Engineering."

"You must be very clever. You look so grown up and accomplished, I'd never have guessed you're a mere student."

Isaac laughed. Though he took her to his room he didn't touch her. Instead, he explained that he had been a deejay for a long time making money for his education. He told her about his disco business and asked her if she wanted to come to the club where he rented out his machines. It was the first time that Isaac had explained himself to a woman.

Nnayiga listened wide-eyed. She had been about to ditch "project Isaac," but the disco business gave it potential. Though Isaac never looked at her as they talked, she was aware of his glances. Once she caught him looking and he was alarmed. Nnayiga realized that Isaac was not the type of man to make a regular customer: he was scared of women. She decided to hold him off sex for as long as possible in order to get the most out of him.

"I can't stay out any longer," she told him.

Isaac changed his shirt and dropped her home.

After three months, Nnayiga decided it was time to be careless. They had bumped into each other many times at the discothèque. Each time, Isaac dropped her home. Twice she let slip that she had left the knife at home but Isaac seemed not to care. The third time, Nnayiga carried a tiny handbag. Her monthly cycle was right and she was desperate. When, on this occasion, Isaac took her to a bar with lodgings upstairs, she drank more wine than usual. Then Isaac decided it was too loud in the foyer, would she mind going upstairs? Nnayiga giggled. She knew that upstairs were only bedrooms rented by the hour, but when they got to the rooms she asked, "They have beds for sofas?" and sat down clumsily.

Isaac did not say a word. Instead, he touched her suggestively. Nnayiga slapped his hand and moved further down the bed. She drank more wine. When Isaac shuffled closer, Nnayiga did not attempt to leave the room even though the door was not locked.

Isaac hugged her and she did not fight him off but when he touched her inner thigh she said, "Stop it." Isaac laughed as she pushed his hand away. He became more daring with every touch. Nnayiga fought him off in a way that ensured he did not give up.

She had been right. Isaac was one of those men who had never come to terms with women's sexuality. If a woman is willing, they drop limp. If she puts up a fight, they became animals. Nnayiga knew that they were a delicate bunch. A woman had to know where to brush her hand as she fought, how to fight helplessly, and when to give in and beg for mercy. As she fought, Nnayiga imagined herself the asexual wife who would fight her husband for the rest of her life. It was a more bearable curse than hooking customers. Finally, she allowed Isaac to overpower her and resorted to whimpering. It was only at this point that Isaac spoke: he asked her to be strong for him, that he would be gentle, that he would not hurt her.

When the nasty smell of his act caught up with him, Nnayiga was sobbing. Isaac cuddled her. "Did I hurt you?" But she sat up, threw his hands off and asked, "How would you like *that* done to you?" Isaac stood up and did the only thing he knew how to do: he emptied his wallet at her. The problem with Nnayiga was that he had got to know her. Her name was Nnayiga, her parents had sent her out into the hostile city to study and make something of herself and she had dreams. She threw the money at him and wept again. Isaac stuffed the money into her bag and asked, "What can I do?"

"Go away."

It was then that he got an idea. "Look, Nnayiga, I'll pay your fees if you want to re-sit your A-levels."

Nnayiga stopped to think. If she stormed out of the room, she would have to throw the money at him but she could not afford that. This could be all the money she would ever get out of the Isaac project. Yet she needed to keep contact in case she needed him later.

Thinking that her silence meant that she was about to take up his offer, Isaac slipped his business card into her handbag.

As if defeated, Nnayiga sighed, "Get out. I'll call you when I've decided." Isaac slunk out of the room, shrinking with shame.

At home, Nnayiga counted the money. It was substantial.

Then she waited.

She did not call Isaac. She did not return to the discothèque. She worked at the takeaway during the day and carried a school-bag in case she bumped into him. Every day, Nnayiga blew on her fingertips like a witch praying, "let it be, let it be."

Two months later, she turned up in Lumumba Hall hysterical. Her sister had thrown her out. She could not go back home to her parents in that state. No, she could not abort: girls die doing abortion. All her dreams of a bright future were shattered.

The image of Nnayiga's dream shattered was too much for Isaac to take. He was turning into his father. That day, Isaac took Nnayiga to the two-roomed house he rented in Banda and moved into Lumumba Hall at the university. He told her not to worry because she would go back to school after having the baby.

As soon as he installed her in his two-roomed house, Nnayiga devised ways of not moving out. Men with an engineering degree and business acumen were not common on the street. Instinct told her that for a man like Isaac, guilt and shame were stronger emotions than love. With skill, she could turn them into affection and respect. When Isaac bought a plot of land in Banda and started building a modern house, Nnayiga dropped the childish demeanor and worked on looking like the madam of a big house. Luckily, pregnancy suited her, she put on weight and her skin glowed. Her clothes grew to maternal lengths. When she heard Isaac say on the phone, "I can't come now, my madam is too close to—" she knew she had made it.

In January 1991, after a long difficult labor, Nnayiga gave birth to identical girls. The twins did not cry when they came into the world. Nnayiga lay shivering and exhausted on the birth bed as the nurses ran up and down trying to encourage the babies to stay. Apart from the moment when each twin emerged and was put on her belly, Nnayiga did not hold her babies. They changed their minds about living and one after the other, they left.

There was only silence as Nnayiga was discharged from hospital. She was too stunned to cry. With the loss of her babies, all earlier scheming and plotting seemed trivial. Her mother carried the bag with the children's clothes. Isaac and his family had already buried the twins. He told Nnayiga that he had instructed the masons to put just the names, Babirye then Nnakato (19-1-91) on each tombstone. Nnayiga did not want to see the graves. Only her mother cried: something about carrying but not holding. Isaac was thankful for the woman's noise. He did not know what to say to Nnayiga. They had gone to hospital to have a baby, then had two but came home empty-handed.

Six months later, Isaac moved Nnayiga into the new house. The floor was still dusty, there was no ceiling, the walls were only plastered and there was no electricity but to Nnayiga it was a palace. Isaac told her that her presence in the house would make it feel like a home.

Eventually, Isaac too moved into the new house. He had come to the conclusion that he might as well keep her as his madam because she was as good as any other woman. He felt as much affection for her as he would ever feel for a woman and he liked the respectability that came with saying that there was a woman at home. Everything else would work itself out.

In the privacy of their home and in their unvoiced grieving, Isaac sometimes called Nnayiga Nnalongo. She started to call him Ssalongo, which brought a smile to his face. "Nnalongo" and "Ssalongo" made them feel like husband and wife. In the months following the twins' deaths, he told Nnayiga that his deepest fear was the mother of his children abandoning them. He said that when she first told him that she was pregnant, he had started to drive carefully.

Their intimate encounters did not change though. They did

not share a bedroom. Mostly, Nnayiga woke up in the depth of the night to find Isaac on top of her. In the darkness, she would try to fight him off to give herself time to get ready. Only once did she mention that if Isaac intended to keep "pouncing" on her then he had better use a condom on other women. She had hoped that he would deny other women but he had only kept quiet. She often smiled to herself thinking that if she ever wanted to get rid of him she would turn into a wanton wife.

In the following six years, Nnayiga had three miscarriages but Isaac did not get rid of her. Doctors said there was nothing wrong with her but Nnayiga was anxious. She was not going to throw away a life of luxury and respectability just because her womb was playing about. To live in such a large house devoid of children made her feel useless. Thankfully, Isaac got the job with MTN and traveled to South Africa for six months' training. When he returned, he traveled across the country helping to install telephone masts. Just as Nnayiga went back to do her A-levels, she got pregnant again. This time it stayed. In 2000, Kizza arrived.

9.

It was as if Mr. Puti Kintu had been alerted that Nnamata was coming to Masaka to find him. He stood, as if posed, near the garbage heap, a few meters away from where the taxi stopped. Nnamata recognized him immediately. He had the kind of face she would never forget. She stepped out of the taxi, stood, and stared. Mr. Kintu had a receding hairline, and what hair remained was cut short. His two-day-old stubble was totally gray. His shirt and trousers were grimy as if he slept on the pile of garbage next to him. Three pens—red, blue, and black—their tops clipped to his breast pocket, were neatly arranged as if he were a professional going to work. He carried a filthy satchel on his shoulders but held a pile of exercise books in his hands. Still Nnamata stared. He turned his head slightly to the right and a smile started to form. Nnamata almost choked; *Isaac turns his head and smiles just like that.* Mr. Kintu was listening. He replied something and picked his nose unconsciously as he listened again, nodding all the time. Then he burst out laughing.

Nnamata looked for some place to sit down. Across the road was a restaurant. She walked toward it. Inside, there were no other customers. The woman behind the counter smiled her relief when Nnamata walked in.

"We make our tea with fresh milk," the woman smiled.

Nnamata stared.

"What will you have, *nyabo*?"

She ordered a Fanta and paid. She did not see the surprise on the woman's face at someone ordering a cold drink so early in the morning. Nnamata sat down on the bench. The woman brought a bottle sweating with condensation, she placed it in front of Nnamata, picked an opener off a bunch of keys around her waist and opened it. The bottle hissed and the woman passed her a pack of straws. Namata picked one, tossed it into the bottle, but did not lift the bottle to drink.

"Would you like something to eat with that?"

Nnamata shook her head and the woman walked away disappointed. When Nnamata saw the woman step outside the shop, she allowed her tears to flow silently. She took a handkerchief out of her handbag, opened it, and covered her face. In the tears flowed many things—the past, Isaac, madness, guilt, pain—but they all rushed at once, not giving her time to work out what hurt most. Then one thing became clearer. She was to blame for Isaac having a mentally ill father. Isaac would hate her more. It was not like Mr. Kintu had killed her: was she the first woman to be forced? Mr. Kintu's family would be hostile after what she did to him. Nnamata did not understand why life would not cease flogging her son. She left Masaka without drinking the Fanta.

Nnamata had been putting off finding Mr. Kintu for a long time. When she returned from Kisumu, where she had lived all that time, and found Isaac struggling on his own to make himself better, she had thought of ways to make amends. Finding his father would show how ashamed she was. But when she got to Luzira Prison, she was told that Mr. Kintu had been transferred to Butabika Hospital in 1970. Nnamata did not know what to feel about the news that Mr. Kintu was mentally unwell. She had not fully decided who Mr. Kintu was to her now—the man who destroyed her future or Isaac's father. That day she went home and refused to think about Mr. Kintu again.

Then Isaac opened that shop, fully stocked, and told her how much to spend and what to put away in the bank and she stopped hassling in the market. Guilt propelled her again. She would find Mr. Kintu, insane or not, with all the pride and confidence that comes from having a son who was not only studying for his A-levels but who had set up his mother with a grocery shop and had a booming disco business. However, Isaac was not yet talking to her. This made it difficult to enjoy his success, knowing that he had scraped that achievement from the depths to which she had flung him. Why add to his struggles by bringing a mentally ill father into it? Nnamata gave up her quest.

When Isaac brought a pregnant woman to his house, Nnamata realized that whatever the circumstances of Mr. Kintu, Isaac needed to know his roots as he was starting a family. She went to Butabika Psychiatric Hospital. There, all the administrators could find were notes that Mr. Kintu had been in and out of the hospital until 1985. His sister who lived in Masaka had looked after him whenever he was released. Nnamata asked for the name and address of the sister. All she had to do was go and find her because, as the nurses told her, "A home with a mentally insane person is not hard to find."

Still Nnamata procrastinated. Part of her hoped that Mr. Kintu was dead so that Isaac did not have to meet him. It would be a neat ending—Isaac not meeting him and she not meeting his family. When Isaac's twins died, she decided there was no rush. Recently she had decided to put herself out of her misery. This time there was no specific reason. She had been lying in bed when the thought came to her. She would face the situation the way a woman faces childbirth. She would wake up early, not open the shop, go to town, catch a taxi to Masaka, and look for Mr. Puti Kintu.

She had not expected to find him standing at a garbage heap, in the middle of Masaka Town, as if he had been tipped off that she was coming so that he could confound any sense of achievement she felt.

Nnamata decided to write a letter first. She did not post it—letters had a way of getting lost on the way. She got in a taxi, went back to the restaurant in Masaka, and asked the woman whether she knew Mr. Puti Kintu's family.

"Who doesn't? He is a son of the village that one. He was born here and when his head muddled up, he returned."

Nnamata noted that the woman had left Mr. Kintu's incarceration out of the story and was glad she had chosen to write rather than meet the family. The woman gave the letter to a boy of six or seven, who sprinted out of the restaurant to deliver it. Nnamata guessed that Mr. Kintu's family was not far from the town center if the child ran that fast. She said to the woman that she would have her drink outside but instead caught a taxi out of Masaka in case the child came back with Mr. Kintu's family asking about who had brought the letter.

Two days later, an elder from Mr. Kintu's family arrived at her shop. There were no questions of how, when, or but—not in the elder's demeanor, not in his words. Everything was about "the child" as if Isaac was a toddler, as if the presence of "a child" had atoned everything. When Nnamata realized that there was no accusation in the elder's attitude, she got the courage to ask, "What is your relation to Mr. Kintu?"

That was the only time a shadow crossed the man's eyes. He pointed at himself: "Me?" as if Nnamata could be possibly talking to anyone else. "We are his parents."

As the elder had used the plural "we," it meant that he was an uncle. The real parent would have used the singular in spite of the shame that comes with acknowledging that a rapist is your own.

Even after all the trouble she had taken to find Mr. Kintu, Nnamata had not plucked up the courage to tell Isaac that she had found his father and that he was mentally ill and that he lived in Masaka and that he was filthy. Nnamata told the elder that Isaac, who worked for a telephone company, had traveled upcountry for mast maintenance. He could not meet him yet. The elder told her to bring Isaac "home" to Masaka as soon as he returned.

A lot of family members were waiting at the family home, where Mr. Puti Kintu was born. When Isaac entered they all stood up, the women ululating, the men's relief clear on their faces, the stares, the *yiiyii and ehe eh bannange, isn't this real blood? Isn't this child Puti himself?* And Mr. Puti Kintu's mother broke down and cried. And she took the first turn to hold Isaac. And she made Isaac sit on the floor so she could sit him on her lap and hold his head into her bosom as if making up for the lost childhood she did not have with him. Then she apologized for the tears because it was a happy day. Then all the elders took their turns saying, *You call me Jjaja because when your grandfather Puti's father let go of our mother's breast, I grabbed it. Puti is our eldest in this house. Sometimes it would be, Puti's father came right after me, right on my back,* or, *this is our very eldest sister, look at her properly, when she speaks up the rest of us shut up; even your grandfather Puti's father who is already asleep, even when he was still with us he never talked back to her,* and it went on until it was Puti's siblings' and cousins' turn, until it was Isaac's brothers and sisters, born to Mr. Puti Kintu's brothers. Then the: *Thank you for bringing him up properly,* to Nnamata began, and *He loves mathematics just like Puti! Oh, ohhhhhh, who has ever seen that?* And, *Thank you for having the heart to bring him home to us munnaffe,* and, *Did you hear he has had twins as well? Do you see the nature of blood?* And everyone was happy because Isaac was Mr. Puti Kintu's real child.

But Mr. Kintu burst into tears when Isaac was introduced to him.

"He's mine, you say?" and he got agitated refusing to sit down, clutching his books as if someone was trying to take them from him. "I swear I've got no child."

There was uncomfortable silence as Mr. Kintu cried.

"Do you remember Nnamata?" a relative asked.

Mr. Kintu stopped crying. He went to a desk, sat down, and picked up a book.

"Silence. I am marking homework," he said. But a mischievous child was not put off by the stern voice.

"What time's your first lesson, Uncle Puti?"

"I've told you—math is the first lesson in the morning, double period. Always." Then he turned to Isaac and asked, "Is Nnamata all right? She has problems with fractions, but I think she'll pass."

"I agree," Isaac nodded.

Mr. Kintu was quiet for a while. Then he turned his head, contemplating.

"She's in trouble. Have you heard?" He pulled his chair nearer to Isaac and looked at him earnestly.

"Is she?" Isaac whispered.

"Yes, but don't tell anyone."

"What sort of trouble?"

"You know, with girls."

"Hmm?"

Mr. Kintu looked at Isaac like he was seeing him for the first time. "You haven't heard, have you?"

"Heard what?"

"You won't set the police on me?"

"I am not that kind of person."

"She's pregnant."

Isaac nodded then asked, "Do you know who the father is?"

Mr. Kintu sprung up as if suddenly alert. He peered through the windows fearfully as if he had heard someone coming to take his life. Then he bolted through the back door leaving his satchel and books behind.

"That's it! We're not going to see him again for at least three days." Mr. Kintu's sister said. "He will be hiding in the bushes around the house watching for the police."

Silence fell after those words. It was as if the word "rape" had fallen large and loud in the center of the room.

Isaac looked at the chair where his father had sat. He had only seen such an old man sprint like a young man once during the war. Army men were chasing the man when he had whizzed past Isaac as if his gray hair was a wig. Now a thick anger gripped him. What was the use of imprisoning a man who was going to be a father? Did they think about the child? But then shame overcame him and he blinked the tears back. He decided that no human being should ever be as torn between right and wrong, fair and unfair as he was at that moment. He needed someone, some object, something to blame but all he could find in that room was sadness.

10.

Kizza started falling sick slowly. It was just a runny nose at first. Nonetheless, Isaac withdrew him from school. Then a cough started but Kizza woke up strong and ate and played. Then the cough grew. At night, Isaac heard it boom-booming like a drum. When it gripped, Kizza coughed relentlessly until Isaac brought him to his own bed. He noticed that Kizza sweated in his sleep. It was now a month since they had taken the HIV test but Isaac had not collected the results.

Isaac took Kizza to Dr. Tembo who said it was just a bad cough and gave him an antibiotic jab. After a week, the cough stopped. But then Isaac noticed that Kizza's hair had lost some of its luster. It was a subtle change, the black had a brown tint and the curls were not as tight. It was a clear sign that Kizza was unwell. Isaac asked his mother, "Have you noticed the change in Kizza?"

"No, what sort of change?"

"He doesn't look right, that hair."

His mother scrutinized the hair, turning Kizza's head this way and that way but she shook her head. "I don't see anything. Children are children: today they're this, tomorrow they're that. Kizza has had a bad cough, that is all."

"Maybe I took him back to school too soon," Isaac said.

Nnamata weighed her words carefully. She knew Isaac's paranoia was looking for the new death's symptoms. On the other hand, she was lucky he had spoken to her at all. Finally she said, "Why don't you take him back to Dr. Tembo for a checkup?"

After a physical examination and a few blood tests, the doctor found nothing wrong with Kizza. But when, two days later, the school rang to say that they suspected Kizza had mumps, Isaac took him back to Tembo. The doctor confessed that he was not sure what was wrong with the boy, but ruled out mumps. He recommended that Kizza be admitted in hospital for overnight observation. The following morning when he came on the ward, Dr. Tembo asked Isaac for Kizza's HIV status.

"His mother died of it, so we can safely presume."

"I can't safely presume," Tembo smiled. "I'll do some tests. I suspect meningitis. If it is, we need to start treatment immediately but I need his HIV serostatus."

For Isaac, Tembo might as well have confirmed that Kizza had it. It was obvious, even to the most optimistic, that meningitis was an HIV symptom. Looking back at the last month, Kizza had shown many typical symptoms.

Isaac was calm as he left the hospital. His wish had been granted. He was confident that after the cold and cough, meningitis would find Kizza a dry twig to snap. By the time he arrived home, Isaac was planning Kizza's funeral.

It was with some dismay then, that Isaac watched Kizza pull through. He pretended to be relieved. Privately, he reassured himself that death can be deceptive: Kizza could seem to be recovering only to be snuffed out suddenly. But then one day, after a week, Isaac came to the hospital to find all the tubes through Kizza's nose removed. Tembo and his mother beamed at him. A week later, Kizza was discharged.

The day Isaac took Kizza back to school he sat in his office dejected. He ignored the two letters on his desk. Instead, he contemplated future hospital runs, Kizza's schooling disrupted and the boy's pain and suffering. What if he died first and left Kizza, sick and at the mercy of the world? He had seen what happened to Nnayiga and he was not willing to go through the same. Who would look after him the way he looked after Nnayiga? Isaac decided that he was not going to be tossed about by nature anymore. He would decide when and how he and his son would vacate the world.

Then, shaking himself free of the melancholy, he turned his attention to the letters on his desk. One was from the Joint Research Centre: he put it aside without opening it. The other, in a brown envelope, was addressed him in Luganda. He opened it. It summoned him, as the only son of Puti Kintu, to represent his father at an elders' council for a family reunion. Dates and venues for the meetings were provided. The reunion was scheduled for the Easter weekend in April. After work, Isaac carried both letters to the car and dropped them in the glove compartment.

BOOK FIVE

MISIRAYIMU (MIISI) KINTU

1.
KANDE, BULEMEEZI

Monday, January 5, 2004
At four o'clock in Mulago Hospital mortuary, the attendant starts to work on the day's new arrivals. They are all still lying on trolleys waiting to be treated, for the lucky ones, and then shelved. First, he arranges the bodies in rows and tags them. He starts with those who had been patients—patient number, name, and ward. Then he moves on to those that he calls the "to whom it may concern" non-patients, unclaimed. In his view, there is nothing as sad as having fussed over your name all your life—my name is . . . *I was named so because or after my* . . . only to be tagged "unknown" in death just because you can't say it.

Kamu has a name, place and date of death. He writes, *Kamu,* but after a cheeky thought he adds, *Kamugye,* because it sounds right. He adds, *Bwaise, D.O.D 5/1/04.* He smiles at his own humor and the parallel he has made between Kamu, a thief, and *kamugye* the squirrel. He slips the string of the tag over the ball of Kamu's dusty big toe: it settles like a necklace and he tightens it.

Kamu arrived at Mulago Hospital two and a half hours ago on the back of a police pickup truck. The police picked him up from Bwaise at one o'clock, five hours after his death. On arrival they had inquired, half-heartedly, in the market and nearby shops whether anyone had seen what happened. Everyone said that Kamu was lying there, dead, when they arrived at work that morning. The police were only putting on a show. They knew no one would tell the truth: who would want to testify in court? Nonetheless, they took down notes in case someone rich or powerful turned up and was related to the deceased and the CID would be involved and people had to be arrested and there would be money to be made from both the bereaved and the suspects. After the inquiries the policemen put their guns down and hauled Kamu's body onto the pickup. They laid him between the benches on either side, climbed on, sat around him, and drove away.

That same afternoon, in Kande where Kamu was born, nature played out a drama so bizarre that Miisi's wife and his sister looked to the supernatural. But not Miisi, Kamu's father. He was rational. There had to be a logical explanation.

The sun had been so high all afternoon that looking through the radiation in the air, nature seemed to be trembling. Miisi was sitting under the lime tree in his backyard, munching roasted groundnuts, watching time go by, when suddenly the sky turned gray. Then a droning noise came. It was not only heavy but it was getting louder. Miisi looked up: there was nothing in the sky yet the droning seemed to be coming closer. He tossed some nuts into his mouth, stood up, walked to the center of the yard, and scanned the sky. Then he saw it. A swift cloud was sailing toward him, droning. As it drew closer, it dropped altitude. It seemed to be heading for his house but Miisi remained rooted to the spot.

As the cloud approached, Miisi saw that it was a swarm of bees. He could even see the individual bees. Each bee flew in its own circle pushing ahead, returning, and pushing ahead again. Yet, in spite of this dizzying flight, the swarm moved forward as one. It continued over the outdoor kitchen, across the backyard toward the main house. For a moment it seemed to head for the back door but then it veered to the right. At the edge of the house, it turned toward the front. The narrow corridor between the house and the hedge forced the swarm to slow down. The bees abandoned their circuitous flight and surged forward, their hum dense and heavy. The window of the outer bedroom on the first floor was open. As if ushered in by an invisible hand, the swarm rose and flew in as a whole.

A child ran out of the house screaming, "We're dead! Bees in the guest room!"

Miisi broke out of his stupor. Muttering, "let me see," as if he did not believe the child, he ran to the house. Inside, the buzzing upstairs was so heavy it felt like walking into a colossal beehive. Miisi ran upstairs. He gingerly opened the door to the balcony and peered in. Thankfully, the door to the guest room where the bees had camped was closed. For a long time, he stood at the door, reluctant to step onto the balcony. Gradually, the droning started to wane. Individual bees buzzed sporadically as if they were finally settling down. That is when Miisi summoned the courage to tip-toe across the balcony to the deck railings and lean forward. He looked below on the ground, then above in the sky and all around to see the reason for the bees' behavior but there was nothing re-markable in the air. Just then the grayness in the sky lifted, and the sun came out and grew hot again. Miisi stood on the balcony, baffled.

2.

Miisi had returned from checking on the bees and was settling under the lime tree again when he was gripped by a bout of sneezing. When it stopped, the depths of his right ear itched. He stuck a finger inside but could not reach the itch. He shook the finger inside his ear until the itch ceased. He decided to go back indoors even though night had not fallen yet. When he got to below the stairs, he looked up and sighed. Why had he not thought about old age when he built the main bedroom upstairs? He lifted one sixty-five-year-old foot up and a pain like a current shot through his right hip. He did not even look forward to going to bed.

Miisi was not an insomniac, in fact, he slept deeply. But in his dreams, his mind broke loose and roamed realms strange and familiar. His childhood was a favorite destination, although sometimes he stumbled into places he had never been in real life. Miisi knew that this relentless return to his childhood in dreams signified something disturbing, but he never revisited the dreams when he woke up.

As a child growing up in a Catholic seminary, Miisi was taught that consciousness during the day, sleeping in the night, and waking up in the morning were pictures of life, death, and resurrection. Sleep was death and death was sleep. At the time, when he slept and his mind roamed, he concluded that his dreams were the image of the restless dead, the ghosts and spirits. This imagery, plus his shadow which stood by him in those frightening days when all that was dear and familiar went away, helped him come to terms with his loss as a child.

Now Miisi hoisted himself up the staircase, wondering why his hip had not bothered him when he had run upstairs to see the bees earlier. He arrived at the top landing and walked along the corridor until he came to the door opening to the balcony. He stood and listened: the bees' hum was low as if they were falling asleep. He opened the door and stepped onto the balcony. In the narrow aperture between the floor and the door, he could see some bees. They seemed lethargic.

Miisi slumped into a basket-chair tucked into a corner. Below him, his two-acre compound rolled down to a sudden drop at the main road. Dusk was gathering under the trees. Just then, a file of children appeared from the patch of flat ground, east of the compound, where boys played football. Each child carried a jerrican of water on his or her head. The older girls, teenagers, led the way carrying a twenty-liter jerrican each while the younger ones took the rear. Now they were so close below that looking down at them he could only see the jerricans lying horizontally, moving. One by one, the children disappeared into the lower house. He could hear them booking who was using the bathroom first, whose turn it was to wash the dishes and who should light the lamps.

He had made the right decision to bring all his grandchildren under one roof, Miisi reassured himself. Now all his grandchildren would grow up as a family. None would ever feel isolated. He might have failed to bring up his own children but if he was careful with his health, this generation would be all right. Every time a son or daughter of his was brought home to be buried, Miisi would ask for the children to be left with him. When he was lucky and found out that a daughter or son was ailing, he visited to talk. It was good for the children to be with their parents but it was not good for children to watch their parents melt away before dying. With this death, even if the spouse were still alive, it was best for them not to worry about the children while they struggled with their affliction.

Just then a stampede came up the stairs. Kidda, his eldest grandson, arrived first. He stopped dead at the door when he saw his grandfather, but the others coming behind him bumped into him, pushing him further onto the balcony. Kidda tried to stem the flow of his cousins and to sound responsible by cautioning, "Stop running in the house," as if he himself had not run in, but the others clambered past him to see the bees.

"Jjaja Nnamuli says that bees have come to visit," Kidda stated. Now everyone crowded the balcony, curious.

Miisi laughed. "Bees coming to visit indeed! Well they made themselves comfortable in that room," he pointed.

Now even the teenage girls had arrived and they stared at the aperture. Little ones knelt on the floor and peered. Suddenly, Kidda made as if to open the door and all the children shrieked and he laughed at their fright. This was Kidda's way of asserting himself as the fearless oldest boy in the house, and Miisi did not tell him off. Instead he listened and watched as each shared their rationale for the bees.

"I think there was once a beehive in this place and Jjaja, I mean the builders, destroyed it when they built this house but now the bees are back to claim their territory: don't joke with them!"

"No," six-year-old Nnattu shook her head. "They came to commit suicide. Wait for tomorrow, they will all be dead."

"Commit suicide? Tsk! But where does Nnattu get these ideas from? As if bees are human!"

"*Wama* Jjaja," Nnattu appealed to her grandfather. "Don't bees commit suicide?"

Miisi was caught. He was not about to crash Nnattu's creativity but at the same time he could not back such an outlandish idea.

"They are possibly going to die."

"See?" Nnattu turned to the others but now even the older girls joined in. They were not allowing her to win.

"Not everything that dies commits suicide; the bees will die because it is their time."

Miisi watched as the children, now having lost interest in the bees, filed out. He was aware that he had ten grandchildren living with him but he would never consciously count them. Sometimes he mentioned their names one by one, talking about their ages, telling about their school progress—Walime is the quiet one, Nnabaale is very caring toward the little ones, Nnakidda speaks above everyone, Baale can sprint, Nnattu, oh, Nnattu, she must win every argument—but that was not counting. If anyone asked how many grandchildren lived in his house he would say, "Oh, how many shall I say? I am rich in blood." Now he sighed contentedly. While death took his children, it had brought his grandchildren close to him. They kept him young and he was grateful for that.

After a while, a boy came upstairs to ask whether Miisi would join the family for supper downstairs.

"I don't have bones to grind up and down the stairs," he complained. "Ask Jjajja Nnamuli and some of you to come and eat with me."

Jjajja Nnamuli was Miisi's sister, who had arrived two months earlier and announced, "Is marriage a prison sentence? *Maama*, I need to take a break too!"

Miisi suspected that she had no intention of going back to her husband but asking about her return would seem like asking her to leave.

Presently, Nnamuli arrived carrying the basket of food. She came with five of Miisi's youngest grandchildren. She was dark and petite where Miisi was light-skinned and tall. Miisi's wife had once remarked how the two were so unalike. Miisi, who had heard that comment all his life and was fed up with it, had answered that it was not uncommon for siblings not to look alike. Perhaps his sister looked like their father while he looked like their mother.

As they ate supper, Nnamuli, agitated over sitting too close to the bees, whispered, "Do you not fear . . . the visitors?"

"Visitors?"

"The bees?"

"They are harmless," Miisi smiled.

"Still, we should keep a respectful distance. We don't know what they want."

"I doubt they'll be joining us for supper. Is any food left in the wraps?"

Nnamuli looked inquiringly at the untouched food on Miisi's plate.

"The children need more food," he explained.

His sister grunted as she made a show of searching the banana leaves. She found morsels of *matooke* and gave them to the nearest child. Then she scratched the pan with the ladle for crusts of groundnut sauce that clogged around the rim and tossed it on the same child's plate. The child attacked the food with the gusto of someone starved. Miisi despaired. He took the food from his plate and distributed it among the children.

"Stop it, I say stop it now!" His sister looked at the children fiercely. "This is why we don't eat with you. These children are drains: they don't realize when they've been fed."

"I've had enough, my stomach has shrunk. Here, Magga, have this."

"Why wouldn't it shrink if it's starved?"

Despite Jjaja Nnamuli's severe look, the boy called Magga stretched his arm toward his grandfather's generosity. Miisi licked his fingers and sat back satisfied. "At this age food is wasted on me, but these . . ." he waved his hand toward the children, "they need to eat until food packs down their legs." Seeing his sister's irritation, Miisi tried to humor her.

"I bet you've already done something about the bees. I mean, the visitors. They're already passive."

"Hmm." His sister would not be drawn in.

"Did you pray or give thanks?"

Unfortunately, a slick of sarcasm floated on Miisi's voice.

"That's the way with the world," Nnamuli's own sarcasm was barely veiled. "Some of us are simple and insecure where others are intelligent and sure. Luckily, the world needs all of us equally."

After the meal, Nnamuli stood up gathering the food-wraps and went downstairs. Miisi went to bed. As he waited for sleep to take him, his mind cast back to the bees. It was peculiar. The year 2004 was only five days old but so far it had thrown up drama after drama. He wondered what it had in store for the future.

When midnight launched the New Year five days earlier, Kande had risen up to resounding applause—drums thundering, people screaming, and others ululating. For more than ten minutes, the village was covered in noise. Village youths had converged at the crossroads near Miisi's house dragging dead Christmas trees decorated with cotton wool and toilet tissue. At midnight, they set the trees ablaze to make a bonfire. At first, Miisi sucked his teeth at their parents' negligence but then he remembered that to some children having parents was a myth, some homes were run by twelve-year-olds and children grew up like weeds.

As the uproar died down, Miisi heard youths hurl insults first at the departing year then at the new arrival. Even to him, the New Year was a troll sitting on the horizon surveying the residents. In time, it would sweep into the village to weed out the luckless and the careless. At the end, another year would sit in the same place and survey its crop. The old year, 2003, had whisked off a daughter and a son from him. Out of the twelve children Miisi had had, only Kamu Kintu and Kusi Nnakintu remained.

The youths stopped shouting at the years and started walking toward Katikamu. Along the way, when they came to a house, they called the names of the residents and told them what the village whispered about them. When they came to Miisi's house the youths called him a Russian idiot and a communist waste of education. At first, Miisi marveled at the success of Western anti-Russian and anti-communist propaganda. But then it dawned on him that the village resented his professed principles. Perhaps to them, his rejection of a lucrative job and a life of comfort in the city seemed a mark of conceit. Miisi choked in mortification as he remembered pontificating to men who had no alternative but to struggle all their lives, that he would rather be poor than hand degrees to students who did not earn them, that he had come to this decision after he had wasted money on a pretentious house.

He cringed as he realized that the ability to take such a stand was exceedingly privileged. He had even inflicted on villagers notions of the uselessness of religion, warned them against the lures of the middle class and the lie of immigration to the West. Miisi had tried to recall exactly how he put these ideas. In retrospect, he should have pointed out that religion was crucial to society in terms of discipline and management of resources, especially at the family level. Immigration redistributed resources and middle-class values built nations. Miisi had closed his eyes in shame. For the first time, he considered abandoning his crusade to build interest in global issues among residents, a crusade that attempted to make his grand education relevant to the community.

After his house, the youths had accused Widow Bakka, the oldest person in the village—no one knew how old Bakka was, ninety-something, perhaps a hundred years old—of defying death. Apparently, instead of dying the widow wiggled, like a snake, out of her old skin into a younger one. Every time she shed her skin, someone in the village died in her stead.

"What are you waiting for, Bakka?" the youth demanded. "Do you think you're a tree, that the longer you live the better timber you'll make?"

Even to Miisi's atheist mind, the young of a community going around the village in the night wishing the old dead at the beginning of the year did not augur well.

Now the bees?

Miisi turned away from the irrational thought. To forge a link between the coincidental events of New Year's Day and the arrival of the bees was tenuous.

Presently, he heard his wife and his sister coming up the stairs. A light flashed through the door, then he heard the balcony door open and close. After ten minutes, he decided that the women were perhaps doing spiritual rituals for the bees. He attempted to turn and lie on his right side but an arrow of pain shot through his hip and he gave it up.

3.

"Wake up, Müsi," his mother whispers. "Get up."

"Why?"

"Got to go."

"Where?"

"The stench is unbearable."

"Stench?"

"I hope it will atone."

"Atone?"

"Are you an echo? I said get up, it's not safe."

"Why?"

"Your brother, Baale. I know the path he took."

"But it's night!"

"Shhh, you'll be safe with me."

"When the police catch you, they will take you away."

"Did you hear the police coming?"

"I hear boots. Listen . . . they're coming," he whispers. "They must have heard you wake up, Mother. Hurry, run to bed."

Müsi's mother jumps back into her bed. She is shivering. "Tell them to go away," her teeth chatter. "I won't do it again."

Müsi gets out of bed, goes to the door, opens it and calls out into the darkness: "Go away, she's sleeping." He closes the door and smiles at his mother even though it is pitch black in their bedroom and she can't see his smile. "They've gone, Mother. They won't touch you."

"Thank you, Miisi. You're the only one I trust."

The shivering is subsiding. Her breathing is even. Miisi is falling asleep again.

"Miisi, do you smell it?"

Miisi pretends to be asleep.

He marvels at himself. He can speak and contain his mother's impulse to flee, yet he is just a baby lying on his back in his basket crib looking at the woven handle.

A squeak, then the rustling of sheets. She is out of bed. She is getting dressed. Miisi should stop her but he cannot be bothered to wake up. He feels her hands seek his underarms. He is airborne. As she swings him onto her back, his arms and legs open in anticipation and grip her body. He should wake the family, but it is so cozy on her back. No doubt they will hear her leave. She has stepped out of the bedroom. One, two, three, four, five steps in the hallway. She unlatches the back door. Someone shouts, "She's escaping. She's got Miisi."

Struggling at the door.

"Let me go."

"Who left the key in the door?"

Strong hands wrench him off her back. He does not wake up. He is laid back in his bed. The house is quiet. Miisi is surprised that he did not wake up through it all. He must be dreaming. It does not make sense: dreaming when he is lying awake in a crib? Yet when he wakes, his mother is gone and there is a vast silence. No one talks to him about his mother. They think he is a baby. Yet, he sees everything. This bothers him. He wants to say, "You think I am a baby, that I don't see what you do to my mother, but I do." But when he speaks they smile at him and make gurgling sounds.

Bump, bumpy, bumping. Miisi wakes up. She's escaped. He did not hear her wake up or swing him onto her back. It is all right. He loves sleeping with his arms and legs wrapped around her. He can feel her buttocks rise and fall rubbing against his own as she walks: it is reassuring. He will not open his eyes: the dark will be frightening. What if a bad animal attacks them? She stops, *bends over slightly, and tosses him further up her back. She tightens the cloth tying him. "Sleep," she whispers. But his left ear, pressed hard on her back, hears deep vibrations running up her spine when she says "sleep." She cradles his bottom in her hands to support him.*

Noises.

"Poor child. On her back all night."

"Where were they this time?"

"On the river banks as usual."

"What is it with her and Kiyira River? One day she will jump in."

"The child should be moved out of her bedroom."

"He won't sleep anywhere else."

Yanked.

Miisi moves from one set of hands to another. He does not open his eyes but he sees everything. His mother is struggling.

"Give me back my child."

"Take the child away."

"Give him back."

"Ah ii . . . she's bitten me."

"Hold her tighter!"

Someone is running with him but Miisi turns and sees his mother's face. There is blame in her eyes. Miisi shakes his head at her, "I didn't call them." Why does she blame him? Can't she see he is just a baby? How could he have set them on her? "I was on your back all night," he cries, but she looks right through him. They hold her hands and tie her. Someone says they should use a strong piece of cloth not a rope. Miisi tries to wiggle out of the hands holding him.

"Don't tie her like that," he shouts.

"He's tired, poor child."

"Leave her alone."

"Oh, the baby smiled at me, did you see that?"

Miisi kicks, throws his body around, and sinks his gums into someone's flesh. The person smiles and gurgles at him.

His mother cries.

He cries too.

• • •

They have brought his mother back from hospital already although they took her just a moment ago. She sleeps all day. Miisi has stolen her tiny red, yellow, blue, and green tablets. He sucks the sweet color off and spits the bitter white out. He is feeding his mother with a spoon even though he is a baby. When people see him, he expects them to marvel and say, "look, a baby is feeding his mother," but they don't, as if it is normal for a baby on his back in the crib to feed his mother. She has grown fat.

4.

Miisi walked leisurely, his hands clasped behind him. He watched his feet come and recede, come and recede from under his *kanzu*. His shadow, in tow, was huge. Miisi was one with himself. A *kanzu* made him feel authentic: African, Ganda, a muntu. He came to the top of Katikamu Hill. On his right, the local Anglican Church was locked and deserted. In the same compound were the Church of Uganda primary and secondary schools. On his left were Katikamu SDA Church and both its primary and secondary schools. The Klezia and the Roman Catholic primary and secondary schools were further away in Kisule. The hill started to descend. Miisi walked down past the teachers' quarters, past the rocky patch of land until he came to the huge *falawo* trees opposite the triangular junction. He turned into Kaleebu's walkway.

As he got to the house, a modest concrete block, Kaleebu's wife saw him and called out in welcome. A child ran out of the house with a folding chair and placed it under the shade of a tree for him. Then Kaleebu appeared in the doorway, dressed in a *kanzu* as well. There was a mixture of surprise and pleasure in his smile.

"What lies has the world been telling?" Kaleebu asked as they sat down.

"Apart from the sun?"

"Is the city roasting too?"

"This year's sun burns right through the loins." Miisi shook his head.

"And the president wants a fourth term."

"Don't start on that leech."

"That man is like balding," Kaleebu said. "Once it arrives it demands more and more space."

"That is our Africa. That is what circumstances have done to us."

"Aha, we Moslems watched as this president heaped insults on Idi Amin. We said, *OK, let's wait and see.* Now we're wondering whether it is the State House that turns every president swinish."

One by one, the members of Kaleebu's family came to greet Miisi. Saying that it was late and that he would lose his appetite, Miisi declined the drink he was offered. This gave him time to consider Kaleebu's words. He knew he had to tread carefully. Kaleebu was still haunted by Amin's regime. Like many Moslems, who formed a minority, he felt implicated whenever a Moslem committed an offense. Miisi was sympathetic. Moslems had been vilified and marginalized during colonial times. Even after independence, Christian Ugandans had taken on the same attitude as the colonialists toward Moslems. Then Idi Amin came along. His horror not only stamped and sealed the horrible beliefs held about Moslems but conjured up new nightmares for them as well. Hence, any political discussion with Kaleebu always veered toward making sense of Amin's regime. In a way, Miisi understood Kaleebu's feelings of persecution. When he had lived in Britain in the 70s, he felt implicated whenever he read in the papers that a black person had stolen, murdered, or raped. Now he answered, "All politicians are the same: once in power they imagine that they're the only ones with brains."

"What has this president done for the country, seriously?"

"At least we can sit here and criticize him."

"But only his tribal region is prospering and he has brought back the Asians."

"At least one region's developing," Miisi said evenly. "I wish

Obote and Amin had developed their regions: we would have fewer problems here in the south. As for the Asians, they have given the city a face-lift. My problem with this man is that he has snuffed out our self-belief."

"But he's taking properties from Ugandans and giving them to Asians. How can that be right?" Kaleebu sat up.

"He's not giving them properties; he is returning their properties," Miisi tried to explain. "The international community will not invest in Uganda until all properties Amin confiscated from Asians have been returned."

Kaleebu kept silent. Finally he said, "I know you'll think that I say this because I am a Moslem and that I stand by Amin blindly, but don't you think this president is taking us back to those old days of 'Boy this' and 'Boy that'? Who doesn't know how cruelly Asians treated us? Maybe you educated people don't but for us who worked in their shops or homes, the idea of having them back is sickening."

"Those days are long gone. Asians return as equals. Besides, they learned to call us 'Boy' from the British."

"The problem with Amin was not that he killed people; who hasn't? Amin's sin was that he killed the untouchables—the educated. Where Amin killed an Archbishop, Obote killed a hundred peasants. Did the world cry out?"

"On second thought, I'll have a glass of water," Miisi said.

"Someone bring us a glass of water," Kaleebu called. Then he carried on, "When the British love you, they wash the ground you tread white with praise, but let them turn against you . . ."

A child brought a glass of orange juice and Miisi was disappointed. Juice would not quench his thirst. He considered repeating his request for a glass of water but decided against it. When he put the glass down, Kaleebu carried on. "The British said that Amin killed his son Moses and ate his heart but Moses's mother returns to Uganda and says that her son is alive *in France.*"

"We cannot blame the West for the way they present Africans in their media: what do you expect? Our savagery is their civilization. It justifies everything. My problem is the Africans who, knowing this, give them the opportunity. If only African buffoons realized how they drag every black person in the world down in the mud with their follies, they would reconsider."

"Of course, Amin was a tyrant. I'll be the first to tell you that, but how much of Amin is myth?"

"Anyone can separate myth from fact."

"Can they? How much of that dehumanization in the media actually dehumanized Amin as a person?"

"Of course no one believes he had people's heads in his fridge, but Namanve was real. Amin was exaggerated because that sort of thing was unexpected so soon after independence. By the time Obote II and the others set in, we were numb, save for Moslems who were feeling it for the first time."

"My friend, you think we Moslems were the people Amin gave the shops to when he took them from the Asians?"

"I am saying that Moslems didn't feel Amin the way we did. Non-Moslem men got circumcised and acquired Moslem names hoping it would protect them: have you forgotten?"

"I'll tell you this, Miisi. Yes, there were people I know who prospered during Amin's regime but there were also Moslems who were killed by Amin and there were Christians who gained from him. You don't realize that the vast majority of Ugandans didn't feel Amin as harshly as you did. We peasants, apart from the lack of soap, sugar, salt, and those little luxuries we could no longer afford, Amin kept away from us. I might be uneducated, but I know that embargoes were clamped on the country. Even if the fools Amin gave the factories and shops to could trade, where would they do it, with whom? However, you the elite had never known a car without petrol and, *Oh the drive-in has been closed,* so you imagined we all suffered the same."

"Surely you must have suffered?"

"We suffered the war from Tanzania and persecution afterwards because we were Moslems."

"Surely—"

"No, Miisi, you are the educated one. Tell me, what was wrong with Amin? He was human. What made him do what he did?"

"I'm not sure."

"Don't tell me you believe he was a monster like the Europeans said?"

"I've never thought it through."

"I'll tell you why you've never thought it through my friend: because Amin was Moslem."

"That is not fair."

"Consider this. Amin came from the smallest and most despised tribe, the Kakwa. He was a northerner. He was uneducated. He was Moslem. I mean, you Christians had adopted the Europeans' view that all Moslems were imbeciles—only good as shopkeepers, drivers, or butchers. It never occurred to you that to forcefully baptize our children when they went to mission schools kept us away from Western education. Did you know that it was Amin who introduced schools for Moslems: that he even went to OIC to ask for an Islamic university so that we could have an education acceptable to us?"

"I am sure he did some good somewhere, but—"

"I'll use your rationale, Miisi. As a president, Amin was first surrounded not only by Christians and the educated, but by southerners, especially us, the arrogant Ganda, who looked down on everyone. Not to mention the Western media that presented him as a cannibal. Is it possible that Amin lashed out to frighten people as much as he was frightened?"

Miisi rubbed his hands up and down his face as if removing something sticky. Kaleebu stopped, ashamed of his outburst. He knew that in Uganda to say anything positive about Idi Amin was blasphemous. He dropped the Idi Amin subject and turned to Obote. "Obote avoided the educated because you people scream so loud that they hear you across the seas," Kaleebu smiled. "Instead, he terrorized us peasants and there were no embargoes this time, were there?"

"You see," Misirayimu started, "this is exactly what happens when a society is gripped with the notion of an almighty God. What would stop their leaders from emulating Him? Can you criticize your God? Can God be held accountable? God-fearing people tend to ape their deity in their own perverted way."

"Ah, there you stray, my friend. When it comes to questioning Allah, we part company."

"This 'God' is unashamedly bent on annihilating other gods: is it surprising that the people who believe in him are intolerant themselves?"

"In this conversation," Kaleebu was shaking his head, "I have hit the wall, my friend. I can't go any further."

"Kaleebu, I listened when you sounded me out on Amin. You made sense. Why can't you listen to me?"

"My friend, I talked about Amin, a man. You're talking about God."

Miisi dropped his head. The evening had become cold. Darkness was falling. Mosquitoes swung above Kaleebu's head. "Time is in a hurry these days," he sighed after a pause.

"It is because we are getting old," Kaleebu laughed, visibly relieved that Miisi had dropped the blasphemous talk.

Miisi drank up his juice and said that he should go home. Kaleebu mumbled something about the night falling like a stone and Miisi said that it was a great metaphor for old age. Presently, he bid Kaleebu goodnight and called his wife to say he was leaving. She said that supper was almost ready, the way the Ganda do even though they would be shocked if you accepted the invitation. Miisi said that he would stay for supper another time.

When he stood up, his shadow sprung up, a giant walking ahead of him. The moon was out early. The two men walked in silence through the darkened coffee *shamba* until they came to the road. When he turned, Miisi's shadow veered and walked by his side, half its size. Kaleebu bid Miisi goodnight.

Miisi was chastising himself for letting the conversation get out of hand. He had come to find out what it was exactly people had against homosexuality but ended up talking about Idi Amin.

He should have never mentioned God. He wondered whether he would ever gather the courage to raise the homosexual issue.

"I've seen you there."

Miisi looked up and saw Nyago waving at him.

"Oh, I hadn't seen you."

"Because darkness is on the black man's side," Nyago laughed. "And by God he has paid for it."

"Come on and join me." Nyago invited. "I'm having a late cup of tea, on my own. Such is the lot of men like me."

"Eh eh, I am going to miss that cup of tea. Where's your wife?" Miisi teased.

"What would I do with my wife?"

"Have tea conversation with her."

"Do you talk to your wife? I mean real conversation?"

"It depends on the woman."

"Maybe women in the city but a peasant's wife: what does she know beyond breastfeeding? Besides," Nyago whispered, "When you talk to her as an equal she gets ideas. Next, she'll be ordering you around. And she'll do it when you are in the company of other men, to show off."

Miisi laughed uncomfortably and started walking home. He claimed that time was moving faster than him, that he should have been home already, that he would return another day for that cup of tea and Nyago expressed pretend disappointment.

When he arrived home, Miisi went straight upstairs to his bedroom. He reached for his pen and paper to prepare an article for his column. It was a wasted evening: his ideas on sexuality were getting nowhere. He wrote in English:

Homophobia: A Result of Fear Imagined or Real

He did not like the title. It did not question the Ugandan notion that homosexuality was a Western export. Nonetheless, Miisi knew that whichever way he presented the idea, religion rather than logic would dictate the readers' response. He wrote:

Homophobia: Cultural Amnesia or Christian Erasure?

He liked the internal rhyme, but how does one translate it into Luganda? He decided to put his thoughts in note form:

Old gripes—this is who we/they are, right/wrong, normal/abnormal, natural/unnatural, ancestors' words as gospel truth—are loosening.

Nothing is above questionable anymore, no truths(?)
What this has revealed is stunning.
The world is more exciting to live in now than decades ago!(?)

He yawned and decided to leave it at that. He might have better ideas tomorrow.

5.

It is dusk. Miisi is sitting on a three-legged stool near the angel's trumpet shrub with his back against the hedge. His double-story house is a ruin. The roof and parts of the walls on the top floor are in disrepair. A man stands above him. Miisi feels imposed upon because he cannot see past the man. The man is covered with bees. He has a single hair on his head as thick as a big rope.

"Get up and come with me," the man says.

Miisi knows he should ask: who are you? Come with you to where? But instead, he whines, "You know my hip is bad," as if he and the man have known each other for a long time.

"If you don't come with me now, you'll have to find me. I am not easy to find."

"But my hip——"

"Hurry up."

The man has started walking. Miisi stands up reluctantly. There is nothing wrong with his hip, yet it has been giving him pain for a long time. He is worried that neighbors are going to see him walking properly: they'll think he is a liar. Miisi hides behind the man covered in bees. It is critical that no one sees him walking without a limp.

They walk through his compound and out toward the main road, only they don't seem to be getting closer. A few bees fly off the man and then settle back. Miisi is not bothered by the bees. It is as if he has lived with men covered in bees all his life.

Miisi and the man are standing on a hillside. They are surrounded by trees. *The place is familiar even though Miisi is sure he has never been there. The bee man touches a tree and looks it up and down. "This tree will be at the center," he says, as he walks around it, still looking it up and down. "It will make the central pole." Miisi is puzzled but the man adds, "Find a tall man, ask him to take ten strides," the bee man takes a stride, "In every direction around this tree and build a dwelling."*

Now they are standing at another end of the hill. Miisi and the bee man have been together on the hillside for years now.

"This is Nnakato," the bee man points to the ground. "You must retrieve her and lay her properly." He looks at Miisi: even his eyes are bees. The eyes are stern as if Miisi is a silly child. "You must observe everything carefully so that when you return with your brothers you can identify the sites. Nnakato is near a rock. You see that tree with a red bark? Don't cut it down. It is the same tree from which she hanged herself. You can sit under it when your head throbs or when you're anxious. Let its water drip on you. Come with me."

They move from site to site instantly like ghosts yet Miisi feels as though they have been touring for a long time. The sun is very bright, but the man's bees are not bothered. Miisi wants to warn him that the sun will kill his bees, but he remains silent out of respect.

They are standing in a wide clearing. The bee man is pointing out Miisi's family. Miisi knows all of them because he buried them there.

"Bring Nnakato over here. That is Baale on my left. Don't disturb him. Lay Nnakato on his left. When you return Kintu, lay him on Nnakato's left. The sun must set behind them. However, Kalemanzira must be laid on Baale's right. Come with me."

Miisi looks back trying to catch a glimpse of Baale but the bee man is hurrying. They stand on a heath. All Miisi can see is desolation. The bee man leads him to a mound. He bends and blows the dust away.

"There he is."

"Who?"

"Your father. Haven't you been looking for him?"

"Oh, him," Miisi remembers looking in rolled mats, behind doors, under tables, behind trees everywhere all his life. His father is a smiling face without a body. The smile is of shame rather than happiness. Miisi looks away.

"How did he get here?"

"Humans walk," says the bee man but Miisi wonders how a smiling face walked. "He loved you."

"Thank God he died. If he loved me he would have killed me."

"He loved you."

"Mother loved me."

"Come with me."

Miisi is seven years old. He is walking behind the bee man. The man's single hair rises on his head but collapses under the weight of the bees and trails on the ground like a snake. Miisi suppresses the childish urge to step on it: the bees would sting his feet. Miisi knows he has been with the bee man for a long time because he has grown a goatee like a Japanese wise man. This worries him because his beard normally thatches the entirety of his jaws. Yet he is still seven years old. The bee man points at a patch of ground overgrown by shrubs.

"That's where the lad is."

The bee man stands away from the grave. The grave hums. It is a metallic hum. Miisi listens: it is the hum of an electricity transformer near his school. Miisi wants to reassure the bee man that the lad is harmless. People are harmless when they are asleep.

"This is my home." The man points to a cave covered in bees. "I'll not return to your house. Go back and find your brothers. Return and build the house. Then wash in the gorge below the hill."

Miisi returns home. In no time, he and his many brothers have built the house but they are all monkeys swinging on trees.

6.

Miisi sat in an easy chair in the garden. His stunted shadow sat behind him. He gazed up at the vacant sky where the sun had been. The iron roof on his kitchen made popping sounds as it contracted after the day's harsh sun. He looked at the angel's trumpets; the flowers that bloomed the previous evening were dying and hung like a slaughtered cow's tongue. Fresher ones were harassed by a constant stream of bees flying in and out of the white trumpets. Dead flowers on the ground hosted flies.

Nnattu brought a cup of tea and two slices of bread. Miisi murmured thanks and put the tray down. He was preoccupied by the multitude of ants that had constructed highways on the ground. The ants carried a delicate cargo of white eggs. There were so many eggs that the highways were covered in white. However, the ants carrying unhatched brothers stopped and kissed every time they met, which was every inch of the way. Miisi looked on bemused: why stop to be polite when you've exposed your posterity to danger? Now here comes a hen.

The hen took slow tentative steps toward the ants. Its beak was open as if it were gasping for water. The hen was ready to jump in case Miisi threw something at it. Finally, it reached the ants. It pecked once, liked it, and made a low glottal noise. A brood of yellow chicks, seven or eight, scurried out of the hedge and joined the hen, pecking madly at the ant eggs. Miisi looked at the ants fleeing but still stopping along the way to wish each other luck. He could shoo mother hen and her chicks away but he lacked the will. Nature is as such: its cruelty to one creature is a windfall to another. No one had shooed nature away from his children. *Let them be eaten*, he thought savagely.

"Jjaja, would you like your tea reheated?" Nnattu asked.

"Oh, wife, what I have done?" Miisi had forgotten about his tea.

"There's a bug in my tea. I wonder whether my little wife has some tea left in her kettle."

"There is."

"But the tea left in the kettle is for my little wife."

"I've had mine already."

"Then I'll have it."

Nnattu picked up the tray and went to get more tea. Miisi bit into a slice of bread. The bread was so hard it grazed the roof of his mouth. Miisi wondered why bakeries in Uganda were obsessed with making bread sweet. He missed the old bakeries of the 60s when bread was not a vulgar cross between scone and cake but proper bread. Nnattu came back with a steaming cup of tea and he beamed at her. "I can't remember what life was like without you." But as he grabbed the cup, a cold shiver ran through him.

"I'll get your jacket," and Nnattu was off to the house before he could stop her. The hen and chicks were pecking frenziedly.

"You're sure you don't want another cup of tea?" he asked as she handed him his sweater. Nnattu shook her head. "Then sit with your husband and tell him stories like a good wife."

Nnattu giggled and rolled her eyes and scratched her arm exaggeratedly, looking up at him. He nodded that he was waiting and finally she called, "In old, old time—"

"Kin, you were our eyes," Miisi replied.

And Nnattu repeated a story he had told her. She forgot parts that she patched with her own imagination. There were parts she was not sure of and she asked him to remind her and he said he didn't know her story and she said he did and they argued and laughed. She sat on his lap. The night sky let out the stars, the bushes released fireflies, and the shrubs released fragrances. When the grass got damp with dew Miisi and his little girl stood up and went into the house.

After supper, he lay on his bed waiting for sleep. An idea of how to illustrate colonization had been brewing in his mind since visiting Kaleebu. He was alarmed at the sheer lack of anger over European colonization among the residents. He sat up and scribbled the title in English:

AFRICANSTEIN

Then he translated the title into Luganda:

EKISODE

Buganda, unlike the rest of Africa, was sweet-talked onto the operating table with praises and promises. Protectorate was the plastic surgery to set the sluggish African body on a faster route to maturity. But once under chloroform, the surgeon was at liberty and did as he pleased. First, he severed the hands then cut off the legs and he put the black limbs into a bin bag and disposed of them. Then he got European limbs and set upon grafting them on the black torso. When the African woke up, the European had moved into his house.

Though the African was too weak to get up, he still said to the European, "I don't like what you are doing, my friend. Please get out of my house." But the European replied, "I am only trying to help, brother. You are still too weak and drowsy to look after your house. I will take charge in the meantime. When you're fully recovered, I promise you will work and run twice as fast as I do."

But the African body rejected the European body parts. Africa says that they are incompatible. The surgeons say that Africa discharged itself too soon from hospital—that is why it is hemorrhaging. It needs a lot more continual blood and water pumped intravenously. Africa says the blood and water are too expensive. The surgeons say, "Nonsense, we did the same to India, see how fast it's running."

When Africa looked in the mirror, it saw that it was hideous. Africa looked in others' eyes to see how they saw it: there was revulsion. That gave Africa permission to self-harm and self-hate. Sometimes, when the world is not looking, the surgeons poke Africa in the wounds. When it falls down the surgeons say, "You see, we told you they were not ready."

We cannot go back to the operating table and ask for the African limbs, Africa must learn to walk on European legs and work with European arms. As time goes by, children will be born with evolved bodies and in time, Africa will evolve according to ekisode's nature and come to its best form. But it will be neither African nor European. Then the pain will settle down.

Miisi was relieved by the reception of his *ekisode* analogy by his fellow villagers. It was the first time he had discussed an article with them before sending it off to the newspaper. Probably, the fact that he had asked for their help with Luganda vocabulary piqued their interest. Either way, Miisi was thankful for their enthusiasm. For the first time, the residents asked pertinent questions such as, "If, because of this ripping, grafting, and stitching, societies like ours are of *ekisode* nature, should we just sit back and wait until evolution smoothens things out?"

"No, not sitting back: we must manage the pain. However, whatever we will do or can do, will be within the scope of *ekisode*. It's important for us to realize that we're operating under a different nature so that we do not compare ourselves unfavorably to others or hold grand expectations."

"How do we manage the pain?"

"Swallow the painkillers as prescribed by the surgeons, keep using our own herbs and do all those things that will not exacerbate the wounds; but all that is just to soothe. Evolution is perfect at perfecting even mistakes."

"In which world are we going to evolve?" Kaleebu was skeptical. "I am not pouring water on your fire, Miisi, but the whole thing sounds too neat for me."

"It's hope though, isn't it?"

"In a perfect world maybe," Kaleebu said, "Where all other continents are asleep and would not interfere."

"Miisi, I say this with a raw mind," Ssekito started. "But if Europeans outwitted us, no matter how despicable their tactics were—isn't it time we came up with a strategy for our own survival rather than sitting here crying *look what they have done to us?*"

"That is for politicians, Ssekito," Kaleebu laughed. "This discussion is intellectual: we're merely thinking aloud, suggesting possibilities."

Despite Kaleebu's cynicism, Miisi was satisfied. At least the residents did not exchange worried looks this time. All he had to do was to tidy up the piece and cut it down to three hundred words before sending it off to his Sunday column, *Obufilosofi bwa Mzei Kintu in Bukkedde*, a Luganda tabloid. Its English sister paper, the New Vision, translated his column as *Local Worldview*, and had asked for an English version. The problem was that the most exciting responses came from the English-language readers. Miisi was wary of a militant feminist at Makerere University who sought a feminist angle in whatever he wrote. She had already called him a chauvinistic dinosaur perpetrating the patriarchy. That was why he had taken care to masculinize Africa this time.

7.

Lower primary pupils are dismissed from the midday parade. It is end of school for them. Boys and girls scatter, screaming. Miisi walks along the lower-school classroom block kicking a pebble with his bare feet. He is about to climb the ramp to the playground when a group of boys fly past challenging, "Fastest to the road, Miisi."

He breaks into a sprint.

Just as he is about to catch up, he sees his mother standing at the fringes of the football pitch waiting for him. He stops running.

She is frowning.

Miisi is seething. He walks toward her to chastise her for embarrassing him. What kind of mother tags along with a boy on his way home when he wants to race his friends down the road? He prepares to say, "Why have you come? I know my way home." But as he gets closer to her, he realizes that it is back. He can see it in the defiant way she holds her head. The condition makes her bold and unwomanly. But when he gets to her, without knowing why, Miisi walks past her.

As he walks home, he keeps looking over his shoulder. She is following him. The boys, huddling away from him, move in a group. He hurries to tell them that he does not know her: that she is just a woman following him, but they run away from him. The village is silent, as if everyone has fled. Miisi knows why. Residents are hiding from him and his mother. They are watching from behind their windows.

The house is quiet as well when he gets there. Someone whispers to him, "Where did you find her?"

"She came to school."

A girl weeps, "She slipped away, I swear, just like that. I turned my head like this, when I looked back she was gone."

The whispering is unnerving. Miisi wants to scream to break it. Someone follows his mother everywhere she goes. She starts to do the dishes but they stop her. She picks up a hoe and starts for the garden but someone asks her, "Where are you going?" She turns back without a word and picks up a knife as if she is going to peel vegetables. Someone asks for it. She refuses to hand it over. The boys struggle with her and take the knife from her.

Now his mother is angry. The way she says nothing, her lips pursed. Miisi knows that look. He wonders why people treat her without respect sometimes. The problem is that he is lying in a cradle. He attempts to climb out to stop them. He screams, "Don't talk to her like that, she's my mother," but a large face dips into the crib. It buries itself into his tummy and blows tickles. Miisi cries but he is giggling. He is horrified at himself; laughing at a time like this! He grabs the face's ears and pulls hard but the face laughs and blows harder and he squeals uncontrollably.

8.

Miisi had no plans for further studies after his MA program in the USSR. In the 60s and 70s, the Soviet Union was a major sponsor of postgraduate study for Ugandans even though anti-Soviet sentiments were high and the British system of education in Uganda looked down on Russian qualifications. Miisi went to Moscow because he had lost his job. Having set up his two wives with income-generating businesses, he ventured into further education. But after the three years in Russia—one year to learn the Russian language and two to do the master's degree—his family in Uganda advised him not to come home—Amin was killing the educated. Rather than stay in Russia, in 1972 Miisi flew to Britain where he waited for Amin to be deposed.

In Britain, Miisi had a lot of idle time on his hands. Then he saw a fellowship advertised in the *Times Educational Supplement* for research in sociology. He put in a half-hearted application: he did not expect to get it. Surprisingly, his proposal, "The Centrality of Bloodletting to Religious Practice', was accepted and he received a large grant. He was able to squeeze on rent and food to send some money home for his children's education. He also had a part-time job at the co-op supermarket as a cleaner.

Miisi's supervisor, Professor Johnstone-Clarke, was keen on the study. He advised Miisi to focus on human sacrifice in African pagan worship but Miisi wanted to focus on Christ and Isaac, the son of Abraham. Professor Johnstone-Clarke argued that these biblical figures had been studied exhaustively and he doubted that Miisi would bring anything new to the field. Miisi suggested focusing on sati but the supervisor said that the study would only be feasible if he took a feminist perspective and focused on women sacrifices. That was when Miisi decided to look at Ikemefuna in *Things Fall Apart* in relation to collective war sacrifice of the young, relating it to child worship in African communities. Since the novel was read as an anthropological text, his supervisor did not raise any objections. Miisi reinforced the subject by looking at the practice of *kiwendo* in ancient Buganda where young men were sacrificed by kings. Miisi presented *kiwendo* as a testostoronal control by the *ba kabaka* in times of population boom.

Besides something to do, Miisi pursued the research study in an attempt to overcome his invisibility. Since arriving in Britain Miisi had felt himself shrivelling. He craved attention. At work, he did outrageous things, dancing at the slightest excuse: he who was never keen on dancing at home. He told colleagues that he had six wives in Uganda: why? Every chance he got Miisi mentioned his PhD study coupled with Cambridge University, to the consternation of his working-class colleagues. The less they believed him, the more outrageous his tales became. On the other hand, he enjoyed the amazement of those who did believe him. "Meet Mezraim my African friend. Mezraim is a clever chap, he's in college."

At university, during group discussions of literary theory, Miisi was so silent other students forgot he was present. At first, he attempted to contribute to the discussions but soon became aware that every time he started to speak such an anxiety fell on the other students that they sat as if bracing themselves. Sometimes, his ideas were met with stony uncomfortable silence as if no one knew what to do with them. In any case, half the time Miisi did not catch the drift of the discussions, as he could never work out their words. Students at Cambridge whistled and hissed their words. Sounds died somewhere in the nose before articulation. He soon realized that here, at the university, speaking was a performance and his Luganda-English stood no chance at all.

Miisi retreated into himself. He started to look at the British with suspicion. This, however, had its roots in his childhood. He had grown up in Magonga Seminary with the Irish White Fathers. As a cross between a son and a pet, the priests indulged him. Every little thing he did, they washed him in praise. He found out later that the Fathers had planned to open an orphanage with him and his sister as the pioneer children. However, the project never received backing from Ireland and was abandoned. Instead, the priests found Miisi a family living in Britain to sponsor him and sent his sister away to the nuns in Nadangira. The Rector, Father John Mary McCann, kept Miisi at the seminary because McCann feared that Miisi would be killed because of a family curse. The British family, the O'Tooles, were extremely generous, paying Miisi's school fees and sending him presents at Christmas.

The priests and the O'Tooles were the first Europeans Miisi came into contact with. They were benevolent, gentle, and loving. To his young mind, the priests looked like Jesus Christ in the pictures and figurines scattered around the seminary. They took on a Christ-like character. And when in history he was taught about the Africans as Hamites who had been cursed by Noah, everything including his family, his people, and the priests fell into place. Miisi learned to associate white skin with goodness, cleverness, and godliness. Europe was heaven on earth. He had wished that the O'Tooles would adopt him outright and lift him out of Africa. He marveled that rather than shun him, the priests and the O'Tooles had chosen to love him. Miisi had worked hard in school to show that despite his Hamitic condition he was clever and could be good.

When he arrived in Britain, Miisi rang the number Mr. O'Toole had sent him in Moscow. A woman's voice answered. She had a difficult accent. He only caught the words "care home" and "are you family?" Mr. O'Toole's voice was very strong when he came to the phone. Unlike the woman, he spoke clearly. He was happy to hear that Miisi was in Britain. "Such a shame what that Idi Amin is doing to your country," Mr. O'Toole had said. But when Miisi asked if he could visit him, Mr. O'Toole hesitated.

"Look, Miisi, I am proud you have achieved so much. I am happy to have been of help but I want to keep it at that. Don't feel indebted to me. You don't have to visit me."

Miisi was taken aback. He agreed and thanked Mr. O'Toole profusely but when he hung up he wondered whether he had offended the old man. How could anyone spend so much money on a person and not wish to meet him? Miisi had dreamed of visiting the O'Tooles all his life. He wanted to show them how well he had used their money. As time passed and Miisi failed to get the jobs he was qualified for, Mr. O'Toole's request not to meet him took on the shape of rejection.

Rejection in Russia was no surprise. Novels he had read and films he had seen in Uganda portrayed Russians as white-haired evil maniacs. He had as much contempt for them as they had for him. Britain and America were the lands of humanity, the places Miisi longed to be. The real Britain took him by surprise. He came to the angry conclusion that the middle- and upper-class colonialists had invented and perpetuated a pseudo-messianic persona which they wore for the colonies, while back home they were different people. It explained why the White Fathers and the O'Tooles had been so good to him in Africa. God became an idea; if there was a God then he was racist. In anger, Miisi walked away from religion.

Miisi had filled the emptiness of the years with imagination. With a few West Indians, Black Americans, and African friends from Cambridge, he reconstructed an idealised picture of Africa fed by the books he read. In the media, an avalanche of negative images of an Africa quickly sinking into anarchy so soon after independence overwhelmed him. Horror stories were broadcast with glee and broke the resolve of so many black activists. Miisi squirmed in the palpable inadequacy of the African—the violence, greed, selfishness, and savagery. To keep his sanity, he and his friends constructed their own narratives of *we, they, us,* and *them*.

In these narratives, Miisi concentrated on those things that made black more human, wholesome, and natural than white. Once he had convinced himself of this, it was not hard to find evidence in the everyday manners, actions, tendencies, and behavior of Europeans.

At the end of 1979, when Miisi was finally able to return home, he had no idea how much he had changed. He was not prepared for the deterioration Uganda had undergone. Raw wounds were everywhere, on everyone. Looking at the impact on his family, he felt like a coward for staying in Britain. The image Miisi had constructed in Britain of the noble African rooted in his cultural values shunning Westernization was a myth. What he returned to were people struggling to survive, who in the process had lost the ability to discern vivid colors of right and wrong. Anything that gave them a chance to survive was moral. To make matters worse, people around him, including his family, called him *muzungu*: Miisi had become European amongst his people.

For two years, Miisi lectured at Makerere University, trying to bury the guilt that in his absence, none of his children had gone beyond O-level study. He could not bring himself to reconcile to his wife in the village to whom he had sent money for the children's school fees. He lived at the university dating different women. His children, knowing the emphasis he put on education, were embarrassed by their own lack and avoided him. His second wife had remarried.

The students at Makerere were more interested in certificates than in education. They hardly attended lectures and kept throwing recycled essays at him. The number of students per class was above two hundred. There were no tutorials, no seminars, and the library was a museum of books from antiquity. Miisi suspected that staff at the university press subsidized their meager salaries by selling exam papers to students. It crossed his mind that he could have stayed in Britain and he was ashamed of it. In 1982

Miisi gave up his university job, left the city, and settled in Kande Village with his first wife. He concentrated on raising cattle and blending in with the peasants.

But blending in was not easy. In rural Bulemeezi, a double-story, multi-bedroomed house and a doctorate from Cambridge were hard to disguise. At first, there was genuine interest as rumor went around the region that Dr. Kintu in the *golofa* house was coming home to stay. But when the villagers found out that his doctorate had nothing to do with medication they sucked their teeth in contempt.

"What's the use of a doctor who can't heal people?"

"It means he's read a lot of books."

"Listen to that, a doctor of books! What use is that to this village?"

Nonetheless, the residents knew Miisi's wife as an unpretentious woman who had struggled with eight children on her own during Amin's regime while Miisi rolled in European luxury, enjoying white women. When he arrived in Kande, the residents smiled and accepted him but set him apart. Whenever they saw him coming to join them, they wore an intelligent look for him, ready to sound intellectual. They found his ideas distant: talking for the sake of talking. However, they were proud to see their ideas and village published in *Bukedde* Sunday paper.

After getting to know him, the residents blamed Miisi's quirks and atheism on communist Russia. And though Miisi was not locally born, they knew enough to trust and respect him. He had been born in Bugerere but because of a tragedy, his home had been razed and the rest of his family, save for one sister were lost. Miisi had been adopted by a Catholic parish that put him in school. When he finished university he had worked for Transafrica, an international freight company. Because of the access to transport across East African nations, he had made money quickly by buying and selling merchandise from Kenya to Uganda, Tanzania, Rwanda, and Burundi. He had been keen to fulfill a childhood ambition of building a big double-storied house no one could burn down. He vowed to fill it with children so that none of his children would grow up alone. When Transafrica went bust, Miisi won a scholarship to study in Russia. That was enough information for them.

Miisi never talked about his research to the residents. What would he say? That he had spent four years exploring the possibility that bloodletting in society was buried deep in the human psyche where spiritual impulses lay? Understandably, the residents had nothing but contempt for Ugandans who got a chance to acquire knowledge and chose to acquire the useless kind. Human sacrifice, bloodletting, and the release of societal anxieties! What was he thinking? Nonetheless, he would have loved the residents to ponder his doctoral view that religious murder is either presented creatively as sacrifice or manipulatively as punishment.

9.

Müsi arrives home from school but home is not home: it is the seminary. This does not make sense. Why did he go to the old school when there is a primary school attached to the seminary? He should not go to his old school. He will never do that again. He turns into the neat paved way of the seminary but the house where he lives with the priests is occupied by his father, who has a large family. This is not right. His father has no right to be at the seminary. The seminary is his and his European friends'. He points this out to Father John Mary, "Take me away from him. Take me to Ireland," but the priest laughs at him. Müsi, now frantic, runs to the backyard but it is his old home. The roof is burned out but the walls are still standing. A crowd is milling around the door hole.

"Take that child away."

Müsi's arm is yanked. He is led away. But then he sees four policemen carry his mother out of the house. There is a rope around her neck. Her eyes, googly, stare at him. The policemen stand on the verandah and swing her body back and forth once, twice, on the third count they launch her into the courtyard. He hears her muffled thud. People scatter. The woman holding his hand lets go. Müsi runs back and sees one of the policemen pull out a whip. The policemen are dressed in the colonial uniform of starched khaki shorts and shirt with lots of pockets. They wear fez hats, black boots, and knee-high socks. The policeman lashes his mother's body. Women scream. Men look away. Müsi shouts at the policeman to stop but instead says, "You're wearing a safari suit," as if the policemen are daft.

"Take that child away," someone says because they don't want him to see.

All the grown-ups descend on him with unnecessary force and carry him away. But the whip is still cracking. Women cry as if the whip is being used on their bodies. The men are useless. "Do something, can't you hear Mother crying?" He catches snippets of whispers, "It's the law . . . The police must lash . . ."

"They've put the rope around my mother's neck so they can take her away," Miisi cries but no one listens. It hurts, it hurts, it hurts not being listened to.

Now the policeman is dragging his mother's body. Her corpse tries to crawl to keep up but it is too slow. It bothers him that his mother's corpse does not fight. She allows herself to be dragged to the grave. All those people staring, no one tries to save her. Yet in the grave she stares up at Miisi pleadingly. He says, "You've done this to yourself, you wanted to die!"

To his horror, he spits into the grave.

10.

Monday, January 12, 2004

Miisi was sitting on the balcony when two men emerged from the depression of the tarred road below his compound and walked toward his house. His heart jumped and he found himself trembling. Perhaps it was because he had never seen the men before. His heart had jumped needlessly because the men seemed uncertain. They wore awkwardly fitting coats with faded trousers. They were peasants dressed to mask that fact. Unfortunately, the effort seemed only to enhance their discomfort. The men came to the steps and disappeared under the balcony. After a short pause, he heard them call. He waited as they were received downstairs, listening out for the expected footsteps on the stairs coming for him. Finally, his sister came.

"There're men here asking for you. I've not told them that you are here, in case you don't want to see them."

Miisi went down the stairs with her. When he had greeted the men, they inquired whether he was Misirayimu Kintu.

"I am."

The men introduced themselves. The oldest, wearing an old-fashioned but new-looking coat, was Magga. Miisi guessed the coat was part of his wedding suit but Magga had not found an excuse to wear the coat since. The other man, whose coat was creased because it had been washed rather than dry-cleaned, was

Kato. Presently, Miisi's wife brought refreshments but the men declined.

"We must do what we came to do first," Magga said.

The men started by each reciting his parentage back to his sixth paternal grandfather who, in both cases, was called Kidda. Miisi thought it was strange: recitation of one's genealogy was done at traditional engagement rites, to eliminate common ancestry between the couple. He had never seen it happen between people who were meeting for the first time. He hoped that the men did not expect him to do the same for he did not even know his immediate grandfather's name. He did not need to worry. Magga, when he had done his own genealogy, looked straight at Miisi, reminded Miisi of his own name, his father's and grandfather's. Magga even knew where Miisi's father and grandfather had lived and where they were buried. Then he recited four more generations of Miisi's grandfathers. Magga's voice shook with emotion as he chronicled the generations. He sat on the floor with his legs folded underneath him as if he sat before the gods. Miisi listened to the names of his ancestors, where they had lived, where they were laid, and tried to picture them. Miisi's sixth grandfather was also Kidda—the common ancestor between the three of them. From then on, their histories merged as Magga talked about Kidda's father, Baale, the youngest son of Nnakato of old. At the mention of Nnakato, Magga's voice fell indicating that he was taking a break. Kato broke in to explain, "This Nnakato was Kintu's *kabeja*. Legend has it that for Kintu, the sun rose and set upon Nnakato. She only gave birth to twins, you see, until Baale came along. In turn, Baale had one child—this Kidda that we three share. Baale had Kidda by a servant called Zaya."

"Zaya was not a servant," Magga corrected as if they could not have a servant in their genealogy.

"Then why was she living in Kintu's home?" Kato challenged.

An awkward moment of silence ensued. Magga did not rise to the challenge. Instead he turned to Miisi and explained, "This Zaya, how she got pregnant with Baale's son when Baale was just about to get married, is unexplained—"

"Baale was a boy, he was playing around like boys do," Kato laughed.

Magga chose to ignore Kato and carried on, "But what we know is that Zaya ran away with the unborn child and settled somewhere in Kyaggwe. When the child was born, he was named Kidda after his grandfather, our forefather Kintu Kidda who was a Ppookino. But I will come back to that."

"Indeed, Kintu, Kidda, and Baale are recurrent names in our clan."

Magga's recitation rose again and he weaved through Baale's life. Baale was indulged by his parents. Apparently, because he was the only child without a twin, he asked for his own twin. His parents adopted a Tutsi, Kalema, as his twin and the two boys grew up together. "Then tragedy fell on the family. Baale dropped dry-dead on his wedding day and Nnakato, unable to take it, committed suicide. That was when it was discovered that Ppookino Kintu had killed the Tutsi, Baale's adoptive twin, and a curse had been cast on him and on his house. Soon, Kintu too lost his mind and disappeared. The rest of the family scattered throughout Buganda and beyond."

Magga once again took a breath while Kato interjected.

"At the time, Buddu was a large province. Our grandfather Kintu Kidda had devoured lands beyond the Kagera River bordering with the Bakaya people in Tanzania. We suspect the family grounds were somewhere close to the border with Tanzania."

Magga pulled out a sheet of paper on which the family tree had been drawn. Miisi was awestricken as he looked at different branches of the family.

"You are at the heart of the family tree," Magga said to Miisi. "We three are descendants of Kintu, of Baale, then of Kidda but you are the only surviving son of the heir lineage as it comes down the bloodline."

"You see Kintu Kidda had chosen Baale as his heir. In essence then, Baale's unborn son Kidda was to be the heir. When you follow that heir's blood it leads to you."

The men waited for Miisi to be awed. When he said nothing,

Kato said softly, "We know that the curse has been harsh on you. Ours is a dreadful inheritance—"

"But then we're blessed with twins," Magga interrupted.

"Yes, there is that," Kato, a twin himself, smiled. "But we would like to say that you should not be hard on your father, he was only trying—"

Miisi laughed cynically.

"He was ill-advised by a quack who had no idea what he was dealing with."

"Indeed, any true medium would know that one man's action toward this curse is a dog barking at an elephant."

"So it is true?" Miisi asked.

Magga and Kato looked at each other.

"What do you mean?"

"That I had an older brother called Baale."

"You were young."

"My mother talks about him in my dreams."

Kato glanced at Magga as if seeking permission to volunteer more information.

"Yes, your oldest brother was Baale and … he died."

"Father sacrificed him."

"He did not. It was the quack. No father would—"

"Abraham almost did."

"Well," Magga smiled uncomfortably, "I don't know about Abraham but your father was told that just one son, the eldest, would break the curse."

"Was Baale the smell in the house?"

"What smell?"

"There was a smell in the house."

"How would you know?"

"I dream."

The men looked at each other, baffled. Then Magga said, "The quack prescribed to keep the embalmed body in the roof to ward off the curse."

"If I believed in this curse you talk about, I would take you outside to my back garden and show you the beds laid out for ten out of my twelve children." Miisi glared at the men as if they had killed his children.

"We know."

"But the reality is," Miisi interrupted Kato firmly, "that five of my children were killed during the war and five have died of this *our new thing*. How can I blame a curse?"

Magga sighed as if he had expected this resistance.

"Regardless of what you believe, Miisi, the sooner we start the restoration the better."

"Restoration? What restoration?" Miisi asked.

"The family seat in Buddu."

"Who is buried in *o* Lwera?" Miisi asked.

The men looked at each other. Then Magga asked, "Has someone been to talk to you?"

Miisi wanted to laugh at their bewildered faces.

"I told you, I dream."

Magga sat up. Then he looked at Kato. Before the men recovered, Miisi, now drunk on their shock, said, "Tell me about the bees then."

"What bees?"

"You know nothing about the bees?" Miisi derided.

"Bees are a myth," said Magga. "Apparently, long, long ago a woman gave birth to a bee in the family ... that sort of thing," Magga laughed. "What I know is that either there was a brother named Kayuki or there was a colony of bees close to the house."

"A swarm of bees arrived here a week ago and camped in a room upstairs," Miisi said.

Magga shivered.

"Then what happened?" Kato asked.

"Nothing. They died. But then I dreamt again."

"Dreamt?"

"A man covered in bees took me to an old place, a hill. He showed me where a Nnakato and a Baale are buried. Then he took me to a moor where a lad Kalemanzira and my father are buried."

There was silence. The men stared at him.

"Before I forget," Miisi could not help laughing at their grave faces, "He told me to take my brothers and build him a dwelling: he gave me the specific measurements and showed me the tree to use and the one where Nnakato hanged herself."

There was silence for a long time. Then Kato stood up rather quickly.

"We have to hurry back and report this to the clan elders. It seems like the ancients came to you before we did." Magga was clearly rattled.

"What did you do with the bees? Dead bees are an omen—death," Kato said.

"My sister, who believes in that sort of thing, buried them. And as you can see, no one has died."

"Wait a minute," Magga whispered to Kintu. "You have no sister."

Miisi glared first at Magga then at Kato for a while. Then he blurted, "I don't like the news you have brought."

"We are sorry," Kato threw a warning glance at Magga as if to say watch what you say. "None of your family survived the fire. The priests wanted you to heal and gave you a playmate."

"Maybe we should wait until you meet the rest of the elders: they'll explain things better." Kato could not wait to leave.

"Don't worry about it. No one will tell me she is not my sister," he smiled. Seeing how shaken the men were, he added, "For a moment there, I got caught up in this whole spiritual situation and played the spiritualist at you. It is true I dream but my dreams are nothing but the rumblings of a disturbed mind. Please don't read anything into them."

"We hear you, Miisi, but the elders will decide what is significant and what is not."

The men left without drinking their juice. Miisi wondered what had come over him to say what he did. He hoped the elders had more common sense than Magga and Kato.

11.

Saturday, January 24, 2004

Miisi opened wide the double doors of the garage and walked around his Toyota, a reconditioned Grande G—locally known as a *Nagoya*—checking the tires. Then he got in and turned the engine. The red needle of the fuel gauge rose to the quarter mark. He turned the engine off. The fuel was saved for emergencies: his depression was not. Depression was the fancy name Miisi brought back from Britain for the slumps that sometimes bothered him. The slumps came on when he allowed himself to dwell on things. Since he met the two cousins, Magga and Kato, he had been dwelling on things. He stepped out of the car and banged the door shut. He closed the garage doors and walked across the compound down to the main road. He knew he should tell the family that he was going out but he lacked the resolve. He crossed the road and stood on the other side waiting for a taxi.

The depression crept on Miisi like a chill. He could not blame it on the cousins' visit twelve days earlier: they only confirmed what had been in his subconscious all along.

A week after their visit, Miisi woke up feeling tired. His mind was a fog as if the drowsiness of a strong medicine had not quite worn off. For a long time, he sat on the bed with his eyes closed.

His wife was dusting in the bedroom. For some reason, her dusting was shrill in his ears. There was a dead taste in his mouth. Seeing how quiet he was, his wife stopped cleaning and joked, "Your foul ancestors are upon you. You're gnashing your teeth."

Miisi stood up, stomped out of the bedroom and sat on the balcony. He did not go downstairs that day. He did not eat at all. The family tiptoed around him. He heard his wife tell the children, "Tread lightly around him upstairs: he's looking for someone to bite."

Miisi knew that he was making the house jittery, he knew that they thought he was just being moody, but he could not snap out of it.

The following day, Miisi once again sat on the balcony, leaning against the wall. To shake himself out of it, he had closed his eyes to imagine beautiful things but instead his mind revisited the 80s bush war that stole away five of his sons. The tragedy was that four of the boys shared a mother, his second wife. At the end of the war, when the bodies of all her progeny with Miisi had been located, exhumed, and reburied, she laughed, "What was all that sex about?"

At first, the bush war was a fable. Miisi had only resettled in the village for one and a half years when one day a green Tata lorry stopped at the crossroads near his house and tipped out a load of soldiers. They spread out in the village like hatched spiders. Word went around that the government suspected rebel activity in the area and the soldiers had come to flush them out. Three days later, when a whole family was killed in the night, villagers started to sleep in the bush.

Nkaada, Miisi's eldest, died first. He was thirty-two. He was the most handsome and, for Miisi, the easiest of all his sons to get along with because Nkaada did not know how to hold a grudge. At the age of four, he contracted the flu, which his mother ignored. Miisi was working and lived in the city with his second woman at the time, estranged from his first wife. When Miisi came home to visit, Nkaada's legs had been sucked thin and soft by polio: the boy dragged himself about on his bottom. Miisi immediately took his other children for immunization. Later, when he returned from Britain, Nkaada had become the village cobbler. Miisi bought him a motorized wheelchair, which Nkaada protected more than his life.

That first evening, before the family left for the bush, Nkaada asked to be lifted into his old wheelchair, the new one was hidden in the ceiling. He told the rest of the family to go and leave him in the house. Nothing happened that night. At dawn, the family crept back embarrassed that they had overreacted. Nonetheless, at dusk, the family disappeared into the bush again. When they returned on the third morning, Nkaada was not in the wheelchair. They searched the house but he was nowhere to be found. Then he crawled out of the outdoor kitchen beaming. He was covered in ash.

"Something warned me to leave the house last night, and they came," he said triumphantly.

"What were they like?"

"That is the funny thing. They were not army. They wore ordinary clothes but had guns. They climbed over the water tank onto the back balcony and into the house. They took nothing though. They did not look in here. It is queer, but I thought I heard Lamula's voice amongst them."

Lamula was Miisi's son who lived in the city.

That evening, as dusk drew near, it became clear that Nkaada was frightened, that he did not want to be left behind. Guilt fell over the house and then grew thorns. The family avoided each other's eyes, they avoided Nkaada's presence. Nkaada's wide eyes, normally languid with laughter, were now dark with resentment. At around six o'clock, after supper, one by one, the young ones stole away to the bush until only Miisi remained downstairs. His wife was upstairs, hiding her tears. Finally, Miisi said, "You're coming with us tonight."

Nkaada shook his head. "Put me in bed. I want to sleep."

"How shall we—?"

"Go, Father, go!"

Miisi called his wife to help lift Nkaada. By the time she got downstairs, Nkaada was wiping his eyes.

"Go, both of you. They won't kill a cripple."

As they started to lift him out of the wheelchair, gunshots rang out in the back garden and Miisi saw an army uniform running behind the kitchen. When he turned, both Nkaada and his wife had vanished. Gunfire came again close to the back door. Moments later, Miisi was behind a bush near the outer compound where the boys played football.

It was a bad raid with bullets flying about for days. As he dodged gunshots, Miisi drifted further from the house. Sanity would prevail: no one would touch a disabled man, he told himself. In those few days Miisi found out that guns had personalities: some cracked, some thundered, and some roared. With the roaring came tiny gunshots, like corn popping. Silence, after gunfire, fell like rain on leaves. Birds were silent. Bushes stood still. Time crawled. Until gunshots came again.

On the fourth day, the first people Miisi saw without guns were strangers, so he stayed put. Then he heard Kaleebu's voice and emerged from the passion-fruit thicket he had occupied for two days. Kaleebu talked about a frontline that had been at Katikamu near the schools but had now been moved to Wobulenzi Town. He didn't know what had happened to his family either. Miisi and Kaleebu walked back home, avoiding the road and open spaces. Everyone they met was going in the opposite direction, toward Bukeeka.

At Miisi's house, the two men slithered along the fringes of the garden watching the house for signs of life. Faint sounds of digging came from behind the outdoor kitchen. When they came closer, the metal of a hoe flashed in the sun and descended repeatedly. Its rhythm was not threatening: someone was digging a deep hole. Four days in the bush had sharpened Miisi's instincts. He could tell a safe bush: the shrub near the kitchen was thick enough.

Miisi ran behind it and saw two of his sons. Ssendi, the fourteen-year-old, stood by a sack while Jumba, two years his senior, dug a hole. When a turn in the wind brought the stench of rotting flesh, Miisi jumped out of the bush. The lads fled. Kaleebu ran after them trying not to call out loud. Miisi remained at the hole with the sack. He felt so light-headed that he leaned against the kitchen wall. When the boys returned, Miisi pointed at the sack.

"Who is that?"

"Who do you think?" Jumba said.

Miisi sat down. The smell was bearable after all.

"Here, help me," Jumba heaved the side of the sack to roll it into the hole but Miisi did not move. Jumba motioned knowingly to Ssendi that their father was such a *muzungu*. Jumba dragged the sack up to the edge of the hole. Then he jumped into the hole with Ssendi. Kaleebu kept watch. The boys lowered the sack and climbed out. Jumba sprinkled earth on the sack and said, "Nkaa-da, brother, wait here until we return. Then we shall give you proper rites." Miisi looked at his son in disbelief. "Don't hold this against us." Jumba carried on as if his father was not there to take lead of the burial. When Jumba had finished he said to Ssendi, "Let's cover him."

Miisi turned to Kaleebu. "We've got to tell people." But Kaleebu started to help Jumba fill the grave. Ssendi was on the watch now. Still, Miisi did not help to fill the hole. Kaleebu went back to watch without a word and Jumba continued to fill the grave while Ssendi carried the cooking stones from the kitchen to mark it.

When they finished, Jumba looked at Miisi and whispered to his brother, "He should've stayed in England."

Miisi slapped him.

Jumba did not flinch, the grin stayed on his face. Ssendi carried on as if he had not seen the slap. Kaleebu watched the horizon. Miisi's hands shook.

"I've got to check my house," Kaleebu said.

"There's no one at your house," Jumba said, the grin still on his face.

"Maybe someone has just arrived."

"But we saw your family on their way toward Bukeeka two days ago."

"Did you say you saw them?"

"Your wife and everyone."

"Well," Kaleebu smiled.

"Let's go then," Miisi said.

"Still, I'll glance at my house one last time," Kaleebu insisted.

"One-last-time is the biggest killer," Jumba laughed at his own wit.

"I'll kill this boy before the guns do," Miisi threatened.

"Where do we go then?" Kaleebu asked.

"That way," Miisi pointed in the direction of Bukeeka and started walking. But the boys stayed put. Miisi stopped and looked back at them. Ssendi looked away. He tugged at a blade of grass. When it came free, he chewed at it frantically. Jumba said, "We're going to Butanza."

Jumba looked at his father as if Miisi was a playmate he had just thrown off the team.

"Kayita's sons did it." Ssendi said in a small voice. "Lamula is with the rebels. He brought them to the house the night before; probably to warn us."

"But Lamula's in the city," Miisi said in disbelief.

No one answered.

"We'll come back. Kayita and his family will pay for what happened to Nkaada," Jumba said.

"There must be a bug in your head, Jumba." Miisi narrowed his eyes.

"It's grief talking. They don't know what they're saying." Kaleebu touched Jumba's shoulder. The boy shrugged him off and turned to Ssendi.

"Come, let's go." To his father he added excitedly, "We're going to *Rambo in the Jango*," and he sparred like he was Muhammad Ali himself. "Friends have enlisted us. The rebels' frontline is a just a few miles away from here."

"You are going to kill me. Knowing that you're somewhere carrying a gun will kill me."

Jumba laughed: "Lamula's been carrying one all this time."

"You go, I disown you," Miisi tried one last attempt but the boys walked on, past the kitchen, past the outside toilet. Miisi last saw them as the shrubs under the mango tree swallowed them.

Miisi and Kaleebu spent that night up a tree. When they saw a large group of women and children coming toward them, they came down and joined the throng. They started their exodus in August 1983 and went around in circles for months until January 1984 when the group was rounded up and put into a concentration camp in Ssemuto. It was a year later, while in the camp, that Miisi learned that Ssendi and Jumba had been killed close to home shortly after enlisting. Miisi was comforted by the fact that the boys had not got the chance for revenge. His mind was about to relive Lamula's death, his other soldier son, when a child came up the stairs and asked whether he would dine on his own.

When Miisi got out of the taxi in Kalagala Bugerere, he could hear the Nile whirling. He was glad he had not brought the car. At the sound of water, his fog began to lift. As he got closer, the whirling turned to rumbling. By the time he reached the riverbank, the roar of water was deafening. He crossed the picnic area and stood on the rocks. The Nile was a steep drop below. Its banks were gray with jagged rocks. The water rushed from his right, plunged over a cliff, and crashed down on the rocks. For a moment at the bottom the water was frothy and confused. Then it sorted itself out and set off for Egypt.

A picture out of a history textbook flashed in Miisi's mind and he smiled. John Hanning Speke, hat and spectacles, stood with one triumphant arm punching the air, the other on his hip. Below the picture was the caption: THE FIRST MAN TO SEE THE SOURCE OF THE NILE. The last time Miisi came there was a plaque saying: JH SPEKE STOOD IN THIS EXACT SPOT SOMEWHERE NEARBY. Someone without a sense of humor must have removed it.

Miisi had been told that he was discovered in this same spot that morning when his home burned down. Over the years, he had refused to consider why his mother left him out here and went back to set the family on fire. Apart from the time when he lived in Britain, Miisi had always visited the Nile and sat in the same spot whenever the slumps bothered him. What he could never explain was why his depression always lifted whenever he came here.

Miisi sat down and his shadow squatted beside him. Spray, like steam, rose from the water below. Once, the wind blew it into his face. It was thin and ephemeral, as fine as perspiration. Miisi was at peace. A sensation, as if he sat on his mother's lap leaning against her chest, overwhelmed him. His eyes began to droop. He tried to stay awake by looking up. In a few hundred yards, the Nile turned sharply making the bank on the other side, covered in dense forest, seem like an island. He lost the fight. He laid back on the grass and fell asleep. When he woke up, night had fallen. He returned home uplifted. The following day, he sent a message to Kamu and Kusi, his two remaining children, asking them to come home urgently.

12.

Saturday, January 31, 2004
Only Kusi came.

Two army cars—an open Jeep full of soldiers and a Mitsubishi Pajero with smoked windows—drove up to the house. The men in the Jeep jumped out and melted into the hedge. The Pajero door opened and Kusi jumped out. She wore camouflage, her forehead was covered by a black beret. She was so lanky and flat-chested that Miisi saw no distinction between her and the men. But when her face cracked into a smile Miisi saw his daughter.

Kusi had joined the rebels at the same time as her brothers. Despite the fact that she was only twelve at the time, she was the only combatant in the family to survive the bush war. When the war ended in '86, she refused to give up her gun, saying she did not know how to do anything else. Besides, Miisi hardly knew her because she had been just a baby when he left for Europe. She had now risen to the rank of general. In public she was known as General Salamander.

"*Mzei!*" Kusi used the Swahili word for "old one." She took the front steps two at a time and she was hugging him.

"Where have you been?" Miisi looked up in her face. He knew he sounded clingy but he could not help himself.

"Busy."

"Do you have to come with so many men?" Miisi swept his hands over the cars.

"They wanted to see what you look like. They read your column."

"Then wait a minute," and he hurried upstairs. In Kusi's presence, Miisi's excitement was almost childlike. When he returned, moisturizer was still wet on his face and his hair was combed. "Do I look all right?" he asked. "I don't want to embarrass you."

Kusi only laughed.

"How is Kande Village?"

"The sun thinks we're barbecue." Miisi led her into the house.

"What are you doing with yourself, apart from writing?"

"Nothing much."

Once in the sitting room, Miisi greeted Kusi again, this time formally. She removed her beret, revealing short curly hair. She knelt down to return his greeting but Miisi told her not to. The children streamed in to greet Kusi, followed by Miisi's sister and his wife. When they had finished, Miisi asked, "What are you *doing* now?"

"Fixing things here and there." Kusi was evasive as usual.

"Major fighting?"

"Up North. Kony is elusive."

"Why you?"

Kusi shrugged.

Miisi scratched his head.

"It's as if there are no men in the army, the way they use you."

Kusi laughed and stood up. Because he did not see her grow up, Miisi had never got used to the fact that Kusi was over six foot tall. She strode outside and called out something in Swahili. Miisi stood up to see. The men carried in groceries through the corridor to the dining area. He went to the backyard and called the family.

"Come, everyone. Come and see what my girl has done."

Kusi had brought two sacks of rice, a sack of sugar, two sacks of maize meal, a carton of soap, salt, the hind-quarter of a cow, and four bunches of *matooke*. Profuse *thank you*s issued from everyone. A child came in carrying a tray with a cup and a teapot.

"Take the tea to the sitting room," Miisi told the child.

"Why not here with us? We want to talk to her as well," Miisi's sister protested.

"We have something important to talk about," Miisi told his sister as if Kusi was a son and they were going to have manly whispers.

"All right, send her to us as soon as you're finished."

As soon as they got in the house, Miisi asked, "Where is Kamu?"

"I've not spoken to him since Christmas," Kusi said. "You know how he cuts himself off from everyone. His phone is switched off."

"Keep an eye on each other, Kusi. There are only two of you left."

"I only arrived from the north this morning and I am going back today. I will not be able to see him but I will keep calling."

"When are you having a child?" Miisi changed subject.

Kusi's head dropped. "Father—"

"Let me finish. I am not asking you to get married. I would not inflict you on any man, I am only asking for a child."

"You're running an orphanage here, *Mzei*."

"None of them is yours. I am asking for yours, at least one."

"It's the time. I don't have it."

"Kusi, everyone knows you're a woman."

"I'll think about it."

"One other thing, and you will not believe this but recently, I found out that we are part of a wider family. Huge!"

Kusi looked uninterested. "What do they want?"

"What do they want? Child, to know us."

"OK, I'll meet them one day." Kusi made to walk away.

"Wait. They've been to see me twice now. They're very traditional. They tell a lot of stories about a curse in the family—"

"Now you're getting old, *Mzei*."

"I've been growing old for some time, Kusi," Miisi laughed.

"But the important thing is, according to them, I am a clan leader and the head of the elders' council."

Kusi laughed. "Of course they will make you a clan head because they think you are rich. Soon all their problems will be brought to you. I can't believe you've fallen for that kind of thing, *Mzei*."

"I've not fallen for anything. First of all, they are not needy and they know that I am poor. Secondly, it gives me something to do, Kusi. I am now writing letters to all family heads, I am organizing meetings for the elders' council, I am meeting new people and learning new things about our clan's history. Besides, it's a chance for me to observe and study traditional spirituality. You have no idea of the implications to knowledge."

"I don't have time for traditional antics," Kusi turned again to walk away.

"Listen, Kusi, and this is important to me. At some point in April we shall visit the family roots, somewhere in Rakai District where we all come from. I need you and Kamu to come along."

"I can't promise anything now, *Mzei*. We'll see when the time comes."

As if to indicate that the visit was over, Kusi took an envelope from her breast pocket and handed it to Miisi. "That's to help with the children's school fees, books, and fuel for the car. Now I must go, *Mzei*. Oh, I liked the *Ekisode* piece," she turned and smiled.

Miisi did not stop waving as the cars drove out of his compound, turned onto the main road, and disappeared. As his arm fell to the side, Miisi felt tears stinging his eyes. Kusi's visits were brief. She executed them with military efficiency. He longed to ask her to stay over so they would talk into the night but Kusi was too restless for that. As Miisi walked back into the house, he remembered that he had promised to send Kusi to her aunt and his wife so they could talk to her. He waved his hands at his forgetfulness.

BOOK SIX

THE HOMECOMING

1.
KIYIIKA, BUDDU

Saturday, March 6, 2004

When the elders parked a plush Mitsubishi Pajero Turbo at the local *kitawuluzi* in Kiyiika Village, residents materialized out of the vegetation and stared. When they announced that they were Nna-kato, the village spirit's descendants, and that they wished to talk to the local councillors, there was a stir. But when they proclaimed their homecoming intentions, the villagers laughed. To them, the three men and their car oozed the fragility born of a cushioned city life and ineptness in matters of a spirit like Nnakato. The woman did not count.

Kiyiika was a shy hamlet. It perched on a hillside teetering on the border with Tanzania. Camouflaged by foliage, it reminded Miisi of the 40s when remote villages were demure, often hidden behind dense shrubbery, barely touched by the wider world. In Kiyiika, vegetation still soared. Trees, shrubs, and bushes were lofty. The hilltop was capped by a wooded area known as Nna-kato's little forest. Human inhabitants were few. They slipped in and out of the flora unobtrusively. For a moment, Miisi felt like he had gone back to childhood.

Waiting outside the *kitawuluzi* for the local councillors, Miisi had never heard nature's sounds so distinctly. Bird songs were so varied it felt as if he were on an island for birds. When the wind came, large banana leaves in the distance whirled like waves on a lake, then the flat coffee leaves flapped. As the wind drew closer, the tiny leaves of a *muvule* above them shivered. Then it blew past the *kitawuluzi* picking up dust and dry leaves, only to dump them a few meters away. The rustling of reed shrubs across the road came last as the wind died into the distance.

The houses, the ones Miisi could see, were roofed with corrugated iron but the walls were built traditionally of wood, reed, and mud. Homes were surrounded and often obscured by large gardens of *matooke* and coffee *shamba*s cut through with tiny paths. The posture of the residents was that of a life without haste, as if there was nothing exciting about the future. Miisi put this preserved state of Kiyiika Village down to the local legend: a community that treated village lore as fact was bound to be frozen in the past.

This was the initial journey by the elders' council to Kiyiika. It was made to locate their place of origin—where Kintu of old had lived. The elders had set off at three in the morning from Kampala. Kiyiika was over seven hours from the city and the roads were deplorable. Miisi had traveled with three other elders—Dr. Kityo Kintu, a retired dermatologist; Kitooke Kintu, a retired civil engineer; and Bweeza, who was not part of the elders' council but turned up for the meetings anyway. Bweeza claimed to have come in place of Kanani Kintu, the head of her branch of the clan, who had declined. The young man, Isaac Newton Kintu, who represented his father, had not secured leave from work to join them.

The elders' council, convened by Miisi, had been meeting weekly for a month now. For Miisi, gaining so many relations overnight was overwhelming. He was planning, after the reunion, to invite the elders' council to his village in Kande so that they could meet his neighbors. It was important to him that the residents back home knew that he came from a large clan.

The journey to Kiyiika had not been without incident. Earlier, as the elders drove through the region, their car had stopped to make way for a herd of cattle when Miisi heard bells tinkling. Moments later, a troupe of hunters emerged with game slumped on their backs, dogs in tow. Miisi had leapt out of the car and pumped the hunters' hands, praising them for keeping tradition alive. Seeing the hunters' confusion, he had said, "I hail from here. This is the home of my ancestors."

"Oh, who do you hail from?" the oldest man had asked.

"Kintu Kidda."

"Kintu Kidda?"

"Kintu, husband of Nnakato." Kitooke stepped out of the car to explain.

"Oh, *our* Nnakato." The old man was not about to be corrected by a stranger in a car.

"That's the one. Her husband was Kintu Kidda, a Ppookino."

"In that case, welcome home," the old man had said. "None of our families is that old. All we know is our Nnakato."

"Kintu died in *o* Lwera, you see," Kitooke explained.

"We thought Kintu was just a story." The old man's words were tinged with sarcasm. "A child of Nnakato is our child. She is the constant feature in this region; the rest of us are wind."

When Miisi got back in the car, Kitooke sighed, "When do these people hope to join the rest of the world?"

"Are you happier for it?" Miisi asked. "I hope there're no Christians or Muslims here. Religion is toxic."

"By the time Kanani is through with them, Kiyiika will be singing *Hallelujah Amen*," said Kityo.

"Kanani should not go anywhere near the residents."

"Who knows? Maybe they would like a local takeaway."

Soon after, the elders had come to Nswera Swamp and driven down into a deep valley. That is when it became clear why they had been advised to take a turbo-engine car: the narrow track in the swamp was muddy and slippery. In the middle was a large stream bridged with *nkoma* tree logs. Kitooke, driving, looked at the logs uncertainly and stopped the car. Bweeza asked what was wrong and Kitooke answered, "I doubt that bridge can take the car."

"Those logs are *nkoma*," Bweeza said as if *nkoma* made the sturdiest bridges in the world.

"Bweeza, they are logs."

"Then you've never heard of *nkoma*."

Just then, locals, concerned that something was wrong, came along. When the party asked them whether there was an alternative route because the bridge seemed unsound, the locals sucked their teeth and walked away.

"Compared to the loaded lorries our bridge carries every day, your car is a toddler," one of them said, clearly offended.

"These *kaperes* from the city!"

So as not to lose face and not to alienate the locals before their mission had begun, Kitooke drove the car onto the logs. The men held their breath. The bridge was sound. Bweeza rolled her eyes.

Finally, four councillors arrived and led the elders inside the *kitawuluzi*. Miisi guessed that on top of serving as the traditional court, the *kitawuluzi* doubled as the community hall. The doorway was a hole in the wall, the floor loose earth. A councillor blew dust off two benches, wiped them down with his hand, and invited the elders to sit.

Firstly, the elders introduced themselves by chronicling their genealogies down to Kintu Kidda whom they now prefixed with the words, "Husband of Nnakato the spirit." This was received with relief and respect but when they stated the clan's desire to reconnect with its roots, the elders were once again derided. Apparently, in the past, many people had come to Kiyiika claiming to be descendants of Nnakato and on a mission to revive the clan. Nothing but clowning came of these efforts.

"One time, a woman came," a councillor explained, "And started doing things up in the forest. We didn't know that she had a child with her. The following day we heard her screaming. When we got there, a python had gripped the child. By the time it let go, the child was dead. Now, there are no pythons in this village."

There was silence as the elders digested this information.

"We're not discouraging you," another councillor broke the silence. "You're welcome to explore both Nnakato's forest and her hill. After all, if you are impostors, Nnakato can look after herself."

For Miisi, listening to the councillors, it was amazing how the Kintu story had mutated over the centuries. Kintu Kidda, the essence of everything, had been erased from Kiyiika's memory while Nnakato had flourished to divine proportions. When he asked the councillors what they knew about Nnakato's legend one of them explained, "Nnakato was a powerful matriarch who gave birth to twins only, apart from her last and favorite son, Baale. But then her family suffered a great tragedy in which family members died, including Baale. Nnakato is said to have taken her life afterwards."

"Some say that Babirye, Nnakato's twin, killed Baale inadvertently and she disappeared: that is where the whole tragedy started," another councillor interjected.

"What we're sure of is that Nnakato is still searching: some say for Babirye, others say it is Baale she seeks."

According to the villagers, the presence of Nnakato the spirit came with emizizo—dos and don'ts. It was taboo to cut trees or collect firewood in her forest.

"When you harvest anything—fruit, vegetables, or honey—leave half behind for her."

When a resident was caught by rain in Nnakato's forest, it was advisable to run because she strolled in the rain. At night, if one heard footsteps behind them, it was best not to look back: it could be Nnakato.

"She has a pet leopard, you see."

The elders sat up.

"It's harmless." The eldest councillor waved their fears away. "You'll be lucky to see it. But if you do, pretend not to have seen it. All it means is that Nnakato is close by."

"Don't keep fire burning in the night."

Pressed by Miisi, the councillors confessed that none of them had actually ever sighted Nnakato the spirit themselves.

"Some people have seen her hanging like a bat on a tree."

"Didn't old Nnabayego see her at high noon bathing in that gorge?"

"There is a gorge?" Miisi asked.

"Yes, it watered the family in Nnakato's time."

The elders exchanged looks. Miisi was bewitched. Here was an ancient story kept alive by the breath of belief. And he, Misirayimu Kintu, was at the center of it. It did not matter that he did not believe the spiritual aspect of it: what mattered was that for some reason, tradition had preserved the history of his ancestry.

"If Nnakato has been calling then this is us answering," Bweeza stated extravagantly.

The councillors still looked skeptical. Miisi expounded on their plans and gave the councillors the schedule for the family reunion. "We will hold the homecoming rites during the Easter weekend—from Good Friday the ninth to Easter Monday the twelfth of April. However, some cousins might arrive earlier and some might leave later. Before then, we shall return to tour both Nnakato's hill and the little forest. There will also be other family members coming to prepare the place. However, any cousins that come will report to you first and inform you of their intentions."

The councillors were happy with this.

"As you can see," Bweeza added, "We are ignorant where Nnakato the spirit is concerned. Could you guide us on how to behave when we're on her land?"

"That we shall do," the councillors promised.

Before leaving, Miisi asked the councillors how far away the border with Tanzania was.

"Get to the top of Nnakato's hill and roll down the other end. At the bottom you'll be in Tanzania."

Miisi whistled. "That's what the British call a close shave. A slight wavering in the colonial pen and Nnakato would be Tanzanian."

"Would the Tanzanians let us claim our heritage?"

"Ask Idi Amin what happened when he tried."

The journey back to Kampala was easier. The elders arrived in *o* Lwera at about six thirty. Men displayed fresh fish and other foodstuffs by the roadside. Miisi reflected on the terrors *o* Lwera once held for travelers. Sayings and proverbs suggested that it was a daunting endless desert. Now, with the modern Masaka Road cutting across its center, *o* Lwera was just a harmless stretch of moorland. He looked through the window to the right; Lake Victoria was a gray line on the horizon.

"You know," Miisi said aloud, "Sometimes I wonder who would name this lake Victoria and call Lutanzige, a tiny one with no relation to Nnalubaale, Albert."

"They pissed on every landmark, these guys," Kitooke said.

"I still can't get over the councillors' trust though," Bweeza changed the subject. "They've handed over hundreds of acres of land and community heritage to us just like that."

"They have not," Kityo clicked his tongue. "Go build a private house on it and see."

"We must put back something in the community," Miisi said quietly. "We could rebuild the *kitawuluzi* or contribute to their schools."

"There you go now thinking that they need our help," Bweeza snapped. "That is how people start feeling inadequate. Soon Kiyiika will be begging. As long as they are not starving or sick I suggest we leave them alone."

The car fell silent.

2.

Kanani woke up tired. He had not yet recovered from the journey to Kiyiika. The uneven ground he had slept on did not help: every inch of his body ached. As he became conscious, he remembered that today was the beginning of the biggest crusade of his life yet Faisi, his indefatigable fighter, was not by his side. He sat up and knelt on his sleeping bag to pray. He asked God to abide by him all weekend as he clashed with the Devil in his clan.

He reached into his bag and retrieved his little wonder, a tiny camping radio/torch/alarm. It was sheathed in a brown leather wallet. He pulled the segmented antenna out to half a meter long and turned on the radio. After a few moments of static jarring as he searched the waves for a clear channel, the news in Luganda came on. There had been a massacre in Bwaise: four local councillors and six other residents had been murdered. Kanani sucked his teeth at how easy yet effective the Devil's work was while he struggled to make even a tiny impact. This made him more determined than ever to save as many souls as he could this weekend. When the news ended, he turned off the radio, unzipped the entrance to his tent, bent his head, and stepped outside.

The morning was still cold because the sun took time to filter through the canopy. In the clearing nearby were four massive open tents. Further in the wooded area, numerous traditional tents made out of sticks and dried banana leaves hung around trees. Kanani guessed that there were at least two hundred cousins camping so far. Apparently, a large group had arrived from Tanzania and they spoke Luganda proper. Looking around, the clan was clearly deep in a spiritual jungle. Kanani saw himself at the forefront of clearing the bush to let "the light" in but fatigue overwhelmed him. There was so much work to do, too little time to do it, and too few people willing to join in. But then, if he failed, the Bible said that stones would preach, spreading the word of God. He dared not fail.

To his left, further clearing had been done up the hill. At the center of the new clearing, the construction of a shrine was underway. Kanani's heart lurched. The elders had assured him that they would be constructing a house on the site: a hostel for descendants who would come in search of their roots. But this was no hostel; the circular architecture of the structure and thatch were suspicious. The framework, including the roof, was already in place. Some men weaved reeds between poles to create spaces that would be filled with the mud to form the walls. On one side of the structure, bales of hay lay ready for the roof. On the other, men kneaded mud-dough with their feet. Kanani turned away in repugnance.

He caught sight of Miisi and stopped. Though dressed traditionally, Cousin Miisi's posture—the way he held his head, the unrelenting humility and friendliness—reminded Kanani of the British missionaries that came to Namirembe Cathedral from time to time. There was no English intrusion in Miisi's speech, but the way he weaved his sentences and his gestures betrayed a distinct Western influence. It is this exoticism that has won him adulation in the clan, Kanani thought contemptuously. Yet if the Devil had taken human form, it was Miisi. To Kanani, despite his professed atheism, Miisi was a more potent weapon for evil than the openly heathen cousins. In the presence of Miisi, Kanani felt he was in the cold and calculating presence of Lucifer. For all his disbelief in the supernatural, Miisi was the so-called chosen one, the one whom the evil spirits spoke through. Yet he had constantly insisted, "My mind is overactive. I must have heard the story of Kintu Kidda as a child before my family died. It must have lain dormant somewhere in the back of my mind."

As for the family curse, Miisi argued that it was a documented fact that in Buganda mental health problems such as depression, schizophrenia, and psychosis ran not only in families but in clans—the so-called *ebyekika*, clan ailings.

Looking at him now, Kanani decided that Miisi was disturbing. That seamless marriage of heathenism and intellectuality was unnatural. Westernisation erased heathenism in Africans; the humility that Miisi possessed came only with Christ's saving grace. Only the Great Deceiver could combine the two. Kanani remembered the first elders' council meeting where he had first met Miisi. Miisi had been hostile right from the start. Kanani had suggested that they open the meeting with a word of prayer when Miisi asked whether any of them knew a traditional prayer.

"We were rescued from our darkness. We now pray to God the Most High through Jesus Christ," Kanani had answered.

"The Most High is a title for the god of the most powerful. Had we conquered Europe and taken our "light" to them, Europeans would be throwing themselves about in trances in the name of *Ddu*nda. Christ would be a pagan god."

"But the Romans—"

"Let's start," Kitooke had interrupted and prayer was abandoned.

Resistance to prayer was a pertinent sign that Cousin Miisi was not innocently misguided but intentionally satanic. Throughout that meeting, Kanani could not keep away the image of Europeans, with their intelligence and poise, throwing themselves about in trances. He had felt sick.

Kanani turned back to his tent. He squeezed toothpaste onto his toothbrush, picked up a mug of water, and went behind the tent to wash up. Then he set off down the hill toward the *kitawuluzi* where cars had been parked.

Paulo, who had slept in the car, was already awake. Despite instructions to keep non-clan members away from the campsite, Kanani asked Paulo to come with him to his tent and to help prepare a place of worship. They laid mats outside Kanani's tent with Bibles and hymnals. By the time they finished, cousins working on the shrine had halted to have breakfast. Kanani asked Paulo to sit outside the tent while he went out to call people to prayer.

He approached a small group first. He greeted them and introduced himself as Kanani Kintu, an elder of the clan who was a Saved Christian. "If anyone cares to reflect on the death of Christ this Good Friday, they can come over there to my tent," he pointed to where Paulo sat.

At first, Kanani's invitations were met with polite smiles. No one accepted but no one refused outright until he came upon the group where Bweeza camped. Bweeza promptly launched at him. "What are you doing, Kanani?"

"Inviting my cousins to morning prayers and to vespers later."

"If we wanted to pray to that god we would have invited a proper bishop. As it is, we hired a medium because we want to reach out to the ancestors."

"We were set free, Magda. We now have a choice to either go to church or to the shrine. I am only offering an alternative."

"Church-going cousins stayed at home. Cardinal Matia Kintu is a brother but he explained that his is a jealous god who can't stand other gods." Now Bweeza's voice rose. "But some Christians are vultures. They stand by as you organize your party. The next thing you know they are waving Bibles at your crowd. Why don't you organize your own reunion, invite the clan at Namirembe, and give us your version of salvation? As it is, Kanani, you are farting in our reunion."

"The cardinal is a cousin?"

"Are you joking?" Bweeza turned to the voice. "We've been

up and down this country looking for our blood. But if a whole cardinal did not pontificate, who are you, Kanani?"

"Kintu is my ancestor too. I came here to acknowledge that. But I am also a child of God. Today, I remember how he sacrificed his only Son for my sins."

"Anyone else would be ashamed of human sacrifice, but not you, Kanani."

"Christ was not human."

Despite Bweeza's attack, Kanani kept a cheerful face and carried on inviting cousins to prayer. Bweeza was tireless. She had so far attempted to usurp him on the elders' council. Thankfully, not even heathens would make a woman an elder. Thwarted, Bweeza had lamented, "Our branch of the clan is headed by a fool just because he's a man."

Miisi had told her that he would sooner forget custom and install her as the elder but the rest of the elders had refused, *no, no, no, that's not done; it does not work!*

When Kanani returned to his tent, he was heartened to see two cousins sitting with Paulo. First, they recited the Lord's Prayer, then there was a reading from the Scriptures followed by a hymn. Kanani talked about God's love as it manifested on the cross and they sang another hymn. He rounded up the prayer with the Grace.

As he and Paulo rolled the mats and put the Bibles away, Kanani felt lifted: legions of angels were on his side. He would dismantle the curse and crash the Devil. This reunion was crop, his job was to bring in the harvest. He looked at Paulo putting things away. Lately he had felt haunted by his grandson. Was this a sign that he, Kanani, was losing his faith? For example, in the past, he would have brought Faisi to the reunion, regardless of what the clan said. They would have overrun this place with the word of God, giving the Devil a bloody nose. Yet, here he was asking people whether they wanted to pray!

"I'll go back to the car park," Paulo said.

As Paulo walked down the hill, Kanani dismissed his anxiety about bringing him along. All would be well.

3.

Isaac took off his shoes to lie down. It was only four o'clock but he
had returned to the tent to catch some sleep. He had been on the
go since the start of the week and was exhausted. Kizza was out
with the other children playing and would not be back to the tent
until after supper, to sleep. He lay down on a mat and propped his
head on his bag for a pillow. He rolled onto his back and tried to
sleep. Then he opened his eyes and stared at the army-green con-
verse of the tent above. Thoughts had started to plague him. He
refused to think about the future. Instead he reflected on how life
had led him to this place. In terms of relations, he was now rich.
It was interesting listening to relatives talk about their mental dis-
orders or other problems with pride as if it were a badge confirm-
ing Kintu as their ancestor. Brothers who did not have a problem
to complain about—to Isaac the clan was made up of brothers,
sisters, and elders—seemed to lack the conviction that they were
true descendants of Kintu.

Before meeting the elders on the council, Isaac had been dis-
missive of his father's family's claim of a family curse. After all,
every family—in a bid to make their roots seem deep and profound—claim some kind of spiritual inheritance. Isaac had never
met a mental health sufferer who accepted his mental condition
as just that—people always claimed that it had to be supernatural.

Then he met the council of elders, all of them more educated than he was but believing, except Elder Miisi who was skeptical. Now, here he was with hundreds of relations, many with stories of their lives, or stories of relatives they had known to suffer the curse. It felt as if all his life he had been walking on a road leading here. He was home.

"Uncle Isaac," a boy broke into his reverie.

Isaac sat up.

"Elder Miisi says that the medium has arrived and you are needed at the shrine."

Isaac stood up, put his fatigue aside, slipped on his shoes, and walked out of the tent.

The shrine was completed.

As Isaac walked toward it, he was overcome by emotion. Did Mayirika occupy this same spot? Did Baale and Kalema play about here? Does the ground remember Kintu's feet? The ground has a memory he was sure: it was beyond comprehension, beyond sight, and beyond touch but he knew it. Otherwise, how else could he explain the hundreds of Kintu's descendants gathered now in this place?

At the threshold, an organic scent from the hay that carpeted the shrine greeted him. It was of the morning earth—open fields and dew. Isaac took his shoes off and walked in. The hay tickled his feet. The stillness and partial darkness inside created an ambience of reverence, as if the ancients hovered. Elder Miisi sat awkwardly on the floor. Next to him, two men sat on a mat. When Isaac sat down, Elder Miisi made the introductions. "Isaac, this is Muganda, the medium. The gentleman next to him is Nsimbi, his assistant." Miisi turned to Muganda and said, "Isaac is our son: he represents his father who cannot be with us. However, Isaac is one of those sons you can rely on as much as an elder."

"Isn't it wonderful to meet such young men?" Muganda shook Isaac's trembling hand.

Muganda took Isaac by surprise. First of all, he was not much older than him. Secondly, Muganda wore slacks and a polo shirt.

The strap of his TAG Heuer watch was thick and wide. His hair and beard were manicured to sharp edges and he spoke in soft tones. Isaac was confused. He had expected an old man, tired from carrying the weight of spirits on his head, with hair in matted dreadlocks because the spirits would not allow him to cut it.

"Muganda and I met at Cambridge a long time ago," Miisi was saying. "Before you came, Isaac, I was asking him whether he completed his course." Now Miisi turned to Muganda, "You arrived just before I finished my research."

"Yeah, I finished the BA and went to Newcastle for an MA," Miisi and Muganda spoke about Britain as if it were a suburb in Kampala. "I see where this is going," Muganda preempted. "You're thinking—how can a British educated man be a medium?"

"No," Miisi denied.

"You're thinking that education should've lifted me above these cheap versions of psychology."

"Normally, when people get a calling like yours," Miisi said, "Which in my view is really an order, they give up everything."

"My 'calling,' as you put it, did not force me to give up anything. I have a job and I travel."

"So, at Cambridge, you were aware that you are a medium?"

"I found out in my third year. Got headaches and hallucinations and I was put on anti-depressants. When I came home for the holidays, my father went native, but I would not. Finally, the healer came to me. As soon as he saw me, he went into this trance saying: this is huge. He asked my father to construct a shrine immediately."

"When did you convert?"

"I've never converted actually. I had a violent episode and my father asked me to lie in the shrine to rest. Twenty-four hours later, I woke up exhausted. Only I did not wake up, I had been up all night hosting all sorts. It took me a week to recover from the exhaustion but the headaches and hallucinations never returned."

"So what is it really like? I mean, do you see, hear, or feel things?" Elder Miisi probed.

"I am a host—an office if you wish. Spirits come on my head, do their thing and go. Unlike you, Miisi, and your dreams, there is no contact whatsoever between me and the energies that occupy me. That is why I need an assistant."

"I don't understand," Elder Miisi said.

"Neither do I," Muganda smiled. "It is not cerebral. My intellectual friends speculate that there are energies out there in the universe and minds like mine are in touch but are too primitive to handle it."

"I am familiar with the idea."

"When the winds come, I stop being. My consciousness is repressed. When they leave, I've no recollection."

At this point, Elders Kitooke and Kityo arrived with Bweeza who had carved out the office of the Great Aunt for herself and had finally edged her way officially onto the elders' council. As Elder Miisi made introductions again, Isaac observed Muganda. He was uncertain about an educated medium, one who spoke such immaculate English. He did not doubt that Muganda had powers—he had already performed exhumation rituals in *o* Lwera and had identified the spot where Nnakato was—but Muganda was too anglicized to inspire confidence.

"At six in the morning we shall exhume Nnakato," Muganda was saying. "My men are experienced in exhumation but Nnakato will take time because she is in a squatting position. We shall dig around her and lift her from the bottom. Then she'll be laid out part by part. At about eight o'clock, two elders will come with me to *o* Lwera to collect the Tutsi and the patriarch. I suggest that we leave Bweeza here to oversee the laying out and wrapping of Nnakato."

"Well said," Bweeza beamed.

Isaac was not surprised that Elder Miisi had opted out of the journey to *o* Lwera. He was a stubborn old man. Isaac feared for him: tradition showed that reluctant mediums paid a heavy price. Elders Kityo and Kitooke agreed to go with Muganda.

Later, as he lay down on a mat to sleep, Isaac mulled over everything. Since locating Kiyiika Village, he had been busy liaising between the elders and Kiyiika's local council. It was through the local council that he found out about the Tanzanian brothers and sisters. Isaac smiled at the thought. When he asked them whether they needed clearing at the embassy, the Tanzanians had asked, "What embassy?" Then they had crossed the border like ants— without travel documents or visas. Elder Miisi had laughed heartily. "Bloody borders! African countries are a European imagination." It was the first time Isaac had heard Miisi speak English.

Isaac had also procured all the materials needed for the reunion. He had hired locals to help with the physical work on the site: clearing the gorge, preparing the campsite, digging makeshift toilets, and erecting traditional tents, which they sold to the clan. For a week before the reunion, residents had worked on the track through the village to make it passable for the expected cars. The amount of money the reunion brought to Kiyiika Village had endeared the clan to the residents. There was even a taxi service from Masaka to Kiyiika for the first time. Kiyiika residents had told Isaac that Nnakato had blessed them for their faithfulness. Yet, throughout those preparations, Isaac had not considered the spiritual dimension of the homecoming. Now, having met the medium in person, he was apprehensive.

4.

Easter Sunday, April 11, 2004

Suubi arrived in Kiyiika on Easter morning, the final day of the rituals, and sat away from everyone. She had only come because Opolot insisted. Such traditional gatherings were her idea of a nightmare—she had heard of the primitive things that took place. The idea of spirits and curses was backward and tedious. Regardless, she hoped that coming would get Ssanyu out of her life.

When she arrived, she was told that cousins arriving for the first time had to put mud on the shrine, for its construction was a collective effort, but Suubi declined. She did not even seek out her branch of the clan. She had convinced herself that since her mind had chosen to bury the past, there was no reason to exhume it. In any case, remembering had been painful—as if a rod were being thrust through her head, piercing the eyeball, right down into her teeth.

Now, looking around the site, Suubi regretted opening up to Opolot about Ssanyu. As soon as she told him about the haunting, Opolot had taken her to meet an aunt, Kizza. Meeting Aunt Kizza was a bizarre experience. The minute the woman took off her headscarf and started talking—her mouth, her smile, the sound of her voice brought back the visits in school and Suubi smiled and said, "You used to whisper!"

But then the fantasy of her parents in England started to grate and her skin itched freakishly because scratching made it worse, yet more memories kept coming—her grandmother's death and then Kulata—like a mudslide, overwhelming her. Then the pain had seared from her head through the eyeballs right into the nerves of her teeth.

"Please stop: it hurts," she said, even though her aunt had already stopped talking when she saw her flinching.

Aunt Kizza had held her. She held very hard as if she could feel Suubi's pain, as if squeezing her would help.

"The pain will go slowly."

"There is a migraine still. It starts in the forehead and stops in the teeth."

"Hmm, hmm. It will go."

Later, when Aunt Kizza invited Suubi to travel to Kiyiika with her branch of the clan, she had declined. She could not risk the pain again. Even the thought of it now felt as if someone was hacking at her mind with a machete.

For a long time, Suubi sat alone, away from the clan, until a sympathetic cousin came and sat with her.

"I don't believe in these things either," the woman began. "But it doesn't hurt to cast mud to the house. Relations are looking for someone to blame in case the curse does not break," the woman paused. "Just go, pick up the mud, and cast it on the wall."

"Is it a house or a shrine?" Suubi asked.

"It is both I guess. It is all about doing something. This is our generation's effort."

"Don't mistake me," Suubi said. "I am neither Christian nor atheist: I am just plain. The supernatural have never intervened in my—" Suubi's heart skipped a beat as the image of the old man who kidnapped her flashed in her mind. She corrected herself, "These things have no place in the modern world."

"As long as there are Africans in the world, there will always be someone seeking these things," the woman laughed.

The two women sat silently for a while. Then Suubi stood

up and walked toward the shrine. The woman made sense, Suubi thought, she had made the journey, she wanted to get rid of Ssanyu, she might as well do the rituals. As she got to the shrine, she noticed that it was vast with a conical roof. The thatch came halfway down the walls. She looked through the doorway. Inside, it was dark but she could see some people meditating while others slept on the floor. The walls inside looked dry: finger marks crisscrossed everywhere without a pattern giving the walls a rough look. Embers in the hearth near the entrance smoldered and an assortment of spears, planted into the floor, formed a row from the central pole to the wall on the right. On the floor, next to the spears, were tiny baskets with offerings and an array of gourds and calabashes.

This is some serious witchcraft, Suubi thought nervously.

Just then, two little boys, sweat streaking down their faces from playing, walked past her, took off their shoes at the threshold and entered the shrine. They went to an earthen pot near the wall. They unhooked a trouted gourd hanging above it, took the lid off the pot and drew water. The first boy drank nonstop until he had to take a breath. The second grabbed the gourd from him and drank as much. When he stopped, he smacked his lips and they giggled. The first one shook the gourd, found there was still some water left, and with his big toe moved the hay carpeting aside, poured the water into the earth floor, and pulled back the hay. They hooked the gourd to the wall, covered the pot, and ran out.

"Me and Kizza, we drank out of a gourd," they shouted to their friends, "And the water is smoked!"

Suubi turned to the right, where the mud plaster was covered with banana leaves against the sun. Nonetheless, the plaster was starting to clog and crack. She poked the surface until she found a soft spot and scooped. She carried the mud toward the shrine and threw it hard on the wall. It stuck and she evened it out with her fingers. She noticed other uneven parts, went back for more mud, and filled them in until the part of the wall she worked on was level. As she washed her hands, a cousin asked if she had just arrived. When Suubi nodded, the cousin went away and came back with food. Suubi's reticent stance relaxed a little. She greeted a group of people camping nearby and returned to her original place to eat.

"It's like pottery, isn't it?" the cousin said as Suubi sat down.

"What is?"

"Putting mud on the shrine."

"I am not looking for new relations," Suubi said after a pause.

"Large families are notoriously nosy. Someone will seek you out."

"My name is Suubi Nnakintu." Suubi's heart lurched when she said Nnakintu but she had so far failed to call herself Nnakato.

"Oh, that name! Are you afflicted? Apparently, Kintu or Nnakintu is an unfortunate name."

"What do you mean, 'afflicted'?"

"Bad luck, haunting, or things in the head that don't make sense. That old man there, his name is Miisi Kintu. He is mad. People say he's the clan medium but he denies it because he is a kivebulaya, a been-to-Europe and is overeducated. He dreamed about all these things but he thinks it is all a coincidence. He had twelve children but only two remain."

"Oh!"

"See that blue tent? Inside is another Kintu, a Christian," the woman laughed. "Apparently he came here to preach the word of God. Can you imagine?"

"Preaching the word of God in this place is like ordering porridge in a bar," Suubi said as she looked around.

"I swear! He comes out in the morning and invites people to pray. Otherwise, he stays in his tent singing Christian songs loudly. This morning only one person turned up but he still held a service. They say he has twins but he thinks the title Ssalongo is evil."

"No, I am not afflicted," Suubi looked away.

"You won't believe how many Kintus and Nnakintus are in this place. Do you have hay fever? Are there twins in your family?"

"I have hay fever. Any drop in temperature sets me off."

"Wait for the evening, one person goes *akchuu* and soon the whole place is sneezing. It's hilarious. It is blood, you know what I mean; we are all the same blood. As for twins, they believe they're extra special because Nnakato of old had so many sets of twins. My name is Nnabaale though. Baale was Nnakato's favorite son."

"The thing is …" Suubi paused as if to think again, "You don't realize that you're cursed until you're exposed to this other way of life. I mean, if we lived on our own, in our cursed world, we wouldn't know. Then the curse would not exist."

"Hmm."

"My father was a twin, Wasswa. He hacked his brother Kato to death with a machete and then killed himself. But to me that is life. You know, like those ten men killed in Bwaise on Friday?"

"My God, that was crazy. Ten people killed and no one was arrested?" Nnabaale said.

Suubi shrugged. "My view is that they came on earth, did their thing and now they have bowed out. Who is to say that things are not right? Nature is as ugly as it is beautiful. People drop dead, people kill each other, people go hungry: you don't dwell, you just exist. But then this other world comes along and gives you ideas. You start to think, *hmm, I am not right, it's not fair.* Things you would never have said before. Soon you start to blame everything on a curse."

"Our own cursed world!" Nnabaale laughed belatedly. "It's just hit me."

"What is a curse to some people is normal to others."

"Hmm."

"With me, I feel as if I was dismembered, you know, chopped into pieces?"

Nnabaale nodded as if she knew what being chopped into pieces was really like.

"And so far I have lived my life in pieces quite OK."

Nnabaale's eyes darted here and there, working out what living in pieces was like, but she nodded again.

"Now this reunion is forcefully grafting and stitching all the pieces back together, which is a good thing, but in some cases, like mine, it does not work. I don't want the pieces back. I have lived without them for too long that I don't know how to live with them."

Nnabaale was still wondering why stitching could not be good for anyone, how living in pieces could possibly be a good thing, and how anyone could not want pieces of themselves back? Suubi continued.

"I'll do the rituals, but as soon as I step out of here, this world will cease for me."

"Sounds like you've worked your life out," Nnabaale smiled kindly. That was all she could manage.

"Before, I had no choice. Life did to me whatever it pleased. Now, there are options. My boyfriend is Atesot. When we marry, I'll become Atesot too."

"I like being Nnabaale now that I know the history."

Just then the truck that had gone to fetch the patriarch and the Tutsi from *o* Lwera arrived. People stood up and started milling around it. Someone sang, *Nyini munno mwali?* and the clan broke out into the traditional homecoming song and someone ululated as if she were Nnakato of old receiving Kintu back. Yet some cousins started sniveling. The hair on the back of Suubi's neck rose. Babirye was hovering, she could feel her. She put her food down and stood up. Nnabaale had run off to join in the singing.

Easter Sunday, April 11, 2004

It was time. Miisi stood up to join the members of the clan stream-ing toward the new graveyard for the main event.

Earlier, when he saw the coffins unloaded off the truck and a wave of emotion run through the clan, he could not suppress a tinge of cynicism. Whose bones were in the coffins? After all, a lot of people had died in *o* Lwera over the centuries and it was not like the medium had carried out a DNA test. But then he had chastised himself: it didn't matter. Facts are immaterial to faith. For a moment then, he regretted the fear that had stopped him from going along to *o* Lwera to look at the remains.

His fear went back to the moment when, on return to Kiyiika Village to tour Nnakato's hill, the elders had come across a tree with a large beehive. The hive sat in an alcove where the tree split into five branches. Bweeza had run back to the car to get tiny baskets into which she dropped smoked coffee beans and coins before placing them below the hive. Then she gave thanks to the spirit Kayuki for revealing himself to the clan. Miisi had stood at a respectful distance, knowing that chances were that there would be at least one beehive in the woods. In any case, in his dream, the bee man or Kayuki as Bweeza referred to him, lived in a cave. But when they found the tree with the pink bark Miisi went numb, especially as there was a rock nearby. All he had said to the other elders was that according to his dream Nnakato had hung on a similar tree and that she would be close to the rock. Then he had pointed out a tree that would make the central pole of the shrine.

"If you believe my dreams, the dwelling should be built here: it should be circular and ten strides in radius."

Perhaps sensing his turmoil, the cousins had allowed him to wrestle with his doubt privately. No one asked provocative questions, there was no sarcasm and no jesting in the car as they traveled back home—just worried silence. That was when a grain of doubt formed. He still could not rule out coincidence, but now and again *what if* crept up on him.

In his instructions regarding the location of the patriarch and the lad in *o* Lwera, Miisi had been true to the dreams, but he stood by the fact that they were just dreams.

"If you find nothing, and I doubt you'll find anything, don't blame me. I've warned you over and over that these are images conjured by a traumatized mind."

Two weeks later, when the party returned having located both bodies, Miisi decided that they were other people's remains. Now he wondered what would happen to his restless sleep after the rituals. He could not wait to see the power of the mind.

"Ready for the main event?" Muganda smiled at Miisi as he made his way to the gathering. Miisi nodded and hurried to join the clan.

When he arrived at the graveyard, he was met with silence. Anticipation and trepidation hung equally in the air. The clan stood facing the three coffins—Kintu's, Nnakato's, and Kalema's. Each coffin was placed alongside a grave. For a moment, Miisi was caught in the awe of being in the presence of history. He saw Kintu's blood flow unbroken through the ages leading to him and he bowed his head. He wanted to whisper something in acknowledgement but did not know how.

When he looked up, he saw three white lambs tethered to a

tree nearby. On another tree were three black male goats. The scene could have come straight out of the Old Testament, he thought. He wished that Kanani could come out of his tent to see it. In a few moments, the animals would pay with their blood for Kintu's sin just as animalkind had done for mankind throughout time. The animals chewed the cud, oblivious. It was Miisi who suffered their looming end. He smiled at the irony. To him, humanity was cursed anyway. The mind was a curse: its ability to go back in time to regret and to hop into the future to hope and worry was not a blessing.

Next to the coffins were bundles of sticks—peeled and smooth. They were as long as chopsticks, only thicker. Miisi had almost missed them. Sheep and goats, black and white, were trademark items for a sacrifice, but the sticks did not make sense. He turned to the clan and wondered which of the cousins had faith in the rituals, which were skeptical, and which were drifting through everything half-consciously.

Muganda greeted the clan and asked them to stand around the graves. He wore a *kanzu*. On top, he had knotted the traditional barkcloth. He wore a necklace of cowries. The watch was gone and in its place were traditional black gem bracelets. He carried a big staff mounted with a traditional curved knife. His feet were bare.

"I speak for Kintu's children—past, present, and to come. We have gathered to lay our father, mother, and brother to rest. We've also come together as children from a single spring to strip ourselves of a heritable curse. As we obtain peace of mind, we seek rest for our mother Nnakato, our father Kintu, and brother Kalema. Ntwire shall let go of the child nursed on Nnakato's breast. Because Kalema found a home and family in Buganda, we shall sever all Ntwire's claims on the lad."

Muganda then instructed each person to pick a stick. His assistant passed them around. Miisi picked one: it was dry and odorless. When everyone held one, Muganda continued,

"Kalema was buried near an oasis. The sticks you hold were

cut out of the *musambya*, the Nile tulip shrubs that grew around his grave. Now, I'll ask you to whisper all your afflictions and rub them into the stick. You may not remember everything at once, so hang onto them."

A stick was placed on each of the coffins.

All around Miisi, cousins whispered feverishly into their sticks. It felt like a Pentecostal congregation whispering in tongues. Just then, a young woman slipped past Miisi. He looked up: she was the woman who had so far stood apart from everything like a teenager forced to go to church. The woman picked up a stick and returned to the back of the gathering. Miisi caught Muganda looking at him with amusement and lowered his eyes, feeling like a child caught with his eyes open during prayer.

Miisi did not whisper any affliction into his stick.

"Can we have the lambs brought forward?" Muganda interrupted the whispering. "For the squeamish, it's time to look away. We're going to harvest their blood."

Miisi turned away before the lambs' legs were bound. It did not help. Presently, a gasp escaped the gathering. Then rapid rustling like kicking came, followed by a slow puffing of blood. Thrice, the rustling and puffing came before fading. Miisi felt nausea rising. Luckily, he held it back.

"We're going to cover the carcasses with barkcloth." Muganda's voice came. There was a pause. "You can turn around now. Everyone, place your stick on top of the carcasses."

Miisi rubbed his stick as if he were making a fire and placed it on the pile. The sticks on the coffins were also placed on the carcasses, so were any that were left over. The gathering was asked to step back. The assistant came forward with a large urn and poured oil on the heap, soaking everything. Muganda struck a match and said, "I now set all that afflicts you on fire." He threw the match on the heap and slowly it was engulfed in flames. "When everything has burned, the ashes will be buried in the four corners of this place but now, join me in laying the dead to rest. First, we lay Kalema. I pour a bowl of the blood we harvested from the sheep into his grave. In so doing, I sever ties with Ntwire and with Ntwire's home. You're no longer Kalemanzira but Kalema. Any force that comes to collect you has been blocked."

Muganda walked to a patch cordoned off by wooden planks. He stopped and pointed with both hands at the demarcated space.

"Here lies your brother, Baale. We shall mark his resting place properly later." Then he moved to the second grave and called out, "Nnakato, you will now lie between your beloved Kintu and Baale; search no more. The rope around your neck has been removed and you shall endure the squatting posture no more."

He moved to the last grave.

"Kintu, your blood has survived the curse. You have children the way a millipede has legs. Now that you're home, we ask that you rest." Now Muganda turned to the gathering and raised his hands. "I call upon the winds of the clan—ghosts, spirits, and all ancestors—to come down on these children like a mother hen comes down on her chicks with her wings and feathers. Guard and guide, undo any evil plots and traps that lie in their paths now and for the rest of their lives."

As Miisi helped to lower the coffins, images of his children lowered into the ground swarmed before him. He busied himself piling earth on the coffins. He did not hear the medium say, "That's enough. If you've put earth on the family, come around." Miisi carried on shovelling until the medium stayed his hand and led him back to the circle.

"My men and I shall sacrifice the goats. Their blood will be poured around the central pole of the shrine and around the wall to buttress the shrine. The goats will be roasted and shared by everyone. I shall see you when you return for the ablution rite."

Suddenly, there was a commotion. Miisi looked up. The reluctant woman, the one he had noticed picking up a stick, had fainted. He ran to help. Muganda ordered everyone away except the elders.

"Go get the large sheets," he told the assistant before turning to the staring people. "Everyone else get back to your tents now unless you want to be caught in this." At that threat, the cousins scattered. "Who knows her? Who came with her?" Muganda asked the elders.

"Her name is Suubi Nnakato: she is from my branch but—" a woman who was lingering shouted.

At the sound of her name, the woman sprang off the ground unnaturally fast and sat back on her haunches. Her eyes were unseeing. She started to bob, then sway. Slowly, her head started to swing. Nsimbi returned with large sheets of barkcloth.

"Come, hold the edge of the sheets," Muganda instructed the elders and they formed a cubicle around the woman to screen her from public view. Miisi held two ends in one corner. This was his chance to observe the transpossession phenomenon.

The woman's body, swinging or rotating, picked up momentum and started hopping about on her hands. Miisi stepped back as the body lurched toward him. The spinning was so unnaturally fast that the woman's head was hardly visible. It was clear to Miisi that the woman did not own her body anymore. He was wondering whether the spinning was the woman's body fighting the suppression of her consciousness when he heard a finger snap. Miisi shouted at Muganda, "Stop her. She's breaking bones!"

Muganda ignored him. Taking his time, the medium took a tiny basket from the assistant and entered into the screen. He pulled up his *kanzu* and knelt down. Having broken several fingers and a wrist, the body now knelt on its knees and spun from the end upwards. Muganda placed the basket in front of the body. He placed a few coins and smoked coffee beans in the basket and requested, "We beg you to introduce yourself."

The spinning started to slow down. When it stopped, Miisi saw that the woman's eyes were narrowed and she breathed with puffing, slow, and deep breaths.

"You're very angry. How have we offended?" Muganda was humble.

When the body did not respond Muganda added, "I beg of you to let go of your host, she has broken several bones."

"Let me kill her."

The voice was as thin as a child's—not older than four.

"But who are you?"

"Babirye, her twin."

Muganda sat back as if his job had been done. Miisi was trying to reconcile the child's voice to the aggression.

"She tried to bind me in your stick." The body moved and Miisi saw a stick that should have been burned lying on the ground. Goosebumps spread all over his arms. The body leaned forward and picked the stick off the ground with its mouth, then spat it out again.

"Nnakato has denied my existence all this time," the child's voice laughed sarcastically. "But then she binds me into a stick to burn me? Me, her sister?" she breathed as if asthmatic.

Miisi felt nausea rise again. He could hear a grating sound somewhere in his head. He asked Bweeza, who stood outside the cubicle, to hold his corner.

"I don't feel well," he whispered to the other elders.

It was as if Bweeza had been waiting for such an opportunity all along. She took Miisi's place with relish. Muganda was still groveling for Suubi's life as Miisi walked away.

6.

Isaac's body still shook from the intense emotions of the rituals. He sat on the ground to try and gather himself together. He looked around the campsite and thought, "This is real." To be within touching distance of almost three centuries' history, to be surrounded by hundreds of relatives whose presence testified to that history. Finally, his own presence on earth was accounted for and his painful life justified. When Isaac looked back at his life—at the friend who stayed with him when he was young, at Ziraba his grandmother and at Sasa—it was not misfortune that he saw, it was intervention. Most of all, the twins, Babirye and Nnakato, had paid him a visit even though they did not stay. There was no doubt that Kintu had tirelessly intervened in his life. Isaac could not contain his trembling.

For him, the homecoming song had set the tone of the rituals. He had heard the song in traditional performances before but its significance only hit home when the patriarch arrived. And when Muganda stepped out of the shrine resplendent in traditional regalia, everything fell into place. Isaac had whispered his father's name, desperately willing Mr. Kintu's mental sickness into the stick. Isaac did not flinch at the slaughter of the sheep. When he saw the blood flow, something snapped and he felt so buoyant that wind could have blown him away. That fire consuming his stick made him so giddy that he sat down and wept. His immersion was only broken when the woman became possessed and Muganda asked everyone to leave. People said that the woman was a twin who had attempted to bind her dead twin's spirit. Imagine that! No one was surprised. The woman had only arrived that day and had carried on as if everyone and everything being done was beneath her. Why come then? These things, you need to be totally committed or you stay away. Otherwise, they rip you apart. There was so much Isaac did not understand, but he was not arrogant enough to turn his ignorance into unbelief.

Later, as roast goat was passed around the camp, a rumor wafted along. Apparently, in Kintu's time, ablution was a rite where each child born to him was thrown into the gorge. If the baby belonged to the family, the gorge threw it back, but if it did not, the gorge swallowed it. Having witnessed the physical manifestation of the curse in Suubi, apprehension settled on the clan. Who was sure that their mother was not a liar? Isaac had read somewhere that twenty per cent of children did not belong to the men they called fathers. Now, the actions of generations of women who married into the family became unfathomable. To Isaac, the idea of surrendering Kizza to the whims of water spirits was unsettling.

Time for ablution came. Every elderly man, with a queue of his offspring behind him, made his way toward the gorge. Isaac held his son's hand and led him there. A few people held back to see what would happen first. Isaac noticed that Elder Miisi cut a forlorn figure standing on his own while men his age led an extensive queue of children and grandchildren to the gorge. Isaac had heard that Elder Miisi had lost most of his children but where were the two who survived? He wanted to go and stand with him but held back.

Muganda started. "You stand before the spring that watered the family in those days. We are going to wash the curse off. Wash your face, hands, and feet. You can have a full bath if you want, but it's not important. Family heads will draw water and make sure that every member of their family is washed. Don't let children near the gorge. I've heard that you were worried we would throw you in," Muganda laughed. "It's true such a ritual took place in the past, but it was for specific children dedicated to certain gods."

When most people had finished washing, Muganda wound up.

"Tomorrow, the locals who've kept your heritage alive will join you in thanksgiving. Those who must rush back home, once you've washed, you can go. I thank you for taking part, for the discipline and for the desire to fight against the fragmentation of your blood. I pray that after today you will keep an eye on each other and hold each other up. I would like to say that you can go and live happily ever after, but I would be lying. What you've done today is to start on the journey of healing. The curse will break. However, in its death throes it might wreak havoc. Our fathers said that an anticipated plunderer makes off with less. Hold each other's arms."

While young people jumped into cars and drove to Masaka to catch the tail end of Easter festivities, Isaac went to bed. As he lay down, he remembered that the results for the blood tests were still in the car. He could have rubbed HIV in the stick, but he did not believe it would go away. For a moment, his mind fancied that after the rituals, the results could be negative. He sat up to go and get them but stopped. It was no use getting delusional and spoiling the moment. He had decided that he and Kizza would check out of the world soon after the reunion. In his view, they had been given the best send-off.

The following day, Isaac was woken up by Bweeza. It was midmorning. Bweeza seemed panicky.

"Son, you're needed in the shrine."

"Is it Suubi the twin?"

"Suubi will be fine. Run to the shrine."

Outside, the morning was slow. It was Easter Monday, the last day of the reunion. Isaac's heart fell. Women cooking in the kitchen area were talking animatedly. A few meters away, sounds of chopping led his eyes to men butchering the meats. Kizza and other children sat on mats eating breakfast. Isaac smiled. The sisters, on finding out that he was a widower, had taken Kizza off his hands saying, "Leave him to us," and Kizza was enjoying having so many children around him. He looked around the campsite: nothing rang wrong or urgent in the air.

When he arrived in the shrine, he saw a lifeless form lying on the floor. It was covered in barkcloth like in death. Fear in the shrine was almost tangible. The assistant was beside himself. Isaac guessed it was Muganda.

"Sit down, Isaac," Elder Kityo whispered.

Elder Miisi sat leaning against the wall, his legs inside a sleeping bag. He looked up at the roof, but his jaws danced.

"What happened?"

"Ntwire's demon," the attendant answered. "It speaks Lunyarwanda only."

Isaac noted that Elder Miisi did not join in the explanations. He still looked up at the roof, his jaws frantic.

"Is he alive?" Isaac whispered.

"I couldn't find a pulse last time I checked but I cannot say he's dead," Elder Kityo said.

Isaac wanted to ask why Muganda was covered as if he were dead but changed his mind. If the elders had not queried it, then it was the right thing to do.

"We're waiting for an interpreter."

"I've never come across anything like this in my entire career," the assistant said. "A spirit that won't speak a language you understand means only one thing; it's come to terrorize."

"I thought it was one of those deaf or dumb demons vindictive people hire because they're aggressive. But then Nsimbi tried sign language and it swore at him in Lunyarwanda," Kityo said.

"We woke you up because we need more hands when it gets roused." Elder Miisi finally looked at Isaac.

7.

Easter Monday, April 12, 2004

It was ten in the morning and the sun was sweetness. Paulo was walking down a narrow trail. The tall bushes on either side leaned into the path so that sometimes he had to push branches out of his face. The skin on his arms was burning: he suspected he had come into contact with a fiery shrub. He was on his way to meet a local lad who had promised to take him to the other side of Nnakato's hill and show him the no-man's land between Uganda and Tanzania. So far, the reunion had been a long weekend of nature walking for him. He had been to all the places fabled for Nnakato's sighting and had been to see *abakomazi* of barkcloth at work. Now he was on his way to Tanzania.

Presently, an elderly man came toward him and Paulo stepped aside to let him pass. The man looked at him curiously then asked authoritatively, "Why aren't you with your clan at this critical moment?" Paulo started to explain that he was not one of them but changed his mind.

"There was nothing wrong when I left a few minutes ago."

"Ah, the elders are hushing it." The man sucked his teeth. "Did you really think that you would come here and in a weekend undo a taboo that took hold hundreds of years ago?"

"What are you talking about?"

"A demon has gripped your medium. He tried to separate the Tutsi father and son—these educated people! Apparently, he learned his trade in Britain."

"What does it want?"

"Blood, what else do demons demand?"

"Have they found it?"

"It wants Tutsi blood but the interpreter would not share his in case the evicted demon needs another host."

"So they're still looking?"

"Mhm."

Paulo ran back. He would share his if the demon would have a half-blood Tutsi. He remembered Bweeza saying that he was significant: this could be it. But when he got there, there was no urgency in the air. All around, people looked relaxed. Nonetheless, Paulo asked for an elder. One came and introduced himself as Kityo. Kalema stated breathlessly, "I am Tutsi. I can give you some blood."

"Calm down, young man. Are you sure?" Kityo whispered.

"Ask my grandfather, Kanani, he will tell you. Bweeza knows me as well." Paulo was forced to whisper too.

Kityo led Paulo to an isolated place and asked him to wait there. He went into the shrine and returned with two other men. He pointed at Paulo. "He claims to be Tutsi. Apparently, Kanani is his grandfather."

"At the moment, we will try anything. Call the assistant."

After listening to the story the assistant said, "A Tutsi with Kintu's blood is perfect. Find Bweeza while I get my instruments."

The assistant returned with a metallic bean-shaped bowl. Kityo, seeing the sealed needle and syringe, nodded his approval. "Sealed—very good."

"We are not the uncouth type," the assistant said tightly.

He asked Paulo to make a fist while he unsealed the needle and syringe. The assistant then tapped at a vein in Paulo's arm until it stood out. He wetted a cotton swab in disinfectant and started cleaning the spot.

"Why don't I draw the blood for you? I am a doctor," Kityo offered.

The assistant stood up. "I am a trained nurse—would you like to see my certificates?"

Just as Nsimbi inserted the needle, Kanani ran out of his tent shouting.

"Leave my grandson out of this! He's not one of us." But Nsimbi continued to draw blood as if he had not heard.

"Keep still," he said to Paulo.

"My grandfather is mad," Paulo smiled.

"Aren't they all?" The attendant pulled the needle out and pressed the spot with cotton. "Hold it," he said while he peeled a strip of plaster to cover it.

"Jjaja, I offered," Paulo explained to his grandfather."

"Do you know what you've done?" Kanani shouted at him hysterically. "Bring that back," he shouted at the assistant who disappeared into the shrine with the blood. Kanani ran after him.

"It won't work, it won't work," but the attendant did not return. "He's not Tutsi. He's Ganda. Don't do it, please," Kanani pleaded but the attendant did not return. "I am telling you my grandson has no Tutsi blood in him whatsoever, don't use his blood, you could bring danger to him." By then, Kanani's hysterics had caught the attention of the rest of the clan.

The attendant returned. He held an urn. In it were herbs and coffee beans.

"Is he Tutsi or Ganda?" he asked Kanani.

Paulo said, "My name's Kalemanzira, but the family calls me Kalema."

A hush fell over the clan. Even the assistant froze. A man, close by, shivered. An elder who had so far stood apart came over and peered at Paulo. Kanani sat down like a sack of charcoal. The assistant walked back into the shrine triumphantly.

"He thinks he is Kalemanzira," Kanani's voice was hollow, "But he is the kind of child our culture calls *mawemuko*."

The assistant flew out of the shrine, tossing the coffee beans and herbs.

8.

Isaac recovered first. Everyone else was still frozen. Paulo was saying, "It can't be true, my grandfather will lie about anything in the name of God," but no one heard. Isaac touched his hand and helped him up. "Look at me," Paulo pleaded with Bweeza as Isaac led him away. "You said I look Tutsi." Bweeza opened her mouth but no words came. He turned to Kanani, "Jjajja," but Kanani did not look at him.

"Come with me," Isaac said quietly. It was instinct probably borne out of coming into the world as a result of an ugly act that made Isaac respond to Paulo's turmoil. He knew that Paulo needed distracting. "Come to my car."

Then, as Isaac and Paulo walked down the hill, the clan came alive and everyone spoke at once. "It is the lad himself . . . he's been here all weekend hovering," Isaac heard someone say as they came to the *kitawuluzi*. They got into Isaac's car and he drove away.

For a long time, they drove through marshy valleys, flat plains, and silent woods. Isaac could not bring himself to look at Paulo let alone say something. Driving on the road, it felt as if the curse had traveled the same road from old Kiyirika to find everyone wherever they were scattered.

"What is *mawemuko*?" Paulo asked.

"You don't know?"

"Uh uh."

"It's sort of . . . incest."

Paulo did not react. Then he gave a short laugh. "She actually told me!"

"Who told you?"

"She's always insisted that I should look to Uncle Job as my father. I am sure one time she said, *he is your father*. But I thought it was just a way of speaking."

"Your grandmother told you that?"

"My mother! Uncle Job is her twin."

For a while, Isaac kept his eyes on the road. Then he stopped the car.

"You need the rituals—shrine-building, burial, stick-rubbing, ablution, quick."

"The medium is dying, remember," Paulo said nonchalantly.

Silence fell again. Then as if to even a score Isaac said, "My father raped my mother. He was thrown in prison and he lost his mind."

"She even named me after him but my grandparents refused."

"Who named you?"

"Because they're so close."

"Who?"

"The twins."

"Which twins?"

"My parents."

"Oh."

"We're back to modernity," Paulo said excitedly as if he had not just said that his parents were twins. "There is a bar on the network."

Isaac did not know what to do with the sudden turn. He looked at Paulo to work him out, then with equal excitement said, "Good!"

In Masaka Town, the network signal got stronger. Paulo stepped out of the car to make a call. Isaac watched him keying the phone then he put it over his ear. Paulo looked uncannily Tutsi: lanky, sharp pointy features, a bridged nose, very dark, even skin, and very dark gums. He got a response, smiled, and moved further away from the car. Paulo seemed to have lived a cosseted life. Isaac felt a pang of envy. Why was Paulo, a child of incest, loved and good-looking while he, a child of mere rape, was shunned and ugly? The call ended and Paulo walked back to the car. Isaac started the engine.

"That was Nyange, my girlfriend."

"I thought you were calling your mother?"

"And say what? *Hallo, Mother. Is it true your brother is my father?*"

Isaac kept silent.

9.

Kanani did not look at Paulo as Isaac led him away. Something heavy, like a boulder, compressed his chest. Everything seemed to be parting from him. He had dealt the Devil a knockout blow but it seemed like he had hurt himself in the process. God's intention for bringing him to the reunion was now clear. He had come clean. Yet, he felt neither relief nor triumph. It had to be the strong presence of evil in this place. It was time to leave.

As he walked back to his tent, he became aware of Miisi following him, but like everything else, the feeling was remote. As he packed his bags, he looked up. Miisi stood outside the tent watching him. Kanani laughed. "You look like a muscle-man waiting to throw me off the premises—only you have no muscles at all."

Miisi said something but Kanani did not catch it. He finished packing and stepped out with his bags. "God works in mysterious ways," Kanani sighed.

"I'll have to drive you to Masaka," Miisi said, removing the pegs of the tent from the ground.

"You don't like me," Kanani said.

The tent collapsed.

"You need to be removed."

"I've become the abomination," Kanani said.

"You're one of us. But at the moment, you have to go so that our grandson can be received by the clan."

"You're only too happy to say that."

"Let's walk down to the car park."

Kanani wanted to say to Miisi, "You can't bully me, I am an elder," but felt too tired to fight. When he got into the car, he bowed his head. "We have nothing to hide anymore."

"How does it feel now?" Miisi asked as he reversed the car.

"Sin is sin," Kanani said emphatically.

"This was not yours to confess."

"We took part in the concealment."

"Your confessions are lies."

"That's for God's work. This concealment was for selfish reasons to cover our shame."

"Why did you come?"

"To witness for God."

The two men talked matter-of-factly, quietly, almost like friends.

"You've been hiding in your tent. You only came out to see if anyone wanted prayers. Why did you bring Paulo?"

"God was in control."

"No, Kanani. You brought him because you thought he was the curse."

"God led me here. It was His will."

"Part of you believed that he needed the rituals, didn't you, Kanani?"

"How could I? Rituals are the Devil's ways."

"You could've asked us for advice."

"You?" Kanani could not contain himself any longer. "You're the Devil Himself, but I am not frightened of you."

"Now you're mad."

"*We praise you, Jesus* . . ." Kanani started singing *Tukutendereza Yesu*, the Awakened's theme song. The song was a comfort in difficult situations.

"It makes sense now—why your children turned to each other in this way."

"*Your blood has washed . . .*"

"I hope there's a God so He can burn you forever."

"*I thank . . .*"

"Shut up!" Miisi banged the dashboard. "Sing that song at me again and I swear I'll turn into Satan himself and abandon you here in the wilderness."

The car fell silent until Miisi and Kanani arrived in Masaka Town.

In Masaka, Kanani was surprised that Miisi waited with him until a taxi came. When Kanani realized that he did not have the fare—Paulo was supposed to drive him home—Miisi gave it to him. But when he got into the taxi Miisi whispered, "Spare the passengers your stories of cavorting with the Devil this weekend."

Kanani stepped out of the taxi and stood before Miisi. His eyes were getting wet but he could not stop himself.

"You may pretend to be skeptical about the curse and the Devil but something evil came upon my children like a bird upon eggs and that boy hatched," his breath came in gasps. Miisi looked away. The taxi filled and drove off. "The day Paulo came home and told me that his name was Kalemanzira, or Kalema if we wished, he might as well have shown me the Mark of the Beast, 666, on his body."

Miisi held Kanani's arm and led him back to his car. When Kanani sat down, tears came down like a stream. Miisi sat with him in the car while he wept. He did not say a word. He did not look at him. Kanani stopped crying and looked at Miisi. Miisi looked straight ahead. Kanani opened his mouth but stopped; he had been about to tell Miisi that he feared that all his faith and good works had been in vain, but instead said, "I am ready," and stepped out of the car. As the taxi drove away, he smiled weakly and waved to Miisi.

10.

When Miisi returned to the campsite, he found Kusi's military presence littered all over the hill. At first, elation surged through his body—Kusi had managed to come to the reunion, however late—but then he was alarmed: Kusi had come with all her army paraphernalia. It was three o'clock and local residents had begun to arrive. Miisi was worried that the little village would be frightened by the presence of so many armed soldiers. What did people think of armed men in their sacred place? Miisi rushed to apologize.

But as he walked through the camp he noticed that the earlier anxiety over Muganda seemed to have thawed. The cousins were clearly waiting for him. He braced himself for the usual curiosities about him being Kusi's father—why had he not mentioned it; where did the name Kusi come from? But she is so tall!

As soon as she saw him, Kusi hurried toward him and threw herself at him. There was an unusual vulnerability in her eyes. She looked tired and her air of self-control was gone.

"Before you complain, *Mzei*, I have done all the rituals I was told to perform. I've put my mud on the shrine. I've buried the patriarch and I've drawn three jerricans of the 'Holy' water from the gorge to take home for everyone. When I get back, the first thing I'll do is to have an ablution."

"It's true. She did as she was told," Elder Kitooke stepped in. Then in an injured tone he asked, "Now, why didn't you tell us that the distinguished General Salamander is our daughter, Miisi?"

"Her name is Kusi. Salamander is her war persona. How is Muganda?" Miisi changed the subject.

"Kusi has a few Tutsis in her personnel. One of them gave us some blood and Muganda is coming around."

"Kusi cannot stay. As you can see, her men are like red ants," Miisi said apologetically.

"I am taking you with me, Father," Kusi said, her in-charge aura back. "There're critical issues I need you to help me with."

"But I can't just leave. I have a duty here."

"Miisi, if our child needs you," Kityo pointed at Kusi, "then she needs you. Everything here is done, all that is left is to make sure that the taboo is disposed of safely. We shall bring you a full report."

"Where is Kamu?"

"He could not come."

"I am not sure—"

"You know my job, Father," Kusi interrupted. "Today I am here, tomorrow I am there. When something should be done, it's done immediately."

"All right then," Miisi, feeling ganged-up on, conceded. "Kitooke, Bweeza, and Kityo, we need to bring the child, Kalema, into the clanfold. We also need to decide how we're going to keep this place going. How do we stay in touch with the Tanzanians? We need to find a caretaker."

"Don't worry. We won't do anything without consulting you."

"Kityo and Kitooke, you must take care of Kalema. He needs careful attention."

"Of course, now go," Kityo waved Miisi on to leave.

In a moment, Miisi was packed but as he walked to Kusi's car he remembered. "About Suubi—Bweeza, what is your plan?"

"Tomorrow, I'll take her back home. I'll stay with her until she is able to use her hands again."

"That is selfless of—"

"I am the Great Aunt. What else is my duty if not to look after lost ones like Suubi?"

"I would like to hear Suubi's side of the story though. As soon as I am finished with Kusi, I'll find her and we shall talk."

Miisi hugged his three cousins. "I think we've done a good job so far," he whispered. "Tell Isaac I will have to see him again to thank him for his good work and," Miisi said as he got in the car, "You must come to my home and visit. I have a lot of little *kaperes*."

As he waved at the elders, Miisi was sure he had seen a distinct look of worry on their faces but he did not dwell on it.

All the way home, he could not get Suubi out of his mind. To him, Suubi's spinning was similar to the lambs' kicking as they were slaughtered. Was transpossession the "slaughtering" of consciousness? He had heard of the "slain in the spirit" phenomenon in the new churches. Had the Christians inadvertently stumbled onto something profound? When Muganda was possessed, he fell as if dead. Was this because his consciousness did not resist being suppressed? Miisi was frustrated. It was all so elusive. How could he retrieve it from Christian perversion when he could not grasp it himself? He could not wait to talk to Suubi about her experiences.

11

When Isaac and Paulo returned to Kiyiika, the place was filled with locals. Outside the shrine, traditional dancers were changing into their costumes. The whole atmosphere was of merrymaking and celebration. It was as if the earlier troubles—Muganda's imminent death and Kalema's presence—had evaporated. Not sure what to do, Paulo stayed in the car. Isaac rushed to the shrine. Muganda was lying on his side, visibly breathing. The death-sheet had been taken off him. Elder Kitooke saw Isaac and whispered, "Elder Miisi has had to leave in a hurry."

"Why?"

"His only surviving son, Kamu, was murdered. We've not told the clan. We don't want to kill their hope so soon."

"Oh, is he not one of the two children he had left? When did he die?"

"Way back on the fifth of January but Miisi didn't know."

"My wife died on the same day." The two men were silent for some time. Then Kitooke remembered. "Is our son Paulo Kalema still with you?"

"In the car."

"It's time to bring him in. Let's go and get him."

"Where did you get the blood for Muganda?"

"Elder Miisi's daughter, Salamander."

"*General* Salamander?"

"The very one."

"She's *the* daughter?"

"He said he had a daughter named Kusi but who knew that Kusi was an army general? Anyway, she had Tutsis among her bodyguards. One of them gave us blood."

When they got to the car, Kitooke opened the door with a large smile. "Where is my son?" Paulo stepped out into his arms. "Let's see how Kintu's blood marked you. Yes, the Tutsi stole you for himself: come." Elder Kitooke now held Paulo's hand as if he were a child. "Come on, Kalema: let me show you off to the clan. And how is Nnakato, your mother?" But before Paulo could answer Elder Kitooke continued, "You see our beliefs; you see Isaac?" Isaac nodded as Kitooke carried on, "These Christians have sowed doubt about our own spirituality but I dare say you are the lad incarnate," he said this as if he had met Kalema of old. "I hear Nnakato, your mother, had only you?"

Kitooke prattled on, suggesting that Kanani's twins were unwitting conduits of the uncanny return of the Tutsi back into the family. Isaac stayed close to Paulo to reassure him.

12.

The eighth hour of the day, two o'clock in the afternoon, was approaching. This was the time when the Ganda committed the dead to earth and turned their backs on them. Kamu's coffin was carried through the front door then around the house to the path that led to the family cemetery. Mourners fell behind the coffin and walked out of the house. Miisi gripped Kusi's hand. His wife and sister wailed loudly but the rest of the mourners bowed their heads in silence.

Miisi, against Kusi's advice, had insisted on examining Kamu's remains. He did so at that moment of wrapping the dead when all mourners are sent out of the house and the body remains with only the heads of the clan, when all the synthetic objects, clothing, jewelry, hair extensions, or weaves are removed from the body—so that it can go back to earth the way it came into the world—and it is then wrapped in barkcloth. One of Kamu's front teeth, after the milk teeth fell out, had arrived before the other and grew so wide that his siblings had nicknamed him "Axe." When the other tooth arrived, it squeezed into a small gap upsetting the arrangement of his teeth. Miisi hoped that this would help him identify Kamu.

He was therefore surprised to find the real Kamu in the coffin, the whole of him—one eye swollen, puffed lip, nose and ears plugged with cotton and the head bandaged—but he was as whole as if he had died the day before. Miisi could not believe that the Mulago Hospital that he knew—corrupt and indifferent to human suffering—could have so preserved the body of an unknown person. He was both glad and heartbroken. It was Kamu in the coffin but it meant that Kamu was truly dead. Miisi stood up and stared, trying to arrange his feelings. He should have felt relief first and then heartbreak but he had a sense of floating. After the death of his daughter the previous year, he had thought that he would never be able to take the death of another child. Yet here he was staring at Kamu's bandaged head without clear emotions.

"He is my son," he said to the clan leader.

"All right then, step outside now, leave him to us."

Now he understood why Kusi did not want him to see the corpse. She had lied about robbers. That attack on Kamu had been sustained; robbers hit to disable so they can get away. Kamu was targeted. It was premeditated murder. He was now sure that Kusi, for all her "I don't know what happened," had not told him the whole truth surrounding Kamu's death. Apparently, she had spent the week leading up to Easter trying to contact Kamu so that they could come to the reunion together. Failing to raise him on the phone, she drove to Nabugabo Road where Kamu sold hardware. The men on the street had said, "Kamu Kintu? *Wuuwi*, he's long gone."

Kusi had said that she found out that day, in Bwaise, that Kamu had been attacked on the night of the 5th of January as he returned home but she did not know why. Frightened, the woman who lived with him at the time had fled. This did not make sense to Miisi. Why would Kamu's woman be frightened? Why did she not try to find Kamu's people? But all Kusi had said was that the woman probably did not know where to find them. When Kusi found her, the woman had told her of the people she suspected of killing Kamu but when Kusi turned up to interrogate the men, she found them dead. That was on Good Friday.

"Are they the same councillors in the Bwaise massacre?" Miisi had asked.

"I think so." But Kusi could not look straight in his eyes. "You never know what people get up to—local councillors in the day, thugs in the night."

Now, as he walked behind Kamu's coffin, realization crept on him. Kusi had killed the men in Bwaise. She would not flinch at administering her sense of justice. Miisi waited for the whole horror of what Kusi had done to overwhelm him. Instead, a spark of satisfaction with her swift execution of justice shot through his heart and his mouth twitched. That was when horror gripped him, at the surge of pride and satisfaction. His decay had set in, Miisi realized. Other people would call it becoming numb but to Miisi it was decaying and to decay was to die.

Miisi remembered the fifth of January clearly. While Kamu lay dead somewhere, the bees saw it fit to lodge in his house. He had laughed at Kato saying that dead bees announced death. Why were the gods so good at displaying omens? Surely if they stopped tragedies, there would be no need for omens?

At two o'clock, when Kamu's coffin was lowered into the grave, Miisi's grip on reality slackened. A new reality was slowly overwriting the existing one. It had happened before. Miisi had gallstone problems, a doctor friend recommended codeine, but when he swallowed the two prescribed tablets he did not feel any relief. After two hours he took another two, which made him sleep fitfully. At one point when he woke up, the floor in his bedroom was a lawn. It was frightening to realize that eyes could lie.

Now, in his mind, the reality of Kamu being buried was like thin white paint. But a new reality, a thick red paint, was spreading over it. Miisi closed his eyes to clear his vision, but it stayed. He had a sense of floating in two worlds. In one, his wife was crying out to Kamu, which meant that he was awake and that Kamu was really dead. In the other, the coffin being lowered held his father's body and Miisi was a child. There were cousins all around but the bush was Kiyiika, which meant he was dreaming. Miisi turned and saw Kusi standing close to him. Recognizing her, he grabbed her hand and the invading reality fled. He recognized the residents—Kaleebu was in charge of the burial, Nyago and his wife minded the grandchildren, the house was behind him rising above the *matooke* plantations, and the ten graves of concrete slabs before them were his children. Miisi heaved a sigh of relief; he had almost lost his mind.

Miisi is walking away from the grave. He is relieved that his father has been committed to the underworld. Mourners are streaming back to the house. Miisi whispers to the woman holding his hand, "I'm lucky he's dead. I won't be sacrificed."

"What?" The woman is puzzled.

"Shhh, keep your voice down. He sacrificed my older brother, Baale. I was next."

"Father?"

"Shhh, they'll hear you!"

"Father, it's me, Kusi."

Miisi hesitates, then shakes his head. "How can I be your father? I am just a child."

The woman becomes agitated. She leads him to a double-story house. Mourners stare. Others are still crying for his father.

"Don't cry for him," Miisi shouts at them. "He was going to kill me too." Another woman, old, joins them and leads him through the back door, through a dining area, and up a staircase.

"Where are you taking me? Are you in league with him?"

"No, he's dead," the old woman says, but the woman who had been holding his hand is crying.

Miisi smiles in relief. The old woman is joined by another old woman. They lead him up the stairs to a bedroom at the end of the corridor. As they enter the bedroom, Miisi sees his father's shirts and trousers in the wardrobe. He panics.

"This is his bedroom."

The women turn onto a balcony and into the room on the right. It is small; the bed is made up with white sheets. He collapses on the bed and realizes that he is too exhausted to keep his eyes open.

Miisi wakes up in a dark room. It is night and the house is silent. He does not know how he got into this room. He sits up and sees a woman sleeping on the floor. A guard. He has been abducted. His father must have brought him here to sacrifice him.

Carefully, he picks up his clothes, steps over the woman, and slips out of the room. The corridor and stairs are familiar but downstairs is a puzzle. The house is dead. There are people sleeping everywhere on the floor but no one wakes up as he walks past. Miisi lifts the heavy bar across the door, then opens the latch and runs out of the house heading toward a hedge. He looks back: he has never known a double-storied shrine. He ducks through the bushes under a mango tree and then runs as fast as he can.

13.

Tuesday, April 13, 2004

It was nine thirty in the evening. Paulo sat on the verandah leaning against the wall of the annex. His stomach growled but he ignored it. The night sky was clear and the stars had come out to play. The man in the moon still held up his axe—to chop firewood—the way he did when Paulo was a boy. Images and words and gestures from his childhood came and went as he searched for clues and hints about his incestuous birth. Ruth sat weeping under the palm tree near the steps to the road. Paulo had reverted to his childhood habit of calling her Ruth. Uncle Job stood over her, his hand on her shoulder. Now, even such an innocuous gesture seemed incestuous. Paulo felt the urge to go over and toss his uncle's hand off his mother's shoulder. His eyes met Uncle Job's. Uncle Job stared back steadily. Paulo looked away in disgust.

Faisi was as unshaken as granite. Amidst the confusion, she was focused. It was as if she had known that one day Kanani would let her down but there was no anger. When Kanani's body arrived from hospital at around midday, neighbors had streamed in to console her but her lack of grief threw them. Not knowing what to do with a cheerful widow, they sat for a polite while and then left. All inquiries about Kanani's death—*How could he die so quickly?*—were met with a clipped, "One moment he was alive, the next he was dead."

Soon after, the twins had arrived and Faisi sang louder to drown Ruth's sobs. The twins did not go to her for soothing. Instead, they hugged each other. Paulo realized then that the thin thread that had tied mother and twins together had snapped. Faisi looked childless already. Yet he could not go to the twins and comfort them in their moment of pain. He walked out of the house and stayed in the annex on his own until his girlfriend and other friends came to keep him company.

The Awakened had turned out in large numbers. They were all the same age as his grandparents. They sang of seeing Him over the other side when He would wipe their tears away. From time to time, Faisi interrupted the singing with a testimony from her marriage. She called Kanani the "calm and cool breeze" that had soothed her life. She talked about his patience, of his unwavering love for her, and of his devotion to God.

By the time Paulo arrived home from the reunion at midday on Tuesday, Kanani was dead. Ruth had rung him several times in the morning before he plucked up the courage to talk to her. When he did, she told him that Kanani had been to see her late Monday evening to tell her what had happened at the reunion. On Tuesday morning, Kanani was found dead on the Cathedral's grounds—heart failure. *Perhaps what he did broke his heart.* Paulo, who had by then run out of emotion, felt nothing for his grandfather's broken heart. He told Ruth that he was OK with her but he did not want to see Uncle Job. To him, Ruth could not have been a willing partner. Even when Ruth told him that she was as much to blame as Job, Paulo would not listen.

"What can we do to ease your pain?" Ruth had cried down the phone.

"Nothing."

"You have no idea how we love you, Paulo. It was wrong and we're ashamed, but you're here and you're ours."

"You're right. I don't understand you two."

"Back then me and Job, we saw ourselves as one person," Ruth tried to explain.

"Hmm? So you are saying that it was only masturbation?"

"What can I say to make sense?"

"Don't make sense, Ruth."

She hesitated at being called Ruth then carried on. "Not giving you away was the only kind thing they did to us. Now they've taken you."

Paulo did not reply.

"Poor Job—now you hate him."

"I am not part of your world where a *mawemuko* can escape himself."

"He did not call you that!"

"Hmm."

"He used to be the easy one. Now he'll not even find the salvation he's been slaving for."

Thirty minutes later, a large group of clan people led by Bweeza arrived. They came to the annex where Paulo sat and fussed over him. That was the moment when Paulo broke down and cried and the elders took turns holding him. Afterwards, when Elder Kityo asked, Paulo led the group to where Ruth and Job sat. He said, "These are the twins." There were hugs and "Welcome into the clan," and Bweeza called them her own children. There was relief among the clan people that they had finally met Elder Kanani's twins. Kitooke whispered, "We've come to be with you because you're ours." Even Job's angry face cracked and he wept. Paulo wondered whether he was crying with shame. Faisi watched the group anxiously. When Job broke down, she stood up and went behind the house. She had not seen him cry since he was a child.

Paulo pointed out the Awakened to the clan so they could avoid them. Nonetheless, the elders went to Faisi and offered her their condolences. Faisi must have warned the Awakened about the presence of these relatives, for soon the vigil fell into three camps: Paulo, the twins, and the Kintu clan in one, Faisi and the Awakened army in another, and then the villagers who had no idea there were camps. Uncle Job seemed to have established a rapport with the elders Kityo and Kitooke while Ruth and Bweeza reminisced through the night about old Nakaseke. Paulo relaxed. He could even bear Uncle Job's presence a little.

When the clan inquired whether Kanani would be "returned home" to Kiyiika, the Awakened pointed out that he had divorced all his worldly kin. He would be buried in the Cathedral's cemetery. The Awakened brethren also said that they would meet all the funeral costs and make all the necessary arrangements.

Despite the long weekend they had spent at Kiyiika, the clan sat through the funeral service at Namirembe Cathedral on Wednesday. The Awakened gave Kanani such a dignified funeral that Uncle Job thanked them in a brief speech. After burial, the clan elders told the twins about the rituals in Kiyiika. They also told Job that he was now an elder and should attend the council meetings, which put a smile on Job's face. The twins said they would let Bweeza know when they were ready to do the rituals.

Faisi did not come home after Kanani's burial. The Awakened had booked her into Namirembe Guest House for a month. Paulo visited her twice but both times he found her in the company of the Awakened. They seemed to be taking good care of her. Paulo feared that her gulu-gulu kind of strength would collapse as soon as the Awakened support stopped. However, after her return and cheerful resumption of sowing, Paulo gave up. The main house remained in a darkened silence.

14.

The thanksgiving party with the locals lasted throughout Monday night. Most clan members left Kiyiika on Tuesday morning but by Wednesday afternoon when Isaac wound everything up some cousins, especially the elderly ones, still lingered. Isaac promised the local councillors that as soon as the elders found time to meet and come up with a plan for Nnakato's site they would be informed. All the clan elders had left earlier on Tuesday to attend the burial of *Mzei* Miisi's son in Bulemeezi. But then at midday, Kalema had rung to say that *Mzei* Kanani had died and Isaac knew that from Bulemeezi, the elders would go to Bukesa to keep Kalema company during the vigil. Bweeza had already taken Suubi home. Isaac sighed. The medium had warned them: Ntwire was leaving, but he was not going empty-handed.

As Isaac drove through Buddu, he tried to maintain the sense of elation of the weekend. He had only been in the county for a week, but the landscape was familiar—Buddu felt as if it had been his home county all his life. But then Masaka Town receded from his rearview mirror and the euphoria started to wear off. Slowly, reality began to crystallize. The reunion had been a screen behind which he had hidden. With Masaka and Nyendo Towns now behind him, the screen was falling away. As *o* Lwera's desolation rushed toward him, he had no option but to contemplate the future he was driving into. He glanced over at Kizza. He lay back in the seat dreamy-eyed, perhaps falling asleep, perhaps regretting that the numerous playmates the reunion had brought were gone.

After Lukaya, a town in *o* Lwera, Isaac became peculiarly aware of the oncoming traffic. As the vehicles drove past, the noise of the engines seemed to cut right through him. He was aware of the mad run of their tires. The very speed of the vehicles seemed so close that he could touch the danger. Some cars had extended bonnets, yet the taxis, which were speedy and light on the ground, had no bonnets at all. Coaches charged like bull elephants, as if the roads belonged to them alone, yet they carried ridiculously overloaded rooftop luggage racks that would easily topple them in a curve. Family cars were less intimidating but once they came level with Isaac, he looked at the passengers and wondered who was waiting for them at home.

He liked lorries; their growl was no-nonsense. They had single front tires and the drivers were elevated twice as high as his truck. They did not have much of a bonnet for a buffer but the fact that the drivers were elevated so high was reassuring. He started to look out for lorries, especially Tatas, which were used by the army, the articulated ones and those with trailers.

After Kayabwe, Isaac became impatient. Lorries were scarce on the road; perhaps merchandise transporters traveled at night. Still there would be one or two on the road soon, he told himself. He first saw one with potential as he drew to Mpigi Town. He accelerated. Four hundred meters away from him, the lorry slowed down and turned off the road. Then he was in Mpigi Town and running out of road distance. He slowed down so much that cars behind him hooted indignantly as they overtook him. He came up to the rise in Nsangi and saw, coming below, a lorry with a trailer. He decided that he was not going to look at the occupants. He realized too late after glancing at Kizza that he shouldn't have. Luckily, Kizza was asleep. As he came down the incline, Isaac accelerated. He did not need to because the incline seemed to pull the truck down. As he came down into the valley, a long hoot came from the lorry. The sound triggered the image of the trains in South Africa, then the train tracks, then the room he trained in, then his grandmother saying that certificates don't rot they just collect dust, Mr. Kintu loved cakes, Sasa's deejay clothes on a hanger . . .

He lay on the road. A lot of feet were running around him.

"Tie the wound on the head."

Isaac's head moved of its own accord, no matter how hard he tried to keep it still, it moved as if it were not attached to him. He did not feel it.

A voice shouted, "Stay down."

That voice was in a dream.

"*Omwana*."

"The child is fine. Stay down."

"*Omwana*."

"He was luckier than you. The car threw him right through the windscreen into the swamp."

"*Omwana*."

"*Owange*," the voice called. "Bring the child here. His father will not stay still on the ground until he sees him."

"That is shock speaking," the other voice said.

"*Omwana*," Isaac said again.

Kizza's head came into view. His hair shimmered in the sun. Isaac looked again: Kizza's head was covered in little grains of sparkling glass. He wanted to rebuke him for playing with glass. There were small grazes on his forehead. His knees were covered in mud. Isaac tried to sit up, to ask Kizza why he was so dirty. Kizza cried half-heartedly. Isaac held Kizza's hand as he lay back. He thought, I have spoiled this boy! *He is crying for nothing*, but he held onto Kizza's hand tight because he wanted to sleep and he had to hold his son's hand. He closed his eyes but the voices around him would not let him rest. He opened his eyes and looked around.

There was shock on people's faces when they looked at him. He felt incredibly heavy. Then it felt cold on his right temple as if cold air was blowing just on that spot. He raised his hand to feel it. It was wet. He looked at his hand and saw blood. That was when he got frightened that he was going to die. He now felt that his head had been tied. He lifted his hand and touched a cloth. He gave up because his hand was heavy; he lay down.

"*Yii* the rich are not human *bannange*: none of the cars will stop to take them to hospital!"

"*Kitalo kino!* A person will die on the roadside because rich people won't help."

"You can't blame them. You take them to hospital, police stop you to ask questions, or want money to let you go because you might have caused the accident."

The view of the world lying on the ground was funny. People above him looked like ghosts. Voices floated above him. Cars ground the road heavily. Bicycles crunched the gravel on the sidewalks. People's feet *pata pata*-ed the ground ineffectively as if they were cats. The sun was too bright. Now noise, further away, of men shouting as if they were heaving something heavy, came. "Push, put it in reverse, *nyola zenno*." And then the distinct revving of his truck. Isaac came alive.

He lifted his head but the ground was a magnet. It pulled the flesh on his left temple off his face. He held his face in place so it did not pour off as he sat up. His face settled back in place once he was upright. He was dizzy and stiff but now he knew what was happening. He held Kizza in one hand. Someone stupid was still saying *stay down*. He looked for the revving noise but could only see the back of his truck. The truck's nose was down in a ditch below the road. Someone must be in the driver's seat, men must be standing in front of the truck trying to push it back into the road, but the mud made the tires, which hardly touched the ground, spin, spraying mud. The truck revved on. The men shouted. I must tell them to leave it alone, Isaac thought.

Just then, someone excited arrived. "Bring them, bring them, fast. This kind gentleman has agreed to take them to hospital."

Isaac was helped up. Now his whole body felt as if it had been padded with weight while he lay down. They were not listening to him about the car. Someone could steal his car. He checked his pockets. His wallet was gone. So was his phone.

"I can't find my wallet; I need to call Mother. The car. I need my mother."

But the man thrust him toward the car and spoke over him to the driver. "Go quickly, he is getting weaker."

It was such a big effort to speak and he was lucky someone was taking him to hospital and Kizza was next to him and Kizza must get in the car first and then he got in. One of the men—he identified himself as a Local Councillor—also got in the car. Isaac gave the local councillor his mother's number, the digits were distinct in his mind as he said them. The man was shouting into the phone.

"*Mukadde*, don't cry, your son and the boy they are fine. I am here with them. I am taking them to hospital my very self. We are heading for Mpigi Hospital Casualty. Maama don't cry. Crying for the living is taboo."

The LC turned to Isaac and said, "Don't sleep. Your mother is hysterical. Say something to her," and he held the phone close to Isaac's ear.

"Maama," Isaac said. "Come, please."

As they were about to drive away a man came with an envelope and the car logbook. He threw them on Isaac's lap through the window and said, "These were in the glove compartment. Take them with you."

Isaac looked down and saw the results envelope.

"What about the bags?" he looked up at the man.

"Bags? Eh, eh forget those! Let's focus on saving your life."

As they drove away the LC shook his head and said, "Those are our people. They come to help and to help themselves."

When Isaac opened his eyes, his mother stood above him fussing over the bedding. The room was crowded with his half-siblings looking disconsolate. He tried to sit up but every inch of him hurt. He fell asleep again.

The next time Isaac woke up he felt lighter and rested. His mother smiled, got off the chair, ran out and called, "*Musawo*, my patient has woken up," and she ran back beaming.

"The doctor is coming. He told me to call him when you wake up," she explained as she came to the bedside. "But now how do you feel yourself, inside?"

"I am fine, just weak." He raised his hand to touch his forehead. Now his whole face hurt.

"You banged your head badly."

The doctor walked in and shook Isaac's hand. She smiled and said, "How do you feel, Mr. Kintu?"

"Just the wound on the head. Everything else is fine."

"Good, good. That is very good. We can give the head some tablets to calm the pain down as we wait for the swelling to go down. We need to x-ray everything to make sure that nothing else is wrong. But before we give you any other medicine; do you have any other complications?"

"Nothing," Isaac said. Then he remembered. "Oh, I have HIV."

"OK," the doctor wrote on the clipboard. "When were you diagnosed?"

Isaac sighed and moved his hands in helpless gesture. He knew that he was going to sound foolish.

"I went for the blood test but I have not—" anticipating that the doctor was going to ask: *How do you know then?* Isaac added quickly, "In fact the envelope with the results, it must be somewhere, I had it."

He turned and saw it in the locker next to the bed. He passed it to the doctor without opening it.

The doctor looked at the envelope and then at him.

Isaac smiled sheepishly. "I could not bring myself to open it but you want to know so go ahead."

The doctor unsealed the envelope wordlessly. Isaac studied her face. A strip of paper, yellow, slipped out first. The doctor looked at it. Her face was emotionless. She looked inside the envelope and retrieved two folded A4 sheets. She unfolded them and read with an impassive face. Isaac's heart pumped like it was flooding. He felt blood in his mouth, nose, and ears. The doctor passed him the yellow strips first. The word negative caught his eyes. It was written three times in bold and in capital letters. The doctor passed him the A4 papers and looked at him with a smile. Isaac opened the large sheets but could not focus.

"Maama," he called Nnamata who had stepped outside during the consultation.

She came in and he passed the sheets and the strips to her without a word because he was blinded by tears. Nnamata fidgeted with the slips and papers expecting the worst until the doctor put her out of her misery.

"Your son is in the clear."

And Nnamata scowled at the sheets and then made to hug Isaac but there was nowhere to hold because he was all swollen. She embraced the doctor, rocked and thanked her over and over because she needed someone to hold on to and vent her emotions. The doctor extricated herself from Nnamata and said, "I will come back when you are composed."

She opened the screen and closed it and Isaac and his mother cried.

Isaac was kept in Mpigi Hospital for five days. He arrived in Kampala via Mmengo. His friend, Kaaya, was driving. It was already dark. At the tipping point, where Namirembe Hill drops into a sharp decline, Isaac asked Kaaya to stop the car. He had never seen the city look so beautiful. He stepped out and crossed the road. He thrust his arms in the pockets of his jacket and stared across the valley. There was no load-shedding, when electricity was rationed, and the whole city was a garden of stars. Kampala's hills rose and fell before him. Even at this time of the night, a sense of expectation hung over the hills. Kampala was going somewhere and he, Isaac, was going along with it. He could stay here and watch the city all night because he had forever. He thought of Kintu and tears came to his eyes. He did not believe that Kintu had made the results negative but Isaac was sure that his ancestor had swerved the truck to save him.

He remembered the moment when he rang Kaaya to tell him the good news. Kaaya had not been surprised.

"Why do you think I was pushing you to have the tests? From the sound of the symptoms you described, I suspected that Nnayiga had died of Lupus but I didn't want to get your hopes up."

"Lupus, is that a new disease too?"

"No," Kaaya laughed.

"Is it contagious?"

"No, it runs in families."

"What? So Kizza might have it!"

"Oh, Isaac! Why don't you take a breath, recover from the accident and from the HIV anxiety, and then take on Lupus later?"

"But—"

"Nine out of ten sufferers are women. Lupus is triggered later in life. Children don't suffer from it."

Now Isaac turned away from the city and walked back to the car. Kaaya smiled with understanding.

"You know, Kaaya, right now you would give me the most beautiful woman in the world and pay me millions and give me an aeroplane on top but I would not stick it into her without a condom."

Kaaya laughed out loud. "Don't worry, you'll get used to it."

"I mean it, Kaaya. I've been snatched out of a crocodile's mouth. From now on, it is me and my son. Sex is not worth it."

15.

Wednesday, April 28, 2004
Suubi's fingers were puffed and stiff at the joints but they did not
hurt anymore. The right wrist still had a niggling pain though.

She lay on the floor with her head propped on Opolot's
lap. As she had been doing in the last two weeks when Opolot
came around, Bweeza had discreetly gone out to check on another cousin, Kalema, who lived in Bukesa. Suubi suspected that
Bweeza was one of those bored old women who go around the
clan looking for someone to mother. Looking back, Suubi could
not believe that in such a short time she had become attached to
the old woman. Their initial encounter, foggy moments when she
had wandered in and out of consciousness, had been the hardest.
Every time Suubi woke up, the same face had come to her whispering, "Nnakato." In the haze, Bweeza had looked like a stern
witch ministering an evil taboo on her. But then Suubi saw the
hospital drip from the corner of her eye and a man bending over
her. The man wore a stethoscope around his neck. The drip and
stethoscope, instruments of civilization, had reassured her and she
fell asleep again. Later, when she was fully awake, the man had
introduced himself as Dr. Kityo Kintu, an elder. He had checked
her pulse and blood pressure and given her some tablets. When
she saw her arms bandaged and tied to pieces of wood, she had

looked at Bweeza enquiringly. Bweeza, misunderstanding Suubi's surprise, had explained that Babirye had almost killed her.

"I knew she would one day," Suubi said resignedly but she could not remember anything.

"Babirye only wants you to use your twin name. She's not a bad spirit."

Bweeza had explained that because Suubi had bound Babirye into a stick, which was never burned, Babirye would always be with her.

"Your twin was furious that you tried to destroy her."

Suubi closed her eyes as she remembered the stick. Tears streamed down her face and Bweeza sat down on the bed and held her like a child. Suubi gave in and she wept silently. Bweeza rocked her saying, "Shhh, it is all over now. Babirye loves you. She just wanted to be with you."

Unfortunately, Babirye was still bound in the stick. Suubi would have to carry it with her always. "Babirye will be savage if I lose it."

"No child, you will not lose it at all. Muganda is going to make the stick easy to carry. Wait and see."

Now Suubi looked at the necklaces, bracelets, and a pair of dangling earrings lying on the table. They looked like jewelry out of a tourist shop. They were made out of tiny round pieces, carved out of the stick. Muganda had colored them in black and white, making them look like beads. Suubi was happy about that; they looked like a matching set of traditional bracelets, necklaces, and earrings. Bweeza had told her that if she wished, Muganda could release Babirye from the stick but it would need an elaborate and expensive ritual. But Suubi could not bear the thought of going near anything like that again. Now that Opolot knew everything about her and Babirye, she had chosen to keep the bracelets and necklaces.

"Here," Opolot took a necklace and slipped it over her head. Suubi slid the earrings through the holes in her ears. "Aha," Opolot said appraising her. "You look Karamajong already."

"Karamajong is the closest I have got to being Atesot," Suubi beamed at the compliment. "But who wears their twin around their neck?"

"So, do I call you Nnakato now?" Opolot asked.

"I am still Suubi."

"You might have twins . . . that would be nice."

"Oh no, I am——"

"Don't worry, we would give them Atesot names for twins—Opio for the eldest boy and Apio for the girl, Ocen for the younger boy and Acen for the girl."

"Call me Acen then. It still means Nnakato."

"OK, Acen." Opolot lifted Suubi's hands and looked at them. "It must've been an awkward fall to break four fingers and both wrists!"

"Babirye was punishing me," Suubi said truthfully.

She had not told Opolot about the transpossession—when it came to witchcraft, Suubi thought, there was a limit to what a woman should divulge to a man she hopes to marry. She looked at the bracelets. It was hard to see her twin in them. The Ssanyu Babirye she saw in her anxiety was emaciated and wretched. Yet Aunt Kizza had told her that Babirye had been a plump and happy baby. Suubi felt guilty that a plump baby had turned into a scrawny spirit.

"Her name was Ssanyu."

"Who?"

"My twin. She was named Ssanyu, which means 'happy.' I was named Suubi which means 'hope' because I was so scrawny at birth that they could only hope that I would live."

16.

When Kusi, her mother, and aunt arrive at Kiyiika, Miisi's mind is at home. Two days earlier, when the Elders Kitooke and Kityo arrived at Kande with the news that Miisi had been found at Kiyiika, Kityo had prepared them for the worst. "Sometimes his mind is there but most times it's not."

The family had mulled over the information silently. Then Nnamuli had asked, "How is he fed?"

"A cousin turned up saying that he had been instructed by the spirits to come and take care of the custodian—Miisi is believed to be the custodian. Apparently, the ancients have hauled him back to take his rightful position."

Kityo had paused as if expecting Miisi's family to marvel at the power of the ancients and how they had hauled Miisi, in spite of his education, back to Kiyiika. The family stared their dismay. Kityo continued, "Those who know the legend well claim that Miisi, in his disturbed state, is the very image of our Kintu when he lived in *o* Lwera. We're trying to make the shrine as comfortable as possible. Cousins are still coming for ablution. They leave money. There is food. But Miisi prefers raw food anyway. He sleeps outside among the trees."

For Miisi's family the idea that he was chosen by the ancients

lost its novelty at that moment. His being forced back to Kiyiika—
because Miisi would not have gone willingly—was cruel and selfish. Loss of mind was death. Miisi had always claimed that to have
a mind was to be alive.

Now as they drive up the hill, Miisi sees them and hurries toward the car. The way he moves suggests that his mind is in sync
with his body. He is relaxed, as if he is at his house in Kande. It is
clear that he does not realize anything is amiss. There is a benign
smile on his face. It is only three weeks since he disappeared but
his hair is thick and gray. It is matted with dirt, rain, and dust. His
beard and moustache, entirely gray, shroud his mouth. His *kanzu*
is filthy. On top of it, he wears a red waistcoat and a purple coat.

"Where did the coat and waistcoat come from?" Kusi whispers, but before anyone answers, Miisi stands before her. He bends
and places both his hands on the driver's window. His smile is
wider and his eyes are shining. He stinks of smoke. Kusi opens the
car door and Miisi steps back. She gets out of the car and hugs
him. Miisi asks, "How is my little army?"

"Asking for you."

"Are they in school?"

"I've moved in with them temporarily."

"Kusi, you are my heir, *kdto*." Miisi clicks his tongue with triumphant defiance. "I am the first Ganda man to elect a daughter
for an heir. Put that down in history!"

Kusi laughs without saying a word. She is not sure whether it
is her father speaking or the madness.

"I had to lose all my sons to realize that my daughter is a better heir than all of them. Now I understand why they died." Now
Miisi raises his voice like a preacher on a pulpit. "My sons had to
die so I could see!"

Again Kusi smiles uneasily.

"Tell them. If anyone ever changes my will, the entire Kintu
wrath will come down on them."

"OK. I'll take the responsibility." Kusi has realized that the sooner she agrees with her father the sooner he will drop the subject.

"I know who I am," Miisi smiles but he is now a different person.

"What about coming home with us?"

"This is home, I am the lamb, the chosen one," he speaks in English.

"The lamb? You don't even believe—"

"All the clan's curses I carry on my head."

At that point, the caretaker comes to Kusi and whispers, "When he starts to speak in English, then you've lost him."

"I named him Ham and sealed his fate. What you don't realize," Miisi closes one eye, "is that children's heads are a space upon which parents inscribe texts. A Hutu gave his child a name translating, 'Tell the world I am not impotent,'" he laughs raucously. "Selfish don't you think?"

The caretaker shakes his head at Kusi but Kusi is not giving up yet.

"*Mzei*, I want to take you home."

"We are not even Hamites. We are Bantu," Miisi continues.

"You're lucky, he is rarely around for that long," the caretaker whispers.

"*He's rarely around for that long,* my good friend tells them as if I am not here." Miisi whispers to himself. "It is a sad situation, isn't it? Average IQ: 70—enough to eat and shit. Fourteen years old at most. They call me mad. But Africans are born to burden others but they're not even apologetic." Now Miisi raises his voice and speaks as if to a crowd, "Mend your ways, you sons of Ham! Turn away from your imbecilic ways and be grateful!" Now he whispers to himself, "But then prophets never know respect in their hometowns. They say to me: *Easy, Mezraim, don't worry, be happy.*"

"He goes on and on. There is no subject under the sun that he has no theory about," the caretaker whispered to Kusi.

"*He goes on and on,* says my good friend, my companion apparently." Miisi clicks his tongue in contempt. "That's all the companionship I have, Kusi. A man so frightened of living that he came to hide behind my back. I might as well talk to the trees, at least they won't patronize me. Kusi, you used to listen to me. He patronizes me," Miisi points at the caretaker, childlike.

"I'll have a word with him."

"What I need is an exercise book, a pencil, and a rubber. A proper writer writes in pencil. That's the first thing you learn. Have you read my column, Kusi? I've received a few compliments on it lately."

The caretaker walks away. Miisi points at him and whispers, "He's beyond salvage, mercy upon us."

"We've got to go, *Mzei*."

"*We've got to go, Father*, she says," Miisi turns away and laughs. "She thinks she is going somewhere, poor child, when in actuality she's waiting to die. I would recommend *Waiting for Godot* but it's another waste of time, isn't it?"

"We're leaving, *Mzei*." Kusi starts to leave but Miisi does not turn around. He rubs his face with both hands, up and down, up and down. Something in his stance suggests that he understands that Kusi is leaving but that he does not want her to. Kusi touches his hand and says, "Father?" Miisi brushes off her hand and turns his back on her. Kusi stands still for a moment and then breaks down. The realization that her father hovers in the middle world between sanity and insanity is hard to take. Still, Miisi does not turn around. He looks up in the sky whispering to himself. When Kusi is composed, she asks the caretaker, "How is his health otherwise?"

"He is fine."

"When he gets a temperature or anything you don't understand, ring these numbers." She gives him her contacts. "It's important to make him feel normal. When he talks to you listen politely, make the right noises, and look like you are following his argument."

"I understand."

"And thank you for everything."

"Duty is duty."

Miisi's wife, who has been crying behind the shrine all along, comes out and tries to bid him farewell but Miisi refuses to acknowledge her or his sister.

"He pushed the gods too far. He kept prodding and prodding until they snapped," his wife says as they pull away.

No one responds. Kusi drives down the rough track until they come to the *kitawuluzi*. She looks back. Miisi is still staring at the sky. She says, "Kamu's death snapped the last cable in his mind."

"Maybe, but still he dug too deep. This knowledge of ours, you just be, but not him," Miisi's wife sniffs. "He pursued knowledge for the sake of knowing. In the end, it ran his mind down."

"It's nothing to do with too much knowledge." Miisi's sister is exasperated. "Miisi was endowed with both cerebral knowledge and a non-cerebral way of knowing. But every time ours popped up, he squeezed and muted. He worshipped cerebral knowledge."

"So he was sacrificed at the altar of knowledge?" Kusi tries to reconcile her mother and aunt.

"For knowing and refusing to know," her aunt says confidently.

ACKNOWLEDGEMENTS

I would like to thank Martha Ludigo-Nyenje for being my first reader and for those first six months in Manchester; Nicole Thiara for reading all the versions of my manuscripts; Commonword/Cultureword's Pete Kalu for the writing group; Martin De Mello, for giving so much more than I can ever give back; the Department of English and Creative Writing, University of Lancaster, for the continuous support; the Literary Consultancy, for Sara Maitland and for Jacob Ross; Kwani?, for the brilliant idea of a manuscript project and for giving this novel a chance; Kate Haines for holding my hand; Geoff Ryman for that letter; James Macdonald Lockhart for giving me a chance; Ellah Wakatama Allfrey for the eagle eyes and for getting more out of me than I thought possible, I was lucky to work with you; Vimbai Shire, thank you; MMU Special Collections for the gem; the City of Manchester for the libraries—don't close them please—Damian Morris for indulging me and for not saying, "What?" when I talk to myself.

And thank you, Jordan Bamundaga, for putting up with a part-time mum.

JENNIFER NANSUBUGA MAKUMBI, a Ugandan novelist and short story writer, has a PhD from Lancaster University. Her first novel, *Kintu*, won the Kwani? Manuscript Project in 2013 and was longlisted for the Etisalat Prize in 2014. Her story "Let's Tell This Story Properly" won the 2014 Commonwealth Short Story Prize. Makumbi lives in Manchester, UK, with her husband, Damian, and her son, Jordan.

AARON BADY is a writer in Oakland, California, and an editor at *The New Inquiry*.

Transit Books is a nonprofit publisher of international and American literature, based in Oakland, California. Founded in 2015, Transit Books is committed to the discovery and promotion of enduring works that carry readers across borders and communities. Visit us online to learn more about our forthcoming titles, events, and opportunities to support our mission.

TRANSITBOOKS.ORG